An Enigma by the Sea

By the same authors

The D Case
No Fixed Abode

An Enigma by the Sea

Carlo Fruttero & Franco Lucentini

Translated by Gregory Dowling

Chatto & Windus
LONDON

This edition first published 1994

1 3 5 7 9 10 8 6 4 2

First published in Italian as *Enigma in luogo di mare*
in 1991 by Arnoldo Mondadori Editore, Milan

First published in the United Kingdom in 1994 by
Chatto & Windus Limited
Random House, 20 Vauxhall Bridge Road, London SW1V 2SA

Random House Australia (Pty) Limited
20 Alfred Street, Milsons Point, Sydney
New South Wales 2061, Australia

Random House New Zealand Limited
18 Poland Road, Glenfield
Auckland 10, New Zealand

Random House South Africa (Pty) Limited
PO Box 337, Bergvlei, South Africa

Random House UK Limited Reg. No. 954009

A CIP catalogue record for this book
is available from the British Library

ISBN 0 7011 4843 8

Typeset by SX Composing Ltd, Rayleigh, Essex
Printed and bound in Great Britain by
Mackays of Chatham plc, Chatham, Kent

Contents

I

A Certain Air of Secrecy

I

A CERTAIN AIR of secrecy hangs over it, which is in part due to the very nature of the place, and in part to its acquired, artificial characteristics.

The rotating stands that the stationery-shops, the tobacconists' and the bijouterie-stalls put out in summer, for example, only ever have one postcard, the same for years now, showing the pine-forest. And since the photographer, in order to give an overall view, resorted to a long aerial shot, all that can be seen is a broad, unbroken band of green alongside the sea. 'Pineta della Gualdana', it reads on the back, with German, English, and French translations.

It looks like a stretch of Tyrrhenian coastline that has somehow remained unspoilt, and thus merits being sent to friends and relatives in far-off lands. But beneath that seamless stratum of interweaving tresses things are very different.

For instance, a Danish tourist, on his way down from Pisa or Volterra, may feel sudden relief on seeing the asphalt darken beneath the coolness of the great green sun-screens, and after a mile or so, he may be attracted by a recess, an unostentatious opening amid the trunks on his right. There are no signs or notices, and the prospect of breaking his journey by entering it and maybe finding his way to the beach for a quick dip in the Mediterranean will strike him as irresistible. He will brake brusquely, turn into the beckoning alley, chug his camper up a slope for a few dozen yards: but beyond the slight mound – actually a dune – are two red and white bars that block the way, and an unostentatious stone building, of one storey, where guards in khaki uniforms control the access to the pine-forest.

One of them, Vannucci, perhaps (a tough, gnarled man in his sixties), will wave one hand in an oscillatory gesture, with the index-finger raised prohibitively, and the Scandinavian will thus understand that he is to back off again, with his skin-peeled, disappointed family. Laboriously manoeuvring the camper around the triangular flower-bed which acts as a bollard, he may see the entrance barrier admit Ciacci (the electrician) in his grey van or the exit barrier rise to emit Grechi (the plumber) in his blue van; he may have time to note, for example, Signor Zeme's white Volvo emerging ponderously from an internal path, or the distant shape of Signor Mongelli cycling forwards to get his newspaper (Vannuccini will come out and hand it to him, a guard with no resemblance whatsoever to Vannucci: tall, large, fair-haired, young).*

But in essence, the only thing that is clear at the guards' lodge is that the pine-forest is private property. Even the wire netting that encloses it on three sides (the fourth opening on to the long beach) is difficult to spot, since it is set back and is now hidden by sprawling masses of pittosporums, arbutus, junipers, sorghums and laurels.

---

* The meticulous (or absent-minded) reader who likes to keep a constant check on 'who's who' will find an annotated list of all the main people and animals in the novel in an Appendix at the end of the book.

The thick scrub, partly arranged in intentional hedges and partly flourishing in spontaneous clusters, almost wholly conceals the hundred and fifty 'villas' that the fencing discreetly protects from outsiders.

Barely visible and rarely seen, the pine-forest is perceived by those who do know of its existence in a variety of ways, as numerous as its birds, insects, shrubs, as the shades of its colours according to the hour and the season. For the various branches of the public administration (the land-registry office, the Tuscan regional authorities, the town council, the inland revenue, etc.), it is simply a residential estate. But take Signor Monforti now (a Milanese ex-businessman who dabbles, or rather dabbled, in the hobby of local history), he is particularly interested in its past vicissitudes, starting with the Medicean statutes where it is first mentioned (1585), and he is still seeking, albeit wearily, listlessly, for some documentary evidence of the raids (this was, for Dante, the meaning of the word 'gualdana') from which its name is supposed to derive.

For the local emergency services, it is a potential hazard, where a fire can break out at any moment in summer. For Ciacci, Grechi, and the handymen and shopkeepers of the near-by village, it is a considerable source of income. For Vannucci, Vannuccini and the other eight guards, it is a secure and undemanding job, except for the period from June to September, when the inhabitants of the hundred and fifty (153, to be precise) residential units are all – or almost all – bustlingly present, with children, guests, foreign domestic staff, cars, and surfboards.

There is a moderate flow of visitors at Christmas and Easter, but for the rest of the year the sun sets on a dark and deserted wood. The 153 villas, all lying low and flat in the thick scrub, are mostly empty, overrun by desperate spiders, rats, millipedes, lizards and even grass-snakes, whose fragile mummies will be found months later in a shower or a corner of the basement.

There are some exceptions: for example Signor Lotti, an ex-jeweller from Florence, who lives here on his own the whole year round, does not like to speak to anyone and wanders the avenues at night on a bicycle, preceded and followed by his four Irish setters, which he commands with a whistle inaudible to the human ear. There is Hans Ludwig Kruysen, the great harpsichordist and organist, who still gives an occasional concert but now spends most of the year with his devoted lady companion in the Gualdana. And by contrast there is the beautiful Signora Neri, abandoned here with her two children by her husband who now lives in Toronto with Signor Mongelli's ex-wife. And there is also old Signora Borst, from Zurich, with her old friend Eladia, from Lugano.

For these and a few other permanent residents, the pine-forest is not an ephemeral, sunlit place where they spend their summer holidays, but a refuge, a hiding-place secluded from the world, though well furnished with all worldly conveniences. And it was the Gualdana's certain air of secrecy that drew them here, for various reasons – the various wounds and hopes of life; and now they themselves help to accentuate that secrecy, with their scattered dots of light peeping from the black backdrop of the winter undergrowth.

This evening for example – it is dusk on a December day – the wind that began to stir at sunset continues to send a plaintive wail down the chimneys, a kind of repeated summons heard indistinctly at odd times and in odd places, and which finally becomes distinguishable as the syllables: '. . . o-liiin!', or perhaps '. . . a-riiin!'. A foreign name, it would seem, and probably female.

There are some who pay no attention and continue to read in their wicker armchairs, to arrange Tarot cards on a table, to battle with a stain on a sofa-cover. Others peer out of their doors, opening new yellow rectangles in the now definitive darkness of the pine-forest.

'. . . a-riiin!' invokes the voice, faint but closer, carried away by the wind. '. . . o-liiin!'

Perhaps a cat, or a pedigree dog that has not returned home.

'It'll be some idiotic baby-sitter who's lost a child,' says Signor Monforti, the owner of lot no. 39 and the villa built thereon.

He speaks wearily and indifferently, continuing to watch, if indeed he was watching it, an old episode of the Perry Mason series that a local station broadcasts at this hour.

His two guests – his sister Sandra and his brother-in-law Ettore, who have come to spend their Christmas holidays here – are agitated by this hypothesis.

'No, really? Then you'd better phone, let's call the guards, let's go and see.'

Perry Mason is phoning too: 75,000 dollars are missing from a safe.

'It's not worth it,' says Monforti. 'There'll be hundreds of people getting in the way, they'll have called the Carabinieri by now.'

The Carabinieri have already arrived in fact, and they are trying to make a militarily manageable picture out of the impossible tangle of shifting shadows that the pine-forest presents to their torches in this north wind. The two longer sides of this irregular trapezium of about 2 miles by 700 yards border respectively on Highway 249 and the sea. An internal network of asphalted path runs lengthwise in the shape of a rough and shaky trident, whose prongs are crossed by five winding minor roads. Another non-asphalted coastal path tortuously follows the dunes along the shore between two low protective hedges of straggling sorghum. In the hedge on the beach side small openings provide access to the residents' shelters and beach-huts, all made of cane, instead of the more common but aesthetically unsuitable cabins and umbrellas.

At around 5 p.m., in the vicinity of one of these openings, Signora Barbara Graham, of English nationality, had spotted an empty cigarette-packet (Philip Morris, the low tar kind) that had been thrown into the bushes despite the various notices and receptacles which, at regular intervals, remind visitors to keep the forest and the beach clean.

As her son Colin, who was accompanying her on her walk, had sat down for the purpose of filling his bucket with sand, Signora Graham took it upon herself to collect the litter and then made her way to the nearest receptacle to deposit it. When she returned, she found the bucket still where she had left it, but of her son, a child of some twenty months, there was no trace.

2

The Carabinieri's small car is parked at the exact spot where the disappearance was first noted and it completely and unnaturally obstructs the path along the dunes. Everything combines to make it look smaller, despite its blazing headlamps and its blue light whirling doggedly away on the roof. Swept clean by the icy gusts of the north wind, the sky bears down with all its brilliant stars on the innumerable pines of the approximately 2 miles by 700 yards of the Gualdana. Marshal Butti knows, from information furnished by his colleagues of the *Guardia Forestale*, that the pines are not in fact innumerable at all; but the statistics none the less speak of 18,300 trunks, varying in age from ten to a hundred and fifty years, without counting aleppo-pines, ilexes, cork-trees, mimosas, laurels, and other trees of average girth, which have grown spontaneously or been planted by the residents. And beneath them, the dense, bristling, hump-backed expanse of scrub.

How can they begin to look for, let alone find, a twenty-month-old child here? The mother, fortunately, is not in a state of shock; she is not crying or screaming. (But – reflects the Marshal – had she been an anxious Mediterranean mother, she would never have let a child of that age out of her sight for even an instant!) She is a tall, washed-out blonde, who answers every question concisely, in good Italian.

How long was the child left alone? No more than a minute, two at the most. What did the lady do then? She started to call him, running up and down a stretch of the coastal path; she went to see if he was on the beach; she went back to the road; she called him again and looked for him; finally she ran home to alert her husband.

The husband is distraught. All his shouting into the wind has left him voiceless, but he cannot desist from uttering his tender invocation which he now repeats softly among the bushes: 'Colin . . . Colin . . . Colin . . .'

His idea is that the boy has not gone far, but is huddled up somewhere, trembling with cold and terrified by the night. He rules out another idea implicitly put forward by the Marshal, who has asked whether the Signora saw anyone in the area before the disappearance. A kidnapping? But they've hardly been to the place before! They only got here this morning! What band of kidnappers could have had the time or means to organise the crime?

And in fact the Grahams – who bought villa no. 97 last March from a dentist in Turin, whose wife found the place deadly dull – know and are known by hardly anyone in the Gualdana. The only people they had informed of their impending arrival were Dalmiero (the only taxi-driver in the village, who picked them up from Pisa airport at midday) and Vannuccini and his wife Ivella, who turned the heating on and cleaned the house for them yesterday.

'Colin . . .' the father starts calling again, in a persuasive, playful tone, as if he were looking for the boy among the armchairs in the living-room, rather than among the hostile, thorny bushes, 'Colin . . . Colin . . .'

Shadowy figures come towards the parked Fiat Uno in straggling clusters, with torches in their hands and collars turned up against the ever-sharper cold.

'He could have got into a hut,' says one male figure. 'We ought to check them all, systematically.'

The adverb sounds like a reproach to the Marshal, who is doing nothing systematic at all because he has another, even more important adverb in his mind: rapidly. Out of consideration for the parents nobody says aloud what is quite clear to everyone.

'Tomorrow they'll find him frozen to death,' mumbles Monforti in a low voice.

'Come on, don't say such things,' protests his sister Sandra, shivering.

'It'll drop below zero tonight, if it hasn't already,' insists her brother lugubriously.

The fact is that Colin (described by Vannuccini as 'robust') is wearing shorts and a denim jacket, because the weather had been deceptively mild before the north wind started up. He must therefore be found as soon as possible. But the Marshal knows from experience in Sardinia that to comb this sort of ground properly and within a reasonable space of time, not even thirty men would suffice, whereas he has just three.

The system-lover, whom Monforti recognises as Signor Zeme with a large cap pulled down over his eyes, offers a new suggestion: 'What we need are dogs, let's ask Signor Lotti if his dogs . . .'

Another cloaked form speaks up curtly from the darkness. It is Signor Lotti.

'Mine are hunting dogs. You'd need properly trained ones here.'

The Marshal who has already discussed the matter with headquarters at Grosseto over the radio, says with equal curtness: 'I've asked, but there aren't any at Grosseto, there are just the *Guardia di Finanza* ones, for drugs. They're sending over the police dogs from Florence, they'll be here in a couple of hours.'

Monforti shrugs and murmurs darkly to his brother-in-law: 'Oh sure, police dogs! What could they possibly sniff out, in this wind?'

They all look at their watches. It is 6.50 p.m. And although there is now this concrete hope of having the dogs, the idea of standing there doing nothing (and without knowing what to say to Colin's parents) seems unbearable to everyone. Signor Zeme therefore returns to his proposal of searching the huts from one end of the beach to the other.

'We could form two teams,' he says. 'One towards Poggiomozzo and the other towards the Capriola.'

These are two small rocky promontories, to the north and south, which geographically enclose this stretch of coast. But complications and points of detail arise at once.

'But there's the Old Ditch,' Signor Mongelli points out. 'So one team ought to set out from the border of the campsite and move this way, while the other one moves in the opposite direction, towards Rome, while a third . . .'

'Rome?' asks Signora Graham, clutching at the only name she recognises amidst these as yet mysterious toponyms.

'Southwards,' says Signor Zeme. 'That way.'

His arm waves upwards to remote stars and then drops as if forced by the wind. Even angrier gusts scatter new objections and counter-proposals, distort the explanations being given to those who continue to turn up out of the darkness. There is now a sizeable crowd around the Carabinieri's car, and an animated buzz of voices.

'Colin . . .' Signor Graham starts up again, sweeping his torchlight over junipers and rosemaries, while the Sergeant and the two Corporals do the same, but over a wider range and with less inadequate bulbs.

As for the Marshal, he stands in silence by the half-open car door, from which there emerges the intimate crackle of the radio. He does not like this inactivity, but neither does he like taking hasty initiatives, 'just for the sake of it', and a search, even if restricted to the huts and the beach, would not be a simple job.

It is quite true that one of the various difficulties to be considered is the Old Ditch, a canal with brickwork banks, five metres wide, which the hydraulic engineers of Grand-Duke Leopold II of Tuscany built in the last century as a drainage system against floods. This canal, crossed by a bridge known – aptly enough – as 'the Grand-Duke's', cuts the Gualdana diagonally from north-east to south-west and flows into the sea between two breakwater barriers formed of large boulders and concrete blocks.

An efficient and rapid search, therefore, would require four teams: two moving from the mouth of the canal in opposite directions; and two coming towards them from the opposite borders, after an exploration of the two adjacent stretches of free beach. Beyond the borders, in fact, the child might have roamed northwards as far as Poggiomozzo (where in summer there is a noisy and much-detested campsite), and southwards as far as the Capriola . . .

Too much overlapping, too many reference points, for amateur searchers who continue to fill the darkness with suggestions that are not only confused but also muffled by mouth-protecting woollen scarves. But even if the shadowy figure with the loudest and most resolute voice (Signor Zeme) were to succeed in taking charge of the situation and were to impose a satisfactory plan of action, he would find himself up against a further series of impediments that Marshal Butti refrains from pointing out to him.

Along the two miles of 'private' beach, there are in theory fifty-one huts to search. In fact, seven of them were unroofed and half-destroyed by the violent gale at the end of October, while four others, closer to the sea, were swept away by the breakers. There are thus forty huts where the child could be sheltering. Each hut is circular in form and divided into three sections; each section is numbered and corresponds to one of the 153 lots on which the 153 'villas' stand (apart from exceptions, contraventions, prerogatives and misappropriations which are not, however, relevant to the search). The door of each section consists of a cane wing that usually closes with a simple iron hook; but at least a third of the residents have an excessive sense of property and prefer to adopt a padlock, a rusty and precarious contraption to which is entrusted the task of conserving battered deckchairs, buckets and deflated mattresses throughout the winter.

Little Colin, if he has indeed sought refuge or shelter in a hut, is most likely to have chosen one of the sections with a door that had either been left open or had got torn off by the gale; but it is equally possible that, finding the sections closed and being unable, on account of his size, to reach the hooks or padlocks, he simply slipped *under* the door, between the frayed canes and the sand.

Consequently the search cannot be restricted to the sections with doors that are either open or can be opened by lifting the hook, but must also include the interiors of the padlocked ones. What will the volunteers' response be, when faced with this obstacle? Will they decide simply to sidestep it, thus rendering the result of the operation entirely haphazard? Or will they take it upon themselves to force the locks, to cut the chains?

The boot of the Uno contains, among other tools, some efficient wire-clippers, but the Marshal has no desire at all to hand them over to the searchers. A bathing-hut by the sea is undoubtedly a different matter from a house, but breaking and entering is bound to contravene some regulation, law, or article of the Penal Code. It is true that chains and padlocks can subsequently be replaced. But at whose expense? The Grahams'? The estate's? Someone might even try to involve the Carabinieri; the residents include several lawyers (some of them highly influential) and foreigners (some of them very important), two highly susceptible categories, much given to quibbles and complaints.

Thus Marshal Butti does not intervene in the discussion and waits in silence for his dogs under the innumerable stars. He overhears, and in his heart commends, the remark of a well-muffled shadowy shape who makes as if to leave the group.

'I'm off, we're doing no good here. We're just getting in the way.'

Monforti's murmured announcement was intended for his sister Sandra, but the hooded sheepskin-coat standing by his side, though almost identical, does not contain the sister in question.

'Ah, you're here too,' says the woman within it.

It is the beautiful Signora Neri, who has hurried here with her thirteen-year-old son to assist in the search.

'I should have stayed in and watched Perry Mason,' Monforti confides to her in a cynical whisper.

'No, come on, we can help surely. Look, come with me, we'll make a team, the two of us.'

She takes him by the arm, guides him through the opening in the sorghum hedge and goes down through the dunes to the nearest hut. She is carrying a torch, which she plays diligently over each of the three sections (nos 82, 83, 84), restoring momentary life to a flabby yellow ball, two folding chairs that rust has rendered unfolding, a gap-toothed rake, a broken mirror.

'Colin . . . Colin . . .' she starts to call in a low voice.

Her companion gives a snort of impatience. 'What's the point of calling? God only knows what's happened to him, poor thing.'

'Gabriele, don't!'

A sudden gust of wind drives her hood back on to her shoulders and her gently glowing face appears set against the coruscating myriads of the sky.

'You're a marvel of creation,' sighs Monforti. 'That's the worst of my troubles.'

'Oh come now!'

She precedes him towards the neatly aligned (and numbered) cane shelters that lie at the end of the dunes and the border of the property. And in fact a board nailed to a post between two wild azalea bushes reads 'Private Property'. At that point the beach proper begins, sloping smoothly and uniformly downwards for about fifty yards.

'I reckon he's drowned. Dragged away by the undertow.'

'Listen, Gabriele . . .' begins Signora Neri.

But a violent gust attacks her almost purposefully, tearing the exasperation from her voice, so that she starts again in a patient, reasoning manner: 'Wait, just look at the sea: with this wind from inland, it's not even stirring.'

And in fact the sea appears above suspicion; it is perfectly calm, the voice of the surge is patient and reasonable as it withdraws and returns, deposits and reabsorbs its thread-like margin of foam. But that innocent air, of one that would never dream of snatching and engulfing a twenty-month-old English child, does not convince Monforti.

'A freak wave,' he insinuates.

'Freak wave, my foot! We're not in Australia!'

'You never know.'

'Gabriele, you may enjoy this . . .'

'Enjoy it?' he suddenly shouts, throwing his arms wide under the starry universe. 'I'm not enjoying myself, OK? I'm not enjoying myself!'

'OK, you're not enjoying yourself, sorry,' she says with resignation.

Monforti trips over an empty petrol-can, one of the many bits of jetsam that the sea has abandoned on the beach during autumn, and kicks it across the sand.

'This beach gets dirtier by the day.'

'They'll be cleaning it up tomorrow, or before Christmas anyway, Vannucci told me so this morning.'

'Oh yes,' Monforti says, with obscure sarcasm, 'Vannucci!'

They move a few more yards in the direction of Capriola, Rome, the South in general, and are about to walk around a huge tree-trunk lying slantwise across the beach when the trunk suddenly gives voice.

'Good evening,' one of its gnarled bumps says amiably, rising to its feet.

It takes them a second or two to realise that it is Signorina Eladia, Signora Borst's friend from the Ticino.

'It's no use looking in the forest,' says Eladia, nodding towards the faint blue flashes of the Uno and the little dots of light flickering in the black weft of the undergrowth. 'Colin must be here, near the sea.'

'Have you seen him on the beach?' asks Signora Neri.

'No, it was this morning, in the cards: I saw water, a lot of water . . .' explains the Signorina, with a wide gesture towards the Tyrrhenian Sea. 'And two figures, a large and a smaller one, who came through the shadows.'

'But that's us!' Monforti laughs improperly, receiving a sharp dig in the ribs from Signora Neri.

An unnecessary dig, since Eladia maintains a humbly, sweetly unswerving faith in her Tarot cards, remaining deaf to all scepticism, superior to all irony.

'No, I don't think so,' she says seriously. 'These two came from the other direction, and there was also a very negative sign, one of great danger. And in fact . . .'

All the possible combinations of the pack mirror for her the infinite combinations of life; indeed, over the years, the roles have been reversed: real life is played out there, among symbolic Kings of Wands and Knights of Coins, while the world holds no interest for her, other than as a dull confirmation, an inevitable adjustment to the pre-announced truths of the Tarot cards.

'Let's hope for the best,' says Signora Neri, looking at the star-crowded sky, as if portentous signs could be expected from there too. 'Do you know these Grahams? Have they got any other children?'

'I only met them once, two months ago, when they came to see about the furniture,' says Eladia. 'But I think they've just got the one boy.'

She squats back down on the trunk – or rather, minuscule as she is in her black fur-coat, she is reabsorbed by it, becoming a confused whorl between two thick, upward-stretching branches.

Signora Neri pulls her hood around her head and holds it tight with one gloved hand. 'It would be terrible,' she says, 'poor woman.'

'Poor silly woman,' says Monforti. 'Have you ever heard of anyone losing a child like that? For a packet of cigarettes – an empty one, what's more.'

'It could happen to anyone,' says Signora Neri.

'Has it happened to you?'

Signora Neri has a son of thirteen and a daughter of twelve.

'What's that got to do with it? Anyway it was a very civilised gesture.'

'All too easy,' replies Monforti, 'to bask in the illusion that this is a civilised place.'

'Well . . .' says Signora Neri.

But then she falls silent and listens.

The wind persists with its decidedly uncivil gusts, shaking and flexing the trees closest to the beach, which have been reduced by years of barbaric weather to stiff, monstrous, inimical shapes. The pine-forest offers a hostilely low profile, like a threatening brow, and above it the sky is an abyss. From its great lair, the sea laps with the meekness of a beast poised to pounce.

Surrounded by these immemorial forces of the Tyrrhenian coast, Natalia Neri is seized with an acute sense of precariousness; she suddenly finds herself doubting the solid reality of the 153 villas, of the fencing, of the road network, of the ten guards, of the regulated estate in which she ordinarily believes. Where are my children? she wonders in sudden alarm. Andrea has joined the others in looking for the child. Giudi is at home with a cold, watching an old episode of Perry Mason (75,000 dollars were missing from a safe).

'I remember when there used to be boars,' says the obscure whorl on the trunk. 'They would come down the Old Ditch to get away from the hunters, and eat the pine kernels.'

Signora Borst's villa (lot no. 126, in the front row nearest the sea) was one of the first to be built, which is why it is now one of those most in need of restoration.

'One night Signor Lopez, our neighbour, heard some strange noises in front of his house and went out to see. He came down all the way to the beach, more or less where we are now. There was no moon, just like now, and he saw what he thought was a huge dog growling. He wasn't afraid of dogs, he always made friends with them at once, so he went towards it, started talking to it, and suddenly it charged him, knocking him right over. It was a boar, wounded and raging. When we heard the yells we came running down and found Lopez disembowelled on the sand. There was nothing we could do for him, poor chap.'

'My God,' says Signora Neri in horror, 'did you know that, Gabriele?'

'Sure,' says Monforti. 'And there are other stories, if you're interested.'

'About boars?'

'No, after the fiftieth or sixtieth villa the boars stopped coming. They're extremely shy beasts and there were too many building sites here, too many cars, too much noise. But there was the fire seven . . . no, eight years ago – anyway before you arrived.'

'I foretold the fire,' recalls Eladia, not at all boastfully. 'The cards spoke quite clearly. And we were all ready, we'd put our money and documents in a bag the day before, and we had our bicycles ready.'

'*Mamma mia*,' says Signora Neri, 'this place is a . . .'

'Sssh,' says Eladia. She has risen from the trunk again and is gazing into the distance, southwards, where the vague pallor of the sand dies into the dark.

'Here you are, they're coming,' she announces without emotion.

'Who?'

'I don't know. Let's signal to them.'

Nervous and also hampered by her gloves, Signora Neri has trouble in turning on her nickel-plated torch, which she finally waves over her head, even though she can still make out nothing on the beach. The north wind has not only accentuated the teeming bustle of the firmament, but has falsified distances even along this modest stretch of the earth's crust, intensifying and thus bringing closer the lights scattered along the promontory of the Capriola (there are a few houses up there too). But from that vivid cluster a little dot now detaches itself, becomes more distinct. It is actually much lower, as well as much closer. And it is moving, it has already left the free beach and is some way along the 'private' one, it is within shouting distance, one can run towards it yelling and stumbling on the sand, it is a shadow, a human figure, a large figure with a smaller figure on its shoulders, it is the guard Vannucci who has found little Colin.

3

Understandably, after poor Signor Lopez's disembowelling by the boar, his widow wanted nothing more to do with the Gualdana; the villa thus passed on to a textile industrialist from Prato, and two years ago, when he went bankrupt, it was bought by Signor Zeme. And it is he now who invites everyone along, to lot no. 122, first row by the sea, since, as he points out, it is within a stone's throw.

Almost everyone thinks this an excellent idea, both because whisky, vodka, etc. seem highly desirable after this long exposure to the freezing wind, and because the occasion is a festive one, the adventure has ended happily, and some kind of celebration seems called for. Colin's parents (the child sits in his mother's arms, looking full of beans and highly pleased with his enterprise) seem in no hurry to go back home; the Carabinieri themselves who, in the meantime, have used their car-horns to summon all the scattered searchers and have sent a radio-message to the van with the dogs (which had already reached Monteriggioni), do not reject the offer. Vannucci, the hero of the evening, naturally asks for nothing better than to recount the various phases of his search and happy discovery all over again. And Monforti's reluctance is finally overcome by the joined forces of his sister Sandra and his brother-in-law Ettore, with the rather less enthusiastic participation of beautiful Signora Neri.

The Uno is left sitting there with the Sergeant inside, irradiating its blue toy-like flashes, and everybody else follows the coast path for a few yards, turns into a narrow path on the right and thus reaches a wide, paved terrace.

Like almost every other villa in the Gualdana, this too is constructed essentially of a few brickwork joints that serve to hold together spectacular glass walls, on the principle that the inhabitants must feel themselves immersed in the vegetation wherever they are in the building. A principle that is much appreciated (as Marshal Butti well knows) by the summer thieves, who slip into the pine-forest from the beach and never fail to find some spectacular window left carelessly open, thus greatly facilitating the removal of video-cameras, money, silverware, sometimes jewellery.

The sliding shutters and the curtains of this particular wall are open and give a full view of the Zeme living-room, a wide rectangle of blue ceramics and white plaster, which has been furnished either entirely at random or with deliberate, arrogant eclecticism.

It looks like a furniture-shop showroom, thinks Signora Neri, who has never been there before, picking her way through the confusion of carved wood, crystalware, wicker-work, plastic and steel, with upholstery ranging from silk to leather and synthetic fibres.

Vannuccini's impression is equally negative, but for practical rather than aesthetic reasons: a few days ago he helped his wife Ivella to shift this mass of clutter to make way for the vacuum-cleaner and now it strikes him that the operation will have to be repeated when the Zemes come back for the Easter and summer holidays.

Marshal Butti thinks nothing of this abundance, which he automatically attributes to the opulence of a place like the Gualdana, and his attention is drawn instead to a person half-hidden in a corner. This is a small, thin woman, who is seated on the very edge of a semicircular leather bench and looks as if she has been set down there, her puny body having no capacity or will to take up a more comfortable position. She is poised in a provisional, hunched attitude, her hands between her knees, and is staring at a television which stands enthroned on a rustic chest. And from the images flickering over the screen, Monforti deduces that she too must have been following the episode of the Perry Mason series (both yesterday and the day before, the local station broadcast Japanese cartoons after Perry Mason). But there would be no point in asking her who stole the 75,000 dollars from the safe, because poor Signora Zeme has for some time suffered from a serious form of depression and everything that happens around her reaches her as if from immense distances, like an echo rolling hollowly down dark gorges and then dispersing across lugubrious deserts.

Monforti realises that those landscapes have not changed since he last saw her in September, and that the treatment they talked about then has borne no fruit. He sees her raise eyes of cement as the living room is suddenly invaded by searchers and rescuers, and he moves towards her in comradely fashion, giving her time to face up to the general cheerfulness, to rustle up a ragged smile, a simulacrum of involvement.

The boy has been found? What boy? Ah, an English boy.

The grey, slender figure now rises to her feet, her eyes slide with glassy indifference over little Colin, resting, blond, beautiful, calm and happy in his mother's arms.

'Listen to Vannucci, he'll tell you all about it!' her husband exhorts her, while he opens a black enamelled bar-cabinet and brings out bottles and glasses. 'He found him.'

Vannucci, an old hunter and thus accustomed to repetition, starts off again at once.

Immediately after calling the Carabinieri, he explains, while it was still light, he followed his instinct and went down to the beach and looked for footprints.

'If there were any, I would see them,' he states with an astute smile, meaning that on the beach, in this season without the bustle of bathers, a small child's footprints could not escape his eyes.

Having found them, he started following them round quirky semicircles and down sudden diagonals, along the water's edge, between the dunes at the verge of the forest, in a circle around some bizarre piece of wreckage, spaced out by a little run, pulled tight by a moment of uncertainty, but always moving southwards, towards the boundary of the Gualdana.

'But then it got too dark, I couldn't see them,' the hunter recalls, and in his demonstrative fervour he bends down to the carpet of Indonesian raffia with yellow and turquoise patterns.

He straightens up again, with a knowing look. 'But I'd brought my torch!'

And so, step by step, he followed the tracks almost as far as the Capriola, and finally discovered the child behind the upturned keel of a resin-boat. He wasn't crying, he wasn't frightened, he just looked as if he were resting after a rather tiring walk.

'I can't speak English,' reveals Vannucci, 'and he doesn't speak Italian. But he let me pick him up without any fuss, he isn't afraid of anything or anyone.'

Signor Graham smiles proudly between sips of whisky. The boy, still in the arms of his mother, who has chosen vodka, looks around imperturbably.

'I couldn't believe that he had got so far,' repeats Vannucci in admiration. 'He walked almost two miles in under an hour.'

He knocks back his vermouth and Signor Zeme refills his glass, then offers the bottle to the Carabinieri, who refuse, make their farewells and leave. And now the other guests, who had all remained on their feet apart from Signora Graham, move towards the spectacular wall by which they had entered.

'Don't go yet, sit down a moment,' says Signor Zeme, gesturing towards a multicoloured group of armchairs and divans in rattan.

'No, thank you, I really must go, I'm expecting a phone-call,' they all reply, more or less. Now that the spot of excitement is over, nobody would know what to say to him.

Monforti hesitates for a moment. Should he stay and talk to Signora Zeme about their respective depressions, discuss the latest developments in analytic therapies and psychotropic drugs? 'Apparently in certain Swiss clinics they're experimenting with a . . .' No, too depressing.

'I don't understand why they keep on coming here,' he says into Signora Neri's ear as they leave. 'It seems she's got a mother or a sister in the Alto Adige: why doesn't her husband take her there? Or to Cortina, or on a cruise to Egypt, anywhere. This pine-forest is a disaster for a depressive.'

'What about you then?'

'But I come because you're here!'

'O Lord.'

As they emerge, the wind swoops down on them as if to punish them for forgetting it, and they turn towards the theatrically illuminated panel where the last scene of the drama has just come to a conclusion. Behind the spectacular picture window they see Signor Zeme replacing the bottles and Signora Zeme depositing herself back in front of the television, where the Japanese puppets continue their stylised combat. Then, amid the keen shafts of wind that abbreviate the farewell rites and cut short the handshakes, everyone walks off with bowed head to his own numbered residence; and the disappearance and rediscovery of the English child remain entrusted to the capricious memory, the unwritten annals, the future mythology of the Gualdana.

II

This Morning on the Wide Pavement

I

THIS MORNING ON the wide pavement in front of the guards' lodge there stands an earthenware pot with an ilex-tree waiting to be transformed into a Christmas tree.

The owner of the nursery, Mazzeschi, had offered to provide a fir, as more in keeping with nordic traditions, observing that the foreign residents would find any other sort of tree out of place, a makeshift solution. But this cowardly conformism ran up against the prevailing rigour of the Gualdana, where the slightest variation from the native flora is considered a betrayal and an example of vulgarity. There are still those who wince at the sight of the cypresses planted fifteen years ago by the late Signori Perroux in front of their villa, and a good few have snubbed a Member of Parliament from Rome, the Hon. Bonanno, who has separated his property from his neighbour's by planting a thuja hedge.

The ilex, including its pot, is three metres high, and Vannucci, Crociani the gardener and Grechi the plumber are all offering suitable suggestions to Vannuccini, as he stands at the top of the ladder, draping the foliage with festoons of coloured lights.

It is a little after eleven. Signora Borst and her friend Eladia arrive on their bicycles and stop for a moment to gaze approvingly at the tree and its decorations, leave a book at the lodge for Signora Neri and proceed on their way to the village to do some shopping. There is a slight sirocco breeze in the air and it is not cold, but the sky is almost completely overcast.

'Higher up, higher up!'

'It's slipping here, put a peg on it!'

Signor Mongelli arrives on his bicycle now, to ask if anyone has seen the electrician. He is told that Ciacci is indeed at the Gualdana, maybe at the Kruysens', and he sets off again into the forest, pedalling energetically.

'You can't see them on this side!'

'No, not like that, it's leaning over!'

Both barriers are raised and Signor Zeme drives out in his white Volvo, slowing down just a fraction and giving a nod of greeting. His wife is sitting beside him, and she is not only less stiff than usual but is actually waving her hands as she talks.

Is she better?

From the top of the ladder Vannuccini confirms this possibility: when his wife, Ivella, called yesterday to do the cleaning, she found her almost normal, compared with the previous occasion, when she hardly said a word, not even hello, didn't do her hair, didn't even want to go out. But now she's thinking of going to see her family in Alto Adige after the holidays, instead of returning to Rome with her husband.

Vannucci finds it natural that she should be feeling better: after all, it was incredible that a woman who was still young and had everything she could ever need to lead a happy life, should have let herself go in that way, without finding the strength to react.

Natural, my arse! Strength to react indeed! Crociani the gardener thinks this is just a load of balls, and shows that the person talking knows nothing about this illness. A cousin of Crociani's, a hard-working woman who got up every day at six, spent years and years like that, sitting in the kitchen staring at her hands, unable to sew on a button, to boil an egg.

Grechi, the plumber, cites the case of Nannini, the petrol-pump attendant, who had to pass his Shell pump on to his nephew, on account of a form of depression which wouldn't go away even after sixty injections and two long stays in a nursing home. And Magnolfi, the builder, has a daughter who's been through it, and Sguanci, the barber's father, is depressed too, it's months since anyone's seen him at the 'Il Molo' bar, and he doesn't even do the football pools any more. And here in the forest, apart from Signora Zeme and Signor Monforti, there are bound to be plenty of other cases. No getting away from it, young and old, rich and poor, it's an illness that can strike anyone, quite at random, and then it may go away all of a sudden or drag on indefinitely, just as it chooses.

This broad medical history doesn't convince Vannucci. Con-artists putting it on, loafers who just don't want to pull their fingers out, that's what all these depressed cases are in his opinion. Or at best, wimps without any strength or willpower.

Him and his strength again. But can't the prat see that losing your willpower is what the illness is all about? And if your will goes, so does the power to have any will, that's the logic of it. And besides – cackles Crociani, turning to the others – who should know better than Vannucci? Isn't the poor bugger in exactly the same situation when it comes to cunt? As everyone knows, he doesn't want to screw any more, and he doesn't even want to want to screw. So is he having injections for it, taking pills or suppositories? No. He's a wimp who isn't even bothered about being one, that's how the illness works!

Vannucci denies this loudly, and he is busily inviting those present to send round their wives and sisters, even their mothers and mothers-in-law, when the Grahams turn up on foot from the forest. The father is holding his son's hand. The mother is pregnant. It is a year since Colin was lost and found again.

2

A year and a day, to be precise. And when Vannucci makes a caressing gesture, with a wrinkled smile of complicity, the child stares at him without any sign of recognition, and then immediately turns to look at a magpie flapping noisily away. He has forgotten all about his adventure on the beach.

'After a year,' says Monforti's brother-in-law, 'he's bound to have forgotten all about it, one of the blessings of infancy.'

He is at the wheel of his own car, next to his wife Sandra. From the back seat Monforti does not let this incautious remark pass without comment. 'That remains to be seen,' he objects, lugubriously rather than polemically. 'Who's to say that the trauma won't come out thirty years later?'

This business of infantile traumas transferred to the unconscious or even simply forgotten, and none the less responsible for serious depressions in later life, is something he has picked up from Signora Zeme, who has recently begun a course of analytic therapy and who phoned him on her arrival yesterday to bring him up to date on her progress.

It's not – she told him – that she has discovered her own trauma yet, but the mere fact of having started to look for it has done her a power of good: it's stirring her, stimulating her, making her more active . . .

Too much so, perhaps. Monforti is perfectly aware that states of euphoria can be a prelude to terrible relapses. But the poor woman's idea of going away for a while to Alto Adige, where her family will be able to help her in her search, seems no worse than any other. He himself should ask Sandra, who is four years older than he is, if she can recall some special and possibly traumatic event that befell him as a child and which no one has ever told him about. Precisely because they didn't want to disturb him, maybe.

'Sandra,' he says, 'you don't—'

'Just a moment,' Sandra interrupts him, as she is writing a shopping-list for the village.

Or could it be – he wonders – that his trouble stems from the very fact that nothing special has ever happened to him? That his life, up to the dark tunnel of depression, had rolled along far too smoothly? Along easy tracks? A happy childhood – he thinks, reviewing things – and an untroubled adolescence; a hit with the girls and successful at his studies; then an active and fruitful role, with Sandra and her husband, managing the firm inherited from his father. And suddenly . . .

'Sorry, what were you saying?' asks his sister, folding up the list. 'Don't I . . .'

'You haven't put your belt on, as usual.'

'Oh no, you're right . . . Anyway we're almost there.'

'The Carabinieri are almost always waiting behind the Shell garage.'

'Really?' she asks, with a tone of shrill vivacity, selected at the last moment instead of a sigh.

She pulls the belt around her shoulder for appearance's sake, and keeps it pulled until they have passed the bend and the lay-by with the Shell station, where in fact no Carabinieri are lurking.

And there is the village.

'It's still a beautiful village!' Sandra says with her usual rapture, not having seen it since September.

'It was a beautiful village until six or seven years ago,' concedes her brother from the back seat. 'Now it's just totally squalid.'

At the wheel, Ettore, the respective husband and brother-in-law, does not pronounce and makes a show of being entirely wrapped up in his driving, although the traffic is much lighter than it is in summer or even at Easter. But from the smile that hovers on his lips, as the car reaches the first houses and continues towards the centre, one would say that he is comparing the two villages: the one Sandra sees and the one Gabriele sees.

SANDRA – Several rows of modern anonymous houses, refined, however, by espaliers of jasmine, trumpet-flowers, bougainvillaea, with several delightful villas in liberty style along the seafront and then . . .

GABRIELE – A miserable suburb of ugly houses which started springing up illegally thirty years ago and which has mushroomed over the last ten, with a few tasteless little detached houses along the seafront and then . . .

SANDRA – . . . and then the natural grace of humble eighteenth- and nineteenth-century architecture, which created a harmonious web of streets and alleyways, *piazze* and *piazzette*, all animated by the colourful display of fruit, jewellery, ornaments, fish, not to mention the designer dresses.

GABRIELE – . . . and then the usual ex-village of ex-fishermen, remade and repainted, spoilt everywhere by nickel-plating, aluminium frames, plate-glass windows and plastic curtains, and of course packed to the brim with stinking pizzerias, rôtisseries, trattorias, fish-shops, not forgetting the discothèque, 'Il Patio'.

SANDRA – The whole place lying at the foot of a hill, on whose steep slopes, as in a Christmas crib, nestles the ancient medieval village, encircled by its almost intact walls and dominated by the ***Collegiata**: a venerable church . . .

GABRIELE – The whole place lying at the foot of a hill, on whose back-breaking slopes, like a wasps' nest, squats the so-called medieval village, encircled by tumble-down walls and dominated by the 'Collegiata': a fancy name for a . . .

SANDRA – . . . a venerable Romanesque church of the XIII century containing a *Sano di Pietro* and a large *Resurrection* attributed to Beccafumi, and dominated in turn by the ****Rocca**, a lofty fortress with battlements where I could live the rest of my days if the Torrianis would only rent me a wing.

GABRIELE – . . . a fancy name for a tiny little black-and-white striped church fronted by two lions (or whatever they are), covered in mould and corroded the way we're all going to be one day, and dominated in turn by the 'Rocca', an absurdly large and banal castle in grey stone which would drive me to suicide if I had to live there like those lunatics, the Marchesi Torriani.

As for the rest, there is little to compare. There is of course the small port with its lighthouse, half-a-dozen fishing-smacks and an infinite number of pleasure boats of all sizes and shapes; there is a Piazza Grande with four plane-trees around a fountain, the town hall and another modest Renaissance church where mass is said once a year; there is the so-called 'meadow of the honey-bees', a vast 'archaeological' site (with remains of Roman walls and a few remnants of a tower against Saracen raids) used as a public car-park.

From there a short road climbs into the real heart of the village, a little square in the shape of an hour-glass named after Fidia Burlamacchi, a local benefactor, but which everyone calls Piazza Garibaldi, on account of the bronze bust set into the wall of a house where the Hero is said to have spent a night.

Here, if one excepts the derisive opinion of a few eccentrics, are to be found the best baker, the best butcher, the best greengrocer and the best pastry-maker in the village, as well as the only stationery-shop, and here the inhabitants of the Gualdana come for their provisions, and also to meet one another and chat.

And indeed Monforti spots almost at once beautiful Signora Neri talking to Signor Zeme by the newspaper-stand, while Signora Zeme stares distractedly upwards, towards the overhanging Rocca, with a thin cigarette in her hand.

Exclamations, greetings and pronouncements on the weather ensue. A shame about the sirocco, there wasn't a trace of a cloud three days ago. And the radio says it's going to get worse, storms are on their way from the Atlantic. Let's hope they're wrong, they often are. On the other hand we could do with some rain: the forest is bone dry.

But the conversation might well grind to a halt at this point, if the poster by the news-stand did not offer a further talking point.

At km 52 along the 'Maremmana':

DEATHTRAP BEND

CLAIMS ANOTHER VICTIM

3

This same poster is the source of worried conjectures on the part of Marshal Aurelio Butti, standing at the window of his office on the first floor. The station is almost opposite the news-stand and the Marshal can see the dark block-capitals distinctly, but as a custodian of law and order, whose task is to prevent rather than repress, his eye reads other, more deadly words:

GARDENER MASSACRES
WIFE AND LOVER
THEN SHOOTS HIMSELF

or alternatively:

YOUNG SKIPPER
KILLS LOVER'S HUSBAND
36 STAB WOUNDS

It has not happened yet but it could happen, given the reports he has received from various sources this morning. The Marshal naturally knows all about the affair that has been going on for months now between the wife of Orfeo Baldacci, the gardener at the Gualdana, and young Dino Fioravanti, who makes a sort of living by hiring his boat out to tourists during the summer months and teaching primary-school children to swim in the winter. A long, lanky fellow, about thirty years old, an odd sort with anarchist leanings, but of the green, ecological kind, and anyway with no previous convictions.

His blond beard has won the heart, or tickled the fancy, of the aforementioned Signora Baldacci, a non-native resident from San Quirico d'Orcia, forty-two years old, restive, dissatisfied with her husband and her own social position, given to exotic clothing, sometimes bordering on the indecent. Having inherited a small property in Val d'Orcia she promptly sold it to a German choreographer, and with the proceeds opened a boutique selling so-called Florentine leghorns imported from Indonesia and took up the study of English and the flute.

As the gardener did not react in any way to these quirks, the Marshal believed him to have resigned himself for the sake of peace and quiet to his cuckold's role. But clearly he was mistaken. Last night, near the 'Il Molo' bar, the two men were involved in an altercation which degenerated into violence, via spitting, shoving, punching, kicking and crude karate-chops.

Fortunately, as neither of them was armed, the brawl concluded with simple grazes and multiple bruising on both sides. And since neither of them has been admitted to hospital or lodged a complaint, there is no reason for Marshal Butti to take any official steps in the matter. Officially, indeed, he knows nothing about it. However, he has heard a report of threats, both of a symbolic kind ('I'll tear your head off!', 'I'll rip your bollocks out!'), and unfortunately of a more realistic and disturbing kind ('I'll shoot the pair of you, you and that bitch!', 'I'll strangle you, I'll slit your guts open, I'll throw you to the fish!').

Furthermore, the husband is a hunter and possesses two shotguns (a Benelli and a Remington), under regular licence. The lover, as a sailor, fisherman and diver, presumably has access to a variety of weapons that could be adopted for cutting or perforating purposes, such as knives, rockets and harpoons, without forgetting his familiarity with ropes and knots. What steps should be taken at this point?

Hardly a month goes by without Headquarters sending some new circular illustrating and insisting on the concept of prevention. But how to effect prevention, in these circumstances?

Butti distractedly swings his regulation pistol which hangs at his side in its black holster. He is a man of courage when the occasion demands it, and has been involved in several gun battles with both organised and disorganised criminals, at times emerging victorious, always with honour. But in this case, unfortunately, there aren't even the grounds for an ordinary summons to the station. He could perhaps fall back on the 'private and informal interview'. But with whom? Just Fioravanti, or with Baldacci as well, or maybe all three, momentarily calling the wife away from her study of the flute?

The idea leaves the Marshal with an unpleasant churning sensation in the pit of his stomach, it gives him a sudden sense of the emptiness and pointlessness of life. And the sight of Signora Zeme (whose condition last year he can recall perfectly, but who now, as she walks along with her husband and Signor Monforti towards the cake-shop looks more or less normal) strikes him almost as a warning.

If the truth be told – the Marshal reflects – what is required is a representative of spiritual rather than temporal power; his Carabiniere uniform is less suited to the occasion than Father Everardo's cowl, which he saw fluttering into the square a little while ago aboard a motor-scooter; its wearer has now stopped to greet the Gualdana visitors by the news-stand.

Another great mouther of the word prevention, the Capuchin priest would rather (and who could disagree?) that pistols and machine-guns were never brought into action. He defines handcuffs as a 'symbol of defeat', and if he had his way he would transform the Force into a corps of social workers, psychiatrists and confessors, organising games and educational amusements. Prevention, my dear Marshal, prevention . . .

But the Marshal has already left the window and is now descending the grey stone steps, with his pistol jostling at his side. There is not a moment to lose, if he wants a preventive consultation with this priest who is for ever bobbing around, preventing here, preventing there.

4

When the Marshal leads Father Everardo away, actually offering to push the scooter along himself (an offer the Capuchin firmly refuses), the residual cluster of Gualdana residents breaks up. Signora Borst and her friend Eladia climb back on to their bicycles loaded with purchases, the Kruysens go back towards the car-park, and Monforti's brother-in-law, at Monforti's request, sets off towards Favilli's shop to buy 2yds of zinc-plated chain and a box of rat-poison. Sandra and Signora Neri decide instead to have a look at 'The Little Blue Man', a shop which opened recently, where they might get an idea for a Christmas present.

Not that the two ladies are absent-minded. They see to all the most important and thought-requiring presents long in advance. But sometimes they too find themselves, with just two shopping days to go till Christmas, clapping a dismayed hand to their mouths and exclaiming, 'O my God, I've still got to get something for Piera!'

However, it is not only this that draws them towards 'The Little Blue Man'. There has also been a kind of telepathic signal, transmitted from the one and instantaneously picked up by the other, suggesting what a good idea it might be to have a quiet moment to themselves for a chat of a – well, private and informal nature.

'She looks much better.'

'Yes, she really seems to be on the mend.'

They are referring to Signora Zeme's state of health, obviously. But neither of them believes what the other says. They are not simply stock remarks, but rather coded messages that they exchange in order to establish immediately at what level the conversation will be conducted.

'You think her husband is right to let her go all the way up there on her own? It's quite a journey.'

'If she feels she can and she wants to, why not? All the better in fact.'

'Yes, it's a good sign, no doubt about it.'

Clearly they are to remain on the surface. At the level of appearances. They are now in front of the shop window, packed with articles that manage to be both dizzyingly miscellaneous and curiously similar: glass tortoises, lighters in the shape of sailing-boats, figs in olive-wood, silver golf-balls, a giant pencil, a miniature elephant . . .

'Who can tell?'

'One can but hope.'

They enter the narrow, neon-lit gut, with its long counters, its long shelves packed tight from the floor to the low ceiling.

'Wasn't there a shoemaker's here once?'

'Yes. Saletti.'

There are two other customers inspecting the necklaces, the thimbles, the cuff-links, the diaries, the paperweights, the backgammon boxes. A woman in a lilac track-suit with a cascade of reddish hair is sitting by a gas-heater, half reading an illustrated magazine and half looking around in desultory reconnaisance. Sandra and Signora Neri wander around silently and separately, stop, retrace their steps, pick things up, examine them, put them back down.

An alabaster clothes-iron. Earthenware scissors. A little table-telephone in solid brass, with a receiver that acts as a bottle-opener.

'Hmph,' they say to each other across one of the counters.
'Well?' they ask each other, meeting at the far end of the shop.

They hesitate, compare, discard.

When they meet up again, they stop with a slight shrug. Sandra picks up at random a nude lady in bronze which is also a corkscrew, then puts it down after looking at the price.

'Expensive too,' she comments more out of commiseration than irony, as if the only way two people like them could react to such senseless junk is with a feeling of bland, dutiful indulgence for the follies of mankind. And a moment later, with a sigh, she comes to the point: 'He keeps on telling me you are his only hope.'

'I know,' sighs Signora Neri in turn. 'That's what he says to me too.'

'We almost managed to persuade him to go somewhere with us this Christmas, just for a change of air, but then he dug his feet in. He wanted to stay here.'

'What can I say?'

'You really wouldn't care to try?'

'No, I really don't feel up to it,' sighs Signora Neri again. 'Put yourself in my shoes.'

'Yes.'

The complicity between them now is that of practical women, who are experts in the cost of living, who know all about grief and are aware how necessary it is to keep it at bay, how necessary it is (and once again it is the Marshal's word) to prevent it.

The subject of this delicate discussion is Monforti, long in love with the beautiful Signora Neri. But what does 'in love' really mean in this case? They both have wavering opinions on the question.

For his sister, Gabriele is a good-looking man, full of

good qualities, very intelligent, at times even too much so (i.e., indistinguishable from an idiot), who has never married because he has never found the 'right woman'. Hence, with the passing of time, his growing sense of emptiness and uselessness, his crisis, his depression. From which he could re-emerge by marrying, or 'setting himself up with', the finally dead-right Natalia Neri.

She on the other hand, sees Gabriele as a good-looking man, full of good qualities, very intelligent, at times even too much so (to the point of folly even), who has never married because of his difficult and touchy character, his deep-rooted pessimism which has degenerated into an incurable form of depression. Marrying, or 'setting herself up with', a man like that would not resolve anything for him and would bring untold troubles and complications upon her.

But each of the women admits that at bottom the other may be right. They are by no means dogmatic, given to absolute judgements, although they are not voluble or insecure either. It is rather that beneath the inflexible little certainties that they rely on for their everyday life (gardeners are all incompetent but one can't do without them, leather suitcases are beautiful but heavy), they have accumulated, through rebuttals and happy surprises, through blunders, come-uppances and sore disappointments, a kind of philosophical relativism, an existential margin to be conceded to error. By now they have understood one thing: that which is might, when all is said and done, prove not to be, and that which would seem to be ruled out *a priori* might, all things considered, turn out to be possible.

'There are your children,' says Sandra, considering a cork Buddha.

'No, that wouldn't be a problem. They've always liked him and he's very sweet and affectionate towards them.'

'Well, yes, he's got a good nature,' his sister concedes. 'I mean, imagine if he were a louse into the bargain!'

'In a way everything would be much simpler, if he were bad,' smiles Natalia. 'No, you know what I mean, what terrifies me is the idea of living with someone who is always so . . . so negative. He knows how to make a joke of it as well, he says that whenever he turns on a tap . . .'

'I know, he expects no water to come out. And of course there's the risk that he could gradually make you like that too.'

'Exactly. I know there are days when he's better, and he says that the whole thing could just clear up from one moment to the next, click, and particularly with me there . . . But how do I know whether this famous click will ever happen?'

Sandra turns the featherweight Buddha round and round in her fingers, then puts it back on the counter.

'There's no way of knowing. Nobody can ever know, with these depressives. You saw Signora Zeme. This morning everything's fine, she's in a euphoric phase, but tomorrow, or this evening, or even this afternoon . . .'

The other lady contemplates a china ashtray in the shape of a half-open tin of sardines. 'I don't know whether I could put up with these continual changes, up and down, black and white, hot and cold. Everything's so uncertain already.'

'I know just what you mean.'

They smile in comradely fashion, veterans of the eternal war against the unpredictability of life.

'But why,' Natalia says heatedly, 'did it have to happen to him, poor thing? And all I manage to do is make him more melancholy, make him feel worse! Why?'

They gaze at each other in this shop where imagination, patience and human industriousness have succeeded in producing nothing but inane horrors. Sandra picks up a glass sunflower that also doubles as a compass. 'But then why anything if it comes to that? Why do we stay here in this hole that just makes me miserable?'

'The Hermit says that depression . . .'

'Oh, look, don't talk to me about the Hermit! He's the most unbearable person I've ever met, I just can't take him. And anyway I reckon he's a fake. Who knows what he gets up to and who with in his hermitage.'

'But Gabriele likes him, after all.'

'Yes, I know, but frankly I can't see . . .'

'You can't deny that as far as intelligence, culture . . .'

'I do deny it, he's just peddling hot air.'

'No, that's not true. For example when he says that *apatia*, which in Greek isn't apathy but . . .'

The sunflower is restored to its place and the two women leave 'The Little Blue Man' without saying goodbye, talking for and against the Hermit, clearly a highly debatable, ambiguous character, who at this very moment is leaving his highly debatable hermitage, seven miles inland from here, to make his way on foot to the Gualdana.

5

A few dozen miles farther north, and also bound for the Gualdana, but by car, there is a woman of an entirely different stamp from Sandra or beautiful Natalia Neri. She too is beautiful, it could be said, but in another way. She is younger, with most of her mistakes still ahead of her. She is greedier, bolder. Maybe stupid, as she herself, at odd moments, suspects. Or maybe just immature. At any rate, highly debatable from several points of view. Her name is Katia, she is on the road from Florence, and when she reaches deathtrap bend she does not notice it because she has never been that way before, has never heard of it.

The bend, which for those coming from the north is downward-sloping, opens up like a wide, inviting parenthesis but closes with a brusque hook to the left. But Katia is not at the wheel and anyway has her mind on other things. She is wondering what she will gain in concrete terms from this 'trip to the seaside' (which is bound to conclude in bed) with this Count Girolamo Delaude (commonly known as Gimo).

Because, of course, only a cretin could ever believe that he's going to get her into the top-model circuit just like that, that he's going to launch her into cinema, etc. But suppose he did manage to get her an engagement with Telegiotto or some other local television network?

'You know,' she says, in order to return to the subject delicately, 'when people tell me that someone like me should . . .'

But Gimo doesn't seem to be listening to her, even though he has never yet missed a chance to tell her what she should or shouldn't be doing, to give her bits of advice and lessons about life, about men, about women, about everything. Besides, it's some time since he last said anything longer than a monosyllable. What's the matter with him? Is he afraid he's gone too far with his promises? One would have to be a cretin not to realise that his attitude has changed.

Katia, who attends an acting course from time to time, wonders what her teacher would suggest at this point. A tone between mischievous and chummy? Or sulky-sweet? Finally she plumps for a tone of maternal solicitude, even though the Count is thirty years older than she is, at least.

'What's the matter, Gimo? Are you tired?'

He jerks his white-streaked head to her for a moment and turns on her a smile of indomitable vigour. 'Me? No, why?'

'I don't know, you're not talking, you're driving like a snail.'

'Of course, one has to be careful here.'

He shows her the deathtrap bend, with its dangerous mule-back camber, its uneven, patched-up surface, points out the red-and-white fencing temporarily replacing a section of stoved-in guardrail.

'People are always getting killed there.'

'Goodness me,' murmurs Katia in a tone between compunction and fear.

After the hook there comes a long flat stretch, then the road starts to climb again, enters a thick wood, seems to want to clamber all the way to the top of this next hill. But it corrects itself, swerving to the left to run alongside a steep slope of yellow tufa.

The Count slows down again, hesitates, turns into the old track which years ago went right up to the crest, and pulls up on the pitted asphalt, overrun by weeds and brambles. He needs a pee, thinks Katia. Unless . . .

She rejects a suspicious-aggressive tone in favour of a languid-surprised one. 'What are you doing? What are we doing?'

'This used to be the road, but it was too steep so they diverted it,' explains Gimo. 'But let's drive on up and I'll show you something beautiful, a real surprise.'

Oh yeah? Does he take me for a cretin? Katia flares. To start with you can bet on it that it's going to be far from a 'surprise' for her. And then she has her doubts as to how beautiful this 'something' will be. And anyway it's not the kind of place where she would ever agree to . . .

'In summer it's all go up here, you've got no idea,' sniggers Gimo, driving at walking pace up the abandoned road.

'What's all go?'

'Tarts, of course. Their base is in Livorno, they bring them up here in a van around midday and come back for them about two a.m. They're all black now. Once there were just three or four old local whores hanging around for the lorry-drivers, but these new ones have put them out of business, at least in high season. These commuters are much younger and I can tell you some of them are really stupendous. Genuine black statuettes.'

'You like black women?' asks Katia, airy-curious.

'Well, you know, they're . . . different, they've got that . . . animal nature.'

'Oh they have, have they?' says Katia, ironic-piqued.

Gimo puts his hand on her thigh, which her tight-fitting stretch trousers put into fleshy relief. 'Don't worry about it, you're quite a little statuette yourself.'

Katia does not reply, does not react, prepares the lashing-outraged tone she is going to need in a minute when Delaude tries to leap on her. What does the imbecile take her for? If anything is to happen at all, it's not going to be till much later, in the exclusive pine-forest where he claims to own an exclusive villa, which she has let herself be talked into visiting without obtaining any kind of guarantee from him for afterwards. And now the filthy lecher wants to get it over with here, in these delightful surroundings, on this exclusive hill for black tarts; he's been thinking about it for the last half hour, charging himself up, setting the snare for the white woman! Chucking her down on to the grass (which doesn't even grow here) or the back seat of the car, like any old whore!

The thought makes her grind her teeth, while the car continues to climb cautiously through the thick bushes that rasp against its side. My God, she'll give it to him: so whatever happened to all that fine talk about style? All those precious lessons about the refinement, restraint and ladylike manners so necessary for a future top model? She'll let him have it: shit, lout and bastard. And she's already letting herself have it: cretin, cretin and triple cretin to fall for it, to actually go and boast to Stefania and Debora about this new acquaintance, oh such a gentleman and so refined, so different from all the others for once.

The car emerges on to the crest of the hill, leaving the last pockmarked strips of asphalt, and pulls up in a clearing of stubble and rocks.

'There you are,' says the Count.

Katia sits there, rigid, her lips and knees tightly closed.

But he gets out, walks round and opens her door; he takes her delicately by the elbow and leads her to the remains of a little wall.

'Just look at this view!' he exclaims, sitting down.

He lights a cigarette, smiling innocently.

She chooses a tone between ecstasy and enchantment, but what comes out is a long sigh of relief. 'Aaah . . .'

Count Delaude, self-styled possessor (actually it is his wife who owns it) of one of the 153 villas of the Gualdana, heaves a sigh of momentary relief as well. Gain time, or rather waste time, see to it that they don't get to the pine-forest before sunset and darkness. This has been his only thought for the last twenty miles. But this brief diversion certainly doesn't solve his problem.

It is just a quarter past one, he checks furtively while pretending to savour in religious silence this view which he knows by heart and which doesn't interest him one jot. Valleys and dales covered in scrub, occasional cottages, olive-groves, fields, stony outlines of villages on distant hills. Nothing special, nothing to take one's breath away. Land, furthermore, that mostly belongs to Vannozza Vettori, a venomous harridan who has not only cleaned him out at bridge on several occasions, but would give a combine-harvester to catch him here with this Katia and go cackling the news to every Tom, Dick and Harry. Not to mention, of course, his wife, who after spending the holidays looking after their estate in Chianti (that too is her property – he doesn't have a lira of his own) would not restrict herself to cackling.

He looks at Katia, who is smoking too but on her feet, with one hand on her hip, in the 'carefree' pose of a supermarket model – which after all is what she is – wearing the pick of this season's articles: orange jacket in nacryl with leather trimmings (L. 94,000); mauve trousers in stretch fabric (39,000); 'Los Angeles' boots (70,000). The ensemble rounded off with a pineapple hairdo, outsize silver ear-rings and green nail varnish.

Beautiful. Yes, beautiful, for anyone interested in the basics, or he wouldn't have hung around her for almost a week. But how could he have even dreamt of arriving at the Gualdana in daylight, with a 'beauty' of this sort? Of stopping at that barrier, with her by his side, and all the residents and other acquaintances bustling in and out? Even up here, visible as they are from the road below, there's a risk that . . .

He looks behind himself, slowly but irresistibly, then shrugs and gazes back at the cloudy horizon.

'What's up? Did you see something?' says Katia, at once alarmed.

'No, nothing, what do you expect?'

Absurd. But for a moment it had struck him as quite possible that a farmhand of Vanozza Vettori's, or Vanozza herself, passing by and recognising him, might have climbed up to investigate.

You're too edgy, too imaginative, he reproves himself, beginning to explain the view to gain another minute: 'That village down there is Poggiali, the one on that hill over there is . . .'

Or was there some slight noise behind them?

'Do you like the countryside?' says Katia.

'Well, you know, I more or less live in it, it's my living . . .'

'It doesn't do anything for me – just makes me sad,' she reveals with a grimace. 'If I had to live here I'd die. My ideal is a big city, people, movement, bright lights. For example I'd be really happy in New York, I'm sure.'

Why didn't I take her to Milan? thinks Delaude, cursing his own avarice but more specifically that of his wife, who sends him a ridiculous monthly cheque which hasn't increased in years, despite inflation. On the other hand there's no getting away from it that a hotel in Milan, with the demands that the aspiring top model would hardly have failed to make, would have cost him at the very least, what with a suite, breakfast and garage . . .

He is still calculating, when Katia impetuously grips his arm.

'Who's behind there?' she asks in a childlike, terrorised whisper.

'Where?'

'There, behind those bushes. There's someone moving.'

'Keep calm,' he says in order to calm himself.

In the silence, noises can definitely be heard from the tangle of broom and oak saplings. Somebody, something, is rustling dry leaves, shifting or trampling on twigs.

'It's not a tiger, they died out years ago round here,' he tries to joke. 'It'll be a pheasant.'

'Let's get away,' whispers Katia.

'At the very worst it'll only be a peeping Tom moving off. We've disappointed him.'

'Listen, I want to get away from here, all right?'

On the way down, they find an old wreck of a car parked halfway across the end of the abandoned road. Gimo squeezes past, cursing but then laughing, because in the side-mirror a figure has appeared, emerging from the wood above them: a miniaturised hulk of a woman in a miniskirt, with a cigarette in her mouth, who at that distance is not so very unlike Vannozza Vettori.

'One of the old guard. Clearly they take advantage of the low season to return to their old haunts.'

'Just what sort of place have you brought me to?' fumes Katia in an outraged-snarling tone. 'And anyway it's gone half-past one. Where are we going to have lunch?'

At Bagliano, he thinks, brightening. And he promises her an exceptional lunch in a picturesque but exclusive trattoria, with two if not three forks in the Michelin Guide. 'Da Mamma Adolfina'.

'It's some distance but well worth it, you'll see!'

Bagliano is not only some distance, but quite out of their way, with a difficult drive along minor roads, full of twists and gradients. Meanwhile the gathering clouds promise early darkness. The fatal barrier of the Gualdana already appears less fatal.

Come black night, thinks Gimo.

III

Every Day at 6 a.m.

I

EVERY DAY AT six a.m., at two p.m. and ten p.m., the two guards on duty at the lodge are replaced by another pair according to a complicated and often bitterly contested system of rotation, which has to take into account holidays, illnesses, the seasons and many other variables.

But at two p.m., particularly during the holiday periods, it is not rare for one of the guards whose turn has finished, or even both of them, to stay where they are rather than go home: ready to run errands in the village, to help out in emergencies or undertake any other suitably paid tasks. Today, for example, when Barabesi and Guerri come along for their shift, it is Vannuccini who remains on hand for the residents. Vannucci, meanwhile, is supposed to call urgently on the Hon. Bonanno, who arrived last night and found several traces of mice – in the kitchen, dining-room and sitting-room, a real invasion – and is counting on him to take the appropriate measures.

Except that the barrier is already raised to admit the gardener, Agostino, and then another gardener close behind him, Diomede. And the ensuing exchange of opinions, ideas and observations soon involves them all.

On average each gardener looks after a dozen villas in the Gualdana, with the exception of Orfeo Baldacci who is in charge of nineteen. However, it is not this record, a much envied but incontestable one, that has sparked off the discussion now raging around the Christmas ilex.

'All I say is he should have done it sooner!'

'But he didn't know about it!'

'Come on, everyone knew about it!'

'That doesn't mean a thing. The husband's always the last to know!'

The theme of the debate, therefore, is last night's sensational incident outside the 'Il Molo' bar, which has already given Marshal Butti cause for serious deliberation.

It might have been sensational, but it didn't make much difference to things, opines Guerri. And anyway, according to Vannuccini, it was too late. Its only result has been to give official confirmation to poor Orfeo's cuckolded status. What he ought to have done, his colleague Diomede reckons, was either react firmly sooner, or go on pretending not to notice, since that was all he'd done up to now.

'But I tell you he didn't know!' his other colleague, Agostino, argues.

'Or maybe he did know, but hoped she would come to her senses,' Vannucci comes in philosophically.

An unbridgeable contrast emerges here, not between guards and gardeners, but between those who are single and those who are married. The latter (Diomede, Vannuccini, Guerri) heatedly support the following theses: 1) if their wife were ever to betray them (an inconceivable notion) they would realise immediately; 2) first of all they would see to it that she got laid up for at least forty days at the hospital in Grosseto or Siena; 3) only afterwards would they settle things with the lover, restricting themselves, however (since the initiative for adultery always comes from the woman), to bashing his face in.

The three single men (Agostino, Barabesi, Vannucci) counter with allusive and disturbing arguments. Wives (present company's excepted of course) are extremely astute in their amorous dealings, capable of the most astounding feats of simulation. When they betray their husbands (present husbands excepted, naturally) the first question is whether it might not be owing to his negligence. Knocking them about is merely the action of a coward and gets one nowhere, leaving aside the fact that many of them are perfectly capable of defending themselves anyway. And as for bashing the lover's face in, one needs to look at each case individually, because there too the would-be basher might easily find himself the bashee. Look at Orfeo, for example.

As if summoned by this *ad hominem* argument, Orfeo Baldacci turns up in his rattling van. The barrier is raised, and although he does not stop but drives straight on towards one of his nineteen villas without even a wave, the conversation none the less dies away in an embarrassed, contrite silence, with no attempt at a nudge or a wink. All of them – even though they do not pose the question of prevention that the Marshal has illustrated to Father Everardo – regret not being able to do anything in such a delicate affair, and with so contrary a character as Orfeo.

But their discomfort also arises from the perception of a strange and desolating phenomenon. When seen from close quarters, traditionally comic situations are not funny, they plump to the ground with a dry thud, like pine cones. A betrayed husband is ridiculous so long as he keeps to his place – a butt of idle gossip and chatter, a figure in a newspaper article, or a television sketch. But Orfeo, in flesh and blood, with his bandaged, scowling face, driving along with his collection of brooms, hoes, rakes and lawnmowers, creates a totally different impression, doesn't raise the ghost of a smile. Quite the reverse.

And so it is that Vannucci, recalled to his duties, drives off quickly towards the Hon. Bonanno's villa, situated on the other side of the Old Ditch. Vannuccini is left wondering whether it is worth his while to stay there, with his moped, waiting for entirely hypothetical errands. There is nothing in fact to give him any inkling of the profitable, untroublesome task he will be entrusted with in a short while by Signor and Signora Zeme.

Or would Signorina Eladia's Tarot cards give him some inkling? After all, what is in store for him is a journey, albeit a short one.

2

Milagros, Signora Borst's Filipino maid, has come to serve the coffee but will not go away again. Standing over Signorina Eladia's shoulder, she too studies the twelve cards the lady has arranged in a wheel in front of herself, according to the astromantic method.

'Ah, lucky the Magician's there!' she approves with her curious accent, more Tuscan than Filipino now, when she sees her favourite card among the twelve.

Signorina Eladia has never managed to convince her that none of the cards of the Major Arcana, not even the Magician, is favourable or unfavourable in itself, but only in combination with the others, with the 'House' that it occupies in the Wheel, and above all with the thirteenth card: the 'controlling' card from the Minor Arcana. For her, that many-coloured figure, with its magic wand and its juggler's table, can only bring good luck.

'The Magician is always good,' she repeats.

'Milagros please!' Signora Borst reproves her, having seen her friend's face cloud over from the start (and become even grimmer when she drew the thirteenth card), and she does not dare to disturb her with the slightest question.

But Eladia gives no sign of having heard. She has not even noticed the coffee, which is getting cold in its cup beside her. Her eyes continue to pass from the card of the Minor Arcana (a Four of Swords) to the wheel where the Major ones are set out, one in each of the Twelve Houses, and her lips remain compressed in an expression of perplexity, of growing apprehension. Even Milagros finally goes off feeling doubtful and uneasy, for once.

Wilhelmine (this is Signora Borst's name) pretends to take up her work again, which consists in painting Christmas pine cones with gold and silver. Actually she is trying to remember whether the astromantic wheel, which Eladia lays out each time they enter a new sign of the zodiac, has ever appeared so threatening as on this December 23rd. Maybe that time there was a fire, seven years ago? No, then Eladia had wanted to be absolutely sure, before giving the alarm, but she had seen the fire (the controlling Arcana card was of Wands) at once.

In any case, she thinks, this Christmas does not look like being a happy one. Because the other cards may be as happy as you like; she can't distinguish them, from where she is sitting, and anyway wouldn't know how to interpret them. But the Four of Swords, outside the wheel, is perfectly visible and gives no grounds for optimism. Its influence is *always* negative.

In the prolonged silence, the ticking of the pendulum-clock on the mantelpiece has become audible and alarming. It is half-past two when Eladia finally raises her eyes.

'Nobody,' she says, 'can tell what is going to happen. But

we must be ready for anything: the wheel is rocking, the Houses are moving, the Fool has overcome the Magician and has unhinged the Four Gates.'

'It's a catastrophe!' shouts Wilhelmine.

Given that the Four Gates, in the wheel, are those of the Four Houses situated at the Four Cardinal Points; given that these Houses are I ('Life') in the West, VII ('The Wife') in the East, X ('The Kingdom') in the North and IV ('The Father') in the South; and having specified that the Houses in question are all 'fortunate': what remains to be seen – as Eladia is now saying – is which Arcana they contain today.

'Yes, but in the meantime there's that horrible card of Swords outside,' says Wilhelmine with a touch of impatience. 'That's the worst, isn't it?'

'Just a moment,' says Eladia, 'let's leave aside the Swords for now. Let's start from the West Gate – from House I, where the MAGICIAN is. When he finds himself in an Unlucky House such as XII ('The Enemies') or even worse VIII ('Death'), he can be fatal; but in fortunate Houses he gives of his best: he is the vital impulse wedded with reason, will-power directed to good.'

'Well, that's a relief.'

'Except,' continues Eladia, 'that at the opposite Gate there's the FOOL, acting as a counterweight. Because the Fool too . . .'

She breaks off to knock back her coffee, stone-cold by now, and starts up again: 'Because the Fool too, in a Lucky House like the VII, is at the peak of his strength. But this strength is blind and thoughtless, this strength is directed towards Chaos! . . . By good luck, at the North Gate there's JUSTICE with her Scales, who should guarantee Equilibrium. But . . . what have we got at the South Gate?'

Signora Borst does not enjoy this kind of suspense, with

its alternate dousing of hot and cold. She wishes her friend would get straight to the point. Besides, she has already seen that at the South there is FORTUNE with her wheel, and she begins to understand the catastrophic mechanism that the controlling card has set in motion.

'Without those Swords,' says Eladia, 'things would be stalled, even though extremely tense. But as it is, the forces of the Irrational have swept away the Magician too, and the Fool has been left to run wild. The Scales of Justice have rocked. And the Wheel of Fortune, with the fall of the Gates, has imposed its alternating motion on the whole system. Do you see?'

Wilhelmine has no desire to go and see whether this rocking is merely symbolic or whether the cards really are moving. But even from where she sits she has the impression that the Magician is passing back and forth from the House of 'Life' to that of the 'Enemies', while the Fool, at the opposite extremity, is passing back and forth from the House of the 'Wife' to that of 'Death'. The suggestion is so intense that her own table, with its three coloured pine cones and its pots of paint, seems to be caught up in the rocking motion. Raising her eyes she finds herself staring at the great window of the living-room, and beyond the window to the stretch of wood that separates lot no. 126 from no. 122, which both stand in the front row by the sea.

'It must be really close to us!' she says with a shiver, wrapping her chequered shawl around herself. 'It couldn't be Signora Zeme, could it?'

'What? Who?'

'The Fool,' says Signora Borst. 'The madwoman.'

No (explains Eladia), the Fool could be anyone: even a child, or an animal. And the same is true of the Magician, the Lover, the Hermit, the Chariot, all the other cards of the

Wheel. It is not possible to make any direct correspondences with real facts or individuals, given the continual shifting of astrological Houses. For example the Lover in House V ('The Children') might seem to be Gabriele Monforti getting better and finally marrying, having children; but in House VI ('Sickness') it could also be Gabriele getting worse, or Signora Baldacci's lover struck down by an incurable illness or even, perhaps, that so-called Count Delaude contracting a disease in some mercenary love-affair . . . And the Hermit, also known as the Capuchin, is already ambiguous for that double correspondence it has with Ugo the Hermit and with Father Everardo; but whereas in House III ('The Brothers') it could play a positive role, in II ('Profit') it is just a trickster or anyway a charlatan, which is what Monforti's sister claims in fact. As for the Chariot, with its driver cracking his whip to goad the two horses . . .

Milagros has come back to collect the cups and she pauses to examine the Chariot. She looks at the driver, studies the horse, and recalls the old converted 2-Chevaux that is always driving around the Gualdana.

'But he's not cracking a whip,' she yells, 'that's Baldacci shooting his wife! . . . Bang, bang! . . . Stone dead.'

Eladia shakes her head impatiently.

'Nothing is what it seems any more,' she says. 'Nothing seems what it is any more. All we can do is wait.'

'Come on now!' the Filipino encourages her, 'when the Magician's around, we needn't be afraid of anything!'

'Milagros, please, go away,' sighs Signora Borst, applying her paintbrush once again to the minuscule scales of the pine cones that Father Everardo has asked her to do for the oratory Christmas-tree.

3

Pine cones fall continuously from the Gualdana's 18,300 pine-trees. Old cones that have opened up and withered on the tree, fully ripe cones crammed with kernels, young cones of a tender green, fresh-formed baby cones, not to mention the oblong cones of the pinasters, compact and grim, as if warped by their bastard stock. They drop with gentle thuds on to the sand or into the rosemary bushes, they crash noisily on to roofs or the paving around villas, they plummet devastatingly amidst the cups of an outdoor coffee-table, irrupting terrorist-fashion into the conversation.

'It's nothing, don't worry,' says Sandra, gathering up the fragments.

'Twelve inches to the left and it would have got you right on the cranium,' remarks her brother.

'Cones have eyes, they say here.'

'An idiotic proverb, like all proverbs. From a height of twenty metres a cone could really hurt someone. And if it were to hit a child on the head . . .'

It may be true in theory, but Sandra just cannot remember ever having heard of anyone, child or adult, being taken urgently to hospital on account of a Gualdana cone. But she is careful not to contradict her brother, as these depressives, these pessimists, are always well stocked with irrefutable arguments in favour of the worst, so that you end up convinced yourself that pine cones are indeed a public menace.

No, Natalia can't be blamed for keeping away, Sandra tells herself, chucking the bits into the rubbish bin, a man like Gabriele can really get you down, he makes you tense and the tension grows and grows, till suddenly . . .

The telephone rings and she starts inordinately.

'See what I mean,' she murmurs in irritation, hurrying towards it.

It is Signora Zeme (wonder what she thinks of the cones?), who has really made up her mind this time, she is leaving this very day and by herself because now, as her analyst confirmed on the phone from Rome, she really must try to handle this new self-awareness all on her own as far as possible, and that means without her husband, who is therefore going to drive her but only as far as Florence where he will put her on the 21.10 *rapido* to Milan where she's already got her seat booked – Vannuccini just has to go and pick up the ticket and the reservation at the agency in Grosseto – and the hotel in Milan is booked too, so tomorrow before setting off again to Bolzano at midday she will also be able to see her neurologist, who is in Milan, and whom she has also phoned and who has been so kind as to give her a morning appointment before he himself goes off on his holidays, since the pills, of course, she can't just stop taking them from one day to the next, even though the analytical treatment has already benefited her enormously, incredible, if one thinks that just a week ago, for example, the idea of moving even just to spend Christmas here . . .

She laughs, talking in an impetuous headlong manner, letting the words gush out as if the flow might cease at any moment and leave her stranded in the sands of dumbness.

The avowed aim of the call is to say goodbye and Happy Christmas before leaving. The real aim (when Monforti is summoned to the receiver by Sandra) is to receive some encouragement from someone who understands her, who knows all about it, a comrade in woes, before she takes the plunge. And indeed, to leave the last word to him, since nothing after all is irrevocable, the departing impulse can still be checked, the nodule of anxiety dissolved in the slough of inaction, of immobility, slumped in front of an episode of Perry Mason.

'I'll drop in on her,' announces Monforti on his way out.

'Good idea,' says Sandra, 'take a little walk. Aren't you going to put your hat on?'

'My hat? But it isn't cold at all.'

'No, I meant for the cones,' his sister teases him affectionately.

Then she remembers the tin of rat-poison Gabriele had insisted she bought this morning, after hearing of the invasion at the Bonannos', and she resignedly starts to sprinkle its contents into the corners of the room. Here and in the near-by villas mice have never been a problem, but she might as well humour him. If only, she thinks, all his problems had to do with mice, pine cones, Carabinieri lurking behind the Shell pump . . .

The door of the Zemes' house is open. Monforti enters and pauses in the hall, coughing to signal his presence. A thread of smoke winds upwards from a thin cigarette abandoned in an ashtray by the phone. He hears distant footsteps, curt noises, then Signora Zeme's voice shouting: 'Antonio! Have you found it?'

'No!' shouts her husband, emerging a second later from a corridor with his head lowered, cursing through gritted teeth: 'Where in Christ's name . . .'

Observing Monforti he gazes at him with scowling, hostile surprise, before summoning up a smile of civil welcome. They cannot find the phial of one of the numerous pyschotropic medicines that mark out Signora Zeme's days.

'Sorry, but until we find these damned drops . . .'

He moves off into another corridor and disappears. At the same instant his wife appears at the sitting-room door.

'The Enzed,' she says to Monforti, to anyone, with a distracted air. 'God knows where I put it.'

She sees the lighted cigarette, picks it up with trembling fingers, inhales, looks at her watch and puts the cigarette back down. 'I have to take it now, otherwise it's no use. Thirty drops.'

This NZ is a supportive tranquilliser to be taken – at an appropriate interval from the others – in anticipation of events that might expose the patient to stress.

'Where can it have got to? It was over there, with all the others, in the drawer of the . . . or maybe last night I had it . . .'

'If I can be of any help . . .' murmurs Monforti, in an attempt to prevent this tangle of desperation from reaching critical proportions. But she doesn't reply, she goes off in the same direction as her husband, leaving the visitor and the dwindling cigarette.

Without moving, Monforti starts to run his eyes over a set of shelves crammed with heterogenous objects: shells, earthenware pots, African statues, oriental masks, a few books, twisted branches picked up off the beach, which the sea has stripped and polished like the bones of fantastic animals.

'Anyone in?' says a voice at the front door, still open.

It is Vannuccini, whom the Signora summoned by phone a little while ago.

'Yes, yes,' Monforti assures him, 'Signora Zeme's in, she's just looking for a . . .'

Signor Zeme reappears, and passes rapidly between the two of them, ignoring them completely and proceeding towards other rooms, drawers, shelves. His wife returns too, and at once shouts to Vannuccini: 'Ah, yes, thank you, just a moment, my husband's on his way, he's just . . .'

She sees the smoking cigarette, stubs it out, twisting it mercilessly into a right angle, and goes out by one of the doors. Another door, in the distance, slams.

Vannuccini volubly explains to Monforti about the task he has been entrusted with. What with the journey there and back – he concludes, shaking his big blond head, and hoping that the agency in Grosseto has already prepared everything – it'll take him at least an hour and a half. Mind you, the Signora has done well to book, with the crowds you get on the trains at peak periods!

Yes, the crowds. Monforti had not thought of this aggravating circumstance, and now it strikes him that the venture is definitely to be advised against: just imagine poor frail Signora Zeme in the crammed carriage, jostled and pressed on all sides, then dragging her suitcase through the violent eddies and swirls of the entrance hall of Milan Central Station, assailed by the terrifying tannoy, the shouts and cries, the unnerving echoes. She can't possibly cope with it, she mustn't leave . . .

'May I?' says someone at the door. 'Is it a good moment?'

It is Father Everardo, looking for the gardener, Orfeo. 'They tell me he's in the forest, but nobody knows where he's got to. He hasn't come this way by any chance?'

They have no idea and are telling him about the missing drops when the telephone starts to ring, brusquely, almost brutally, in the small hallway. The three men stiffen, ill at ease until Signor Zeme appears, snatches up the receiver, pronounces a few curt yesses and noes, concludes with a 'No, not even at the agency in Viterbo! We'll see after the holidays, perhaps!' and bangs it down again, turning a sullen face on the visitors, and scowling even harder when his wife enters in tears.

'They're nowhere around, they're nowhere, I can't find them,' she repeats in anguish.

She stands there, her arms hanging from her shoulders like dead branches.

'But listen,' says her husband, 'are you quite sure they're not in the chest . . .'

'Come, come,' says the priest, 'We'll help you look, they must be somewhere, after all.'

Vannuccini shakes his head again, dismayed by the amount of furniture and knick-knackery cluttering every room of this house, but Father Everardo urges him into the sitting-room, invites Monforti to search the bathrooms, sends Zeme into the bedrooms, even into the spare ones, and takes Signora Zeme with him to inspect the rooms in the basement.

'But they can't possibly be there, I never go down there,' she says plaintively, descending the first steps.

'Come on, let's have a look all the same, you'll never find anything if you don't look.'

The deserted hallway becomes a recipient for echoes from all directions, then, about ten minutes later, acts as assembly point for the mortified searchers.

As Signora Zeme sinks sidelong on to the bench by the phone one of her feet slips from its brown shoe and lies there on the cold summer tiles like a bony relic on the shore.

'At this point I wonder . . .' begins Signor Zeme gravely, turning to the priest.

He says no more, but everybody understands. The journey would be madness. But (Monforti says to himself) couldn't, shouldn't it be her husband who decides to take her to Florence, to Milan, to the neurologist, to her sister's or somewhere, anywhere, for God's sake?

'No, I'm going,' groans the woman, 'I'm going, I'm leaving . . .'

'But Signora,' says Father Everardo.

She looks up at them in silence, those four men standing over her, dominating her, hemming her in with their disapproval. And suddenly she jerks awkwardly to her feet, thrown off balance by the missing shoe. 'Antonio, it was you!' she shouts at her husband. 'You hid them to stop me going! Where have you put them, tell me at once where you've put them!'

'Now keep calm,' says the priest.

'Don't give me calm, it was him! He wants to keep me here! He wants to stop me doing what I want to do, just for once, he wants to go on stifling me as he's always done! To destroy me! To . . .'

She tries, still standing, to thrust her foot into the shoe blindly, shifts it with her toe, then pushes it away angrily.

'Magda, please,' says her husband. 'Wait, I'll help you . . .'

He kneels down, but something in his tone (infinitely patient, or perhaps cunningly querulous, plaintive, recriminatory?) arouses in Monforti a feeling of dislike, of visceral repugnance for the rough, honest fellow that Signor Zeme had been in his eyes until a moment ago. He is suddenly certain that it is he, and only he, that is the cause of his wife's depression, the perpetual trauma that the poor woman must absolutely get away from. Now he understands: Signora Zeme's journey isn't a whim, a sudden euphoric quirk, but an attempt to escape. And it is quite possible that in the deadly winding tunnels that lie beneath their married life her husband really did hide those drops, that for some dark aim of his own he really did . . .

'Is this the medicine by any chance?' says Vannuccini, who had wandered off without anyone noticing.

He holds up a brown phial and Signora Zeme runs limping towards him.

'The Enzed! How clever! Wonderful! Thank you! Thank you so much!'

'It was on a shelf in the kitchen, behind the jars.'

'Ah, you see,' she shouts, clutching the phial. 'You see.'

Monforti is reminded of Signora Graham clutching to her breast the child Vannucci found a year ago; but he also grasps the ambiguity of the cry: has she remembered that she put the Enzed behind the jars? Or has it confirmed for her that her husband hid it there?

Signor Zeme gets clumsily back to his feet, walks away, comes back with a glass of water which he hands to Father Everardo, who has already taken possession of the phial and now shakes the drops of colourless liquid from it, counting them in a low voice, one by one. Everybody listens in total silence to this numerical prayer, eight, nine, ten . . . fourteen, fifteen, sixteen . . . twenty-eight, twenty-nine, thirty!

And then, like the frenzy of movement that seizes everyone at the end of mass, Zeme takes out his wallet and gives Vannuccini some money, his wife kicks off the other shoe as well and walks off talking about her suitcase but then comes straight back to embrace the priest, ordering her husband to confirm her arrival at the hotel in Milan and urging Vannuccini to hurry back from Grosseto, with or without the booking for tomorrow's train, repeating Happy Christmas, Happy New Year in all directions, until, shoeless and vulnerable, she approaches Monforti, takes him by the arm as if inviting him to dance, but does not say a word, looks at him so as to allow him to peer into the depths of her fear.

'Yes, sure,' says Monforti, 'go, don't worry, just go.'

'All's well then,' says the priest setting off again on his scooter. And as Vannuccini too roars off, a large pine cone drops on to the mudguard of his moped with a resounding 'clang'. This, thinks Monforti walking back home, is a decision too. A fallen cone cannot fall again.

Only – he reflects, turning right instead of left in order to prolong his stroll – only that in the life of a depressive nothing is ever really decided, everything is continually cancelled and redisputed within the space of a day, an hour, a minute . . .

4

After ascertaining the damage (carpets gnawed and books minced, a sofa riddled, even wardrobes nibbled); after sealing the opening by which the rodents had infiltrated the house (a rust-eaten ventilation grating in the boiler-room); and after placing his means of slaughter (poisoned grain and pastry, contrivances with spring-released and sluice-gate snares, cages with sliding backs) in strategic points about the house, Vannucci does not spare the Bonanno family his remonstrances.

First of all, he points out to the Honourable Member's wife and two daughters, they should not have left any sort of food in the larder. Not even in tins. Since, he explains, 'they can smell it all the same, and then they take it out on whatever they find'. And secondly, in September, before leaving, they should have called him to come and check that everything was properly closed and sealed.

'Because,' he says knowingly, 'of course it's true the tiniest mice can get in anywhere if they want to. But through that grating . . .'

A glance from the Hon. Bonanno halts him, but it is too late. The three women – three lanky, indistinct figures, apparently of an age in their drabness – are staring at him with anxiety behind three pairs of thick lenses.

'The tiniest . . . mice?' stammer the two girls together. 'Then, the ones that got through the grating . . .'

'What were they like? . . . What are they like? . . .' asks their mother, ashen-faced. 'You mean they're . . .'

'Tiny, tiny,' Vannucci collects himself. 'That's what I said, isn't it? Tiny! They're always the ones that do the most damage. And then here in the forest, you might get a few medium-sized ones in the houses,' he says opening his thumb and index-finger four or five inches at the most, 'but big ones, no, never!'

'No big ones?'

'Definitely not,' confirms the Honourable Member. He knows nothing at all about the pine-forest (because when he is here he spends practically the whole day on the phone to Rome, or poring over his fax-machine), but he mainly hopes not to have to spend another night in the armchair with the light on, keeping watch over his wife and daughters barricaded in the double bed.

Meanwhile Vannucci, under the women's panic-stricken eyes, has knelt down in the sitting-room to place one last trap, large enough for a rabbit.

'There you go,' he says, standing up again. 'I've finished then. And don't worry madam, don't worry ladies. Because as the saying goes, there are more traps than mice here now!'

When Bonanno ushers him into the study in order to pay him for his trouble, Vannucci adds in a low voice: 'I said what you told me to, *Onorevole*, but they're big rats, you know? Did you see the droppings? Anyway, let's wait and catch one so we can see what sort they are. Because if they're water-rats, though I don't think so, seeing as we're quite a way from the Old Ditch, you can get rid of them more easily. But if they're roof-rats, which aren't so big mind you, or maybe martens . . .'

'For goodness sake, how many sorts are there? They should have told me this when I bought the land! Instead . . .'

'No, because you see, *Onorevole*: the ones that get into the houses, like I was saying, aren't that common. Otherwise you'd have to count the ones they call "big-moles", for example.'

'Big-moles?'

'Yes, that's what we call them, but they're not really moles: they're rats that make their nests in the trees. But then there are squirrels too, aren't there? And dormice that live in the hazel-trees. Then in autumn you get the boars, though there aren't so many of those now, and there's shrews, there's badgers, there's even a porcupine, imagine that. It's an old porcupine that goes about at night, like all porcupines, but you hardly ever come across him now: when he goes, who knows whether there'll ever be another one. But there are still frogs, there are tortoises, *frustoni*, which are great big snakes . . . Well, I mean! A pine-forest is a pine-forest, after all.'

'I know perfectly well it is,' says the Hon. Bonanno, somewhat piqued since he is not only a member of the Ist Commission (Constitutional Affairs) but also the XIth (Agriculture and Forestry), in place of Under-secretary Ciaffi, and thus boasts knowledge in the ecological field. 'But it strikes me that here things overstep the limit!'

5

'Two firemen meet in the fire station yard, where there's a tiny Christmas-tree with just one candle lit. One says to the other . . .'

'Firemen aren't funny.'

There is a long silence, during which two men load two suitcases and two bags into the back of an old Land Rover parked in front of a gate. One of them, in a buckskin jacket, is about thirty-five, the other is about ten years older and is wearing a thick, white, cable-knit pullover, which hangs almost halfway down his thighs. Leaning against a gate, a woman in jeans keeps a vague eye on their activity and the hopping of sparrows under the thin acacias along the driveway.

The two men climb into the car.

'Two lorry-drivers are driving in the fog: one says to the other . . .'

'Lorry-drivers aren't funny.'

'Two priests get into a car. The one at the wheel goes searching through his cassock, can't find the keys, pulls out his breviary and says to the other . . .'

'Priests don't work. Come on, let's get going.'

The man in the white pullover waves goodbye as the car drives off, and the woman closes the gate again, picks up a ball from a corner of the garden and goes back into the house.

'Have they gone?' comes another woman's voice from a near-by room.

'Yes,' says the first woman, stopping in front of an enormous Christmas-tree that takes up half the entrance-hall.

'Thank God. I couldn't take any more of it. I've never seen them with such writer's block,' says the second woman coming into the hall herself.

'The fact is they work too hard, they get tired, the jokes don't come to them, and then they get even more depressed,' says the first, straightening a pair of candles. 'It's a vicious circle.'

'Let's hope the Gualdana unblocks them.'

'Either they get unblocked or they'll split up, which would be a catastrophe. By now people are used to seeing them together.'

'But if the jokes don't come to them, they could get someone else to write them. Isn't that what almost everyone does?'

'But they say that if they don't find them themselves they don't enjoy telling them, and then the audience doesn't enjoy hearing them either. No, all we can do is hope that by working peacefully up there . . .'

Dramatic shouts of children tear them from the tree and

draw them automatically, but without excessive haste, towards a room at the end of the corridor.

'Pity. We would have had a good Christmas together.'

'Let's hope they get unblocked by the New Year.'

The two men in the car are blocked in a long queue, at the entrance to the Rome–Civitavecchia motorway.

'Will the heating be on?'

'Yes, Graziella phoned the guards.'

'When?'

'Two hours ago, as soon as we made up our minds.'

'It'll still be like an ice-house.'

'There's always the fireplace.'

'Will the beds be made?'

'No. We'll have to make them ourselves tonight at least.'

A painful silence ensues. From the distant toll-booths there comes the wailing sound of car-horns which snakes its way down the long queue, getting louder as it goes, until it reaches the two men. The one in the buckskin jacket, who is at the wheel, shrugs.

'What do they do that for?' he says. 'It's pointless.'

'A slave-protest.'

'Got it: a sketch about slaves. We're all of us slaves to everything, without exception. At the slave-market two slave-buyers, loaded down with chains themselves, meet and . . .'

'Slaves aren't funny.'

During the next pause the chorus of car-horns sweeps on past them, fades in the distance behind them, and a resigned silence falls again.

6

What is art? This question – which he sometimes imprudently raises himself, trying the aesthetic approach with tourists of various nationalities – is one that Delaude has never known how to answer. He has always got round it by merely indicating, if he is outdoors, the nearest monument – Giotto's campanile, San Miniato al Monte, or whatever – and saying with solemn simplicity: 'Look, there's art for you.' Or, if he is in some closed and more demanding place, by using another infallible escape route: 'But I live there, I live in the midst of it, I breathe it. How do you expect me to know what it is?'

But now, as he approaches the ruins of an ancient church with Katia, he begins to glimpse a simple truth: art is for taking time. The meal at 'Mamma Adolfina' was fairly lengthy because in winter, since there are fewer customers, there are fewer waiters, and what with nibbles, hors-d'oeuvres, etc., the pace of things was not exactly pressing. Then coffee. Then the liqueur offered by the house and sipped at leisure. Then the lavatory. Then, having exhausted all possible delays, back to the car. Another call at a service-station to fill up again just in case and check the oil, battery, tyres. And then nothing else to do at all, with at least an hour of full daylight still to go.

It was San Guglielmo that saved him. Halfway along a straight stretch, there was a yellow arrow at the side of the road. 'San Guglielmo, Romanesque Church XII Century.' Manna from heaven.

He turned without hesitation into the stony track and stopped the car.

'What is it? What are you doing, Gimo? Another load of tarts again?'

'No, no, this is a really old church, it would be a pity not to have a look at it, since we're so close. Come on, get out.'

'But why do we have to walk?'

'Can't you see the state the road is in? Come on, it's just a few hundred yards and we're there.'

'Have you been here before?'

'Sure I have,' lies Gimo. 'It's a real jewel, well worth a look.'

The path soon turns into a furrow through the burnt stubble and climbs gently towards the scrub that fringes a long, low hill. But from the crest brambly undergrowth rolls gently downwards and beyond it, in a kind of trough, they can just make out the ruins of San Guglielmo.

'Oh look, look at the little lambs!' shouts Katia.

Here and there amidst the olive-trees to their left there are indeed some sheep, both old and young.

'Look at the black one!'

She is rather less excited by the twelfth-century ruin, even though the apse is almost intact and retains a somewhat melancholy grandeur. All that remains of the doorway is a large battered aperture; beyond it stand two single pillars supporting nothing, amidst blocks of fallen stone and sharp-edged grey chippings. The roof has gone completely. One section of wall still stands with two crumbling ivy-choked windows, and the ivy, with other creepers, straggles over most of the ruins, all around which runs a vague path, which looks far from well-beaten.

'This must have been the bell-tower,' says Gimo standing in front of a large heap of rubble.

But he has nothing else to say. He knows and cares no more about this church than he does about any other, whether romanesque, gothic or baroque. And he has not the faintest idea who San Guglielmo was and why on earth a temple should have been erected in his honour in this out-of-the-way hole.

Black birds rise cawing from a near-by field and flap to

the scrub lying black against the sky on the hill above them. A dog barks in the distance, maybe at the sheep, then everything falls still and silent, settling back into its sluggish cycles.

Gimo notes a niche at the back of the apse with a seat fretted by the centuries, and having pushed away nettles and dark weeds he settles himself there with a sigh. He suddenly feels worn out, with a real weariness, not simulated in order to waste time. He doesn't even want to smoke and Katia's enthusiastic voice affects him painfully.

'It's fantastic! It would be wonderful!'

What is she on about, what does the girl want?

The girl has suddenly thought that the ruins of San Guglielmo would be an ideal background for a 'feature'. What sort of 'feature'? Well, a fashion one of course, for an autumn-winter fashion collection. Bruno, a photographer friend of hers, would go crazy over a location like this, and Giancarlo too, another photographer, would rave over the romantic contrast.

'Don't you think so? Isn't it sensational?'

'Yes,' Delaude admits weakly. 'Yes, sure.'

'I really must show them this place, come on, quickly, give me the car-keys, I'll go and get the polaroid, you could snap a few poses, just as an example, couldn't you?'

'Yes,' he nods from his corroded niche. 'Yes, I think so.'

'Hurry up, quickly, before the light goes. You're a genius to have found this place.'

The genius hands her the keys and the top model rushes off, tearing resolutely, emphatically through the passivity of the sheep, the gnarled age of the olive-trees. In six months, in some fifth-rate magazine, she, and maybe a lot of other similar girls, will appear in similar garish jackets, similar multi-coloured trousers, leaning against one of these pillars, framed by one of these ivy-entwined windows.

Good, Gimo says to himself, calculating that what with one pose and another, at least half an hour will trickle by and the risk of getting to the Gualdana too early can now be considered over. Good. San Guglielmo has lent a hand.

But this miracle doesn't greatly cheer him, to tell the truth. For some reason he finds he does not care that much. He tells himself idly that the true miracle, should the Saint choose to perform one, would be to find himself here, in this same niche, looking at the same olive-trees and the same darkening fields, the same bank of clouds driven on the sea-wind . . . but in the twelfth century, far from this world of service-stations and deathtrap bends, polaroids, pseudo Mamma Adolfinas, top and not-quite-so-top models and super-store Katias.

7

The light thickening through the thousands of tree-trunks is now of the same hue as the asphalt rolling dustily beneath the bicycle-wheels, and Natalia Neri, on her way back from the Kruysens' villa, feels herself penetrated by the universal grey, which is on the point of yielding to black.

Ah, the colours, the marvellous colours of the Gualdana, that so enrapture people from May to the end of September!

But in winter, at this opaque hour, the pine-forest reneges on all its promises of picturesque hospitality and exclusive sanctuary. The rigid verticality of the trunks, the miles of wire-fencing, the entrance and exit barriers superintended by uniformed guards, instead suggest a prison.

And is hers a life-sentence? wonders Signora Neri, not for the first time. As ever she remains in doubt as to whether it is still too early to abandon this questionable refuge, and to try and set up a normal life, or already too late.

But now she is anxious to get back, because the lonely stretch of road alongside the Old Ditch, up to the Grand-Duke's Bridge, is not only depressing but sinister, in this lessening light. And when she reaches the bridge she is not at all happy to see the motionless shape of a man leaning on the parapet. Indeed, she feels an unpleasant tickling sensation at the roots of her hair. A nasty encounter in the forest? No, come on, it'll just be a guard or one of the residents, maybe Mongelli, standing there brooding bitterly over things as he gazes at the stagnant water.

The Grand-Duke's Bridge is actually an awkward brick gangway over what was once a sluice. Even for a bicycle it is a tight squeeze, and Signora Neri prefers to get off rather than risk bumping into the indistinct figure with his elbows on the parapet.

It turns out to be Monforti, after all. And although it cannot be defined as 'nasty', an encounter with this other depressive can hardly be thought of as desirable, just at this moment.

But the roles, strangely enough, are at once reversed.

'What a lovely colour in your cheeks,' he says appreciatively, smiling broadly.

'It's just the cycling,' she says with a self-deprecating grimace.

'You're the only living thing in this dreary waste.' He indicates the dead waters of the Old Ditch, cluttered with paper, plastic bags and other floating ignominies from inland.

'And what are you looking for there?' she asks with a touch of sarcasm. 'Hope to find your trauma down there?'

Monforti gazes at her in surprise, and remains silent for a moment before replying affectionately: 'No, I was keeping an eye on the moorhens, there's a nest down there.'

He indicates a spot where the canal curves gently through marsh plants and low bushes.

'Last year we saw three, with your son. They're extremely shy and quick, they scud along the water like hovercraft.'

A sudden trembling emotion drives Natalia then to tell him that her children have grown up, that they get bored here, they don't know what to do, whom to see, even though she's just left them at the Kruysens', where they're happy to go because luckily they love music, but even so, staying there for two hours to listen to a musician, however famous he might be, is hardly the most one can hope for from life at that age.

'The two Bonanno girls were there too,' she concludes dejectedly, leaning her elbows on the Grand-Duke's brick parapet beside him.

'Is it true the mice wrought havoc in their house?'

'Yes, and they're none too sure they were just mice either. The poor things are terrified.'

The water lies motionless and resigned beneath them, as if it had forgotten for ever the spates and floods that induced Leopoldo II's engineers to build the canal.

'What do you think, have I done everything wrong?'

Monforti squeezes her arm tenderly. 'Don't do the same as I do, don't keep re-editing the film of your life. You'll never stop.'

He winks at her cheerfully. 'The trick,' he says, 'is to persuade yourself that the film could never have been any different, that it's always the same, whenever you look at it.'

'Like Perry Mason?'

'More or less.'

A seagull flies listlessly for a brief stretch over those unpromising waters, then veers away towards the sea.

'It must be fate,' says Natalia.

'Or Eladia's Tarot cards,' jokes Monforti.

'So, just to stay in the same TV series, let's go round to Signora Borst's for a cup of tea and a chat about the weather. I have to return a book to her. Come along.'

She sets off first, pushing the bicycle.

'It hasn't rained for weeks,' he says with a last glance at the dead water. 'And this sirocco doesn't strike me as very promising.'

'Maybe Eladia will be able to tell us some more.'

IV

A While Ago a Black Dot

I

A WHILE AGO a black dot appeared over there in the distance, on the public beach towards Poggiomozzo, and it has gradually become more conspicuous as it approaches the Gualdana. Now it is making its way along the private beach towards the Old Ditch, where it climbs down and disappears for a moment or two among the rocks and stones that clog the estuary. It is an animal, perhaps.

Or if it is human, as it would seem to be when it emerges from the Ditch against the light and continues on its way, why should it have chosen that uneven route? It could have used the crossing offered farther up by the Grand-Duke's Bridge.

It is indeed a man, although clearly not a resident. Wearing black, with a battered hat, shabby shoes, a tattered haversack over his shoulders and a peeling stick in his hand, he looks like a ragged wayfarer of bygone days. But it is not a vagabond or a tramp that he suggests so much as a pilgrim, making for a precise goal, which in this case appears to be Signora Borst's villa. That is the direction he now takes slantwise across the beach, ignoring Signor Lotti's dogs that come running towards him, barking.

Does he already know that they will not reach him? The fact is the four animals – summoned, most likely, by their invisible master's inaudible whistle – do a rapid about-turn and make off as quickly as they had come.

The man continues towards the villa. But when he reaches the gravel path, instead of going to the door and knocking, he turns left and makes a cautious circuit of the building, hiding among the plants. Thus he passes in front of the kitchen, where the light is already on, and he sees Milagros busily arranging canapés on a tray. He goes on past a row of dark windows, with the shutters closed. And after turning the corner he finds himself next to the large sitting-room window.

Here, only the fireplace is lit. But the last light of the afternoon allows him to make out Signora Borst at her little table, with her bright-coloured shawl, Signorina Eladia at her Tarot cards, and various guests sitting around the room. The man, who has stopped to spy from behind a laurel, seems to be about to walk up to the window and knock on the glass. But then he resumes his circuit until he reaches an unlocked door at the back, by which he furtively enters.

The guests seen through the window are five in number and nearly all familiar, starting with Father Everardo. He, in fact, had only come to collect his pine cones but happily agreed to stay and have some tea. His forays in search of Orfeo had left him cold and tired.

Besides, Father Everardo is always pleased to linger at Casa Borst, even though (and this perturbs him a little) he is not exactly sure why. The villa, so close to the sea, is damp and somewhat shabby, and the character of the two women can hardly be described as warm or expansive. Their constant, unchanging kindness sometimes seems not so much a virtue as a sort of mild sickness, like a chronic cold borne with discretion – a little cough here, a repressed sneeze there. But the fact remains that at their house one is always welcomed under that zodiacal sign which (if it existed) might be termed that of the smile: a calm, genuine, though inexplicable smile.

After settling comfortably in his armchair, while Signora Borst added the finishing dabs of paint, the priest allowed his thoughts to drift, pondering on the destiny of these two foreign ladies: on the unknown chain of events, the accidents of fate that brought them all the way here, to this pine-forest and this pre-Christmas Eve, one painting her half-dozen cones and the other reading fortunes in the Tarot cards.

He then dutifully admired the alternate silver and gold gilding of each scale, and expressed his gratitude in such terms as to include the yellow envelope, with its generous cheque, which he will find, as every year, at the bottom of the basket ... True Christian charity, he reflected, even though he does not know whether the two Swiss ladies are Calvinists, Lutherans or what. Or maybe theirs is just a vague, eclectic spiritualism, if one considers the complex amalgam of beliefs, superstitions and magic expressed in that wheel of bizarre figures from which Eladia is unable to tear her eyes for long.

At this point he was struck by another doubt, which if not exactly malicious, was at least slightly ungenerous towards his hostesses. Might not the amiable welcome they reserve for all visitors, whether occasional or regular, be attributable to total indifference? Almost as if every peal of the doorbell were already programmed, every new arrival already announced by the stars, laid down by the Wheel of the Tarot cards from the dawn of time? As if the two women told themselves that whoever comes, or whoever goes, nothing can ever change anything for anyone?

This new meditation was aptly interrupted by a peal and the arrival of Signora Neri, accompanied by Signor Monforti, with the news that the mice had wrought havoc at the Bonannos'. An unprecedented invasion.

'But maybe the cards had foreseen it?' joked Monforti with unusual good humour, moving over to sit next to Eladia.

'Everything is always there in the cards,' she said seriously, turning also to Father Everardo and Signora Neri. 'But in certain situations, with a conjunction of signs that are all orientated . . . ambiguously, that are all potentially . . . threatening, it is impossible to foresee the specific shape that events will take. Here for example,' she added, indicating the Wheel, 'it is clear that we are in for something truly . . . something extremely . . .'

Another ring at the door made her turn, however, and when she recognised Signora Graham's voice, she swiftly put a finger to her lips: 'Not in front of her!' One of her rules, in fact, is never to refer to dangerous, or at any rate unpleasant, conjunctions, in the presence of pregnant women.

Signora Graham explained that she had taken advantage of her daily stroll along the coast road to come and exchange the season's greetings. But without the other child, of course, who was now too lively to take on visits. In any case, she would only stay a moment, she said, as she . . .

No, no, Eladia and Signora Borst at once protested: she must stay for some tea, since Milagros was already preparing it for everybody.

Neither of them, however, expressed any regret at the absence of 'the other child', Father Everardo noted with fellow-feeling; he gets on fine with children at the oratory, at the play-school and in church, but is more than happy to do without them at teatime. When Signor Mongelli appeared (he too had just 'dropped by to wish everybody a Happy Christmas'), the priest noted a touch of surprise and embarrassment in everybody's eyes, including those of the all-foreseeing ladies of the house. Actually, it struck him, he himself was the only one who could have foreseen this arrival, since poor Mongelli had confided to him the other day that he couldn't bear his lonely existence any longer, two years after . . .

But maybe it was written in the cards and the stars that Father Everardo's reflections were to be continually interrupted. At this point Signora Graham, in order to get the conversation going again after Signor Mongelli's arrival, started to praise the Tarot cards as works of art.

'They're really beautiful,' she said.

'Don't you believe it, Signora Gramme!' Milagros contradicted her, entering with the tea. 'There's nothing beautiful there, no, there's a very bad ugly Wheel, says the Signorina. Oh, there's going to be sorry things, do you come to the point?'

Nobody has ever managed to convince the girl that this favourite expression of hers not only does not mean 'do you understand?' or 'do you get the point?', as she firmly believes, but is entirely meaningless. However, that was not why Signora Borst loudly rebuked her, breaking into the Capuchin priest's thoughts: 'Milagros! How often have we told you not to . . .'

But the evil had been done. Eladia, while the maid was sent off to fetch the canapés, had to admit that obscure threats hung over the Gualdana and maybe the surrounding area as well, if not the entire Maremma. And she is now in mid-explanation when a door suddenly springs open at the far end of the sitting-room.

'Here I am, friends!' thunders a mantled and indistinct figure from the dark threshold, holding high a lantern with a flickering wick. 'I am Cratès the Door-Opener!'

Without removing his battered hat and still leaning on his pilgrim's staff, the ex-black dot (since, without any doubt, it is the individual we saw walking along the beach and then slipping furtively into the villa) moves forward and sits down on the floor by the fire. He puts the lantern and staff down by his side and begins to rummage in his haversack.

Nobody else has said a word yet. Only Signora Graham murmured 'Oh dear!' in surprise as the door flew open, but she was reassured by the benevolent smiles of the ladies of the house. Father Everardo and Monforti smiled too, though rather less benevolently, while Signor Mongelli confined himself to raising his eyebrows.

As for Milagros, who has returned with the canapés, she stands there for a moment with her mouth open. Then she goes straight to the stranger – who in the meantime has taken a crust of bread and a handful of dried figs from his haversack and begun to feed himself as if in his own house – and bends down to peer under the hat.

'Ah, I thought so,' she starts laughing, 'it's Sor Ugo doing that joke again, opening the doors! So it's a real sign of trouble!'

Ugo de Meis, alias Ugo the Hermit, alias (on this occasion) Cratès the Theban, known as the Door-Opener, nods as he chews.

'For those who do not live by nature's laws,' he says, 'there will always be trouble, dear Milagros.'

2

None of the gardeners in the Gualdana is a real gardener. Before this less renowned and wilder part of Tuscany was discovered and promptly civilised with villas, cottages, hotels, camp-sites and various other settlements, the natives mainly devoted themselves to agriculture: they were woodcutters, swineherds, gamekeepers, pine cone pickers, fishermen, bicycle repairmen, cobblers, who all gradually switched over to geraniums and plumbago.

Orfeo Baldacci is no exception; he too is an ex-peasant who grew up in the tough school of artichokes, sunflowers and olive-trees and deep down is still convinced that ornamental flowers are things for cemeteries, showy stuff that women and townsfolk are inexplicably fond of. Over the years he has learnt a little, though reluctantly and condescendingly. He now has some knowledge of beds, borders, and espaliers and is acquainted with rare or odd flowers, whose names, as pronounced by him with the appropriate vernacular adaptations, would leave Linnaeus puzzled.

But on the whole the Gualdana poses no serious problems. Apart from the shameful thujas of the Hon. Bonanno and three vast English lawns, which represent the very height of absurdity in a Mediterranean pine-forest, the residents remain faithful to the local vegetation amidst which Orfeo moves with complete ease. He does not love the sea and attributes to a kind of collective madness the fact that so many people, including of course his wife, spend hours and hours on the beach, frying their brains in the sun between one dip and another. Consequently he detests the summer, when all these lunatics settle in their villas, go swarming around the avenues and paths, visit one another, admire everybody's gardens but their own and in the end take it out on him. 'Orfeo, can you explain why the Perscarmonas' bougainvillaea is so splendid and ours so feeble?'

Orfeo has spent part of the afternoon at the Melis' villa reinforcing the cover over their wretched bougainvillaea, a great sheet of transparent plastic that the wind can mangle and tear just as it likes and which has to be fixed down each time with ropes, nails, hooks and pegs. The sirocco that has been blowing since this morning does not seem dangerous but a shoulder-blade and a knee tell the ex-peasant that the weather is going to get worse and it would be unfortunate if Signora Melis were to arrive tomorrow or the next day and be confronted with a scene of ruin and neglect the moment she stepped from the car. It's always the women who make life difficult. It's always the women who nag at him with their absurd claims, obsessions, demands.

Orfeo tears his mind from the bitter pills his wife is forcing him to swallow and tries to concentrate all his animosity on Signora Melis, who refuses to grasp the fact that up against that wall, exposed in that fashion, it is impossible to grow a bougainvillaea properly. What exasperates him is the fact that in this case it is the pure and simple truth. Like everybody else he is capable of lying, but unlike his colleagues, who are all extremely loquacious and tend to justify their failures with endless explanations, he is a man of few words and thus held to be entirely trustworthy. The few remarks he does make between one grunt and another – it was the January frost, the March gale, the red lice at the roots – never sound like excuses and are never doubted. And yet this Melis woman, who on other occasions has happily swallowed some enormous whoppers (the one about the mimosa was laughable), this time of all times just won't believe him.

Sweeping the pine needles off the paved terrace around the villa would be a waste of effort, particularly with the pricking signals that his knee is continuing to send him; and besides time is passing, the day is beginning to droop. He climbs back into his van with a grunt and sets off under the massing gloom of the green fronds. Winter is his season, it is in winter that the pine-forest returns to its ancient, solemn, rustling absorption, without the jarring contrast of car-metals against the aromatic bushes and immemorial trunks;

without the overweening laughter, the shouts, the multinational rebukes of all those tanned women.

Five-sixths of the villas are empty and lifeless, and when one glimpses the occasional strip of wall or segment of roof, it is easy to imagine they are already ruins, overrun by the scrub, which, in its green tenacity, has the power to submerge and slowly crumble everything in its path.

But Orfeo Baldacci has a very definite villa in mind, one that is even less visible than the others, squatting down behind a dune. There he has to finish off another little job (which he promised the owners for the New Year); and there – more importantly – he will tonight, after so much vain talk, move on to definite deeds.

3

Ugo the Hermit – real name Professor Ugo de Meis, forty-five years old, from Borgomanero (Novara), and ex-teacher at the secondary schools of that town – has been a hermit in the Maremma for an indeterminate number of years. Some say nine, some twelve. At first, it seems, he used to come here just in the summer and as a simple camper. But later, having got to know some families in the area, including the Gherardinis, he was able to settle permanently on a hill that belonged to them, in the isolated little house where he still lives.

His hermitic vocation is a subject of discussion too, not only in the Gualdana but in the village and the hinterland as well. For some he is a mere charlatan and parasite. For others he is a kind of saint. For yet others he is simply a poor wretch, a man who has been disappointed by life, but who genuinely considers himself a master of wisdom.

'A depressive who doesn't know it,' Monforti defines him sarcastically.

He himself has always claimed to be a follower of Diogenes, the cynical philosopher who lived in a barrel and during the day wandered the streets with a lighted lantern looking for a man. Until quite recently, however, he had never given any intimation of knowing anything else about Diogenes. The barrel and lantern were all he needed to set himself against Father Everardo, in his capacity as lay anchorite: opposed to the world and its vanities, averse to any mercenary work, but all in the name of a pure naturist ideal.

Then, imprudently, Everardo had gone and told him that someone, he couldn't remember whether it was Schopenhauer or maybe Zeller in his monumental *Philosophy of the Greeks in its Historical Development*, had compared Diogenes' followers to the preaching and mendicant monks of the Middle Ages, even calling them 'the Capuchins of antiquity'.

He was to regret it.

The very same day (according to Monforti's sister, who had heard it from a cousin of the Gherardinis) de Meis had rushed to the Salvanis (another notable family with a villa in the hinterland) in order to read up on the subject in their library. He had consulted Zeller, Schopenhauer, and then, so as to do the job properly, Lübker's *Reallexicon*. He had borrowed *The Lives of the Famous Philosophers* by the ancient Laertius.

And ever since, it has seemed as if it were no longer just Ugo from Borgomanero coming down from his hovel on the hill to preach and beg, but the entire band of Cynic philosophers of the fourth and third centuries BC, up to Bion of Boristhenes and Menippus the Phoenician.

One day, for example, it will be the founder of the school, Antisthenes called 'the Cur', knocking at the door of the Kruysens . . .

Another day it may be Diogenes in person, called 'the mad Socrates', ringing at Signora Neri's door . . .

Today – as we have just seen – it is Cratès slipping into the Borsts' house without knocking or ringing. He was not known to the Athenians as 'the Door-Opener' for nothing. This most faithful of Diogenes' followers was in fact so highly appreciated for his wisdom, so sought after for his advice, that not only did all doors open before him, but in the end, to simplify matters, he started to open them himself and to enter people's houses quite unceremoniously. At least this is what we find recounted in Laertius' *Lives* and Apuleius' *Florilegio*.

'Wonderful, most interesting,' says Signora Graham, who, while the Filipino maid distributed canapés and served tea, has had the situation explained to her quietly by Monforti. 'But why should this gentleman's arrival confirm the fact that there will be trouble? Were the Cynics soothsayers as well? Did they read Tarot cards too?'

'Not that I know,' says Monforti, with a questioning look at the pseudo-Cratès. 'But since our friend in his guise as the Door-Opener does nothing but foretell disasters . . .'

But his friend interrupts him in order to present himself formally to Signora Graham, whom he has not met before.

'Cratès from Thebes,' he states, remaining seated by the fire, but courteously removing his hat. 'And where are you from, and what is your name, stranger? Are you new in this land?'

'Almost new, O Cratès,' says Signora Graham, remaining quite self-possessed. 'I'm from Chatham in Kent and my name is Barbara. Are you Theban then?'

'Yes, from Thebes in Boeotia. Although quite early on, after distributing all my wealth to the poor, I moved to Athens to follow the teaching of Diogenes. Now I live in the Maremma of Grosseto under the name of Ugo the Hermit.'

'Delighted to meet you, Signor Ugo.'

'The pleasure is mine, dear lady.'

The ladies of the house and Signora Neri approve, clapping their hands.

'A very proper introduction,' comments Signora Neri, 'despite the double identity of the person being introduced.'

'The Cynics were cynics but gentlemen,' agrees Father Everardo with a slight smile. 'But I wonder, like Signor Monforti, whether they did not perhaps exaggerate in their pessimism. Why always expect the worst? It's like going out with an umbrella even though the sun is shining.'

Receiving an ironic glance from Signora Neri, Monforti recalls that he himself has this habit and remains silent.

'But apart from the future life,' Mongelli comes in rather unexpectedly, as a practising Catholic, 'hasn't Christianity itself always said that this world is a vale of tears?'

'Certainly,' smiles Father Everardo, sipping his tea. 'It's just that today . . . well, let's say that today, we try above all to prevent the tears.'

Ugo the Hermit, who refused tea and has now pulled out a battered tin mug, shakes it in denial: 'No, no, Father, say rather that you too try to delude yourselves. Fine way of preventing things! And as for the umbrella, let me remind you . . . Just one moment, my dear, I can't find the thyme,' he says to Milagros who is there waiting to fill his cup with boiling water. 'Ah, here it is . . .' he announces, exhibiting a little bundle and turning to Signora Graham. 'It's thyme from the city of Hamper, as Cratès joked in a famous epigram.'

'Hamper?' Signora Graham asks politely, the only one present who has not heard Cratès' epigram at least a dozen times.

'Hamper is the haversack!' explains Milagros, ruining the effect. 'Even the brickwalls know it round here!'

Which does not prevent the Hermit from reciting *in extenso*, after thrusting two little sprigs into the water:

A town there is by name of Hamper,
That offers nothing rare or rich,
But thyme, dried figs, and staling bread
And garlic bulbs – all that's required
For Cratès aye to live at ease.

Signora Graham finds the epigram beautiful though she has some reservations as to the garlic. On the other hand, she assures him, she has nothing against thyme, but why exclude tea? Isn't that in accordance with nature as well?

'Not in Greece or in Tuscany,' says the Hermit, darting a glance of reproof at everybody. 'Or are you going to say that you find Bonanno's thujas and Signora Melis' bougainvillaea natural here too?'

'That's below the belt, dear Ugo!' Signora Neri says, laughing.

'But not entirely wrong,' admits Monforti impartially. And to avoid any further macrobiotic epigrams, he brings the conversation back to the weather. 'Is it true or not, as Father Everardo was saying, that the Cynic is so pessimistic as to go out with an umbrella even though the sun is shining?'

The hermit puts his cup by the fire and gets to his feet excitedly. 'On the contrary!' he replies. 'The Cynic, supposing he owns an umbrella, first gets used to doing without it even when it rains. After which he throws it away, thus ridding himself of the fear of losing it. Where is the excess of pessimism in that? It is simply the most reasonable way of facing the variability of the weather and . . .' he concludes with a gesture towards Eladia's cards, '. . . the whims of fortune.'

'Better not to have than to lose,' murmurs Mongelli

darkly, embarrassing everyone again. The allusion to Signora Mongelli's flight with Signora Neri's husband could hardly be more obvious.

'Well, I wouldn't be quite so absolute . . .' begins Father Everardo, who as the poor fellow's confessor has already discussed this desolate point of view with him.

But the disciple of Diogenes cannot miss this opportunity to reel off his master's fundamental apology, for Signora Graham's benefit, even though the others know it by heart.

'On this question, Stobeus in his *Chosen Passages* and Seneca in his treatise on the *Tranquillity of the Soul*,' he cuts in firmly, 'refer to Diogenes' famous apology, or rather dialogue with Fortune. Do you remember how it goes?'

'Of course we do? Another thing the walls know,' laughs Milagros, who has sat down to follow the conversation. 'It says they meet in the road.'

'Who?' asks Signora Borst, who had dozed off.

'Diogenes with his lantern and Fortune with her wheel! They meet in the road. Then Fortune says . . . what does she say? . . . ah: "O Diogenes," she says, "be careful, because today my wheel don't like you much!"'

'Well,' says the Hermit, 'what she actually says is "my wheel is against you", but it comes to the same thing. And so what does the other one say, contemptuously?'

'So the other one – Diogenes of course – he says contemptuously: "O Fortune, do what you want! Diogenes hasn't got nothing you can take from him".'

'. . . "has nothing you can take from him." Very good. And so?'

'And so he goes off all calm, and she's left there embarrassed saying: "*Mamma mia*! That chap, my wheel won't never do nothing to him"!'

'Very good! *Brava*!'

As everybody applauds and compliments her, the girl

quickly collects the plates and goes back somewhat flustered to the kitchen.

The Hermit turns to the others with a complacent smile. '*Apatia*,' he comments, 'in Greek does not mean apathy but impassibility, perfect tranquillity of the spirit: that is the true and only aim that the Wise Man . . .'

But Signora Borst is threatening to doze off again, Father Everardo is showing signs of impatience, and Signorina Eladia shakes her head as she considers her Tarot cards: 'I wonder if Diogenes himself,' she says, 'would have remained apathetic if faced with a Wheel like this.'

4

On his risky journey towards Grosseto Vannuccini could: have turned into the main coast road that runs between a double row of pine-trees and consequently lost control of the moped, thus crashing into a trunk; or have chosen the inland road that follows the bank of a canal for miles, and plunged into it after skidding; or have been run over by a van that he failed to give way to at a crossroads, or have been cut down by a Ferrari which, at another crossroads, failed to give way to him.

In increasingly realistic detail Signora Zeme can see the pine-tree, the canal, the van (a white one, from a furniture shop), the Ferrari (black, merciless, with a Brescian number plate), and finally the moment comes when she just drops on to the side of the bed.

'Are you tired, do you want to rest for a while?' says Signor Zeme.

'No. I've had enough. I'm not going.'

'What do you mean, you're not going?' he says. 'We've almost finished.'

He is standing by the built-in wardrobe, which has all four doors and numerous drawers open. The second and third drawer of the Venetian-style commode are open too.

'I'm not well.'

'But just a moment ago everything was just . . .'

'I'm not well, I'm not well, I'm not well.'

'*How* are you not well, Magda? *How?* In what way? How do you feel?'

Magda waves the question away with a floppy gesture of her hand, like a last fragment of a cornice crumbling from a ruined house, and then crosses her arms over her chest, rocking to and fro.

'You can't understand,' she says, 'it can't be explained.'

'Do you feel sick?'

'Yes. That too.'

'So I'll go and get the Eteraxil! Don't you want the Eteraxil?'

'No, don't say another word, please.'

'But if you're sick, Eteraxil is the . . .'

'Don't speak to me, I beg you.'

Signor Zeme leaves the room resolutely in search of the Eteraxil, which could be anywhere in the villa – replaced, hidden, dropped, forgotten, in the most unlikely nooks and crannies. Magda is left alone to rock in the storm, to hold her head above the great waves that cannot be seen, cannot be heard, cannot be touched, cannot be explained, dark masses of liquid that fling themselves from all directions. Higher and higher. To prevent herself from being submerged she gets up again and starts to walk back and forth among the suitcases and scattered articles of clothing, with her arms still hugged across her chest. She trips here and there, but manages not to fall, not to let herself be sucked back into those black vortexes that have already swept away all the pine-forests, cities, people, phones and trains – all shreds of order of all universes.

Heavy yet insubstantial footsteps intrude; a voice gets through to her, indistinct but urgent.

'Vannuccini has phoned. He's got the tickets.'

Signora Zeme rocks herself, clutched tight in her thin arms.

'Did you hear? The tickets are there, the bookings are made, Vannuccini will be here in a moment.'

'God . . .' implores Signora Zeme, 'God . . .'

Her eyes straggle around the disorder of the room.

'But we'll never make it!' she shouts. 'It's impossible!'

'Magda. Almost everything's packed. We'll be ready in a couple of minutes.'

'No, no,' she protests, 'there's too much stuff, what do I want with all this stuff?'

She kneels down and yanks a multicoloured pile of jumpers and cardigans from a medium-size suitcase, hurls them on to the bed, then from a second case pulls out a neatly folded skirt, unfolds it instantly with outstretched arms, throws it away impatiently.

'And this thing? And this? No, I was crazy, and you too, couldn't you . . .?'

'But I tried to . . .'

'We'll have to start all over again, reorganise everything, with two cases like that I'd never be able to . . .'

'But exactly, that's what I was . . .'

'Just one. No, a bag. They're up there, pull them all down.'

Signor Zeme climbs up an aluminium step-ladder, reaches the upper cupboards and deposits three bags on the carpet, two of cloth and one of leather.

'This one . . . no, too heavy . . . this one, yes, this one. So: the two pairs of pyjamas . . . no, just one pair and one night-dress . . . socks . . . underwear . . . too many hankies . . . six blouses? No, it's pointless . . . no, the pullover no, too thick, it's always far too hot in their house . . . trousers . . .? What do you think, shall I take them?'

'I don't know,' answers Signor Zeme. 'They might be useful.'

'But suppose I put them on for the journey? Eh? What do you think?'

'Yes, maybe.'

'No, better not, it's always too hot on the train, my legs would swell . . . Oh, my God, the shoes!'

Five neatly ranged little bags are left at the bottom of the first suitcase.

'Now where am I going to put these? Where?'

Signora Zeme leans back against the bed and closes her eyes. She can see Vannuccini quite clearly on his way back, bent over the handlebars, his large head magnified by the helmet, and the double row of pine-trees no longer frightens her, the canal, now on the left, is not threatening, but the real danger lurks in the Tavernelle village, a few miles from here, with its bar-trattoria and adjoining general store, where Vannuccini is bound to pull up, dismount, take off his helmet, enter and drink a glass of wine, no, of whisky, and there at a table four or five of his friends will be sitting, all faceless, all hunters, and they'll start chatting to him about hunting, ducks and boars, and then guns and dogs, and they'll go on and on, they won't stop, while in the dark the minutes rush by like empty and now unreachable carriages, lost for ever.

'No,' the lady says in a whisper, with her eyes closed, 'I'm not going.'

5

'Two exhausted explorers are making their way through the jungle. They come across a clearing where there's a group of huts and one says to the other . . .'

'There are no such things as explorers nowadays. Just stupid tourists.'

'All right: two stupid tourists are going through the jungle in their Land Rover and . . .'

'It's the jungle that doesn't work.'

'OK, OK: two stupid tourists are approaching the North Pole on their snow-mobile, when a giant bear . . .'

'No, not the bear.'

'A seal.'

'You don't understand. It's the North Pole that doesn't work any more, that doesn't exist any more. Dip the headlights.'

The man in the fawn jacket obeys mechanically and continues driving in silence towards a barrier of hills.

'It's incredible,' says the man in the white pullover after a while, 'how many different blacks there are in actual fact.'

'Sorry, what do you mean?'

'This sky is black, isn't it?'

'Yes, and so?'

'But the hills over there are much blacker.'

'Ah. Well, that'll be because of the contrast with the lights.'

'No, it's another black. Completely different.'

'It's just the same with the other colours, there's a whole range of greens, of reds.'

'But with black, and with white too, you'd think you could be sure of things. This pullover's white, that dashboard's black, and that's all there is to it. But instead . . .'

'It's because you don't have the eye for it, you're not a painter.'

'I know.'

'You don't see the different shades.'

'I know, I know. It doesn't matter. I was just remarking.'

The lights scattered along the black hills here and there cluster together into villages, or gradually emphasise their lonely detachment, or sink down and flatten out to emerge as road-markers. Beyond half a dozen lamp-posts there is also a yellow traffic-light flashing on and off to indicate a pedestrian crossing.

'We're at the Tavernelle,' the driver announces. 'Two and a half miles from home. An hour and a half. Not bad.'

'And suppose we'd taken two, what difference would it have made?'

'None. Just remarking.'

The car slows down and stops in an open space bordered by high eucalyptus trees and the side of an old house.

'Cigarettes,' says the driver. 'And while we're here we might as well do some shopping. They have most things here.'

'Good idea. So we'll have the whole of tomorrow for work.'

'But we're not going to eat at home tonight? I don't feel like cooking.'

'We can go to the village, there's bound to be somewhere open.'

'"Da Febo", maybe. Or "Al Bastione". Or if not, just a pizzeria.'

'No, I can't take another pizzeria.'

'Or maybe here at the Tavernelle. You can eat quite well here.'

'Let's see.'

They enter the little bar. A group of men are drinking, talking and paying no attention to the Perry Mason episode being shown by a television on a high shelf. To the left is the door into the shop, where general goods – hams, loaves, dolls, rubber boots – bask under the livid white of the neon. The landlady straightens up from her boxes of beer and serves them. Passing on from the bar, beyond Perry Mason, they glimpse the deserted restaurant room, decorated with festoons of coloured paper pulled tight against the ceiling. In the unlit fireplace stands a crib with a few model figures, a pink rubber elephant, a cuddly tiger.

'Uh-uh,' says the man in the pullover.

They go out and stock up with cigarettes at the tobacconist's on the opposite corner of the square.

6

Gimo covers the last stretch of road in a state of split personality. Without knowing why, and without wondering about it either, he has lost all interest in the girl by his side, a stranger whom he could chuck out of the car as easily as he would a paper cup, just leave her lying on the side of the road. But once a decision has been taken – though God knows when and where – that something is to be done, then that something must be carried through. Gimo performs. He is a shell, a passive container of impulses that are out of his active control. Overtaking, changing gear, braking, dipping headlights, undipping headlights, everything runs its course without any involvement on his part. He is not dazed, or confused, but even his ideas follow pre-set paths, as if programmed by some remotely-operated computer. When the thought of coffee presents itself to him, the sequence unfolds in flashback. As for wine, there is always a crate in the basement from his wife's vineyards, and upstairs there is bound to be some whisky, sherry and gin left, and maybe still some of that exceptional Calvados Pierre brought in September. But coffee? It is impossible to remember from one visit to the next whether there is any coffee left in the larder.

And then an instant connection is made with the flashing traffic-lights over there. The Tavernelle village. The general store, with its adjoining trattoria.

Gimo diligently performs the manoeuvres to park under the eucalyptus trees that border this side of the square.

'Why are you stopping here?' Katia asks him.

Gimo's voice performs promptly: 'I'm buying some coffee for tomorrow morning. Do you take coffee in the morning?'

Katia hesitates at the implications of this, then decides that the appropriate tone is a factual one. 'Yes, with a little milk.'

'Some milk as well then.'

'And oranges, if you can get any. Or a carton of orange-juice.'

'Right,' says Gimo's voice, 'oranges.'

Get out, go up the two steps, enter . . .

No. Step back and pretend to be absorbed in examining a funeral announcement on the wall – Aida Passerini widow Mosca, 87 years old – while two men come out, two Gualdanesi, who have certainly just arrived for their holidays too and are known to Gimo, although they probably don't know him. But one can never be sure. Let them go.

Go up the steps again and enter. Done. It's the bar and there's a group of excited villagers sitting around a little table. They are not so much arguing as barking. Nobody behind the bar. Pass through to the adjacent grocery-shop. Done. The landlady is there, arranging packets of biscuits on a shelf. Order coffee, milk, orange-juice, biscuits, but something for this evening too, so as not to have to go out again: some farmhouse bread with ham and cheese will do fine, after the late lunch at 'Mamma Adolfina's'. Done. Go back with the landlady to the bar, where the till is. Pay. Wait for the change, while the men drown each other's voices with tones of ever-rising thunder: some village affair, wives, husbands, adultery. On the right, mistletoe hanging at the entrance to the restaurant. Christmas decorations. A crib in the unlit fireplace. Above it, a stuffed boar's head. Collect the change. Done. Go out, get back into the car.

'Did you get everything?'

'Everything. And something for afterwards too.'

Katia receives the word 'afterwards' as allusive, thinks of champagne and decides a smile is called for.

Kiss her? No. A hand on her thigh? Yes. Done. Gimo continues with mechanical diligence to perform the necessary actions for taking off the handbrake, starting the engine up, turning on the headlights and . . .

An idea.

That pair he saw a moment ago have come out from the tobacconist's opposite and climbed back into their Land Rover with a Roman numberplate and are now taking the main road northwards: heading for the Gualdana, obviously. Take advantage of this. Follow them at a suitable distance but accelerate at the opportune moment, in such a way as to enter on their tail before the guards lower the barrier again. And so with a brisk wave to Vannucci, or Vannuccini, or whoever it is, it will be possible to pass through without having to stop even for an instant. Since the lodge is on the left, nobody will be able to make out the girl next to him or even realise that there is anyone next to him.

Performance.

After a mile and a half of straight road, a double bend, another straight stretch, here comes the entrance to the pine-forest. Accelerate. There goes the Land Rover's left indicator as it approaches the turning. Fall in behind, but wait a few seconds at the beginning of the short slope. Now! . . . Perfect: the barrier is raised, the other car is passing through and Gimo follows close behind, waving his arm to Barabesi who responds likewise.

Done. Distance himself again from the other car which goes straight on and then turn into the left fork, avoiding a grey cat as it crosses the path.

'Good thing it wasn't black,' says Katia. 'Are you superstitious?'

Deny.

'Pity there aren't any lamp-posts. How come there aren't any lamp-posts? I'd be afraid to stay in a place like this, without lamp-posts.'

Ignore. Take care not to confuse the Valenzanis' driveway with his own. Slide under the cane shelter, switch off the headlights, get out.

'But I can't see a thing! Isn't there a light?'

Take the indistinct shape by one arm, guide it through the bushes to a door. While rummaging for the keys, point out the heady scent of the pines.

'Tell the truth, all I can smell is burning.'

Sniff. There is a smell of burning. Express the opinion that somewhere upwind, someone is barbecuing steaks. And usher this stranger through the door, switch on the light, close the door again, decongest the heart, lungs, throat, jaws with a deep breath.

7

But when Vannuccini arrived with the tickets the choice had been made, the bag – not that one, another one – was ready, though still open, and after two further variations and a final addition Signor Zeme managed, with some strain, to close the zip.

'Ah, the label.'

'It's there.'

'Name and address, in case I leave it somewhere,' smiles Signora Zeme, checking that the leather rectangle is properly attached to one of the handles. 'It's happened to me before.'

'It can happen to anyone,' says her husband.

'Once,' confesses Vannuccini, 'I took the wrong train, I thought I was going to Florence and I ended up in Lucca.'

'Oh Lord,' says Signora Zeme in fright, 'and suppose I end up in Turin?'

'Magda, you're not going to end up in Turin, don't worry,' says her husband with a glance at Vannuccini, who blushes. 'Come on, let's offer our express-courier a whisky.'

'No, there's no time, sorry Vannuccini, but it's late.'

'But it'll only take two minutes and anyway we've got loads of time. I need a whisky too at this point.'

'No, no, you've got to drive! And he's already had one at the Tavernelle.'

'Me?' says Vannuccini in bewilderment. 'But I didn't . . .'

Signora Zeme silences him with an imperious gesture. 'All right, all right, let's forget about the whisky, please, we must go, let's be off, quickly.'

It is Vannuccini who takes the bag down and puts it into the boot of the Volvo, while Signor Zeme locks the door of the house, goes down the stone steps and takes his seat at the wheel.

'Happy Christmas! Happy Christmas!' shouts Signora Zeme, leaning out of the window as if Vannuccini were already far away. 'Give my regards to Ivella!'

But as soon as the car has set off she remembers she hasn't bought a present for Ivella or for Luca, their little boy.

'Oh my God, how could I, what can we do, can you see to it tomorrow?'

'All right.'

'Perfume for her, or a toy for the boy. Will you find something?'

'Yes, yes, don't worry.'

'No, better still, I can do it at the station in Florence, if we get there early enough.'

'Yes, all right, we'll see when we get there.'

The exit barrier rises in little jerks, while Barabesi waves out of the lodge window. The car sets off again.

'Wait.'

Signor Zeme stops again before the little slope, just beyond the Christmas ilex with its festoons of red, green and blue flashing bulbs that quiver in the wind.

'Do you need to say something to the guards?'

'No, no, nothing, there'll be tips later, but you can see to that, or when I get back I can see to it, let's go, let's go, let's go. Tell them the tree is lovely.

'All right.'

So finally the white circle of the headlights bleaches the last bushes of the Gualdana, flickers over the trunks of the last pines, strikes the asphalt of the main road, straightens, tapers to a long blade that lunges swiftly into the darkness.

8

Signora Graham and Signor Mongelli have each gone back to their own homes, after expressing their thanks for the tea and Eladia's explanations of the Tarot cards. As for Father Everardo, he had asked the guards to tell Orfeo, when he showed up again, that he was there and would like to speak to him. But they had phoned from the lodge a while ago just to say that Baldacci hadn't been seen since.

Should he wait a little longer? The gardener is unlikely to

be still working at this hour and in this darkness. But if he had left the forest they would have seen him, wouldn't they?

Not necessarily, says Monforti. The cars leaving are not checked as thoroughly as those entering. Often, at rush hour, the exit barrier stays up. And besides Orfeo doesn't live very far away: he could have left his van here, if he intends to continue the job tomorrow, and have gone away on foot. Maybe along the beach.

But if it is not indiscreet to ask, asks the Hermit, why is Everardo so keen to see him? Is it some little job for the monastery?

'Ugo!' Signora Borst and Signora Neri protest together, hypocritically, to make it clear to the Father that Orfeo's story is common knowledge by now, so there is no need for excessive discretion.

The priest admits to knowing that Orfeo has some problems and that he hopes to be of help. But he sticks firmly to generalities.

'Nowadays when people never, or hardly ever, go to confession,' he says, 'people get locked up with their unhappiness: and hence the upsurge in the number of desperate acts, the increasing frequency of depressive states for which they invent new and highly complicated treatments by the day, when the simple practice of confession could . . .'

As a chronic and, so to speak, professional depressive, Monforti already knows all about therapeutic confessions. The argument, in any case, does not interest him. Instead, he tries to follow the low-voiced conversation that Natalia has started up with Eladia, though little more than fragments reach him:

'Let's hope poor Orfeo doesn't . . . But couldn't this forecast of trouble be specifically connected with . . .? Or with . . . by train, on her own, in the state she . . . Don't you think?'

'Impossible to say. The signs are too confused to . . . Men, things, animals: it's all a tangle of . . .'

'But what kind of animals? Not mice? Because those poor Bonanno girls . . . Or one of those barn owls that apparently make their way into . . . Or those dogs belonging to . . .'

'I don't know. With the cards it isn't always possible to distinguish between . . .'

Generalities again. Pointless chatter. But, as always at the Borsts', there is a dreamy, rarefied atmosphere as of a club or an old café in the provinces: a place of subdued conviviality, where it really makes no difference whether one decides to muck in or to stay on the sidelines . . . to be there or not to be there . . . or even to be (reflects Monforti *à la* Hamlet) or not to be.

The Hermit meanwhile is making fun of Pachomius the Great, the founder of monachism in Upper Egypt, along with Isaac of Syria, Simeon the New Theologian and various others of the ancient, celebrated 'Desert Fathers'. From which one can deduce that Everardo, having exhausted the theme of confession, must have passed on to that of climatic conditions. Like St Jerome, in fact, the Fathers attributed to humidity and/or certain winds such as the *ramshin* and the *shulūq* (the Italian 'sirocco') the fatal *akedìa* (our 'depression', not the common accidie) that afflicted so many authorities and cenobites in the deserts of Syria, Palestine, Egypt, Mesopotamia.

'But in that case,' jeers the Hermit, 'wouldn't all those wonderful people have done better to stay at home? Because if a little wind was enough to throw them . . .'

Monforti has always given little credence to the influence of winds, and in particular of the sirocco, on his psychic state. Today, for example, he ought to feel terrible. But he feels almost fine, and listens with serene detachment, even with amused interest, to the Desert Fathers' recriminations against the demon of *akedìa*:

Like those tangles of brushwood that the wind drags hither and thither over the sands and the rocks, so the monks assailed by this demon go wandering without a goal and without rest.

Nilus of Mount Sinai

Those wretches affected by this malaise try to remain seated in meditation and prayer. But the merest voice, the merest sound from without is enough to make the cenobite climb up to the window of his cell and the anchorite peer from the entrance of his cave: and thus are they plunged into the blackest despair.

Evagrius Ponticus

Akedìa drives us to begin everything and to conclude nothing. It makes every place desirable apart from that where we are; every occupation pleasant, apart from the one we are engaged upon; every argument boring, apart from the idlest of chatter; the whole of humankind consoling and charitable, apart from those nearest to us.

John of Gaza

And this in truth is the worst demon of all. It is the death of the soul and of intelligence.

Simeon the New Theologian

It is the depths of Hell.

St Theodore the Studite

My!

A little shaken in spite of all, Monforti breathes with relief when the Capuchin rises to return to the monastery, since Orfeo is untraceable. And when Natalia too goes off on her bicycle, he decides to accompany the Hermit for a part of the way. These Cynics were a little repetitive, in their programmatic pessimism, but basically they were cheerful people, they were always prepared to joke, and their follower from Borgomanero – whatever his sister Sandra might say – is pleasant company. Today he has really gone all out, poor chap, to pull off his old number: 'Cratès the Door-Opener'.

'And now, Ugo, are you going to walk all the way back to your hermitage?'

'Of course. The distance is not much greater than that between Piraeus and Athens, which Antisthenes used to cover twice a day to go and hear Socrates. And what did Socrates say, in fact, with regard to journeys on foot?'

Unlike his sister, Monforti is not put off by these didactic questions capped with a threatening pause: it must be a hangover from de Meis's teaching days at the secondary school.

'I don't know,' he says, humouring him.

'He said that if one put together all the paces one takes in one's own home or in one's neighbourhood over a few days, one would easily reach Olympia in the Peloponnese.'

'Wonderful.'

Thus they set off along the coastal path, by now almost indistinguishable, in the dim light of the Hermit's lamp. Monforti has his battery torch with him but does not switch it on because, he has to admit, Diogenes' wick lights things up in a different, more picturesque way.

'But,' he says as they continue towards the Old Ditch, 'you're not going to have bread and thyme for dinner too? Or bread and garlic?'

'No, no. That is to say: in my role as Cratès I am strictly vegetarian, like my wife; but I don't . . .'

'Your wife?'

'Cratès' wife, I mean. A girl from a rich family, named

Hipparchia, who . . . Do you know the story? I must tell you it because it's a very good one. But I was saying: unlike the Door-Opener and Bion, who recommended a diet based solely on beans and fresh water, the other Cynics paid attention to practical matters. "The rich man," said Diogenes, "feeds when he wants to and on what he wants; the Cynic, when he can and on what he finds".'

'Magnificent. So why don't you come and have dinner with us? My sister will be very happy to hear the story of Hipparchia.'

He accepts with pleasure and Monforti turns on his torch, and leads the way into the pine-forest and towards his home. After all, he thinks, Sandra will prefer to see him turning up in the company of the Hermit, rather than a prey to the demon of *akedìa*.

9

Inside the white Volvo everything is black: the leather seats, the carpet, the dashboard, the gear and brake levers, the silent radio.

'Do you want some music?' says Signor Zeme.

'Yes, why not,' murmurs Signora Zeme emerging from her black taciturnity.

The luminescent bar of the scanner starts probing around the dial: eight seconds of rock-music, advertisements, a soprano, rock again, a man talking about sport, eight seconds of violins . . .

'Here?'

'Yes, yes, that's fine,' Signora Zeme brightens up. 'You know that in Sweden they've started to prescribe music as a complementary therapy? Monforti told me about it. Or in Switzerland, I can't remember, but I can ask the neurologist tomorrow, he should know, shouldn't he?'

'Probably.'

'I wonder how they find out what suits you, maybe they make you listen to a bit of everything and then they decide, a little Mozart or Verdi in the morning, half a sonata by Beethoven after meals and Chopin before bed, or Wagner, I don't know, but it would be worth trying, I'll ask the neurologist, also because I used to love music as a girl, I often went to concerts with my sister, so maybe if instead of you I had married someone who at least encouraged, or not even encouraged me, just took me once to hear *La Bohème*, for instance, or got me a season ticket for the concerts at the Conservatoire, I'm sure nothing would have happened, the depression just wouldn't have come, that's the truth of it.'

A breach opens in the violins, and the piano at once makes its snaking entrance.

'I should take up the piano again but I haven't touched it for over twenty years now, I'd have to start practically from scratch and then of course we'd have to buy one and God knows where we could put it in our flat with all the stuff that's in it, one day I'm going to get rid of everything, I can't take it any longer, living among all that clutter, I've had enough, away with the lot of it, in fact let's get out of that wretched penthouse, much too big, absurd for two people without children, and let's sell the Gualdana too, I've been saying so for years, with children it would all have been different but it's certainly not my fault and you've never forgiven me, that's the truth of it, although basically you're right because I've ruined your life, you really wanted children, you would definitely have been a much better father than mine was, though that's not saying much, because my father was a disaster as a father, you could even say he was the ruin of me, he couldn't have cared less about me, all he did was shout, never show any interest, never any advice or encouragement, besides it was the same with my sister, he would have liked to have boys, that's the truth of it, and in fact it was quite something if he gave us a present at Christmas or for our birthday and by the way, don't forget, you must get a present for Vannuccini's boy, he's five, you can look in that shop in the little road behind the town hall, you know the one? Just beyond the pasta shop, you know the one I mean?'

'Yes,' says Signor Zeme, 'I know.'

Black hills loom up and sink back against the black sky, the headlights illuminate bends marked by black-and-white striped fencing, tracks that disappear into black woods. There is hardly any traffic and Signor Zeme drives grimly, poised on the shifting razor-edge of his wife's anxieties, between the fear of being late and the terror of excessive speed.

'That's enough of that stuff,' says the black profile of Signora Zeme, cutting through an outburst of brass.

She presses the lighter on the dashboard, takes one of her slim cigarettes from her bag, changes her mind, takes out a little silver box with an enamelled lid, which she opens and then closes again with a sharp sound. Snap.

'Empty, it's always empty but it doesn't matter, I don't try and kid myself any more, peppermints and sweets are never going to help me break the habit, I smoke a lot, so much the worse, or rather so much the better, at least with a nice throat cancer I'd solve all my problems as well as yours, or in the lungs, like poor Anita who, all right, suffered almost a year with that horrid chemotherapy, but if nothing else at least everyone took her seriously, it was an illness you could see, you could touch, she lost her hair . . .'

Snap. She has lit the cigarette but she continues to open and close the lid of the box – snap, snap – as if to give rhythm and some kind of check to the torrential flow of her words, before they burst their banks and die away in another swamp of fatal silence.

'. . . whereas with depression it's no good, it's in your head and they all come and say pull yourself together, snap out of it, no one believes in it, nobody understands how bad you feel, I mean really bad, bad, at bottom you don't even believe in it yourself, it just seems an idea, something imaginary.'

Snap, snap.

'You're going too fast, you took that bend too quickly, what's the matter, are we late? Tell me, it's late, isn't it, do you think I might miss the train?'

'No,' says Signor Zeme. 'You won't miss anything, just try and keep calm.'

'Calm? But I'll never be calm again, and who knows when I'll feel able to drive again, even though by now with all these drugs they'll never renew my licence, but anyway you could go a little slower at least, you have to be careful here, the deathtrap bend is somewhere around here, isn't it here?'

'Not yet,' says Signor Zeme, slowing down. 'And anyway it's dangerous in the other direction, coming downhill.'

Snap, repeats the box, snap, snap. And Magda Zeme's invisible, implacable scanner switches on again, starts to run to and fro along the band of her life, picking out mistakes from her past, regrets, missed opportunities, returning to the gift for little Vannuccini, insisting on the french-window of the bedroom which doesn't close properly, recalling the oppressive smog of Milan, pausing on possible piano or guitar lessons, eight seconds of children not had, eight seconds of voluntary work in a community for drug addicts, or maybe a boutique selling Asiatic fabrics, or a resolutory metastasis, or even a resolutory accident at the deathtrap bend or any other bend, and then her indifferent father, her sister who is basically selfish herself, inept neurologists, and again Ivella Vannuccini, too many cigarettes, a pair of ear-rings lost God knows where in the Gualdana, and always that box opening and closing again, opening and closing amidst neglected commitments, long-lost friends, far-off moments of happiness, snap, snap, snap, snap, while the dark profile talks, remembers, questions herself, tortures herself without an instant of rest, until the next torturing silence.

V

Where Women Are Concerned

I

WHERE WOMEN ARE concerned, Count Girolamo Delaude, generally known as Gimo, could in one sense be considered a puritan. He has never understood, for example, the perverse pleasure that some of his acquaintances derive from going all out to get their wives' best friends or their best friends' wives into bed; he has never shared the vanity of other acquaintances, who, out of pure exhibitionism, set their sights on the most beautiful woman at the party, the beach or the club; he has never allowed his amorous initiatives to be contaminated by such incongruous motivations as revenge, retaliation, snobbery or the virile or social affirmation of the self. From his early youth, Gimo has always fornicated, so to speak, without any ulterior motives, remaining strictly faithful to his motto: 'C . . . is c . . .'

But like all idealistic formulas (one's country is one's country, one's mother is one's mother), this too has a fatal tendency to crumple when it collides with the petty, prosaic aspects of reality. The merest trifle is enough to spoil a moment of happiness, Gimo now reflects, his eyes gazing down at the plastic sandals adorning his feet. But what was this 'trifle'? Where did the pin come from that pricked the rose-coloured balloon?

There he was, happy and contented under the blankets after a good half-hour of finely-gauged effusions, all carried through to the happiest of outcomes; there he lay, enjoying softly strategic contacts with Katia's malleable body, this charming, splendid girl whose satisfied moans and sighs had only just died away in the room. A moment of total abandonment, to be savoured in silence, while his finger wandered around a conspicuous breast and his mind around the concept: 'Old Gimo is still up to it.'

Then the breast was withdrawn and the girl stretched out on her back, yawning from head to foot.

'And now I'm going to have a nice hot shower.'

That was the pin, Gimo thinks. Because the electric water-heater takes a while to warm up and when they arrived, he completely forgot (c . . . at that moment being c . . .) to turn it on.

'So I'm supposed to have a cold one!'

First pout. First sulk.

'Well, while it's heating up we can have a drink.'

And with the condescension of a grande dame, she said: 'Oh all right, let's have a drink and forget about it.'

And he offered her his old tartan dressing-gown taken from a damp built-in wardrobe.

'And what are you going to wear?'

'Oh, I'll put my old loden jacket back on.'

And there they both were in the living-room. Vodka? No thank you. Sparkling wine from his vineyards? Not that either. Sherry? She doesn't like it. So what does she like? Coke, obviously.

'I'm afraid there isn't any.'

'Well, a fruit-juice then. There's bound to be some fruit-juice, isn't there?'

'No, I'm afraid not. But wait . . . there's the orange-juice I got for tomorrow morning.'

'No, in the evening orange-juice doesn't agree with me, it all stays up here.'

Second pout. Second sulk. A little laugh that is far from affectionate.

'You know you look really funny, in that get-up.'

Naked under a thigh-length jacket, his bare feet in his half-unstitched sandals. But then she herself, in that fusty old dressing-gown, isn't exactly what you might call the tops: and the armchair she's gone and sat in could do with a new cover; and on the wall behind her Gimo notices the damp mark caused by a barn-owl's nest. Not too large, fortunately. But sprawling like a sinful stain on a sheet in a cheap hotel. Squalid.

'It must be the barn-owls . . .'

'What barn-owls, what are you talking about?'

He explains about the barn-owls, huge nocturnal predators that damage the roof-tiles wherever they happen to nest. They tend to choose towers and castles, but in the Gualdana they have also settled in a couple of villas, including of course the ones with sloping rather than flat roofs.

'Come on, let's go and see if we can spot anything.'

'Me?' shivers the delicate little bundle. 'But it's windy, it's cold, you go if you want.'

Third pout, third sulk.

And old Gimo, dressed as he is, takes down his 'Crickett' torch from its hook in the hallway and goes out into the wind which is bringing a few drops of rain. There must already have been a brief downpour in the meantime, because the paving glistens with viscid reflections. Gimo turns the corner of the house, tries to identify the spot where the stain has spread, plays his band of light along the edge of the roof.

There is nothing to see, of course. At this hour the barn-owls will be out hunting mice and the tiles all look perfectly in order, from down below. He will have to phone Crociani to come and check it over as soon as he can. Gimo turns off the dynamo torch and gazes at the starless sky, teeming with dim ragged clouds, driven headlong by the sirocco. Is it going to rain again?

The pine-forest is completely dark apart from a light gleaming through the pines a hundred yards away. The villa belonging to Max & Fortini, the two providential comedians who enabled him to get through the barrier so smoothly. A real stroke of luck. A good duo of entertainers, although, to tell the truth, Gimo has only ever seen them twice on television, and never at the theatre.

When he goes back in he is greeted by a storm of canned laughter. Katia has turned the television on and is watching a variety programme of games and advertisements.

'What is it? Anything interesting?'

She does not reply, just laughs. The dressing-gown has fallen open at the front, revealing her splendid thighs.

'What are you watching?'

'Bindo and Bicci,' she says without turning. 'They're on every evening for two hours on Telegiotto: "Shoulder to Shoulder", a kind of revue.'

Old Gimo approaches her, slips one hand under her mass of hair, which Katia at once shakes off with a movement of infantile irritation.

'Leave off, let me watch.'

On the screen two adults in coloured jackets with sequined seams are about to come to blows when a girl intervenes, separating them by waving a vacuum-cleaner.

'The show-girl,' says Katia contemptuously. 'I know her, she was Miss Fucecchio last year. She's terrible. I'd be much better. She doesn't know how to move, just look at her, I mean she's useless!'

The dressing-gown has come open at the top now, giving a glimpse of those top tits.

'But quite frankly those two are pretty awful as well,' says Gimo. 'My neighbours are much better.'

'What neighbours, what do you mean?'

'Max & Fortini.'

Katia jerks round. 'You know Max & Fortini? They're your neighbours in Florence? But they live in Rome!'

'Not in Florence, here. And you saw them too, they were in that car in front of us, when we came in. At this moment,' reveals Gimo, smiling, with a vague gesture towards the window, 'they're a hundred metres from us.'

The effect is all he could have hoped for. Katia gets up, her eyes still diffident but now ready to widen ecstatically. 'And do you talk to them? Do you really know them?'

'Of course I do, they've been coming to the Gualdana for years.'

All pouts cancelled, all sulks withdrawn, the girl throws her arms around his neck with leaps of jubilation, that justify all risks.

'Max & Fortini! It's incredible! But will you introduce me to them? Will you let me meet them?'

'Of course,' says Gimo with tender grandeur.

The promise (he senses) is a highly risky one, loaded like the sky with threatening clouds, with winds that could carry one anywhere. But meanwhile the purity of his new ideal affirms itself once again, once again c . . . is about to be c . . .

2

Naturally the so-called *rapido* has arrived forty minutes late. Naturally all the carriages, including no. 7 with its reserved seats, are full of people and luggage blocking the gangways and corridors. And naturally Signora Zeme's seat, when finally reached, turns out to be occupied by a character who will not budge until he has put on his glasses, pulled out his reservation-card, and discovered that his seat no. 54 next to the window is in carriage 6.

But the first door has been slammed and the noise now starts to echo threateningly down the train. And thus Signor Zeme, having squeezed his wife's cumbersome bag on to the laden rack and having picked up the bundle of magazines bought at the station, which in the confusion had slipped to the floor, just has time to push his way through the passengers in the corridor and reach the doorway, from where he leaps to the ground.

'It's a disgrace, an utter disgrace!' he shouts to the stationmaster who is giving the departure signal.

He stays there to bid goodbye, waving his arm, until the last carriage has slid past him, and then walks slowly down the platform. He arrives, pale and sweaty, in the hall. Before facing the return journey he walks along to the bar where he orders and knocks back a double whisky, since Signora Zeme is no longer there to stop him doing so.

3

'Two robots, an old one and a young one meet up in front of the . . .'

'How can you tell the difference?'

'The old one has got a long white beard.'

'No.'

'A long beard of rusty tin. And he walks with a stick.'

'No.'

'An iron rod. A great long spanner.'

'No.'

The man in the white pullover (Fortini) throws a pine cone into the fireplace, then a second and a third: the flames flare up, crackling.

'Robots aren't funny. Too many of them nowadays.'

'That's just the point,' says the man in the fawn jacket (Max), 'that's the point. I saw them as characters who've become traditional, like the two ship-wrecked sailors on the raft, the two drunks clinging on to the lamp-post. They're funny just because they're not funny any more.'

'You don't say.'

A pine kernel bursts with a sharp crack and from the pile of firewood a blazing cone tumbles down and rolls sparkling to the edge of the fireplace.

'It could be a skull,' observes Max, trying to grasp it with the tongs. 'Dracula's head burning.'

'Horror isn't funny any more.'

'I was just remarking. Or even a hedgehog. You know they eat roast hedgehogs here?'

'Who?'

'Whoever finds them, woodcutters, builders, the guards, anyone. Apparently they're delicious.'

'What is there to eat?' says Fortini.

'Here on the fire? Nothing.'

'No, in general. What have we got in the house?'

'The provisions for tomorrow. But weren't you saying you didn't feel like cooking?'

'But I don't feel like going out either. It's raining, and anyway the restaurants here are always freezing in winter, they never have anything more than a little gas stove.'

'There's spaghetti. There's tuna-fish. And there must be some tins of soup, peas . . .'

'Paper plates?'

'Loads. If we want to we can.'

'The fact is,' meditates Fortini, his eyes fixed on the

frenetic flurry of the flames, 'that I hate trattorie, I hate luxury restaurants, I hate pizzerias, I hate self-service buffets.'

'So let's stay in, let's organise a picnic by the fire.'

'Don't call it a picnic. I hate picnics.'

'A tidbit.'

'Ugh.'

'A snack.'

'Give us a break!'

'Mess-break.'

'That's it, mess-break's the word.'

'Two soldiers,' says Max, 'are walking along carrying the heavy mess-tin with the stew in it. One of them stops, lets go of the . . .'

'Soldiers aren't funny.'

'Two Roman soldiers. Tenth Legion. Julius Caesar.'

Fortini shakes his head, rummages with the tongs amid the palpitating red and grey of the embers.

'Greek hoplites?' tries Max.

'No.'

'Napoleonic grenadiers?'

'No.'

'Marines?'

'No,' says Fortini, standing up. 'Come on, let's go into the kitchen.'

4

And a hundred yards away, in Girolamo Delaude's kitchen, there are packets of spaghetti, tins of tuna-fish and peas, as well as the cold meats and cheese bought at the Tavernelle store. But Katia is adamant.

'No, I feel like a pizza.'

'But I tell you the pizzas here are inedible, they don't know how to make them.'

'It doesn't matter, I always like them.'

'I'll cook you some spaghetti.'

'You! You reckon you can cook!'

'Well, why not, I manage.'

'Oh yeah, I'm sure.'

'Well, you cook it then.'

'Oh yes, and then wash up as well,' snorts Katia, turning her back on the kitchen with its egg-yellow tiles.

'There's chilli, there's garlic!' Gimo shouts after her, opening a wall-cupboard. And then, his voice dropping, 'And anchovies too.'

All no good. It must be a custom, a post-erotic rite of these new generations. Pizza, for them, is pizza: an absolute ideal.

'And it's started to rain!' he tries again from the corridor. 'Listen! Can't you hear it pouring down?'

And from the bathroom, where she's combing her hair: 'So we'll take an umbrella.'

'But look, just tell me why we're going out on a night like this. Tell me what we do if we don't find a pizzeria open, which is more than likely?'

'Never mind then, we'll come back and eat your ham. But at least we'll have tried, won't we? At least, we'll have put our nose out of this putrefied pine-forest! Come on, get dressed, I'm hungry.'

All those women on strict diets, all those women getting by on crackers, on low-fat yoghurt and raw vegetables, and he had to pick this guzzling gannet whom he is now going to have to slip through the barrier again. Another gamble, not only more pointless but riskier than the first one, because on the way out the lodge is on the right and obviously it is the passenger, not the driver who draws the immediate attention of the guard on duty.

Gimo relapses into his earlier tremulous and diligent schizophrenia. Pull on trousers, socks, shoes. Take the Crickett down from its hook, leave with the pizzaholic, close the door. Done.

'What do you mean, raining? It's not raining at all.'

Reply that that is precisely how the sirocco works: a cloud, a downpour, another cloud, another downpour.

'What's that light over there? Is that their villa, is that Max & Fortini's villa?'

Reply that it is. Get ready for the next question.

'What do you say – shall we go over and see them now?'

Reply absolutely not, because they may be working, or anyway tired and irritable. Better to wait till tomorrow. Light the way for the pizzaholic through the bushes, reach the cane shelter and the car. Get in. Start the engine. Leave. Done.

Desperately search for nonchalant words, for an airy, playful tone with which to ask the girl to curl up with her head down, so as to be invisible when they pass through. Give up the idea, drive on, gradually abandon the shrouded security of the dark pine-forest, get closer and closer to the bottleneck, to the guards' square lodge, to the Christmas-tree rocking forlornly in the wind, to the lowered barrier.

The guard is not visible, however; he emerges a few seconds later from an inner room (it is Guerri) where he was probably watching television. He just glances at the car as it leaves, presses the button and rushes back to enjoy the fun of Bindo and Bicci.

Gimo stamps down on the accelerator and starts laughing.

'What are you laughing at?'

'I was thinking of Max & Fortini.'

'Those two,' says Katia, laughing herself, 'they kill me, they really do.'

5

On the way back to the Gualdana Signor Zeme follows a lorry for a long stretch. There is little traffic on the road and at several points it might well be in order to overtake, but Zeme continues to behave as if the passenger-seat beside him contained not a wooden puppet but Magda with her sudden transmigrations from aboulia to apprehension, from total silence to loud alarm. Cautious, restrained driving, prompted by the same meticulous solicitude as ever.

The two red lights on the lorry, which bumble along calmly, almost sleepily, in front of him, limit the vastness of the night, encourage brief thoughts. In the black cockpit of the Volvo, the driver lazily begins to assess the quality of the silence around himself: a calm, relaxed silence like an animal skin, soft and still, without the constant menace of the endless voice of suffering.

But what about a little music? He sets the radio-scanner in motion and the silence steps back with a yawn, serenely allows eight seconds of rock-music to pass over it, eight seconds of different rock, eight seconds of advertisement, eight seconds of double-bass . . .

'Come on, snap out of it, let's go.'

Signor Zeme straightens up in the driving seat, brusquely accelerates and gets ready to overtake the lorry's two red dots.

6

With just a rough cloak around you
You will come a-roaming with me
As once Hipparchia did with cynic Cratès.

*

In fact (as this poignant fragment from a lost comedy of Menander's testifies) the charming Hipparchia, after marrying the Door-Opener against her rich parents' wishes (they gave their consent only after threats of suicide), adopted the customs of the Cynics in all respects and went around with her husband dressed in just a *tribon* (a cloak of rough cloth, which served the ambulant philosophers as a bed too) with nothing at all underneath.

This gave rise to a spicy episode at the house of Lisimacus, who had invited Cratès to dinner with his young wife and various other philosophers, including Theodore the Atheist, an ex-Cynic who had gone over to the laxity of the Cyrenian school.

Now Hipparchia was an atheist too, or at least agnostic, like all the Cynics. But Theodore was getting on her nerves with the vacuous, eccentric sophisms he was always trying to trip her up with. She decided to face him on his own ground.

'Can the same action,' she asked, 'be lawful for Theodore and unlawful for Hipparchia?'

'No,' admitted Theodore (for fear, presumably, of being taken for a male chauvinist).

'Therefore,' she said, 'since it is lawful for Theodore to slap himself, it cannot be unlawful for Hipparchia to slap him.'

And wham, a resounding smack.

He remained quite unruffled. But it must have immediately come into his mind that whereas he, as a Cyrenian, was wearing a *chiton* (a loose-fitting belted tunic) under his cloak, his interlocutor had nothing at all.

'Quite right,' he said. 'And since it is lawful for Theodore to take off his own cloak, it cannot be unlawful for him to take . . .'

The cloak was already off or almost, when Hipparchia

managed to grab it back and cover herself. But – her biographer reports – she did not appear flustered or ashamed, as would have been natural for a young woman of her rank. And when everybody present marvelled at her 'aplomb' (*eustatheia*), when Theodore asked with admiration, in the words of Euripides, if she was 'the same woman who had recently abandoned her work with the distaff and the loom', she answered courteously: 'Yes, Theodore, it is I. And do you think I did wrong to concern myself with my education, instead of wasting yet more time spinning and weaving?'

The story of Hipparchia, recounted in a lively fashion over dinner, won Sandra over to its narrator, and she even wishes to know more. How did Cratès take the joke with the cloak? How had they met, he and the future lady-philosopher? What other stories do they tell about her?

But it is getting late, Monforti says solicitously, and their guest has to walk several miles back to his hill. Unless he will accept a lift?

His brother-in-law Ettore says it will be no trouble for him to drive Ugo over, but the Hermit explains that his principles will not allow it. Up there, he says, he has an old bicycle and sometimes he even uses it. But no motorised vehicles, not even a scooter like Father Everardo's.

'On account of pollution?' asks Sandra.

No, no, pollution for him is like bad weather, it doesn't bother him in the slightest, a Cynic can't be worrying himself about lead and asbestos! Tough on those who are against them. For him it's more a question of . . . But yes, it is getting late, and he had better set off.

A question of what? wonders Monforti, who has accompanied him as far as the coast path and now watches him go off with his flapping cloak, his pilgrim's staff and his lamp, more flickering than ever in this sirocco, which seems to be turning into a southwesterly wind.

Of style, he tells himself eventually. Because it cannot be denied that poor de Meis has found his own road, has succeeded in creating a dignified, if somewhat bizarre character for himself. After all, how could one imagine him, in his Cynic's uniform, on a motorbike or at the wheel of a Uno? On an old bike, just about.

This reminds him of his plan for a cycling trip with Natalia and her two children, perpetually postponed for motives of depression. But if his condition continues to improve like this, why not propose that she should come alone, maybe on foot and 'with just a rough cloak around her'?

But, as ever, it is either too early or too late, he thinks, absorbedly making his way back home. The idea of beautiful Signora Neri in a *tribon* with nothing on beneath merely serves to agitate him.

7

A couple of miles south of the village, on what were once fields cultivated with wheat and colza, there rises a forest of sheds and warehouses which might be said to serve a primarily symbolic function: that of reminding the resident, no less than the tourist, of the industrious squalor on which the smooth running of his daily life so greatly depends.

In order to set the prow of a defective motorboat leaping once more towards Elba or Corsica, to get the cantankerous engine of a BMW re-chugging on its way towards Duccio da Buoninsegna or Piero della Francesca, to restore an unhinged wardrobe or a rat-gnawed divan to a semblance of life, one has no choice but to come here!

It is the 'industrial zone', where carpenters and smiths, plumbers and car-dealers, tyre-vendors and upholsterers rumble and rasp side by side. Their rough grey workshops have sprung up more or less at random, giving rise to short narrow alleys, geometrically bewildering yards, wide avenues that suddenly run out of asphalt and dwindle towards reed-beds; and although the 'zone' itself is heralded by a large notice-board, once one enters its cramped and crooked jumble, anonymity is the rule. No addresses here, no Via Kennedy 23 or Piazza Einstein 5B, no roads dedicated to Progress or Technology. One finds one's way by indications of the medieval type. Lilli's electrical repair shop? Well, it's almost directly opposite Ilario, the marble-worker, just beyond Malentacchi's, the oilburner man.

Now of course the area is dark and deserted. There is no one to ask for directions.

But the driver of the Panda that turns up at this moment – a well-wrapped woman, of whom nothing can be seen but a great mass of dark hair – does not seem to need any. She makes her way directly towards a vaguely hexagonal yard, where a high lamp-post provides lighting for the entire zone, then slips into a lane flanked by huts of wood or concrete, turns into a wider road, drives on between miscellaneous buildings, and only when she comes to a crossroads does she hesitate for a moment.

'Left,' says the man sitting by her side.

After Malentacchi's (NAPHTHA, DIESEL-OIL AND KEROSENE BURNERS states the sign) comes Lilli's workshop, marked simply by a rough board with the words: ELECTRICAL REPAIRS. On the other side of the grey metal gate, there is a courtyard of trampled earth where junk of the most varied and incomprehensible kind is stacked in precarious heaps around an old van. And at the far end of the courtyard the Panda's headlights illuminate a shed with high, wide, sliding doors, half metal and half glass, inset with a smaller man-sized door.

The passenger gets out and pushes the gate to let the car

into the yard. Then he walks on, searching for a key in his pocket; he opens the little door, enters and turns on the light. After parking the car, the driver joins him. One behind the other they climb a little iron staircase from the garage to an upper room. The light downstairs goes off as the one upstairs comes on.

We are in Lilli's office, it seems, although a gas-cooker, a fridge and a folding bed in one corner suggest that it is also used for living purposes.

One might suppose that the conscientious artesan, when work mounts up or is particularly pressing, spends the night here instead of returning to the village; or (considering the present situation) that the room serves him for discreet encounters, by day or night, safe from the curiosity and gossip of his fellow villagers.

Except that the young man who was brought here in the Panda and who is now sitting sulkily behind the desk, while his driver makes up the bed with two sheets that she has taken from a bag, is not the stocky dark-haired electrician. He is a lanky blond with a Nazarene beard and hair, and a sharp face which, despite slightly protruding watery eyes and numerous plasters, is not without a certain romantic charm.

And from the dialogue he now embarks on with his bed-maker, it transpires that it is he – or rather they – who often use the room for their encounters, as they are both good friends of Lilli, but that tonight the bed is for his use only.

'I'll be back tomorrow morning or I'll phone as soon as I hear anything,' she concludes. 'You just make sure you don't move or let anyone see you round here, because you never know.'

'In that case,' he says through his teeth, 'I shouldn't let anyone see me anywhere.'

'First I just have to find out what he intends to do. Anyway, it's even possible that he's come back in the meantime.'

'And what if he asks you where you've been?'

'I'll tell him I went out to look for him. But anyway I must go now. I'll put the goat's milk and the soya shoots for tomorrow in the fridge.'

'But wait . . . Listen . . . Supposing he has come back, or anyway when he gets back . . . you could tell him . . . promise him that from now on . . . I don't mean always but every so often . . . you . . . once in a while, at least. Do you get what I mean?'

'No,' she says curtly, slamming the fridge shut and turning round to stare at him, grim-faced.

She is a middle-aged woman of average height, olive-skinned, with a mass of jet-black hair and a figure that one can tell is generous under the purple woollen poncho. Her eyes, also jet-black, now flare threateningly.

'No,' she repeats. 'What exactly do you mean?'

He stands up.

'I'm saying,' he says, 'that you shouldn't always say no, when he asks you. After all, he is your husband.'

'But he doesn't even ask me for it any more!'

'Because he knows you wouldn't let him have it anyway!'

'So I should let him have it, in your opinion? Is that what . . .'

'Yes! Because maybe that's the thing that's really driving him mad. Whereas if you – I don't say always, but . . .'

'Listen, Dino, just listen carefully . . .'

'No, Amelia, you listen carefully to me!'

At this point, it is perfectly clear that the long-haired, lanky man is Dino Fioravanti, and the woman in the purple poncho is Amelia Baldacci, the wife of Orfeo the gardener. It is also clear that when Orfeo did not come home this evening, his wife guessed that he had gone to look for Fioravanti in order to bump him off, with the gun he always keeps in the van for firing at processionary moths' nests. So she too set off in search of her lover and, finding him at the 'Il Molo' bar, persuaded him to take shelter in Lilli's workshop rather than go back to his own house, where Orfeo is probably waiting to shoot him.

But what is not clear are the couple's motives with regard to the husband's demands and the wife's absolute refusal to satisfy him. It is a matter of principle, says Amelia Baldacci, with which Fioravanti has always agreed. Yes, says Fioravanti, but now it's a question of preventing further violence, and non-violence is also a matter of principle.

'Why don't you just admit you're afraid?' she shouts.

'That's the limit, it really is! It was you who came and scared me with this story of the gun!' he shouts. And when the woman finally stomps off, slamming the door behind her, he sits there thinking how much simpler things would be if she just let Orfeo have it every so often.

8

The pizzas at the pizzeria-spaghetteria 'Las Vegas' are indeed not the kind that one remembers for the rest of one's life, but Katia takes care to munch her way through the tough, burnt crust as well so as not to give the Count the satisfaction of 'I told you so'. Similarly she makes it a point of honour to assume a pleased air as she drains the last drops of Coke while looking around: the place is actually a graveyard, with wretched coloured lights, a ridiculously low sottofondo of rock and no more than four or five local youths, as coarse as the benches and rickety tables they are sitting at.

The village itself is a graveyard, though Katia remembers it as a cheery bedlam, with all the shops open till midnight under the illuminated castle. But it must have been a Sunday in summer, two (no, three) years ago, when she was going out with Aldo (no, with Nicola) and had that green jumpsuit with white flowers and nothing under it but a fluorescent tanga.

They walk out of the pizzeria into the wind and slanting rain, and the only consoling thought that Katia manages to clutch on to as she gazes past the flapping windscreen-wiper at the deserted streets (the outskirts of a village on the outskirts of everywhere) is: at least I don't have to live here, or I'd shoot myself!

She is not enjoying herself, she has not enjoyed herself, the 'trip' has proved a semi-failure, like so many other similar 'trips'. An attentive reader of biographies of singers, actresses, top models and television presenters, Katia is fully aware that in order to open up new horizons in her life, in order to 'make it', a modern girl of course has to slog, to study, etc.; but above all she has to be an unscrupulous calculator. She is sure that she has long since got rid of all scruples, and the proof is this fellow here, this Count driving by her side, whom, despite having been to bed with him, she just cannot manage to think of as 'Gimo'. But it is her skills as a calculator that she is beginning to doubt.

With that marketing manager things did not turn out as planned. And they didn't turn out with that director's assistant from Telegiotto either, nor with that freelance photographer from the Botticelli fashion-centre. All people who should have led to 'contacts' of great promotional importance and whom in fact Katia, in her private thoughts or conversations with friends, never once considered as men but as 'contacts' and nothing else. Just that in practice these famous contacts all come down to one and one only kind of contact. And the horizons that should open up all come down to the same single horizon: a ceiling, whether with central or concealed lighting.

Am I a fool? Katia asks herself. But at this time of night, in this desolate seaside resort, the question is purely rhetorical. Yes, she is a fool, rather than a whore, because at least whores know how to manage their affairs: straight business agreements, payment in advance and off with the knickers. Whereas she whips them off every time with no contracts signed and no calculations made.

If she ever manages to make it as a top model or a show-girl, she will do well to be very vague about this period of her life. 'They were tough years,' she will have to tell the journalist. 'It took a great deal of courage to face certain challenges, certain sacrifices.' After all, that's what they all say, alluding generally to 'disappointments', 'mistakes', 'moments of crisis and dejection'.

'Are you tired? Sleepy?' her latest 'mistake' asks her.

Katia straightens her chin and shoulders: courage is shown in these things too. 'No, of course not, I could go on till four a.m. There's nowhere to dance round here, is there?'

The 'mistake' trembles, and stammers that in winter everywhere closes, at Punta Ala, the Argentario, everywhere. As if she didn't know perfectly well.

'Do you take your wife dancing in the summer?'

And at the mere mention of his wife, he trembles again. 'Well, you know how it is, in summer we usually rent the villa out, we stay in the country, I look after the management, the horses, we have lots of guests . . .'

'Paying?'

'Well, yes, paying, foreigners mostly.'

'Quite a little business, eh?' says Katia, thinking that these people really know how to make their calculations.

'Well . . .' mumbles the riding-master.

Kinder than many others, more polite, poor Count. And maybe not quite so useless as a 'contact', if he can introduce her to Max & Fortini tomorrow. A drink around midday, or a walk along the beach after coffee. 'How did you meet them?' the interviewer will ask her one day. 'Pure chance,' she will answer. 'I was staying with friends in that stupendous pine-forest, the Gualdana, where they have a dream-villa too . . .'

And now they are approaching the entrance to the stupendous pine-forest. The Count slows down and trembles, trembles and slows down, so that Katia is almost tempted to crouch and make herself invisible this time, rewarding him for previously having had the good manners not to ask her to do so. But there is no need, another car is going in and once again the Count darts swiftly forward so as to tag on behind, once again he takes advantage of the raised barrier to slip into the forest himself, once again, as soon as the first car whizzes off, he whizzes off after it.

'Lucky,' says Katia.

Too soon, because an instant later: screech, bang, slam, crash, and Katia's forehead bumps, not too hard, into the windscreen.

9

For the last quarter of an hour on Telepadùle a breeder has been showing off his white Maremman sheepdogs, a breed that has recently and rightly come into favour again – thanks to the English, mind you, always the first when it comes to dogs and horses. But just as he is settling in front of the television to find out a little more about them, Guard Roggiolani, who has taken over from Guerri for the night-shift, hears a tremendous clang of metal above the howling of the sirocco outside and the barking of the animals inside. He bounds back through the control-room and out of the lodge.

Thirty yards beyond the barrier there has been an accident. Signor Zeme's white Volvo, which he let in barely a minute ago, has been violently struck from behind by Count Delaude's grey Fiat, which was following hot on its wheels.

Roggiolani runs towards them. Road accidents in the Gualdana are not rare, there is always someone knocking his rear or front bumper against one of the 18,300 pine-trees, or cutting in front of someone as they emerge without due care from a bend or private driveway, not to mention what the motorbikes and push-bikes get up to. But a nose-to-tail crash is fairly unusual.

Nothing serious, however, since Signor Zeme is already getting out of his car and the Count opens his door without any problems.

'How did it happen?' asks Roggiolani.

The two men ignore him, grim-faced, each absorbed in his own incredulous choler, busily considering their respective damages. Quite a smash. The heavy Volvo naturally has come off better; it just has its back bumper damaged, its registration number and maybe its boot pushed a little out of square; but the Count's car is in a sorry state: its bonnet crumpled, its left headlight shattered, its left mudguard twisted so that it is touching the tyre.

'Quite a smash,' says Roggiolani.

The two men, standing between the two cars, say nothing, still in shock or maybe simply poised between wrath and resignation. Is there going to be an angry exchange of words? An altercation in which he, Roggiolani, will have to act as peacemaker?

No, of course not. They are not lorry-drivers but civilised inhabitants of the Gualdana. The Count naturally blames himself: he was driving too close, he admits grouchily. Zeme, equally grouchy, acknowledges that he braked too sharply, when he saw a porcupine, a beast this size, crossing the road in front of him.

'Oh, old prickle-back,' confirms Roggiolani, who every so often finds its long quills scattered around the forest.

But they pay no attention to him, they start talking about insurance, Zeme pulls out a piece of paper and props himself deliberately on the boot (which is actually all wet) with the evident intention of taking down the other man's name and address and also Dalvo Roggiolani's particulars, as the only witness.

But the situation changes with the sudden appearance of a second witness, a woman who emerges from the Count's car. It is not the Countess but a tall, pissed-off brunette massaging her forehead, who says: 'Well then?'

The Count suddenly sees Roggiolani and says, 'A guest of my daughter's.'

In the meantime another fat shower patters down and Zeme suggests: 'Listen, it's wet out here, wouldn't we do better to put things off till tomorrow morning?'

'Yes, of course. I'll come round to your place,' the Count agrees at once, taking the brunette by the arm.

'No, I'll come,' says Zeme, his hand already on the door handle.

'No, no, I insist, it's no trouble . . . ,' insists the Count.

'No, I mean it, I'd rather come round myself,' Zeme cuts him short, closing the door and driving off smoothly.

Roggiolani stands by to see if the Fiat will manage to start. With a bump like that the engine might have suffered and anyway the twisted mudguard is likely to prevent the wheel from turning.

'Yes, yes, we'll see how it is now,' says the Count.

'I could get the hammer,' Roggiolani offers, 'and with two good bangs . . .'

'Yes, yes, thank you,' says the Count, pushing his daughter's guest into the car. Which, though lopsided and one-eyed, starts up docilely and rumbles off into the wood, so that all is left for Roggiolani to do is to get a broom and sweep up the bits of glass left at the scene of the accident.

10

'So there are porcupines here!' says Katia, in an incredulous-scandalised tone.

'Yes, they have a den somewhere.'

'You can be walking calmly along through the trees and be faced with a porcupine!'

'Yes, it can happen.'

'I've never seen one.'

'You only ever see them at night.'

'Are they dangerous?'

'Just look what they've done to my car,' says Gimo sourly.

'What do you mean, it was your fault, you were driving much too close.'

'It was that idiot, he shouldn't have braked so suddenly.'

'But with that porcupine in front . . .'

'Be quiet,' orders Gimo.

He strains his ears and once again, as they meet a bump in the asphalt, he thinks he can hear the rasping throb of the mudguard against the wheel.

'Jesus, it's touching, I know it is!'

'Don't swear, I don't like it.'

'But it's scraping off all the tread!'

'Well, you're insured, aren't you?'

'Not for my own damages.'

'And suppose I had smashed my head against the windscreen, would you have had to pay the hospital fees?' Katia asks, rubbing her forehead.

Gimo does not answer; this further disaster, however

hypothetical, is too much for his mind to take in at that moment.

When they reach the shelter, he inspects the damage again. A mess, a real mess. He can't possibly go back to Florence in this state. But only when he gets into the house, only after closing the door, does he recall that he is not alone, that he has to take into account this extra 'thing', this girl who seems to be growing, protruding in all directions, dangling jaggedly, absurdly, from this disastrous nocturnal encounter.

So he sits down and starts to reflect with funereal concentration.

'First thing tomorrow morning I'll go to Sirio, the mechanic, hoping that he's about and can do the job for me even though it's Christmas Eve. Second thing: I'll call a taxi to take you to Grosseto and there you can get the train to Florence or Rome, if you were wanting to go to Rome.'

He hadn't foreseen the third thing.

'Hey, sunshine, are you joking?'

Katia's voice bristles with instant quills.

'No, I'm afraid there's nothing else for it. I'm sorry too, but you must see that in an emergency like this . . .'

'I don't see anything! All I can see is that you've taken me for a tart!'

'No, look, what do you mean, I've had the bad luck to . . .'

'Well, if I'm a tart, then you'll have to pay me, and pay handsomely, because as a tart Katia comes expensive, she's not like one of your Nigerians up in the wood there, do you get me?'

'Katia, do me a favour, you can see how things are . . .'

'A favour??? You have the face to ask a favour from me??? You ask me!!!'

She has reached the yelling stage now. And saliva-spraying, fist-raising and tempestuous heel-stamping as she marches up and down the living-room. This is not the moment to react, to snap back at her seething irrationality, as she dishonestly denies Gimo's virility, dwells on his age, his thinning hair, his wrinkled stomach, endows his wife with both a repugnant appearance and a frenetic propensity for adultery, hints at a phone-call or even a letter which will bring aforesaid wife up to date on what has happened today and demand – from her no less! – the payment for Katia's services.

Gimo smiles despite himself.

'What are you laughing at, shit-face!'

'You don't know her.'

'And I've no desire to, becuase if she could marry someone like you . . .'

And suddenly she has made up her mind: she won't leave, there won't be any taxis or trains, she'll stay here until she's been introduced to Max & Fortini, or otherwise until she's been lavishly paid, get the message? Even if it means staying here Christmas Day as well and if needs be until the New Year, with the risk that whoever turns up with the cheque will find themselves faced with the scandal of a completely demolished villa, torn to pieces, chair by chair, plate by plate, because a girl who gets treated in this fashion can't be held responsible for her nerves, get the message? And for a start, she'll move right away into another room, with different sheets and blankets, and she'll lock the door so as not to have anything to do with this worm, this filthy, slavering, miserable scrounger, the nastiest kind of lecher, get the message?

Doors slam, drawers open and close and finally a key clicks wrathfully in the lock. Gimo is alone.

When everything is quiet within the villa the wind repossesses the silence with yet stronger gusts and Gimo welcomes it as an intemperate but faithful friend; he sits for a long time listening to the variations between bushes, trunks and branches. Nature is nature, after all – solemn, grandiose, and eternal, for ever putting the fleeting tribulations of fleeting men into perspective. So what has actually happened? Nothing serious, no big deal.

Gimo yawns deliberately and stands up. It's time to go to bed, and tomorrow when things are calmer, well, he'll see. But then, as he stands at the foot of the double bed, gazing at the twisted sheets and the slewed pillows, he notes a stuffy smell, the dregs of which contain the perfume 'Velvet', that he himself gave Katia just a few days ago. Better open the window for a while and let the wind carry it away, and meanwhile he'll go back and drink something to settle that wretched pizza and that filthy white wine.

There's the rare Calvados that Pierre brought, there are a few month-old magazines, and there's an illustrated book which Gimo now picks up and flips through: *Ireland, the Paradise of Horses*. Green meadows, low walls, horses.

At this time of night (it's almost one o'clock), there is almost nothing on TV but advertisements for second-hand cars and new furniture, but Telegiotto is showing a faded film about pirates. Gimo stays on that channel and when he wakes up it is almost two.

His stomach is burning; neither the pizza nor the Calvados have settled down; but by way of compensation, worries, both ancient and recent, have loomed up, in a writhing heap: a gambling debt with Vannozza Vettori, a trifle but which will have to be paid; his step-daughter Griselda, who now treats him quite openly as a good-for-nothing parasite; his wife, who will have to be told about the accident and who will end up finding out the rest of it, either from the guards or from Katia.

Gimo rests his eyes on the Irish horses cantering across

the table, on a woman selling beauty products on television, and then struggles, stiffly and creakily, to his feet. He tiptoes over to the room where the girl is holed up and listens through the door: she might be awake and ready to make peace. But the handle does not give and no noise filters through the hollow wood. Gimo risks a soft signal with his finger-tips, but then gives up and goes back to the living-room for another sip of Calvados.

He is not at all sleepy but agitated, as always happens whenever the tiny autonomous segments into which he usually manages to divide his life – this evening, in two hours' time, tomorrow morning – come brusquely back together, presenting him with a snythesis like a brimming rubbish-bin, an illegal dumping-ground swamped in toxic waste. Katia is right, his wife is right, Griselda is right, Vannozza is right, the architect Salvini is right, they're all right to see him as a worm, a louse, an ineffectual scrounger, a womaniser with perpetual egg on his face and fleas in his ears, and above all, as essentially, congenitally a shit, an irredeemable numbskull. Not to mention the bad luck that follows him everywhere and which in any case aggravates rather than justifies matters.

On the wall opposite him, the damp patch seems to have grown; it has annexed another large piece of plaster high up on the left, but at this moment he cannot hear the patter of the rain. Gimo goes out with the torch and a large night bird disturbed by the beam flaps away from somewhere close by and disappears among the trees. A bat or a barn-owl? And maybe the barn-owls, like other owls, are heralds of misfortune? But he's already had more than his fair share today, even if 'c . . . is c . . .' and Katia after all 'let him have it'.

A new, distressful inspection of the car reveals even worse damage than he had previously noticed. Gimo pushes and presses the metal and fibre-glass with his foot, but these materials, which had yielded like wax to Zeme's car, now resist him with exasperating firmness, refusing to budge an inch. And all because of a porcupine, that wretched 'old prickle-back' that chose tonight of all nights to go for a stroll, that moment of all moments and that exact spot of the pine-forest of all spots. No getting away from it: bad luck, thinks Gimo with gloomy conviction, is bad luck.

He switches off the torch and stands there in the definitive dark of the Gualdana. Max & Fortini's light has gone off too, while the wind now carries a louder, more clamorous roar from the sea. The sky is completely overcast, and over there, towards the south-west, distant flashes silently herald the storm. It has stopped raining. Gimo takes a few irresolute paces, breathes deeply, but nothing clears up – not his headache, nor his heartburn, nor Katia, nor the smashed car, nor his wife, nor the rubbish-bin, the dumping-ground swathed in obscene fumes that is, and always will be, his life.

II

The *shulūq*, or sirocco, the wind feared by the desert fathers for its baleful influence on the human spirit, is also known for its highly changeable character, its tendency – which can be remarked both during the ascendant (or spring) equinox and during the descendant (or autumn) equinox – to give way to the contiguous south-west wind, the *libeccio* (from the Greek *libykos*, from Libya), also known as the *garbino* or, contemptuously, *libicocco*. But a similar phenomenon sometimes occurs in the winter months, giving rise to what is commonly defined as a 'freak *libecciata*'.

The *libicocco* is a violent and, above all, unpredictable

wind. Roggiolani, for example, who used to be a fisherman, before he came and buried himself in the Gualdana lodge, often tells tales of *libecciate* off the coast of Montecristo or the Giglio in tones that are positively, though unconsciously, Homeric. He and his mates sitting or lying about on deck, awaiting the dawn, the boat rocking in gently swaying waters – and suddenly, without any warning, the smack of the first gust, the frenzied rush to draw in the nets, the prow swung effortfully towards the nearest promontory of the island amid the turmoil of the first waves, the lightning flashes, the blinding rain.

It is not the first rumbles of thunder that awake him tonight, but the unequivocal lashing against the lodge windows and down the chimney: it's him again, the old, unexpected enemy. Sitting up in his camp-bed, Roggiolani listens, happy to be out of danger, grateful to Vannucci who recommended him for this peaceful guard's job, and yet not unresponsive to the call of those adventures on the high sea.

He gets up at last and goes to the door on the pretext of checking the Christmas-tree, which could be toppled by a gust of wind.

Even at this distance the roar of the sea is deafening and all 18,300 pine-trees creak and groan simultaneously, all the countless shrubs seem on the point of taking flight. The coloured lights of the 'Christmas ilex' sway with the swaying branches, and needles, berries, leaves, twigs and ever stiffer streaks of rain can be seen scurrying through their polychrome aureola.

Roggiolani runs and tests the resistance of the ilex in its pot, goes back inside to switch off the lights, and a thunderbolt that falls catastrophically close by induces him to switch off the lights outside the lodge as well. Everything is more violent and savage than ever when he scampers back under the overhanging roof in his oilskins.

The thunder rolls plurally as if spilling out from an immense sack of sounds and further flashes of lightning capture the spectres of great trees in desperate postures. Nothing seems capable of resisting the powers that have been unleashed, and when the electricity goes off in the whole area the end of the world is nigh.

In fact, nothing serious happens. The waves hurled upon the beach will sweep over it until they lap at the row of huts, a dozen of which as usual will be unroofed and cleft asunder by the wind. Thousands of pine cones and several large branches will fall, and rain will form huge puddles in the dips in the roads. A few windows left open will get shattered, a few dogs howl in terror, a bicycle or a ladder leaning against an outside wall will go crashing down. But none of the villas in the Gualdana caves in or is ripped from its foundations, no roof launches itself skywards.

In the front row by the sea, Villa Borst just emits a flicker of emergency candlelight, while at the Zemes' all is peaceful and quiet, as it is at the Kruysens' and the Grahams'; these northerners, little Colin included, are clearly superior to mere Mediterranean squalls. Deep sleep, or maybe indifference, or irritated resignation, probably explain why no reaction to the storm is to be seen at Monforti's, Gimo's, Mongelli's or Max & Fortini's. Only at Casa Bonanno is the entire family up, all of them with their hearts in their mouths after a thunderbolt fell on each of their pillows, and all of them now staring at a second and more horrific surprise: two torches and a candle pick out an enormous rat squealing horribly in one of Vannucci's traps in the sitting-room. Signora Neri wakes with a start, goes to see if the children (as if they were still three or four years old) are as scared as she is, and then goes back to bed thinking of the possible collocation of the *libecciata* in the Wheel of the Tarot cards. It seem legitimate to imagine that Orfeo is curled up snugly under the blankets, maybe with his back to his faithless wife, and it can be hoped that Ugo the Hermit got back in time to his distant hermitage, or at least that his Cynic's cloak is able to protect him from the wrath of God.

Roggiolani permits himself another few minutes of the spectacle, then returns to the lodge, gropes his way back to his bed and lies down amidst the thunder, the lightning, the howling, with a smile on his lips.

VI

A Man and a Boy Are Gazing

I

A MAN AND a boy are gazing at the sea after the storm. It has stopped raining, although heavy slate clouds are still in control of the sky and could decide, from one moment to the next, to punish the Gualdana and the surrounding area again.

'Vannucci says that two fishing-boats didn't get back,' reveals the boy. 'They didn't make it.'

It is Andrea, Signora Neri's son, and his tone, though serious, is charged with melodramatic expectations: he would like to enrich his thirteen years with a drama at sea. Monforti, standing beside him, thinks that the two robust motor-boats probably found shelter at Portoferraio or Piombino, but does not say so. He knows that in this case his hypothesis – optimistic for once – would have a depressing effect.

'Let's hope for the best,' he says. 'Let's hope they don't share the fate of the *Viktor Hansen*.'

'The *Viktor Hansen*?'

Adventure is in the air, in the wind that has not ceased to waft from the sands of Libya, in the salty spray tossed up by the hubbub of the waves, in Andrea's excited voice: 'What's the *Viktor Hansen*? A ship?'

How can one refuse to indulge a boy wrapped in a yellow oilskin and still open to epic in his every freckle? With an effort, which becomes less burdensome as he proceeds, Monforti does what all singers of ancient deeds must do: without actually lying he colours, or rather 'pumps up', the pale drooping jellyfish of reality.

About fifteen years ago, after an even stronger *libecciata* than this one, a little cargo ship drifted and ran aground on the beach of the Gualdana, over there, beyond the Old Ditch, in that stretch of sand where all the wrecks get dragged in the end by the current. It had obviously been abandoned by the crew, though no one knew when or where, and no one came to claim the low-tonnage hulk, in its white and blue paint, with the name *Viktor Hansen* at the stern. The harbour-master's office couldn't be bothered to tug it out to sea, or perhaps they didn't have the authority to do so; papers were shuffled between one maritime authority and another, while the carcase stayed where it was, leaning further and further into the sand, getting more and more derelict, feared by anxious parents, loved by children who finally had a real shipwreck for their endless games. Year after year, storm after storm, the plating rotted, the keel sank, the iron of the superstructures rusted and crumbled, until the seagulls stopped flying over it, the fish stopped darting around it, and the *Viktor Hansen* was gradually swallowed by the sand and disappeared.

'But is it still there?' asked the enthralled listener.

'I imagine so,' responds the conscientious narrator.

'But can you see it?'

'I don't think so, not any more. You'd have to dig under water.'

Andrea ponders on this maritime mystery. 'But who was this Viktor Hansen? A Dane?'

'Probably. Some little shipping merchant in Copenhagen, or his father perhaps. But it was an old wreck, which might have changed hands countless times.'

'Did it have a flag?'

'I don't remember, but it was probably Cypriot or Liberian.'

'I'd like to have a piece of it, a piece of the *Viktor Hansen*,' says Andrea, examining the beach avidly.

At the very height of the storm, around dawn, the waves had reached as far as the line of huts, smashing several and carrying others away; now the sea is still swollen but its grey and yellow tongues remain a few yards off and the beach is a uniform, glistening band, under the incessant fretwork of foam. Here and there along the dunes, there are other people besides Monforti and Andrea contemplating the aftermath of the *libecciata*; in the distance, Signor Graham is identifiable by the child holding on to him, and, a little nearer at hand stands Milagros, Signora Borst's maid, wearing an exaggerated fur hat. Lower down, on the sleek strip that the waves continue to lick flat, Guard Barabesi walks slowly along in rubber boots, his eyes turned towards the battered row of shelters and huts.

'Shall we go down too?' suggests Andrea, who would like to be closer to the scene of action that the sea constitutes today.

But Monforti is not wearing rubber boots, and he and the boy resume their stroll along the humps and bumps of the coast path, bestrewn with branches and fronds torn down by the *libeccio*. Ahead of them, a window can be heard to bang. On days like this it is normal, the whole of the Gualdana echoes with doors and windows banging. And indeed a moment later there is another sharp slam, which Andrea remarks on.

'Don't they know how to close them?' he says, a line his

mother must have repeated to him countless times. And when the window bangs again he runs along a path through the bushes.

'Where the devil are you going?' Monforti shouts in vain.

It is the Zemes' villa.

The yellow blot runs, disappears, reappears in leaps and bounds in front of the house, and then halts beside a french window on the right.

'What are you doing . . . ?'

'Come and see!' shouts the boy, stepping back on to the path and waving urgently to him.

Irritated, Monforti moves forward with the intention of yanking back the unauthorised explorer and sees, beyond the half-open sliding shutter, the french window with one pane shattered.

'Look! They've been burgled!'

Through the gap, they can see a room that has been ransacked. Around the double bed, which is untouched, it appears as if the *libeccio* has whirled freely, leaving bags and suitcases overturned, drawers open, clothes scattered, in addition to countless pine needles floating in pools of water.

'Isn't this the Zemes' house?' says Andrea.

'Yes.'

'Are they here?'

'He should be. Unless he stayed in Florence. He was taking his wife to the station last night.'

'Let's go and see if the car is in the garage.'

All he can do is follow the yellow grasshopper, which has already leapt towards the forest side of the house, where the front door is situated and, just beyond it, the ramp of the basement garage.

'The car's here,' announces Andrea with a touch of disappointment.

Through the windows of the closed sliding door, the white shape of the Volvo can be seen.

'But if he's here, where did he sleep?' says Andrea, perking up, trying to keep this land-mystery 'pumped up'.

'How do I know, he may have been in another room.'

One cannot tell him the probable truth: that the mess is the result of a much-suffered departure, uncertain till the very last moment; and that poor old Zeme, on his return from Florence, had no desire to face the scene again and went to sleep in a single bedroom.

The boy has disappeared; he comes back a minute later.

'I've been all round the house,' he reports breathlessly. 'All the windows are closed.'

'And so?'

'Well, if he was sleeping in another room he might not have heard the thieves. Shall we ring?'

Monforti looks at his watch, as does Andrea: it is ten to ten.

'No.'

'He ought to be up by now.'

'No. He's probably dead tired and having a lie-in.'

'But anyway we ought to tell him.'

'No, you can't disturb people like that, come on, let's leave him.'

They go off into the pine-forest, and when they hear the window bang again, Andrea looks reproachfully at Monforti. 'We could have closed it at least. Or told Barabesi.'

'Listen, when I get home I'll try and phone him, all right?'

'OK.'

'And then I'll tell you.'

'OK.'

But as soon as Monforti gets home and tells his sister about the scene of chaos in the room, the roles are reversed.

'But why bother phoning him about a broken window?' she says at once. 'He'll be sleeping.'

Without answering he dials the number, counts a dozen rings, and hangs up pensively.

'He's not there.'

'He'll have gone to the village.'

'Without noticing a thing? And anyway how? The car's in the garage.'

'Someone else will have given him a lift. I've got to go there shortly, come with me and I bet you we'll find him doing his shopping, if you're so concerned.'

How concerned am I? wonders Monforti, strolling with his hands in his pockets into the living-room. Actually he is not at all concerned, he concludes; and in fact it does not even cross his mind to report the episode to Ettore, who is sitting there calmly reading a paper. But the problem has not been stated in its proper terms. Sandra is really insinuating that this natural worry of his over a neighbour who has been visited, and perhaps attacked, by burglars, is a prelude to a phase of euphoric anxiety. But Monforti is certain that this is not the case: if anything he might have been affected by Andrea's excitability. The boy gets bored at the Gualdana, with that marvellous, enviable boredom of adolescence, and last night's storm, followed by the wreck of the *Viktor Hansen*, have all put him in a state of mind to keep that broken window 'pumped-up', to transfigure it into a break-in by thieves or bandits.

Outside the large windows the light is pallid, the various greens of the forest all seem equally dull. Monforti flops into an armchair, picks up another newspaper (yesterday's perhaps) and starts to leaf through it without the slightest interest.

But half an hour later, just so as to know, he tells his sister to stop at the barrier, he gets out, and asks about it at the lodge. Have they seen Signor Zeme go out this morning?

No, he was seen returning last night from Florence and he had a little accident, his car was bumped into by Count Delaude. Nothing serious, Roggiolani saw the whole thing. But has he been by since then, maybe on a bike? No. And he hasn't phoned? No.

'Could be in a coma, with his spine broken,' says Monforti to his sister. 'When you get hit from behind you never know. At the time it might just seem like a little tap on the neck, but then . . .'

With agility, Sandra changes the subject to this evening's dinner, which neither she nor Ettore feel like transforming into a great gastronomic event.

'Let's just have something at home, the three of us, before midnight mass, shall we?'

'Eh? What were you saying, sorry?'

'Do you want to eat out, by any chance, do you want me to book at the Uncino or the Tavernelle?'

'No, good Lord, much better at home.'

'Anyway I'll stock up for the next day as well, so there'll be no need to . . .'

Monforti loses interest, if he ever had any, in these culinary calculations and when they get to the village he leaves Sandra to make her resolute and zig-zagging way from shop to shop.

'We'll meet up here in an hour or so,' she shouts at him, already some distance away.

'Here' is the Piazza Grande, the vast esplanade that slopes gently down to the port and the canal, where dozens of boats of all sizes pitch against one another in a continual tinkling of metal rings. The wind assails the occasional passers-by as they come round corners and sweeps them into alleys, or thrusts them rudely into doorways.

At the 'Il Molo' bar the customers, who do not include Zeme (but then why should they?), are discussing the freak *libecciata*, the havoc wrought in the village on chimney-pots, windows, roofs. But there has been no drama out at sea, the two fishing-boats caught off the isle of Elba took shelter at Portoferraio and called from there a little while ago. Monforti thinks he might let Andrea know of the lucky escape, but instead dials Zeme's number. No answer. The man could have collapsed while taking a bath, or while dragging himself to the phone to call for help . . .

Outside, a little old lady, with head bent, is battling crab-like up the wind-swept street; it could be, but isn't, Marshal Butti's mother, whom Monforti assisted months ago at a critical juncture, while she was struggling with a heavy load of mineral-water bottles. At that age, it's so easy to fall, break a leg, end up in hospital or even . . .

The old lady disappears into a haberdasher's shop right opposite the Carabinieri station and Monforti, deciding that this is not a phase of euphoric anxiety but – if anything (and it isn't necessarily anything) – of anxious euphoria, rings at the door of the station.

2

Katia wakes up with the thought of vendetta alive and kicking in her breast. The thunder and lightning of the night never penetrated beyond the borders of her sleep but it is as if they had none the less managed to inflame rather than dampen her anger. I'll show him, just wait, she thinks as she opens her eyes.

She dresses in two minutes and immediately goes in search of the enemy, so as to resume their fight at the exact point at which they left off last night. But there is no sign of him in the double room. The adjoining bathroom is empty. As are the living-room and the kitchen.

The girl then starts to prowl aggressively from room to room, inspecting each one. After all, it is here that she is going to be living for the next few days if the situation doesn't change. Two more bedrooms. A third bathroom. And then down the stairs into the basement, where the oil-heater hums sullenly: three more small rooms, a shower, a washing-machine, an ironing-board, a little window banging in the wind . . . Of course there is no trace of the louse here either, and Katia goes back upstairs in vexation. He must have gone to the village to get his clapped-out old car repaired.

At this point she realises that while walking around she has continued to switch on light after light, as if it were night. But it is past nine o'clock and daylight, however reticent, is filtering through the slats of the shutters. Open up then, let the fresh air come and sweep away the fug, the smell of sedimented damp.

The rain has intensified the aroma of pine which now rushes into the house and Katia takes great lungfuls of it, calculating it as a healthy advance-payment on what is due to her. If nothing else, at least she'll have had some clean air. Then she looks out of the french window in the kitchen and gets a surprise: beyond a withered lawn and a dozen dripping shrubs, she can see the shelter with the car still parked there. Already mended? No, impossible. So the old wrinkly must have cycled to the village to plead with the mechanic in person. They'll be here any minute with the breakdown van to tow away the car.

The clatter of a loose window calls her back in, even though – she reflects – one window more, one window less, the house isn't hers and for all she cares the whole place can get smashed to bits. The wind is getting on her nerves, and she is irritated by the idea that even the weather is being unkind to her. Later, for example, it might be nice to take a walk through the wood and along the beach, but this heavy, dark sky and rumbling sea don't entice her in the least.

She prepares her breakfast with meticulous care, arranging everything on a plastic tray adorned with the answer to a television quiz she saw last year: Van Gogh's *Sunflowers*. She drinks her orange-juice, munches her biscuits, sips her milky coffee. She doesn't touch the cheese or ham, which could come in useful at lunchtime if she has to stay here. But now, this aspect of her plan is beginning to worry her. In theory, it would be a perfect calculation not to move from the old codger's villa until she has been paid off; but in practice, how will she manage to eat during the occupation?

In the wall cupboards she finds a few tins, some half-empty packets of pasta, just about enough to survive for a couple of days. But it would be simpler if Gimo came back now with a nice present in red or gold wrapping paper, and they made things up, and he took her to meet Max & Fortini. It would be better, much better.

3

A sudden outburst of squealing from the basement tells the Hon. Bonanno (his wife and daughters have taken shelter with the Kruysens) that another of the beasts has got caught in a trap. The eighth so far. The other seven have already been tied up in a bag and taken away by Vannucci, who dropped by a while ago to check the efficiency of his devices and to load them with fresh bait, as well as to utter words of hope and encouragement.

For a start it's lucky – he said – that the rodents that got into the house are what they call 'big-moles': huge rats that live in the trees and never go into houses, as he was explaining yesterday. That is, *normally* they never go in, or at least it's never happened round here before. So it's just an *anomalous* or freak invasion, which means that once the present invaders have been driven out it is unlikely ever to happen again.

Vannucci uses the adjective 'anomalous' airily, having learnt it recently, and does not miss the chance to apply it to last night's *libecciata*. The two anomalies could even be linked, he explained jokingly: in the sense that the 'big-moles' (equipped like all rats with a sixth sense) might have foreseen the storm well in advance and so abandoned the near-by trees, entering the Bonannos' house in search of shelter.

But this playful hypothesis must have suggested another one. Before leaving he re-examined the rusty, twisted grating that the rats presumably entered by.

'Unless someone chose to play a nasty trick on you, *Onorevole*?' he asked, and his eyes moved from the grating to the sack at his feet, squirming with squealing 'big-moles', which he was about to carry away and set free in some suitable place. Someone could have done the exact opposite: have caught the animals in the forest and then emptied the sack through the unhinged grating. But who?

Bonanno turned pale.

'Under-secretary Ciaffi!' he thought immediately. But not being able to confide in Vannucci, he fell into a grim silence, while Vannucci explained that it was probably best to wait before mending the grating – whether it had been tampered with or not. That line of escape might encourage the 'freaks' to beat it by themselves. And then if any more fell into a trap, all the *Onorevole* had to do was take the whole thing over to a tree and open the little hatch: he'd see straightaway what the *normal* behaviour of a 'big-mole' was.

The Hon. Giampaolo Bonanno is not a coward. Having

found the cage containing the squealing animal (even larger than the others) in the basement, he follows his instructions and takes the whole thing a long way from the house, to the bottom of a huge pine-tree. He opens the hatch cautiously.

In an instant, and with a shriek of relief, the red beast (though far less beastly when seen in its natural setting, where it seems much less threatening in size) is out and scuttling up the ruddy bark of the pine, vanishing with a flip of its tail at the first bifurcation.

Down below, the Hon. Bonanno has no further doubts. A hired henchman unhinged the grating and then infested the house with rats in order to ruin his Christmas, frighten his family, and – above all – distract him from those political tasks to which, both by telephone and fax, he gives his untiring attention even during the holidays. As for the instigator, it can only be his fellow party-member – and even fellow faction-member within the party – but also his fiercest rival and persecutor: the Under-secretary for Agriculture and Forestry, the Hon. Severino Ciaffi.

How can he take his revenge and at the same time protect himself from further attacks? Appeal to the *questori* of the Chamber? The Party leaders? But unfortunately Bonanno knows that he cannot count on any of those careerists and careerists' lackeys: it is after all no coincidence that they gave the Under-secretaryship to a nonentity like Ciaffi, while he himself got shoved on to the XI Commission to replace Ciaffi and had his request for an armed escort turned down. And to think that just one police-guard would have been enough to catch the henchman red-handed (or – he laughs bitterly – rat-handed).

On the other hand his certainty, though absolute, is only a moral one. He would need some concrete proof, even if indirect, such as . . .

Ah, but yes, here is some:

This closes the terrain, and is like poison
To nocturnal mole, and to the greedy rat.

They are lines from the poem *Field-Farming* by Luigi Alamanni (1495–1556), widely consulted by Ministers and Under-secretaries at the Ministry of Agriculture. Quoting a few hendecasyllables always makes a good impression in statements to the press, and even more so in television interviews, as it suggests broad cultural awareness in addition to specific competence.

He himself knows whole chunks of it by heart, though he cannot recall what it is that 'closes the terrain' (maybe a thuja bush like his?) and is poisonous to *moles* and *rats*. But anyway that is what gave Ciaffi the idea for his criminal plan with the 'big-moles'! After which, in his position, it must have been very easy to get hold of an accomplice in the person of some state-forester or guard, by dangling the possibility of promotion before his eyes.

Maybe a guard from this very area? The circle of suspected henchmen is narrowing. And Bonanno begins to consider the elementary, if somewhat humiliating and (for an MP) degrading, idea of going to the local Carabinieri station.

4

None of the desks, wardrobes or cupboards in the whole villa contains the tiniest little radio or cassette-player to give a lonely girl a bit of company. Katia has searched the place from top to bottom, and then gone over it all again, just to pass the time. The owner of the house has not returned, either alone or with the mechanic. The car is still there, under the shelter, and the wind is still blowing, the sea still growling.

He could at least phone, let her know what's happening, the pig. But the phone has remained silent, and if she wanted to use it to call the lodge, or perhaps a taxi, a friend in Florence, her Aunt Ines, she couldn't. It's one of those old machines with a rotating dial, and in the hole corresponding to the number 5 there's a little lock to stop it being mis-used by strangers. How mean can you get?

In the living-room three or four magazines are mouldering away, one of them about fashion, and devoted mainly to the return of the hat, of which Katia is a resolute opponent. And she has already picked up the illustrated book, *Ireland, the Paradise of Horses*, twice; it's now the third time. But those highly unenticing pictures (grey cottages, rocks, riders filing along a country path) rekindle her longing to travel – New York, above all, but also Bali, the Maldives, Bermuda ... Without forgetting Disneyland. Florence is undoubtedly the most beautiful city in the world but it must be even more beautiful to see it again after a long journey to distant lands. 'And tell me sincerely, Katia,' the interviewer of Telegiotto will ask her, 'what do you like most of all about your job as a top model?' 'The travel! The chance to see those virgin beaches, those emerald isles set in the dazzling blue of the ocean!'

But the sopping stain in the wall has assumed the dimensions not of an island but of a continent, and this is the depressing geography of her existence right now. Forget about sun-kissed palm-trees! A howling wind that never lets up, a sky so dark she has to keep the light on at midday, a deserted house with nothing but barn-owls and silence for company.

'And tell me sincerely, Katia,' the interviewer of Telegarbage will ask her, 'what was the most difficult moment in your career as a top tart, whoops, top model?'

'When I realised that that bastard had gone off, by taxi or whatever, not giving a damn about me or my threats. He guessed I wasn't really the type to smash up a house or loot it out of spite, and risk getting reported to the police or thrown out by the Carabinieri. And besides, what could I do?'

The book on the paradise of horses slips to the floor with a thud but Katia does not retrieve it; she too has slipped into an absorbed yet lucid despondency. Create a scandal? Come off it. This isn't the King of England she's dealing with, he's a nobody, and no magazine would ever publish an article, an interview, or even a single line on the fact that he's betrayed his wife with some poor fool. And as for the Countess, she must be used to these little flings of Gimo's, quite apart from the fact that she probably pays him back in the same coin. At best she'll slap his face, stop his pocket money for a while, he'll beg for forgiveness on bended knees and they'll all hug and kiss happily under the mistletoe. No, there's no possible revenge; once again Katia has to acknowledge the fact that she's got her calculations wrong.

To try and shake off her mortification and in any case to escape from these cold, inhospitable rooms she decides to go out, leaving the french window ajar. A short stroll, with her ears cocked for the sound of the pick-up truck arriving.

There is not a soul to be seen among the rain-darkened trees, and anyway dripping bushes and scrub screen everything. These are people who really care about their privacy, and Katia can guess only too well why. It may be splendid in summer, but right now this pine-forest is just a total but total graveyard. A cat, not a black one luckily, crosses her path without even looking at her. Some invisible beast of a bird flies off through the branches cawing. Countless soaking pine cones are just begging to be kicked, and so, kick by kick, Katia makes her way to Max & Fortini's villa, where she recognises their Land Rover under the usual cane shelter.

'And tell us, Katia,' the interviewer of Teletriumph will ask her, 'just how did you meet them?'

'Well, thanks to a chain of events that concern my private life only, I found myself in that pine-forest of theirs, all on my own, with hardly a lira and my morale down round my ankles, or lower. Total but total blues. But I wouldn't be beaten, I forced myself to react, I said to myself: Katia, if you don't find the courage to go and ring that doorbell . . .'

But courage cannot be plucked up from nowhere, as somebody once said, and anyway it would not be the same sort of courage as is required, for example, to go tearing up and down the Garfagnana on a Kawasaki clutching on to that madman, Giancarlo . . .

Katia perches half-on, half-off the low rustic fence that encircles lot no. 114, supporting the usual barrier of brush, arbutus, myrtle. She cannot be seen from the house, which is anyway some distance away and set at an angle to her, whereas if she turns and peers through the greenery she can make out a lawn with an empty swimming-pool in the middle. What do they want with a swimming-pool when the sea is so near? For the children, maybe. They are both married, they both have children, and that would be the really legendary opportunity, a truly fantastic pretext: hey, I saw this child crying, he fell off his bike and broke his arm (no, better a twisted ankle, a sprained wrist) and so I picked him up and brought him here, he says he lives here . . .

But no childish yells or imperious motherly cries reach her behind the bush – just two adult voices, carried on the wind like pine needles.

'St Peter and St Paul,' says the first voice, 'meet in the VIP lounge at an airport, and one says to the other . . .'

'It's not funny,' the second voice interrupts curtly.

Katia straightens up, her heart in her mouth. Good God, it's their voices, it's really them, Max & Fortini in person! And suppose they come out of the gap in the hedge and find her there eavesdropping, spying? Momentarily paralysed, she has the presence of mind to bend as if to tie her shoelaces. But nobody emerges, everything falls silent again for a couple of minutes.

'The prophets Ezekiel and Isaiah,' says the first voice, 'are taking part in the pole-vault at the Olympics, and when Ezekiel takes his run-up . . .'

'It's not funny,' interrupts the second voice.

Katia holds her breath: they're working, they're creating! In the open air, to clear their minds. And she (she – Katia!) has had the incredible, amazing good fortune to . . .

'Two comedians that nobody finds funny any more,' says the first voice, 'keep on walking around an empty swimming-pool. At a certain point the first one lets the second walk ahead of him and sends him sprawling with a powerful kick. Then the second one, from down below . . .'

'It's not funny.'

But behind the bush Katia bursts into uncontrollable laughter.

5

A relationship, for Marshal Aurelio Butti, is simply a blanket term to describe a bond of consanguinity between persons, often necessary in discussing crimes of a domestic nature. However, it would never cross his mind to use the word *relationship* to describe the affectionate if at times exasperating rapport between himself and his old mother, with whom, as a childless widower, he shares the accommodation at the rear of the station. And the idea that he and his mother, in the accommodation in question, *handle* the aforesaid relationship, which, furthermore, is to be considered as a *valid and constructive one*, would strike him as actually obscene.

But it is in such terms that Dino Fioravanti, male, 27 years of age, unmarried, and Amelia Baldacci, female, maiden-name Picchi, 42 years of age, who presented themselves spontaneously at the station half an hour ago, insist on describing their intrigue, carried out to the detriment of Orfeo Baldacci.

What detriment? they object. Theirs is a valid and constructive relationship, which they handle primarily on a cultural level even if . . .

Cultural?

Yes, confirms Signora Baldacci, suggesting by her tone that she knows there is no point in trying to explain certain things to a Marshal of Carabinieri. Primarily on a cultural level, even if a human one in a wider sense.

But in what sense exactly?

In the widest possible sense, she repeats through clenched teeth. In any case, in so far as it is a strictly interpersonal relationship, it only concerns the two of them.

The Marshal controls the strong impulse he feels to expel the pair of them interpersonally with his boot.

So why, he says, have they come to him?

But listen, she says (since it is almost always she who speaks, Fioravanti rarely managing to get a word in edgeways), she has already explained this to the Corporal and also to him. Her husband hasn't been seen since yesterday, he's got that double-barrelled shotgun he always carries around in his van, and after his violent outburst the other night, they can't be blamed for thinking the worst.

Does she mean he might have committed suicide?

No, of course not. Suicide has never even crossed her mind because Orfeo isn't the type. But he is the type to wait for Dino outside his house and shoot him the moment he sees him! So last night, he – Dino, that is – went and hid in Lilli's workshop and slept there.

Alone?

Yes, she went back home. But Orfeo hasn't turned up this morning, and so they've come here to ask what they ought to do. They can't go on like this, can they? The Carabinieri should protect them, instead of sitting there asking them all sorts of questions about their relationship.

The Marshal continues to control himself and tries to reflect. It is possible that last night, after Father Everardo had looked for him in vain, Orfeo went off and got drunk somewhere and stayed there to sleep it off. If it weren't for the shotgun there would be nothing to worry about. But on the other hand, shotguns are normal working tools for the gardeners in the Gualdana; they often use them with special cartridges to shoot away the foliage from the nests of the processionary-moths: those caterpillars that not only ruin the trees, but can also give you a nasty sting, if they fall on your neck.

Except that it is a little early to go shooting at moths, the season is more around February-March. And anyway, with all this talk of their valid relationship, neither Baldacci nor Fioravanti (is it she who won't let him speak?) have explained the point that interests him most.

So, he says sarcastically, they want the Carabinieri to protect their cultural interests.

The woman tightens her lips and falls contemptuously silent, while Fioravanti finally stammers out *sottovoce:* 'I just say you should protect us.'

'If you like, I'll put you both in a cell. Safer than that . . .'

'Oh yeah?' shouts the woman furiously, getting to her feet.

But the man does not move, as if he sees no reason for ruling out the idea.

'You know,' he says, rubbing his hands over the plasters on his forehead, 'I hate violence.'

'But you gave him a pretty good thrashing all the same, when he came looking for you at "Il Molo",' says the Marshal, standing up himself.

Then he gestures to the young man to stay where he is, goes to the door, and calls the corporal on duty in the ante-room. 'Macchia,' he says, 'this lady is to wait in there with you. I need another word or two with Signor Fioravanti.'

'Signor Monforti's in there,' says Corporal Macchia.

The presence in the ante-room of such a distinguished visitor as Signor Monforti (whom the Marshal went immediately to greet, asking him to wait just a few minutes) prevented Signora Baldacci from flying off the handle. As for Fioravanti, he now seems much more at his ease.

'Marshal, as far as I'm concerned, if you advise me to stay here until Orfeo . . .'

But the Marshal is thinking of something else now. Who is to say that Orfeo's disappearance – if he really has disappeared – is not the work of these two themselves? And that perhaps they 'presented themselves spontaneously' in order to divert suspicion? It would not be the first time such a thing had happened.

'Listen,' he says, 'I still don't understand how things are with Orfeo. How long has this affair . . . excuse me . . . how long has this relationship been going on between you and his wife?'

Fioravanti shrugs his shoulders as if to say that, unlike Amelia, he's quite prepared to call an affair an affair.

'About six months,' he says. 'I mean, we knew each other before that, because ever since she opened her shop she's been interested in ecology, macrobiotics, yoga meditation ... But you know the way things happen, Marshal: after a while ...'

'... the relationship became wider,' the officer helps him out. 'And when did Orfeo get to hear of it?'

'Well, almost immediately. Because in the village, people started talking about it, and so Amelia told him the whole story quite openly. We hate lies.'

'Congratulations. And what did he do then?'

'Nothing, he shouted a bit, he wanted to give her a belting, but she isn't the sort to give in. She told him that if he wanted, she would go on being his wife as usual, otherwise she would leave him. And since he's always at work, and just needs a wife in bed and in the kitchen ... Well, he seemed resigned to it, it seemed like he wasn't going to make a big fuss about it. But now here he is wanting to shoot me.'

'After six months! But why? That's what I want to know. There must be a reason, mustn't there?'

'Yes ...'

'But you won't tell me.'

The other man looked at the door uncertainly and somewhat timorously. 'Well, I don't know,' he says evasively at last, 'it must be that ... I mean: I hate violence, as I was saying, but since I had to thump him the other evening, to defend myself ... I guess he wants to get his own back for that, right?'

'Oh yes?' the Marshal bursts out. And with the risk, or with the intention, of being heard in the ante-room, he clarifies the following points in a loud threatening voice:

1) Fioravanti and Signora Baldacci take him for an idiot. It is clear in fact that they both know the real reason why Orfeo, after tolerating their intrigue for so long, attacked Fioravanti the other evening outside the 'Il Molo' bar.

2) If Orfeo has disappeared, there is nothing to say that they are not behind his disappearance, for two good reasons: in the first place, their version of events is riddled with holes and contradictions; and in the second place, neither of them can say where they were and what they were doing from yesterday evening to this morning, since Fioravanti, who usually lives in the village with his parents, claims that he spent the night in Lilli's workshop, but is unable to prove it.

Therefore, he concludes, opening the door again and escorting the young man into the ante-room, they need have no worry, they'll be watched over all right. But for the rest, they can do whatever they like.

'You, dear lady, can go back home, and for the moment you can stay in your workshop perhaps,' he dismisses them before turning to Monforti. 'Please, come this way, Signor Monforti. I'm sorry if I've kept you waiting.'

6

'Two comedians meet a maiden who has lost her way in the wood and she tells them a sad, sad story. Her . . . escort . . .'

'Brackets: a worm.'

'Brackets: a disgusting worm, since he sloped off without even leaving her a note, dumping her there on her own, with no means of transport or subsistence in a place cut off from the rest of the world where the poor girl doesn't know a soul.'

'The two comedians, who have hearts as big as anything . . .'

'Let's say . . . two absolute bricks.'

'They take pity on her, and after drying her tears take her into their own little hut.'

'But could it be that they . . .?'

'Brackets: the hapless girl asks herself after a while.'

'Could it be that they too have unmentionable intentions?'

Katia has never enjoyed herself so much. As if following a game of tennis, her head jerks from Max to Fortini, who have now assumed disgustingly lubricious expressions. In real life, they are even better than on television or at the cinema, even more fun.

'Little Katia', says Fortini, his eyes and mouth reduced to cruel slits, 'could in fact have fallen into the hands of two sadomasochistic rapists.'

Katia laughs, but a little shiver runs down her spine.

'And suppose instead,' whispers Max, letting a line of saliva dribble down his chin, 'they were two psychopaths addicted to cocaine and cannibalism?'

Katia laughs with imperfect naturalness. There is a moment's silence, during which the steady booming of the sea and the irregular gusts of wind reassert themselves.

'*Uuuuuuh* goes the *libeccio*,' moans Fortini. '*Uuuuuuh* . . .'

'So many girls today,' sighs Max, 'get themselves into awkward situations by trusting complete strangers.'

'But I . . .' begins Katia in a forced little voice.

'But you,' she recovers, 'you're . . . you're famous, I know you!'

'Oh yes?' says Max, his face suddenly stony.

'You think so?' says Fortini, with a sinister leer.

Katia cannot manage to laugh. No, she thinks, it's not possible, they're pulling my leg.

Max stands up.

'Girl,' he says harshly, 'you may as well be told. We need you, now, at once.'

'For special services,' Fortini specifies mellifluously.

Katia looks at them, blushes, tries to view things as an unscrupulous calculator. Why not, after all? At least the contact this time – or rather, the *double* contact – would be with important people, with Max & Fortini in flesh and blood, and her career . . .

But then she gets brusquely to her feet herself. No, it's not possible, career or no career, she could never do it with Max & Fortini, just because they *are* Max & Fortini . . . She stares them straight in the eyes. First one and then the other.

'No,' she says, 'I can't, I couldn't.'

The two comedians sit down on the floor, their heads in their hands.

'I can't cook,' groans Max.

'And I hate cooking,' groans Fortini.

'And I hate eating what he cooks.'

'And I detest restaurants.'

'We hoped you'd cook some spaghetti for us, I'm getting hungry.'

'With capers and anchovies, maybe.'

'No, garlic, oil and chilli.'

'And then you'd stay on to do the washing-up, of course.'

'Since you don't know where to go.'

'And we thought you could do something about dinner too, unless your Count returns.'

'But of course if she doesn't want to be our servant . . .' says Max to Fortini.

'I know, girls today are independent, proud.'

'And anyway they don't know how to cook, all they know about are pizzas. She'd make us eat pizza day and night. It's much better this way, far better that she leaves us.'

'But it's not true!' shouts Katia. 'It's not true at all! I'm a very good cook, my grandmother . . .'

'Incredible,' Max interrupts her, 'she's even got a grandmother.'

'But then,' says Fortini, amazed, 'then she's . . . then you're . . . you're Little Red Riding Hood!'

'And we two are the wolves,' says Max.

Katia laughs happily and strokes their heads. 'You're two lambs,' she says, 'two adorable lambkins.'

'No, ducky, not that,' says Fortini.

'It's not funny, you see?' says Max.

'Where's the kitchen?' says Katia.

7

Depression, for Marshal Butti and the Carabinieri in general, constitutes a police problem in so far as 'people affected by this illness – which consists of a morbid anxiety, often accompanied by delirious ideas – can reach such extremes of suffering that their emotional state finds release in acts of senseless fury: the so-called *raptus melancholicus*'.

What form do such fits take, and against whom are they directed?

In the most recent case that the Marshal has had to deal with, that of Nannini, the petrol-pump attendant, the depressive's senseless fury fortunately restricted itself to the classic 'destruction of inanimate objects'. Armed with a heavy hand-drill, Nannini hurled himself against the pumps of his own service-station, smashing the glass and causing irreparable damage to the counters.

But it is not rare for such fits to lead to suicide and, as a corollary, to the multiple murder of relatives. In which case – as the exhaustive *Police Handbook* at the station explains – the act of folly may have its roots in a double determination.

On the one hand 'the state of permanent anxiety and anguished expectancy in which the invalid lives may cause him to view the existence of his relatives in the same gloomy light, so that it will strike him as a meritorious act to liberate them from so dismal a present life and spare them a similar future.' And on the other hand 'even when there are no delirious ideas, the invalid may be driven to the murder by the thought, often well-founded, that his wife and children will be left in poverty when he, the support of the family, has committed suicide.'

Cases of suicide preceded by multiple murders have been known among the Carabinieri themselves (although the *Handbook* makes no mention of them) and the Marshal is well aware that this illness spares no category or social class. But he also knows that such fits are relatively rare, while there are cases of invalids who make a complete recovery: for example (or so at least it is hoped), the daughter of Magnolfi the builder.

As for Signor Monforti, who has just finished explaining the purpose of his visit, he seems to have improved greatly in the time he has known him.

Only last summer his anxiety was at its acutest, he foresaw accidents everywhere, individual and collective calamities. That time when the Marshal saw him at the newspaper-stand and thanked him warmly for helping his mother, Monforti had at once drawn a terrifying picture of what could happen to an old woman who insisted on carrying a pack of six bottles of mineral water: a broken femur was the very least. Even on subsequent, more friendly encounters, in the square or on the café terrace, he had rarely failed to alarm him with his pitch-black, if not exactly delirious, ideas.

But now, as he tells him about the broken window, the ransacked bedroom and the 'absence' of Signor Zeme (he was careful not to talk about a 'disappearance', unlike that couple in the case of Orfeo) his greatest concern seems to be to stick to the actual facts, without wandering off into rash or alarmist hypotheses.

'My idea,' he now concludes reasonably, 'is that in the rush to leave, the bedroom was left all topsy-turvy, with the cupboards open, the drawers on the floor, and neither the shutters nor the french window closed properly. And then the *libecciata* did the rest, while he was sleeping in the living-room or somewhere else.'

'Yes, it seems a plausible explanation.'

'As for the fact that he isn't there now or at any rate doesn't answer the phone, I really can't say . . . You know me, dear Marshal, and you know that I get easily alarmed. But I wouldn't like . . . Well, in any case, I thought it best to inform you.'

The Marshal nods. 'And you were quite right to do so,' he says. 'You phoned half an hour ago, you said? Let's try again now.'

After all, Monforti's apprehensions are not always unreasonable, he thinks as he dials the number. Last summer, for example, it had struck him that the bust of Garibaldi was leaning forward a little, on the façade of the building opposite the Carabinieri station. And his alarmed warning had indeed served to prevent it from falling.

As it turns out, Zeme does not answer, and there is no answer from the Delaude villa either, where Zeme might have gone to discuss last night's accident.

'You were saying, Signor Monforti, that his wife's departure in that state must have upset him. And that their house, on account of his wife, contains sleeping-pills and drugs of all descriptions. So, after all, you wouldn't rule out . . .'

'No, I wasn't thinking of that. I hardly know Zeme at all, but he really doesn't strike me as the type.'

This is the second time in less than an hour, the officer reflects, that he has been told about people who might have disappeared but who don't seem the type to have committed suicide. He is irritated by what the coincidence obviously suggests: that with all the work he has to get through (and with Sergeant Farinelli on Christmas leave), here he is wasting his time on idle chatter and groundless fears.

'I was just thinking,' Monforti continues, 'that after a sleepless night, Zeme might have taken a strong tablet so as to sleep on this morning. In which case he may have unplugged the phone so as not to be woken by Delaude, whom he was supposed to see this morning.'

'Yes, quite likely.'

'Or by his wife, it strikes me now, who might have phoned from Milan to pester him with all sorts of catastrophic predictions. Because, Marshal, you have no idea, you cannot imagine just how depressing, anguishing and destructive we depressives can be for our own relatives. And that poor chap . . .'

The Marshal recalls the terrible impression that Signora Zeme made on him just a year ago, when he saw her for the first time. She was then in that state 'characterised by inhibited mobility', defined in the *Police Handbook* as 'dazed melancholy', in which 'the condition of passivity can reach the point of total paralysis of the will'. Except that from that same state, the manual specifies, there is often a return 'to delirious predictions of impending catastrophes, imminent losses of money or social position, financial collapse, etc., which renew the sufferer's fury and impel him to acts of violence: from the mechanical destruction of objects to acts of arson, aggression against other people, etc.'.

Difficult to say which of the two states is preferable for the relatives, thinks the officer. But he imagines that cases of suicide cannot be unknown among the relatives themselves (whether 'the type' or not, and although the *Handbook* makes no mention of them). And he wonders curiously what his own reactions would be if his mother were given to the 'mechanical destruction of objects', rather than just to pestering him with accusations of neglecting to look after his uniform (which she never tires of brushing, cleaning and pressing because, as she also never tires of repeating: 'You may not be a Colonel, Aurelio, but you're still an Officer of the Law!').

'But now you mention it,' he asks, 'couldn't it have been the Signora herself who broke the french window, by hurling some heavy object? Because, leaving aside the *libecciata*, you said that the chaotic state of the room could be explained by the fury of their departure. But suppose this fury was accompanied by one of those destructive impulses which unfortunately . . .'

Monforti looks at him in surprise. 'The destruction of inanimate objects? I had no idea you were an expert on the subject. But anyway yes, I hadn't thought about the window but it strikes me as perfectly possible, the crisis may have been even more awful than I imagined. And so . . . I don't know . . . there is no excluding the possibility that at the end of such a terrible day, returning from Florence already desperate, at the end of his tether, and finding that chaos there to greet him . . . with all those sleeping-pills and tranquillisers on hand and then tripping over, I don't know, a phial of Tavor or Sedipnòl . . . But I wouldn't want my imagination to run away with me,' he checks himself, shrugging his shoulders and accepting a cigarette.

The Marshal lights one himself and pauses for a moment in thought.

'Listen,' he says, 'right now I have to stay here, and I haven't even got a Corporal I can send out. But I would be happier if someone had a look. The french window is still open?'

'Yes, I mean, I pulled down the sliding shutters from outside, but it's open. Do you want me to go in?'

'Better if a guard does it, they're licensed guards and they know what to do, if they actually . . . But I wouldn't want to alarm everyone by phoning them myself. If you're going back now, could you tell them?'

'Of course. And I'll let you know at once if Zeme is . . . I mean, if he's there or not. Or if anyone has heard anything in the meantime.'

'Fine. Thank you. Anyway in the afternoon I was thinking of dropping by to look for Orfeo, the gardener, who . . .'

'. . . has also disappeared, from what I understand,' smiles Monforti. 'But in his case I wouldn't let the idea of suicide worry you. He really isn't the type.'

VII

Milagros, After Serving the Coffee

I

MILAGROS, AFTER SERVING the coffee, has hurried back to her bedroom. She is now gazing into the mirror, admiring herself in the soft, synthetic fur coat, the elegant boots with matching handbag that Signora Borst and Signorina Eladia have just given her as a Christmas present. 'I don't know,' she repeats to herself in raptures, 'if I come to the point!'

Signora Borst, contrary to her usual habits, but in anticipation of midnight mass, has gone to her room to rest for an hour or so.

Eladia is on her own in the living-room with her Tarot cards. Her expression is tense. On the table, the twelve cards of the astromantic wheel have not changed. But the thirteenth, the ill-omened Four of Swords connected with the oscillations of yesterday (and, there can be no doubt, with the tremendous storm last night), has returned to the pack which the Signorina is now slowly shuffling.

Certainly the situation remains serious. It is rare for an astral tempest like the one recorded yesterday by the wheel not to conclude in tragedy. However, if the new controlling

Arcana were of Cups (corresponding element: *Air*), or better still of Wands (element *Fire*, unlikely in this season in the pine-forest, but useful against the opposite element) it would mean that there was still a way out. Even the ambiguous and unreliable Coins (*Earth*) would leave some hope.

But if the Arcana should once again be of baleful Swords (*Water*) . . .

Eladia continues to shuffle and reshuffle, without resolving to draw out the new card. Even among the Arcana of Swords, she reflects, there are still two that are not always ill-omened. For example the King, who is usually the incarnation of merciless power, but whose figure, in the beneficent meaning of the Arcana, can represent 'illustrious or influential people, such as priests, magistrates, officers'.

Except that a priest can also be a forewarning of a funeral, a magistrate of a trial, and an officer – if of the Carabinieri – of a serious crime. Eladia would prefer, if possible, the figure of the Knight, which in general symbolises unscrupulous adventurers, but which – and on this point the best treatises all agree – 'in its beneficent meaning indicates explorers, sportsmen, non-commissioned officers'.

She draws the card impulsively and stares at it for a long while, before setting it down beside the wheel.

It is the Two of Swords.

The worst card of all, with a wheel like this. Because – and on this point too the treatises all agree – 'it does not just mean that something terrible will happen, but that it has already happened, although it is not yet known what it is'.

2

The connotations might be less sinister than those of a Two of Swords, but none the less a car with the word CARABINIERI driving around the Gualdana would undoubtedly give rise to alarmed speculation. The residents, who are on the whole a law-abiding lot, would imagine all sorts of things, would pester the lodge with inquisitive phone-calls.

Officer Butti therefore leaves the Uno at the entrance-barrier and he and Vannuccini get into the car with Monforti, who is not worried by the hazards of driving within the forest.

'Orfeo?'

'Still no news. A little while ago the Tavellas were looking for him too.'

'Here at the Gualdana?'

'Yes, they have a factory at Piacenza and he looks after the gardens. There's a pump that doesn't . . .'

'All right, we'll deal with that later.'

When the Marshal's finger formally presses the bell, Monforti's hope is that the door will be answered by a cheerful and surprised Signor Zeme. This had been his hope when he came here two hours earlier with Vannuccini, who, as a licensed guard had scrupulously rung at the door for quite a while before entering. And now, just as on the previous occasion, there is no answer, nobody comes. Zeme has not returned in the meantime.

The Marshal gives a nod to the guard, who inserts the spare key that is kept at the lodge for each villa into the lock. The door opens on to the gloom of the hall and Vannuccini switches on the light.

Monforti passes from disappointment to apprehension. True, he checked the villa thoroughly with Vannuccini, and reported to Butti that it was empty; but now he is suddenly afraid that he may not have searched with sufficient skill and imagination. Following the Marshal from room to room, he would not be surprised to stumble across a pair of feet or a bloodless hand in some overlooked corner. 'My God, I never noticed, I didn't look there.' A pathetic excuse, which luckily he is not required to make. There is definitely nobody in the house, alive or dead.

None of the beds shows any signs of having been used. Three of them have their mattresses rolled up, two are untouched, with unwrinkled bedspreads. There are no blankets lying around anywhere and in the kitchen there is no sign of a breakfast having been consumed this morning, the cups and jars are all in their places, the sink empty.

'It almost looks as if he never came back,' murmurs the Marshal.

'But Roggiolani . . .' says Vannuccini.

'I know, I know.'

All the shutters, doors and windows are closed tight, except of course the bedroom shutter and french window, neither of which shows any signs of having been forced. Someone simply forgot to close them and the wind did the rest. In the room the disorder has become order in Monforti's eyes, as he contemplates it for the third time. Broken glass, clothes, overturned drawers, but all in the same position as this morning and that is sufficient for the magma to set into the lava of normality, to dissipate all threatening vibes. The Marshal opens a couple of drawers at random, then gives up.

'We need to know if anything is missing, jewels, money . . .'

On one of the bedside tables there is a metal rack full of medicines, the top of the chest of drawers is cluttered with a number of other boxes and phials.

'Does the Signora take all this stuff?'

'Well, it's not stuff you take all the time,' explains Monforti. 'Every day, of course, you take a range of drops, capsules, tablets, but after a while they no longer have any effect, you have to change treatment, and so the old products stay there, because maybe after three months . . .'

'And are any of them . . . dangerous?'

Monforti fumbles with the cheery, colourful packages, turning them round. 'Who can say . . . Milovan . . . Quantril . . . I've heard of some of them, and used them too . . . But they're always bringing out new ones and I'd be hard put to say . . . Abraten . . .? Who knows.'

The three men give one last look around, more than anything else to try and justify to themselves this scarcely indispensable, if not exactly superfluous inspection.

Vannuccini peers down at the bits of broken glass strewn amongst the pine needles.

'Shall I sweep it up?'

The Marshal thinks for a moment. 'No, let's leave everything as it is.'

He has noted that there are no signs of a scuffle, the clothes – all female – are untorn, and there are no other indications to suggest a kidnapping. But other hypotheses cannot be ruled out, which might require the intervention of specialists, and the first thing specialists ask in that freezing tone of theirs is whether anything has been moved or taken away. Not to mention the fact that Zeme, like Orfeo, could turn up again or get in touch from one moment to the next. Not to mention, if the truth be told, that this is the most likely thing to happen.

'All right, we may as well go.'

Monforti breathes again. For the last half hour he has been troubled by the same thought as the Marshal: that at any moment Signor Zeme could appear at the door. But a grim-faced Zeme, indignant at this ridiculous intrusion, which is all the fault of one person – Monforti. Try and explain to him about Andrea and the *Viktor Hansen* . . .

In the hall, a camel-hair coat with matching scarf and an old hooded raincoat are hanging on the wooden knobs of the coat-stand.

'Are these things kept here all year round?'

'Only the Signora's raincoat, I think,' says Vannuccini. 'The other one's her husband's, he was wearing it when he left yesterday.'

Vannuccini bends down to pick up a hogskin glove, then, seeing the other glove dangling from one of the coat pockets, he pulls it out, stetches it until it matches the first one exactly and puts the pair down on the shelf by the telephone. But along with the glove two bits of paper have flipped out of the pocket and fallen to the floor; the Marshal takes it upon himself to pick them up.

And when he puts his glasses on calmly in order to examine them, Monforti makes a little gesture of reluctance: he moves imperceptibly to one side, looking away, as if abstaining, not wishing to cross the slender but decisive border between an inspection and an official search.

'A receipt from the bar at the station of S. Maria Novella, with yesterday's date,' says Butti. 'And there's the platform ticket from the station itself.'

Are these two banal pieces of paper already 'clues'? Monforti wonders. Will they be confiscated by the Marshal in anticipation of God knows what grim verification?

But the searcher puts them casually into his own pocket, and from the pocket of the coat on the hook he draws, just as casually, a wallet swollen with coins and banknotes. He weighs it, decides not to open it, replaces it.

'Anyway, they got to Florence, the wife left, and afterwards he came back here.'

'And in fact Roggiolani saw him . . .'

'I know, I know. But he didn't go to bed and later, we don't know what time, he went out again, without a coat or hat.'

What's in that wardrobe?

The guard at once throws open a built-in wardrobe where

jackets, anoraks and a rubberised cape are hanging, but naturally he is unable to say whether anything is missing.

'Can we get into the garage from here?'

'Yes, down those stairs.'

'Let's see the car.'

During his previous inspection, Monforti had vividly imagined a suicide by means of a tube attached to the exhaust-pipe. But the garage, despite the strong smell of petrol, was and remains a garage, not a mortuary chamber. The white Volvo sits there, tightly boxed in, just enough room around it for two bicycles, a small lawnmower and a few garden tools.

The Marshal notes that the sliding door is closed on the inside, he glances at the dent in the boot, and then spots a paper bag on the front passenger seat. Inside the bag there is a transparent plastic box, tied with a Christmas ribbon containing a folding Pinocchio in a foetal position.

'It must be the present for my son Luca,' explains Vannuccini, 'the Signora was talking about it when they left.'

The Marshal examines the receipt in the bag, which reads, 'S. M. Novella Gift-Shop' and nods. The toy too turns out to have been bought at Florence station yesterday.

'Let's leave it here for now,' he says, putting the box back in the bag and the bag on the seat, but slipping the receipt into his pocket with the other two.

'Tomorrow he'll give it to him himself,' says Monforti, 'provided . . .'

Upstairs the telephone rings.

'The phone!' shouts Vannuccini, running back up the stairs, followed by the other two.

Three, five, six rings. At the seventh the guard, with his hand already on the receiver, is seized by sudden paralysis. He looks at Monforti, he looks at the Marshal. There is an eighth ring, which has a peremptory tone of reproval.

'Give it to me,' says Butti.

'Hello,' he says. Then he replies: 'No, Signor Zeme isn't here at the moment . . . I'm one of the guards. No, I couldn't say. But who is this? . . . Signora D'Alessio? From Bolzano?

'Ah,' he says. 'Yes, I see, the Signora's sister, yes . . . Well, listen, Signora, we know that he got back from Florence last night but this morning he left early and he isn't here now . . . We're here for a matter . . . No, no, there's been a freak *libecciata* and several houses have been damaged, we've come here on account of a window that . . . Certainly Signora, we'll inform him that he must phone urgently because . . . What? . . . But the train . . . Yes, I see.'

Then he says again: 'Ah, yes . . . No, absolutely . . . Of course, Signora D'Allesio.'

And after a long pause and several other monosyllables and a few more 'of course Signoras' and the conclusion that 'I'm quite sure it will turn out to be so, however, let the lodge know at any time, keep us informed, and on our part, the moment your brother-in-law . . . Of course, the name and the number in the address book, quite, don't worry, good evening,' the self-styled guard takes off his Carabiniere's hat and sits down on the bench by the phone.

'That was the sister, from Bolzano. She says they went to pick her up at the station as agreed but she wasn't on the train, she didn't get there, she hasn't phoned, they've heard nothing else.'

He raises his hand, wiggling three fingers.

'That's three so far,' he says, but as if he didn't believe it.

And Vannuccini too lets out a sceptical expression, '*mammeglio*', which in this part of Tuscany and in these circumstances means 'A likely story'. And Monforti himself seems inclined to play things down, Signora Zeme must have missed the train, but she'll turn up on the next one.

'Yes, that's what her sister thinks too,' says Butti.

'From Milan there's another train that gets there this evening at nine o'clock, but it's not direct. The next Intercity is tomorrow morning. Anyway if she gets there they'll let us know, and meanwhile we'll let her husband know . . .'

He looks doubtfully at the gloves, the silent telephone.

'Provided her husband turns up in the meantime.'

They all three fall silent and Monforti wonders whether the other two are reflecting on the curious problem of establishing a link between two untraceable people. The husband God knows where, and his wife . . . This morning, wandering dazedly among all the trains leaving Milan in the pre-holiday turmoil, she got on the wrong one and is just now discovering with a cry that she is in Ancona, Schaffhausen . . . Last night, wandering dazedly in the streets near the station she forgot the name of the hotel and is now roaming Milan with her heavy luggage, her clothes rumpled, her face haggard . . .

'But supposing she doesn't turn up on the next train,' he says, 'we can at least find out whether the hotel she booked in at . . .'

'Which hotel?' says Butti. 'Do you know?'

'No, I don't, but I imagine that if the registers were to be checked . . .'

'It's possible,' concedes Butti, 'but I'd wait a while, don't you think?'

'Yes, of course.'

'You told me that this morning she had an appointment with a specialist?'

'Yes, but . . .'

'Do you know him? Can we call him if necessary?'

'No, I think . . . I mean, I know his name and we can always find the name of his surgery, but I heard that he was going to leave straight after the appointment, he was going on holiday himself.'

'All right,' says the Marshal, 'we'll find some way of tracing him, if necessary, but I don't think it will be necessary. In any case . . .'

From the black leather address book by the phone he copies into his notebook the name and address of the sister in Barbiano (Bolzano), and dictates it to Vannuccini, who also takes it down.

'If necessary . . .'

He stands up again and puts his hat back on.

'And what shall we do about the shutters on that window, Marshal?' asks the guard Vannuccini. 'Shall I close them again?'

Butti thinks of those hypothetical specialists, but then shrugs. 'Yes, you might as well.'

'If a burglar were to come by . . .' insinuates Monforti.

Vannuccini carries out the task with a '*mammeglio*' which in this part of Tuscany and in this circumstance could mean, 'That'd be all we needed'.

And then with a last glance at the empty, silent, locked villa, they get back into the car, reverse down the gravelled path, reach the asphalt and the first fork. Monforti stops the car.

'Humph,' says the Marshal. 'It might be an idea to go and talk to this Count about the accident.'

From where they are not a single roof of a single villa is visible. The pine-forest still rustles in the wind but it is like a huge victorious animal that is shaking off the last flagging attacks of an enfeebled enemy. The pounding of the sea is less aggressive and up above things are improving too; the tattered grey rags that are beginning to appear between clouds are, if one looks carefully, already sky.

To the left an abstracted trio of strollers appears. It is Signor and Signora Graham walking slowly along, with

Colin between them, held firmly by both hands – the progenitor of all disappearances. It seems a good omen, somehow.

3

Two neurosurgeons, two oil-tankers, two dustbin-men, a cat and a mouse, a bottle and a glass . . . Dozens and dozens of possible pairings, of gags in embryo, all quashed at birth by a curt, plaintive or angry 'it's not funny'. But Katia, just at the thought of those two voices, of those two knitted brows, bursts out laughing as she gathers up her few things in Count Delaude's villa.

She is totally but totally happy. She has cooked for Max & Fortini, she has eaten at the same table with Max & Fortini ('Two French cooks knock at the door of an enclosed convent and a novice-nun . . .' 'It's not funny.' 'Two managers are eating lamb dumplings prepared by a professional poisoner . . .' 'It's not funny'), she has prepared coffee and washed up, striving all the time to obey the strict injunction not to laugh, not to be there, to make the two workers forget all about her. But it was they who then suggested she should move in and be taken on temporarily, until she finds something better, as a 'humble not to mention unpaid maid-of-all-work'. Katia laughs, as she puts her little jars and tubes into the dressing-case.

Gimo hasn't turned up again, but who cares. Actually, it's thanks to him that Katia's life (yes, her life!) has taken such a turn for the better. As an unscrupulous calculator she still runs over the advantages that might accrue from this meeting, but she does it in short spurts, confusedly, almost out of a sense of duty. The truth is she is savouring the sheer pleasure of disinterestedness, the excited astonishment of one who feels herself swept along by good luck and trustingly allows herself to be carried towards joyful outcomes.

When the bell rings she goes dancing to the door. Poor old Gimo, back at last: she'll throw her arms around his neck, tell him all about her stroke of luck and leave him with a nice kiss on his forehead. All forgiven and forgotten. Not the slightest inkling that her merry warbles are delighting the ears of Carabinieri.

A second later this jolting blow to the stomach unleashes a sort of emotional *libecciata* in her. The worm, the shit, the louse has had the face to call the Carabinieri to see her off! She'll take a hammer to him, cleave his skull with a pick-axe when she sees him again! And she will see him again, if she has to go to hell to find him!

'What is it? What do you want?'

Now that they want to chuck her out, Katia decides irrevocably that she will not budge from this hole. They'll have to use force.

The Carabiniere (there is only one in fact) raises his hand to his cap and salutes her. 'Marshal Butti. I'd like to speak to Count Delaude. Is he in?'

Total but total amazement. 'But didn't he send you?'

'No, we need some information from him.'

'What information?'

Butti looks questioningly at a big fair-haired man in a khaki uniform who shakes his head. Obviously one of the guards of this exclusive pine-forest, who has never seen her before.

'The Count isn't at home?'

'No,' says Katia, still on the defensive, 'he isn't.'

'You live here, you're . . . a guest, can you tell me when we may find him?'

'I don't know,' says Katia, lowering her arms, 'to tell the truth I was expecting him too. I haven't seen him since dinner last night. When we got back from that pizzeria.'

'But do you know where he's gone?'

'No, I don't know, this morning when I woke up in my bedroom, I mean, when I went to look for him in his bedroom, he wasn't there, and since then . . .'

'He hasn't phoned?'

'No,' says Katia, jutting out her lower lip. 'He hasn't shown up at all, he's disappeared. I thought, I think that . . .'

'And so,' says the Marshal in amazement, 'we've reached number four.'

'Four what?'

The three of them, (there's another one in civilian clothes, with a yellow pullover under his raincoat, who looks like a real civilian) gaze at her without answering, then the Marshal half-smiles, half-sighs. 'Maybe,' he says, 'you can give us a hand.'

Back to pre-historic times. A Count and a girl returned to the pine-forest last night, did they? Near the lodge did they have an accident? A nose-to-tail crash? With a white Volvo? Did the crasher and crash-victim both get out of their respective cars? Did the girl get out as well? Did she hear if the crash-victim expressed his intention of calling on the crasher in the course of the morning, December 24th? Did the above-mentioned crash-victim turn up?

'I haven't seen him,' says Katia. 'Nobody came, at least not while I was here.'

'And how long was that?'

'Well, till eleven o'clock more or less. After that I don't know.'

So, just to draw things out a bit: the Signorina is unable to give any information on a possible meeting between the crash-victim and crasher? And furthermore she has no idea where the latter might be? And she doesn't know what garage he might have contacted to get the vehicle repaired?

'He always goes to Sirio,' the fair-haired man cuts in. 'The one behind Lilli's, in the industrial zone.'

The third man observes that, whether he contacted Sirio or anyone else, on Christmas Eve it's very unlikely, if not impossible . . .

'In any case you'll be staying here?' says the Marshal. 'When the Count comes, would you please . . .'

'Well, actually, I just came to pick up my stuff, I'm going.'

Irrevocably. She wants nothing more to do with Gimo, with his car, his business, his villa. Just forget all about him.

'But . . .' begins the Carabiniere, examining her from head to foot.

Katia appreciates his hesitation and is tempted to help him out; indeed she would like to tell him about this turning-point in her life, let him know where she is going. But her first duty now is to protect the privacy of Max & Fortini while they try to escape from their creative block. Nosy-parkers, photographers, autograph-hunters and also Carabinieri must be kept away. Her lips remain firmly sealed, and the Marshal, when he realises that not another word is going to emerge from them, salutes her respectfully and turns on his heels with the other two.

Katia gets back to her packing, and laughs as she thinks: a crasher and a crash-victim meet in a pine-forest . . .

4

The absence of Count Girolamo Delaude is puzzling enough, but the presence in his villa of so variously remarkable a girl as Katia is likely to arouse far more speculation. However, in the circumstances any speculation would border fatally on gossip, inadmissible on duty, and therefore when Vannuccini lets out a clucking '*mammeglio*', the Marshal quickly cuts him short. 'How many gardens does Orfeo look after here?'

'Nineteen.'

'So we'll have to go over them one by one until we find the van at least.'

'At this time of day?'

Not only the wind but the light is diminishing too, and if a search is to be conducted it is clear that it will be a fairly limited and somewhat pointless one. Orfeo, Vannuccini further points out, is a funny kind of bloke. When the pine-forest was still riddled with snakes, for example, he used to come here to catch the adders and sell their poison, or he used to go nude-bathing in November with the burgomaster of Cologne . . .

'What do you mean?' the Marshal cuts him short, irritated by this list of eccentricities.

'Nothing, but if he's made up his mind to hide the van, it'll be tough, I tell you.'

They have stopped at a crossroads where a peeling cork-tree protected by a stone parapet acts as a traffic bollard.

'Well, we've got to start somewhere,' says the Marshal brusquely. 'Come on, which is the nearest villa?'

Near by is the wide road that leads to the Grand-Duke's Bridge; on the other side of it, to the left, is the Kruysens' villa, almost opposite the Tavellas, where Orfeo might have called to check the irrigation pump, which is apparently . . .

When they get out of the car they see a man on the bridge staring at the slimy flow of the canal.

'Good evening, *Onorevole*,' Vannuccini greets him, crossing the ancient footbridge first.

The man automatically lifts a cell-phone to his ear, as if he were only able to catch the human voice by that means. 'Ah, good evening,' he says uncertainly.

'See how the Ditch has risen with last night's flood?' Vannuccini continues, unaware that he has not been recognised. 'Still, we needed it, didn't we?'

'We needed it, we needed it,' the Hon. Bonanno confirms with a sharp glance at the Marshal. And he asks Vannuccini, who is wearing the same uniform as Vannucci, an innocent ecological question. 'Are there water-rats, here in the Old Ditch?'

'Oh yes, there are,' grins the guard, 'but they aren't your sort, *Onorevole*. Yours are . . .'

'Don't talk to me about them,' says Bonanno.

And he at once starts to talk about them himself, in a tone which is intended to be airy, almost amused, but which soon slips into the emphatic cadences of a parliamentary peroration.

'I don't know,' he concludes, 'but the fact is that my girls refuse to spend another night there, they're traumatised!'

'*Mammeglio!*' exclaims Vannuccini sympathetically.

'I'm not sure,' states Bonanno, seeking the Marshal's eyes, 'but in my opinion there's something at the bottom of all this, and I'm not the only one to think so. An invasion of rats on so large a scale cannot possibly be the result of pure chance.'

But the Marshal's eyes are following a broken box that is being dragged by the slow dark current around the wide curve of the canal, through marsh-weeds, canes, bare tamarisks. And suddenly the *Onorevole*'s voice is wafting into his ear an elaborate intrigue between different political factions, a conspiracy with Roman and Maremman connections, and then killers, enormous rats, corrupt forest-guards . . .

Marshal Butti's attitude towards the political powers-that-be could be described as one of respectful indifference, not unlike his feelings when attending (under orders) a ballet-performance once in the Boboli gardens in Florence. Stuff for specialists, which at his level usually only dribbles down in the form of occasional nuisances connected with patrol and escort duties. But this Hon. Bonanno, whose constituency is in the Abruzzi and who only comes to the Gualdana on holiday, is now dribbling something much bigger than a mere nuisance down on to him: a discreet inquiry.

'With the maximum discretion,' he repeats in a far from discreet voice, as he starts to back away between the two low walls of the bridge, already merging into the shades of the evening. 'I must urge the maximum discretion.'

The Marshal salutes him with all the zeal he knows he will be unable to bring to the inquiry. The request is absurd. The *Onorevole*'s suspicions may be perfectly logical from the point of view of Roman political life, but offer no practical grounds at all to work on. Where would one start? Whom would one question?

'Well, well,' grins Vannuccini colloquially, with the intonation he will use later at the lodge and in the village bars. 'The Marshal has been promoted rat-catcher!'

Although veiled by the twilight, Butti's glance is like a whiplash. In uniform and on duty, there are familiarities that just cannot be allowed; the guard has broken a rule which, though unwritten, remains fundamental for the good of all: mockery is a power to be exercised at the appropriate times and places.

'The inquiry must be undertaken,' the Marshal answers severely, 'and unless there be proof to the contrary the licensed guards of the Gualdana are obliged to give me their assistance, should I so require. And with the necessary discretion.'

Vannuccini falls silent, mortified. Beyond the pale shape of the box, now jammed in the tall reeds, at the point where the canal straightens for its last run towards the sea, a seagull swoops to make its own nutritional inquiries, and with motionless wings traces a few perfect circles around some half visible object amidst the withered branches of bramble and tufted stems.

'What is it? It looks like a car.'

'It's on the towpath, it could be the tractor that keeps it clean.'

'And could it be Orfeo – Orfeo's van?' says Monforti.

'Let's go and see.'

The ruts and bumps of the towpath take them jolting along to Orfeo's van, and from there their eyes rove freely towards the mouth of the Old Ditch and Orfeo himself.

'There he is! It's him!'

Orfeo is a small upright shape on one of the breakwater cubes against which the sea-storm is spending its last spumes.

'What's he doing, fishing?'

'No, he's never been a fisherman.'

The Marshal gets out of the car and sets off alone along the last stretch of towpath, which soon merges into the sand of the beach. Monforti and Vannuccini see him walk round the first rocks set there to protect the mouth, jump up onto the crenellated concrete barrier, and then pass from one lop-sided cube to another until he reaches Orfeo, still immobile.

Not a word can be heard at that distance, but very few words are passed anyway. Orfeo continues to stare stonily out to sea; he never turns his head although at a certain point he lowers it and remains seated in that position, with his neck bent, until some minutes later the silhouette of the Marshal detaches itself from his, stands out clearly against the cloudy horizon for a second or two before returning to the sand, then the towpath.

'What's he gone up there for?'

'I don't know, he didn't tell me.'

'But is he going back home to his wife?'

'He says he is, but last night he slept here because he

didn't feel like going back and anyway he had some more work to do here. He wouldn't tell me anything else.'

'He's a funny sort of chap,' sniggers Vannuccini. 'He's a freak too. A freak cuckold.'

5

Since 'The case of the sleepwalking taxi-driver' is one of the silliest in the series, Monforti finds it even more irritating that his brother-in-law should continue to be engrossed in it while he tells him the latest developments in the Zeme case.

'Odd, I agree, but such things happen every day,' he says coolly, without dragging his eyes away from Perry Mason who is phoning his secretary. 'And then the explanation always turns out to be quite simple.'

His sister Sandra is not watching the programme, but continues to write and seal belated Christmas and New Year cards.

'Sorry, but these greeting-cards go on for ever,' she says, raising her head for a moment. 'Anyway I wouldn't worry too much either, if I were you. It's all too likely that the poor woman, in the state she was, missed the train and had to take the next one. Or changed her mind this morning and is now on her way back here. Her husband might have gone to pick her up in Florence.'

'On foot?' Monforti is about to ask her ironically. But he reflects that, leaving aside Delaude's flight, there could actually be a connection between the wife's failure to arrive and the husband's absence. She could have phoned him early this morning, in fact, and told him she'd decided to come back, and he . . .

But with this Perry Mason fan and this card-fiend there's no way of discussing it. So – he decides, putting his coat back on – he'll go and talk things over pleasantly with Natalia whom he hasn't seen since last night. There could be no better pretext.

Andrea and his sister Giudi are stuck in front of the television too (where Perry is yet again, or still, phoning his secretary). And Natalia, like Sandra, is busy with a heap of envelopes and coloured cards. But her welcome is less discouraging.

'What a good thing you came. Otherwise I'd be here all evening with this lot,' she says, gathering up the cards that have already been written and putting away the others. 'Lucky old you, never sending any.'

'But I've got the excuse of my depression! Actually I pretend to be depressed for this very reason, didn't you ever guess?'

The children start laughing and lose all interest in the sleepwalking taxi-driver. Andrea wants to know about Zeme. Monforti tells him.

But after a while, although he is careful to slide over the more sinister theories and indeed endeavours to lighten the atmosphere with news of Orfeo's reappearance and the comic involvement of the Carabinieri in the rat-story, he realises that Andrea is troubled. His investigative zeal is not what it was this morning. As for Giudi, who is a year younger than her brother, she gazes with unconcealed aversion at the black bushes and even blacker trunks in the darkness outside the window.

Of course, the narrator rebukes himself, remembering the very different effect that certain stories used to have on him as a boy, according to whether he heard them in full daylight or when it was already dark. How could they fail to imagine, he asks himself retrospectively, that those oleander bushes conceal Signor Zeme's bloody corpse, or that his wife's ghost is about to emerge from behind that pine-tree?

Anyway, he concludes hastily, the most plausible explanation is that offered by his sister, Sandra: this morning Signora Zeme phoned her husband to tell him she had decided to return, and he went to fetch her at Florence.

'On foot?' asks Natalia in a low voice, when her children have settled back in front of the television.

'He could have got a lift from someone,' he says, in an equally low voice. 'I don't know, suppose . . . but even on foot it isn't impossible, if you think about it for a moment.'

'What do you mean? I don't understand.'

'I'm just saying that if I were to fetch you, I'd go to Florence on foot,' says Monforti, not caring whether the children hear him or not.

6

In a dream he had God knows how long ago (at his age it is impossible to remember), Hans Ludwig Kruysen was at the keyboard of a majestic organ, in a large deserted church, when a light touch on his shoulder made him turn round. No one was there. The church, which he now recognised, was the Marienkirche of Lübeck and the organ was the largest of the three, in the lofty gothic gallery at the far end of the central aisle. Behind the solemn stained-glass windows darkness was falling.

The balustrade of the gallery was missing (after the war, when the church had been entirely rebuilt, they must have forgotten to replace it) but none the less he walked right to the very edge. He knew that the touch would be repeated and he waited, thanking the gods who were mercifully consenting to free him from these last, interminable years of tedium and decline. Below him, from that height and in that gloom, the stone pavement was barely visible.

The light touch was repeated.

The fall, one incalculable instant later, ended with a blinding flash and the immediate cessation of everything. At that point of the universe which for so many years had been Hans Ludwig Kruysen, there was nothing now but a deep quiet. Never, in his whole existence, had the old organist imagined such deep satisfaction and happiness.

Time rolled on and nothing moved. Nothing harmed the astral perfection of that silence. Except (had it just started or had it been going on all the time, without his noticing?) a kind of imperceptible buzz . . .

Could it be Signor Lotti's whistle, which somehow became audible here? Or a normal but distant household appliance, probably a vacuum-cleaner which Vannuccini's wife, under the direction of his wife Ute, was passing over one of the ground-floor rooms?

It was thus, still dreaming, that Signor Kruysen realised he still existed and the intense disappointment woke him.

But since then, the burden of his years and ailments, although increasing, has become less unbearable. Through having been there, not simply through having heard tell of it, he knows the place of cosmic quiet and silent music that awaits him. It does not bother him to have to travel all that way to get there.

Meanwhile, without any regret whatsoever, he has left his famous and antique harpsichord, entrusting it to Ute's care, since she is still young; it is a highly sensitive Ruckers and his arthritic fingers can no longer do justice to it. To deceive himself that he is playing, he now mostly makes do with a rickety old piano on which Ute, before she married him – or rather before she became his nurse, poor girl – used to practise, still using Cramer's *Studies*.

As for the organ, this year too he has had to promise to

play it at midnight mass, in the village church, on condition that he can arrive and leave without any ceremony whatsoever. But he will limit himself to one keyboard and, in order not to have to struggle with the stops, he will select them beforehand. He will use the pedals as best he can. At any rate he hopes not to butcher Frescobaldi's *Toccata* (No. IV, from the 2nd Book) which he has chosen for the Elevation; and for the rest, in memory of Lübeck, he will simplify in his own way the six Christmas chorales by the great Buxtehude. He will have to forgo Bach, whose toccatas and chorales he would never dare to touch again.

'*Puer natus est in Bethlehem*,' he says encouragingly to the Bonanno girls, whom Ute is keeping here until better news should come on the rat-front. And they reciprocate with one of those tremulous, admiring and stupefied smiles of the poor in spirit, who whether one likes it or not are a guarantee of the kingdom of heaven.

7

Although priests are not funny, Katia has managed to persuade Max & Fortini to take her to midnight mass. Maybe some good gag will come to them all the same. Then she regretted joking like that, about the church and priests, at Christmas of all times. But she can at least say she did so for a good cause.

She is curious to see who will be there, who else will come from the Gualdana, and above all, of course, she is eager to be seen with the two famous artists. But she feels like going to church anyway, apart from this; at Easter for example she always goes and last year, feeling really low, she even took communion. Max & Fortini never go apparently, not even with their wives, but they're wrong. Maybe this evening will do them both good and it may help Fortini to get over his block, you never know.

Only she can't go dressed like a tart, can she? So looking in the spare room she found a decent dress of Signora Fortini's which looked fine on her and asked if she could wear it and they said of course she could, by all means, in fact, let's see: 'A girl finds two dresses, one yellow and one red . . .'

Lord how funny those two are. They're really nice people, she listened to them while they were phoning their wives and children to wish them a Happy Christmas but saying such hilarious things about everything, even about her – calling her an out-of-work *au pair*, but a good one, pretty even, sent by Baby Jesus – so that she suddenly felt like crying at the thought that people like that had taken her into their house, the wives must be really nice too, and the children, oh God, let's hope it lasts.

Although the Gherardinis and the Salvanis had invited him most warmly to dinner, Ugo the Hermit had gone to neither house, on the pretext that this evening he had to limit himself strictly to boiled roots and dried figs.

Actually he would have been happy to accept, were it not for the fact that on such occasions there were always too many people making too much noise and having too much fun. As for the stiff, dull Vettoris, he has decided not to go there because, as Diogenes said of certain Athenians, 'the last time I dined with them they didn't show enough gratitude'.

Instead, he thinks as he lights the fire in the only room of his hut on the hill, and really does boil his roots, he'll go to midnight mass in the village. He'll have to take the bicycle, unfortunately, because at night, what with the journey there and back, twenty-two kilometres is too far to walk. But he is eager to hear Everardo's sermon, which will give him fresh targets for his jibes, and also he doesn't want to miss old Kruysen's music, since there's no saying whether he'll still be around next year.

Besides, who can say whether he himself will still be around, or whether he'll end up following the teachings of Egesias the Cyrenian, also known as the Peisithanatos?

Although his wife, busy with the stove and the saucepans, has her back to him, Orfeo can imagine her obstinate eyes, her tight lips, her hard inflexible jawline. He knows that she'll give him nothing to eat this evening either, although since he came in not a single word has been exchanged.

But he'll leave things for tonight. It's Christmas. He'll go to mass later to hear that Father Everardo, who he hears was looking for him yesterday, and who's going to be preaching tonight. He'll ask him what he had to say to him.

But from tomorrow on . . .

That whore standing there cooking her broccoli as if nothing was the matter – she doesn't know what he intends to do, now he's back. She's got no idea what strength he's regained in the secrecy of the pine-forest. She thinks she can go on keeping him under her thumb, she and that idiotic criminal who screws her, and that other one or those other ones, all of them hand-in-glove with her. He knows perfectly well that there are others, and he'll make her pay for them all. Don't give him broccoli.

VIII

On Summer Nights the Steep Medieval Quarter

I

ON SUMMER NIGHTS, the steep medieval quarter that dominates the village with its Castle and, further down the hill, the Romanesque church of Santa Maria delle Preci, is illuminated in sumptuous scenographic fashion at the expense of the Town Council. And there is no doubt that Tourism, Business and even the Industrial Zone all benefit from it.

But suppose this lavish use of energy-resources – the Parish authorities remark – were to be extended to religious feasts and in particular to Christmas night, would not the Faith benefit as well?

Quite possibly – the Town Council replies – but in this case is it not up to the Parish authorities? *Unicuique suum!*

The quarrel has been going on for ages. And so tonight, as ever, the people make their way through the tangle of alleyways and then along the single winding road up to the church, in the dark or almost. The sky is now clear, but the moon, although half-full, is not yet high enough to compensate for municipal stinginess.

Besides, many prefer it like that. The silent, slow,

nocturnal ascent is part of the ritual. And the confused tramping of feet (cars and motorbikes have to be parked at the bottom), the subdued exchanges of words or occasional greetings between wayfarers who, despite the darkness, have managed to recognise one another, give the walk a suggestion of an ancient medieval pilgrimage.

But in the churchyard the atmosphere changes. In front of the beautiful, and not over-restored XIII-century façade, the rectangular gravelled yard is, for better or worse, lit by a couple of municipal lamp-posts. And the villagers, who mostly get there very early, are quite happy to stand about chatting. While awaiting the sacred, the profane is given free and often lively rein.

This time there is something very serious to discuss, something that apparently happened last night, during the *libecciata*, although the first news of it only got out a few hours ago: the kidnapping of an important Roman industrialist, Signor Zeme, who was carried off together with his wife from his villa in the Gualdana, by Sardinian immigrants according to some, or – which is more likely – by the Calabrian *'ndrangheta*. There is already said to have been a phone-call from the Alto Adige demanding a ransom.

But if they carried off the wife as well (the owner of the 'Il Molo' bar objects), who are they asking to pay the ransom?

Her family (explain the better-informed), who live in Alto Adige and who contacted Marshal Butti at once.

But this explanation is contradicted by the appearance of the Marshal in person, arriving with his old mother on his arm and calmly entering the church. Wouldn't he be consulting his superiors in Grosseto, or at any rate be taken up with his investigations, if the situation were so serious?

In order to understand a little more (or perhaps less) one would have to be able to follow the coil of rumours back to their original source in the village: Ivella Vannuccini, maiden name Sguanci, and daughter of the barber of that ilk. Which latter, having received from aforesaid daughter an already highly-coloured, embellished version of what her husband had told her, did not fail to add further colour and embellishments for the benefit of his clientele. Who in turn . . .

As for the Gualdana residents – except for Maestro Kruysen, who was driven here with his wife by the parish priest and who is already trying the organ out – they are only now beginning to arrive. But most go straight into the church, like poor Signor Mongelli, always by himself now, beautiful Signora Neri with Signor Monforti (but how come her children aren't here?) or the Hon. Bonanno with his family. And the few who linger in the yard, talking strictly among themselves without looking around, discourage questions. Even Milagros, the Filipino maid, usually ready to chat with anyone in the village, stands haughtily apart in a fur coat and hat, talking to an unknown girl, who seems Tuscan from her accent but from Florence, while her mistresses discuss Tarot cards with the famous comedians, Max & Fortini.

Fortunately here comes Orfeo; his conjugal affairs are of no interest to anyone now, but since he works all day at the Gualdana, he might bring fresh news. However, he merely enquires whether Father Everardo has arrived yet, and being told that he has, goes straight into the church.

It is now midnight and everyone finally troops in, taking their seats in the nave or, according to the local custom, standing in the aisles or at the back. The organ welcomes those present with the first of the *Weihnachtschoräle* ('Nun komm, der Heiden Heiland') by the great Buxtehude.

2

Majestic organ notes resound around the porter's lodge in the Gualdana too, though broadcast televisually from the Cathedral of Siena. One could change channel, but there's little choice tonight. No westerns, no soft porn, no documentaries on dog-breeds. You have to take your pick: a priest preaching, or some saint's life, or make do with a film about the early Christians, naked amid the lions. Flick by flick, guard Roggiolani comes back to the high mass in the Cathedral of Siena, which is a live show after all, even though it doesn't count as a real mass, except for the seriously ill.

The fire is dying in the hearth; Roggiolani bends over and pokes it, then leans back in his fake-leather armchair and yawns in boredom. How about something to eat? But he isn't hungry yet, and, besides, the diet that Doctor Scalambra put him on after his indigestion last Sunday is scarcely enticing. Rice and boiled chicken, stewed apples. While Scalambra himself cheerfully smokes his sixty cigarettes a day. As a national health doctor, shouldn't he feel duty-bound to set a good example?

From one corner of the large window on the right the moon appears, half-full but pale, wan, as if it had worn itself out struggling free from the last tatters of clouds. Roggiolani goes out to look around and notes that the weather has really taken a turn for the better, there are a good many stars visible and the noise of the sea has resumed its subdued, innocuous rhythm.

But then the organ music, with the distant accompaniment of the undertow, is joined by a livelier, more insistent sound. The guard hurries back in, turns the volume down, lifts the receiver.

'Hello?'

It is Signora D'Alessio-Pettinati, still with no news of her sister, or her brother-in-law, who is not answering from Rome either. Any news from the Gualdana?

Roggiolani is afraid there is none. He is fully aware of the situation, if he had heard anything, he would have called her himself. But so far . . . Yes, if there is any news he will call at once. At any hour of the night. Of course.

The guard puts the receiver down but does not turn the volume back up. Is it worth phoning the Carabinieri again? His colleagues on the previous shift have already told them that Signora Zeme did not arrive on the 21.00 train. And anyway at this time of night, nobody will answer, they'll have put the recorded message on by now.

But Corporal Macchia answers, and takes note of his information.

Both of them take the opportunity of a little chat, bemoaning the tedium of the evening's programmes, while on the screen the mass continues silently.

3

Impeccably celebrated by the parish priest with the assistance of Father Everardo, stupendously accompanied by Signor Kruysen and enlivened by the epistle of St Paul to Titus (which Milagros is reading in her purest Grosseto accent), the mass at Santa Maria delle Preci proceeds to the satisfaction of everyone but Orfeo.

He, to tell the truth, had only come for a word with Father Everardo before the sermon. But he found him already fully occupied as Father Albino's helper. If he wanted a word with him, they told him, he would have to wait until the end of mass. So he took a place in one of the pews at the back, where he now sits sullenly and listlessly, making it clear that he is not going to stand up even for the Gospel: just as he did not stand or make the sign of the cross for the veneration of the altar, or beat his breast during the act of penitence, or pull out a lira when the Bonanno girls went round for the collection.

And yet Monforti, who has been watching him for a while now, remembers seeing him in an attitude of total respect and even kneeling just last Easter. He must have fallen out with God over his wife, poor chap, as opposed to Signor Mongelli, who has grown ever more religious and devotional.

As for Monforti himself, he only ever comes to church – when he does come – to accompany his sister or brother-in-law, or Signora Neri with the children. But in order not to hurt the feelings of those who take a more active part in the ritual, he then stands at the back by the door, among the less committedly faithful, or at any rate, the less ostensibly devout. Thus it is that he finds himself next to Marshal Butti, soldierly and impassive in the uniform he keeps for important occasions. The Marshal's mother is sitting in the front pew with Signora Neri. And near the door, in his raggedest cloak but with no stick or lantern, since he cycled over, the Hermit stands, with his battered hat in one hand.

The Epistle is over; Milagros returns demurely to her place with Katia and her mistresses, while everybody except Orfeo stands up for the Gospel.

Father Albino begins to read. Mary wraps the child in swaddling clothes and lays him in the manger. The Angel of the Lord pours his light down on the humble shepherds to whom he brings the tidings of great joy. The multitudes of the heavenly host who then appear glorify God and call for peace on earth. Maestro Kruysen intones the admirable *Puer natus est in Bethlehem.*

And then Father Everardo approaches the microphone on

the altar-rail. He invokes peace for the world, particularly the Third, and then passes on to illustrate the inescapable links between peace and justice, social justice above all.

But, perhaps partly due to the faulty nature of the microphone, the sermon does not grip. Many go back to chronicling the double kidnapping of the Zemes, while others find themselves, to their surprise, thinking about their own affairs.

Signora Neri is a little worried over Andrea's health; he had declared himself too tired to come and had shuffled off to bed, with the result that Giudi stayed at home as well. Could he be sickening for something?

Sandra and her husband wonder instead whether the two children, who are so fond of Gabriele, might not have done it on purpose so as to leave him alone with their mother. He is, after all, definitely on the mend. And so why – thinks Sandra – don't she and Ettore themselves go off to Cortina as originally planned? If things, God willing, were to go well with Natalia, they would only be in the way.

Mongelli knows that things will never go well for him: his faith is a comfort to him but will also prevent him from remarrying, in the highly unlikely event ... And bitterly following the thread of these thoughts through, he ends up wishing that his ex-wife, happily remarried, will pay for it in the next life.

Similarly, the Hon. Bonanno, although the 'big-moles' have apparently abandoned his villa at last, wishes unimaginable chastisements down on Under-secretary Ciaffi.

Katia is bored to tears and looks at her new friend, who is indulging in a secret yawn next to her. ('It could do with some spice,' admits Milagros in a whisper.) Luckily Max & Fortini, leaning against a pillar near by, do not look as if they blame her. God only knows what funny things they're thinking.

Signora Borst dozes while Eladia reflects that now that midnight has passed, the die is inevitably cast: the Two of Swords does not forgive. Monforti feels the wing-tip of depression brush him once again. And the Hermit, next to him, thinks back to Egesias, known as Peisithanatos or 'persuader of death', whose pessimistic doctrine led to countless suicides, including his own: death from dejection, from boredom . . .

But at a certain point, even the most distracted members of the congregation – some earlier than others – realise that Father Everardo has returned from his theoretical and soporific tour of the Third World. He is talking of the marsh, in fact, and in particular of the Sienese and Grossetan marshland – the Maremma: from the mouth of the Cecina to the mountains of the Uccellina and the area of the Albegna.

But the precise moment of his return had passed unobserved, so the congregation struggles to get its bearings. What has the marshland of Siena or of Grosseto got to do with the developing countries? What have Pia and Sapìa, the respective wives of Paganello Pannocchieschi and Ghinibaldo Saracino got to do with it all? Who the devil is the blessed Pietro Pettinaio?

The fact is that the preacher has chosen to give his homily a dialectic course. World peace, above all, for which everyone must pray and work as best they can. But then the warning that the corner of the Earth in which we must first of all demonstrate our love of peace is our own.

'It would be too easy to reserve our love for . . . our most distant neighbour!' he said, with a happily chosen oxymoron, lost however amid the general inattention.

But now, the congregation has gradually managed to get things clear. The wife of the brutal Paganello is Pia de' Tolomei, from Siena, whom the ancient marsh of Luni 'undid' in

Dante's *Divine Comedy*, in the sense that her husband, out of jealousy, had her thrown into a ravine situated there. Was the murderer's jealousy justified or not?

'Nobody knows,' says the preacher, 'but on all occasions, whatever wrong has been committed, the Christian's first duty is to flee from all intentions or desire of revenge.'

Everyone listens demurely, but, although stories of faithlessness are not in short supply in the village, they all wonder immediately whether the admonition is directed at Orfeo. Only Mongelli thinks of his own ex-wife, and is dismayed at the idea that he had been wishing eternal damnation on her just a moment ago.

The story of Sapìa, also from Siena but banished to the Val d'Elsa for her Guelph sympathies, meanwhile leads the Hon. Bonanno to repent, appalled at the extremes of wickedness that political hatred can lead to. Confined in a castle tower, this vindictive gentlewoman witnessed the bloody defeat of her own townspeople, with more than a thousand of them butchered before her very eyes, and her only reaction was to utter words to the effect: 'This is the most beautiful day in my life!'

And it is from here that Father Everardo, with a further reference to Dante's poem (*Purg.* XIII, 128), evokes the figure of another honorary Maremman, the blessed Pietro Pettinaio, through whose intercession Sapìa was able to spare herself many torments in Purgatory.

This Pettinaio or Pettinagno – he explains – was a wealthy merchant (of combs – *pettini* – as the name suggests, which he imported from Pisa) who one fine day gave all he had to the poor, withdrew to a hut outside Siena, and then making his way from there down the valley of the Ombrone started to preach in the countryside, feeding himself on berries and roots like the ancient Desert Fathers. And wherever he preached, he brought peace, smoothing over family quarrels, settling disputes between neighbours, curbing hatred, re-establishing friendships . . . So that for those who listened to him, one could say, it was always Christmas night.

This ingenious return to the starting-point makes it clear that the homily is coming to an end. Monforti and the Hermit exchange a smile, as if to say that Everardo hasn't done so badly, after all. The skilful references to the Maremma and the long-forgotten Comb-Seller (beatified in 1802) have ended by arousing Orfeo himself, who . . .

No. Orfeo has indeed sat up in his pew, but now he has got to his feet and is walking out, turning his back scornfully on the preacher. His expression is darker than ever. And the look he bestows on Monforti and the Hermit, as he passes in front of them on his way out, is so grim as to be frightening. But just whom has he got it in for, precisely?

4

There have been no more phone-calls to the lodge and, for almost an hour, the barriers have not had to be raised to let any cars in or out. On the television, with the volume turned back up a little, the mass from Siena seems more or less at halfway point.

Roggiolani goes out to stretch his legs. It'll be some time yet – he calculates, starting off down the road that leads into the woods – before the first of the mass-goers return.

Around him everything is peaceful, but suddenly the guard finds himself in the middle of a noiseless turbulence. Emerging like ghosts from the undergrowth, four dogs (but it seems as if there are more) swirl around him, shaking their heads, tails, and fur, panting softly, pushing and shoving, jumping over one another, eyes and noses to the ground in a tight, eager carousel.

They are Signor Lotti's dogs, magnificent beasts, kept like princes, but who could do with the odd trip out of the Gualdana or an occasional hunt. Otherwise, what's the point of keeping them so fit? Strange beasts, with strange names, who never show any affection, never seem to want to be patted or to play, so that it is difficult, apart from their beauty, to see what satisfaction their owner derives from them.

Roggiolani eyes the road, expecting to see him turn up on his bicycle. He would be happy to stop for a little chat, even though Signor Lotti is a laconic type, quite as strange as his setters. But nobody appears. Instead, the dogs break off their loop-the-loop, stiffen for a second and then disappear just as they came, lissom mahogany shadows, galloping off at a peremptory summons which is inaudible to the guard, who now turns round to go back to his lodge.

Lotti finds them swarming round him a minute later but he continues to pedal with no fear of colliding with them or being collided with, so fluidly do the animals move, ready to make the tiniest adjustment. Thus they run into the night, one moment flanking the bicycle's headlamp, the next launching themselves lithely on one of their mysterious explorations to left or right of the road. Their owner makes towards the sea, turns into the narrow path along the dunes and when he comes up against a sudden slope, dismounts and proceeds on foot. At the top of the dune he is alone.

A pinaster projects its wind-twisted trunk over the path and several thick branches form crooked rungs at various heights. Lotti chooses one of these seats to rest, and gazes at the sea which the moon is just beginning to streak with silver, then summons his dogs and gets back on his bicycle.

But after another dune, and then a second, the dogs have still not returned.

No light seeps from the villas in the front row, squatting in the scrub, and the only sound that disturbs the silence is the bland, monotonous pounding of the waves on the beach. Lotti sends out his signal and waits. The dogs do not return, something even stronger than the summons is holding them somewhere. Lotti turns his bicycle and goes back along the path, stops at the deformed pinaster, calls once, twice – and finally, from the direction of the sea, not from the forest, he hears a vigorous rustling of disturbed bushes. But the dog who appears is alone, and it halts in front of him, wagging its tail slowly, staring into his eyes with one lifted paw. It is Onice.

Lotti gathers that he is a messenger and allows himself to be led through the rosemary and juniper bushes, goes down towards the beach where the dog at once abandons him, bounding off towards the other three, who are standing motionless in a semicircle. It is more or less the spot where the *Viktor Hansen* sank into the sand, and where the play of currents brings together all kinds of wreckage after the storms, even from far-off places, tree-trunks, chairs, whole cabins, rubber dinghies, once a huge catamaran.

But such objects, it is clear, would not be enough to catch the nervous attention of Onice, Diaspro, Giada and Opale. It could perhaps be the carcase of a dog or a sheep, swept away by the floodwaters, as happened last summer at this very spot.

But the dark shape that can be glimpsed lying half in and half out of the water, on the shifting, moon-gleaming margin, is something larger than a dog or a sheep. Larger even than a man. Or at least – Lotti estimates as he approaches – than a man of normal size.

5

Corporal Macchia's arrival would have passed unobserved at Santa Maria delle Preci had it not been preceded by the noise of the Uno up the hill and then the scrunch of its wheels on the churchyard gravel.

But even so, the officer's entrance did not arouse much curiosity. Those who turned to stare saw him move in silently next to the Marshal, with the air of one who has come to hear mass himself. So they all turned back to the altar, where the coadjutor and another assistant were arranging the missal, the altar cloth and the chalice ready for the Eucharist. As for the Hermit, now sitting in Orfeo's place, he is waiting for the *Toccata* of Frescobaldi which Maestro Kruysen will play at the Elevation, and meanwhile he rests, preparing himself for the long journey back.

Only Monforti notices that the two Carabinieri are engaged in a whispered conversation. And now he realises that the Marshal is staring at him insistently, as if he had something to communicate. As unobtrusively as possible, he moves closer to the door until he ends up next to him.

'There's some news from the Gualdana,' the officer murmurs, 'and it would be useful if you could come as well, in case an identification should be needed.'

They've found Zeme, Monforti at once understands, *but as a corpse. I was right.*

'I'm at your disposal,' he whispers. 'But,' he continues, turning towards Corporal Macchia, 'when the mass is over my sister will have to be told and . . .'

The Marshal nods but explains that the Corporal will have to go with them. 'If you would like to tell your relatives yourself – and,' he adds a little awkwardly, 'my mother as well . . . Meanwhile we'll go outside, we'll wait for you in the car.'

*

As they wind their way down the tortuous road, without the siren blaring and without speeding, the Marshal gives the details of the case. A resident, Signor Lotti, whom Signor Monforti will no doubt be acquainted with . . .

'Not that well. At the Gualdana we mainly know his four dogs . . .'

Quite. Because it seems that it was these very dogs who led him to discover a half-submerged body on the beach at the water's edge: the corpse of a man who, from a first description given by this Lotti to the guard Roggiolani, would appear to be . . .

'. . . Signor Zeme.'

Yes. But the guard, when he phoned the station a few minutes ago, had yet to visit the spot; and besides, he hardly knew Zeme, having taken up his post at the Gualdana only very recently. He saw him for the first time in fact last night, when the accident occurred with Delaude, and he only remembers him as a tall, burly man, with thinning grey hair.

'Which corresponds.'

In any case the Marshal thought that since Signor Monforti knew him better than anyone else . . .

'. . . the culprit is Monforti himself.'

Marshal Butti is perhaps the person in the village who knows Monforti best, and the joke amuses him. However, Corporal Macchia, who is now driving fast along the straight road, appears somewhat taken aback.

6

During Roggiolani's absence, the lodge is closed but the barriers are both kept raised, and next to the Christmas ilex Lotti is waiting, already mounted on his bicycle and surrounded by his dogs. When he sees the Uno come up the slope with its blue light, he waves his arm in a broad sweep and pedals off energetically.

'Follow him,' says the Marshal to the Corporal.

The winding route is dappled confusingly with shadow and moonlight, and at this reduced speed it appears even more labyrinthine to the two Carabinieri.

'We're heading towards the Old Ditch,' explains Monforti. And there in fact is the narrow bridge, which they cross. They then follow their guide towards the narrow coastal path. 'It must be round about where the *Viktor Hansen* is. Everything turns up there.'

'Turns up?' asks the officer.

'I mean that if Zeme was swept away last night by the storm from the beach near his house, that's where the currents would have dragged him.'

'In a word,' says the other man, 'you were right to imagine the worst.'

'Quite,' concedes Monforti.

But when one of his worst conjectures finds confirmation, he feels no satisfaction. If anything he feels a kind of low-spirited relief, because at last that tingling anxiety, that murky agglomeration of future looming over the world, has found a definite outlet, has contracted into a well-defined past that can be confronted. The broken glass in the Zemes' house this morning shook him more than does the idea now of staring at Zeme's corpse, given up by the sea.

However, when they leave the car on the coast path and go down together to the beach, he remains a certain distance from the body, and waits while the authorities carry out the preliminary investigations. But in any case, yes: the man lying face-downwards at Roggiolani's feet, a large man with half of his body alternately covered and uncovered by the wash of the waves, certainly appears to be Antonio Zeme: deceased husband – he thinks with bureaucratic detachment – of the untraceable Signora Zeme.

The fact that he is deceased has been ascertained by Lotti and by Roggiolani, both of whom, furthermore, declare that they left the body in the same position they found it in.

'Right,' says the Marshal, 'let's start with the photos. They probably won't come to much,' he says to Monforti, 'but it's the procedure, as with road accidents.'

The Corporal goes to the Uno and comes back with a camera already mounted on a tripod, which however he has some difficulty in setting up since one or other of the legs keep sinking into the wet sand.

Lotti's dogs stand there, unmoving, some distance away with their master. Monforti, in the flashes of the camera, hardly glances at the dismal bundle lying there on the shore.

Would he have noticed it – he wonders – if, on this lovers' night, he had strolled down here with Natalia after mass? A couple of miles out at sea, the navigation lights of a fishing-boat move slowly from left to right, but the throb of the diesel-engine sounds very close, rolling unimpeded over the water and nuzzling the beach with its cordial, familiar tone. They'll have had good fishing, after the turmoil of the *libecciata*. Christmas Eve or not, it was a chance not to be missed.

The moonglow continues to spread over the sea. A long curling line of silver rears silently over the surface, breaks against a sandbank twenty yards from the shore, and the starry burst sends spuming crests rushing forwards, which slap against the body, covering it almost up to its shoulders, and then draw back in the light of a final flash.

Monforti goes rigid. Only now has he noticed that the man, so to speak, has no feet.

'Don't get your shoes wet,' says Butti, seeing him approach. 'We'll pull him out of the water now and turn him over. And then you can confirm whether . . .'

'It's not him,' says Monforti.

'But . . .'

'It can't be Zeme. Just look where his feet are.'

The corpse is wearing what for a man of his apparent stature would be a normal jacket, but which is in reality a long coat. And his trousers, which the raging sea has almost torn from him, extend well below his heels. His real height – the Marshal realises – is not above five foot seven or eight at the most.

With the help of Corporal Macchia, he drags the body on to the dry sand and first of all proceeds to go through his pockets, in search of a wallet or anything similar that might help to identify him. But he finds nothing. If there ever was anything, the sea has carried it off.

When the body is turned on to its back, Roggiolani switches on his huge torch to illuminate the face.

'My God, what a mess,' he says, taking off his woollen cap as a mark of respect.

Although still masked by sand, the face appears pounded and flayed as if the dead man has been bashed repeatedly against jagged obstacles. The nose is clearly fractured. A sandy strip of skin hangs down from his forehead over his right eye.

The Corporal pulls out his handkerchief and starts the laborious task of cleaning the sand off the face. The Marshal says nothing, looking at his own splattered trousers, his 'best' shoes full of water. Lotti and his four setters stand in a circle at a respectful distance.

Monforti too has remained a little way off, but he cannot drag his eyes away. 'He must have smashed into the breakwaters of the Old Ditch,' he says.

'No, I reckon it was the wreck of the *Viktor Hansen*,' says Roggiolani. 'That's the only thing that could have reduced him to that state.'

'I've been saying for years that it's a hazard,' cuts in Lotti, 'but nobody does anything about removing it.'

The strongest *libecciate* and siroccos eat treacherously away at the sand, shifting the sea-bottom, and sometimes bring the rusty superstructure of the old ship to the surface again; now they all strain their eyes, trying to spot it amidst the liquid furls.

'Tomorrow we'll put the buoys out,' says Roggiolani energetically. 'It might not be the bathing-season but it's dangerous all the same.'

Getting up every so often to rinse his handkerchief, Corporal Macchia has meanwhile finished cleaning the disfigured face, rearranging the strips of torn skin and pushing the straggles of thin hair from the forehead. The eyes are open. The corpse, which is no longer Zeme but God knows who, drowned and dragged here from God knows where, maybe from Marina di Grosseto or even further, perhaps from the Argentario, is now ready for its final photograph.

The Corporal sets up the camera again to frame it half-length, and the flashlight, for a fraction of a second, restores a definite even if spectral identity to the disfigured features.

Monforti knits his brows. Lotti makes a gesture as if about to speak up again. But it is Roggiolani, quickly stepping forwards a pace, who identifies the dead man that is not Zeme.

'Christ,' he shouts, 'it's the other one!'

'Which other one?' says the Marshal.

'The other one in the accident. The one who crashed into the Volvo. It's Signor Delaude, that's who it is!'

Signor Lotti has approached as well, with his pressing retinue of dogs. 'Yes,' he confirms with decision, 'that's Delaude, I've known him since we were at school together. It's old Gimo, no doubt about it.'

7

When the doors of the mortuary van are slammed shut again, and Girolamo Delaude's corpse sets off on its final journey, leaving the pine-forest of the Gualdana in reverse gear and for ever, the Pleiades have already set, and Monforti's watch tells him it is four a.m.

Removal. Transference. Repression. These words, with their various material and figurative senses, much loved by psychiatrists and analysts, begin to dance and blur in Monforti's mind as he watches the van depart. He imagines (tiredness makes his mind wander) those investigators searching for the repressed in the legal archives of Grosseto, where the roll of photos taken by Corporal Macchia will end up, carefully conserved for years to come. The roll of the unconscious catalogued for every man, every woman, in an endless register . . .

There is nobody on the beach now except Monforti and Marshal Butti, who linger there, numb with cold, their faces turned to the indifferent audience of the sea. The show is over. Lotti went off some time ago, lest the damp should get through to his dogs. Roggiolani, after accompanying the van through the maze of the forest, has gone back to the lodge to warm himself by the fire. Doctor Scalambra, tossing the stub of his twentieth cigarette this December 25th on to the stones of the coast road, thrust his head into his Teutonic knight's black helmet, straddled his Honda 1000, and left the scene as well.

'Come along, I'll give you a lift,' says the Marshal, abruptly turning his back on the sea and starting to walk back up to the pine-forest. On the road the Corporal is waiting, with the engine gently throbbing and the blue light whirling dutifully and quietly, as on the night when Colin Graham disappeared a year ago.

Reassuring, these Carabinieri, thinks Monforti. Even though there's been no happy ending this time. But it's nice to think that if a man disappears mysteriously from his villa on a stormy night and another one turns up as a wave-tossed corpse, there are people who don't lose their heads, who get things going, who act, do something about it. If Oedipus had been able to call the Carabinieri to look into things after his road-accident with Laius, if Hamlet had gone to the Marshal of Elsinore for a preliminary investigation into the suspicious death of his father . . .

'It's consoling to see you at work.'

From his tone of voice, the Marshal realises that Monforti is not being ironic.

'It's the regular procedure,' he says simply.

Quite: the procedure. Since yesterday morning Monforti has been in close contact with the procedure and hasn't found it at all bad. He has got extremely cold, he is very tired, he has seen, both in glimpses and in full detail, some macabre sights but he feels curiously at ease. It certainly wouldn't have had the same effect, he thinks with a smile, if he had found himself here in the company of Father Everardo, the Hermit or Eladia, with their respective procedures. Maybe, he thinks with another smile, I'm a Carabiniere manqué, that's what I should have gone in for . . .

'All right?'

Butti is holding the door of the Uno open for him.

'Thank you. I've changed my mind, I'll walk back home, it'll warm me up.'

'As you like.'

Instead of shaking his hand, the Marshal unexpectedly squeezes his arm. 'Thanks for the help and Merry Christmas all the same.'

'Ah, yes, Merry Christmas.'

The interior of the car is all a radiophonic crackle; the radio set has been hard at it tonight as well, from the first call to inform the Headquarters in Grosseto. And there are more calls awaiting Butti over the next few hours, in an increasingly intricate lattice of reports, replies, requests, provisions, orders, check-ups. And long waits, many long waits.

No, thinks Monforti giving up his career as a Carabiniere, it's not for me, at best I could take a minor role in an old TV episode of Perry Mason, exchange a few words over the phone – not even with him, the lawyer, but with his secretary.

The car reverses until it finds one of the access roads, and a few seconds later that last noise fades away and in the dead, spectral pine-forest the birds begin to make their voices heard.

'*Has the wife been told?*' chirps Perry Mason's secretary.

'*Yes, via the Carabinieri of Castellina in Chianti, where she has her holiday-farm business. But she wasn't exactly cut up by the news. She just said that she'll come to the mortuary in Grosseto tomorrow for the identification. She had no idea that her husband was at the Gualdana.*'

'*And that dark-haired girl who came with him the other evening? She must be the last to have seen him alive.*'

'*It seems she's still in the wood, staying with someone else, but at the moment she can't be traced. In any case, the first thing to do is to ascertain the cause of death.*'

'*But didn't Delaude drown?*'

'*We'll know that for certain after the autopsy; tomorrow morning the police doctor . . .*'

'*But I don't know him, I didn't see him on the beach. And the Public Prosecutor should surely have come tearing down from Malibu, with wailing sirens, in our TV episode.*'

'*But Tuscany is not California, my dear lady. And in any*

case, here it was impossible to do very much; it's not as if the corpse had been found in a locked room, with fingerprints and footprint-casts there for the taking, bullet cartridges to pick up, and so on. There was just a beach strewn with seaweed, branches, rubbish, globules of diesel-oil. There was nothing suspicious about the circumstances.'

'And so your Butti thought it was accidental or voluntary death, one or the other.'

'Exactly. And the prosecutor, whom he has known for ages and has the highest respect for, authorised the removal, once the preliminary investigations laid down by the procedure had been carried out, of course.'

'But this motorcycling doctor, this Scalambra fellow? I must say I liked the way he arrived, very striking. That figure emerging from the bushes and moving down towards the beach, the black helmet gleaming in the moonlight . . . It was like seeing death in person.'

'But a moment later he took off the helmet, tossed it on to the sand, stuck a cigarette into his mouth and Butti was there ready with his lighter, and out came the doctor's regular quip, "Ah, a breath of fresh air!" after the first drag. Actually he's an old friend of the Marshal and works with him from time to time; in fact the Marshal, as the procedure allows, summoned him to stand in for the police doctor, having of course obtained the consent of the latter and of the prosecutor and Headquarters in Grosseto. I repeat: the circumstances were . . .'

'I understand: accident or suicide.'

The phone-call is interrupted brusquely. A rustle in the bushes to his left has halted Monforti, who attributes it to a cat, a hedgehog, or a rare marten. But meanwhile he stands motionless among the motionless trunks, behind which it is often easy to imagine 18,300 murderers lurking with weapons already raised to cleave one's skull.

'Where are we?' Signora Zeme asks in anguish. *'Have we crossed the Grand-Duke's Bridge already, is the Cork-tree Crossroads still ahead of us? My God, my God, we've got no reference-points, we're lost, we'll never find the way home, my house, my bed, my God, my God!'*

'Keep calm, Signora, keep calm.'

Monforti starts walking again, pressing his heels down firmly, in the certainty that sooner or later something will help him get his bearings.

'Keep calm, Signora, you'll be found too, and your husband as well. The procedure is lengthy but in the end efficient. One step after another, one thing at a time, think of Dr Scalambra who 1) throws away the stub 2) opens his bag 3) pulls on his transparent gloves 4) bends over the corpse 5) says ohohoh.'

'I don't trust Dr Scalambra, he doesn't believe in psychotropic drugs, or in psychoanalysis, he only believes in engines, in that Honda of his that looks like a rib of a spaceship, he's too fond of risks.'

'And yet not only has he never had an accident, he's also extremely professional, well-balanced and alert; and after 1) taking the corpse's temperature (the same as the sea: therefore the body had been in the water for several hours); 2) observing the absence of rigor mortis (but the process could have started and then been interrupted); 3) recording on the machine in the Uno as general a description of the corpse as was possible in the light of the moon and Corporal Macchia's torch; after all this he went on to examine the cuts, lacerations and excoriations on the head alone.'

'Ohohohoh, ohohohoh,' Signora Zeme insists anxiously, *'but is that all Scalambra can say?'*

'Be patient a little longer, Signora, it's a delicate job and although Scalambra knows that only the autopsy will be able to give incontrovertible results, he has none the less

done his best now to obtain as precise a picture as possible of the situation, since these first indications might be extremely useful to his friend Butti.'

Monforti recognises the two round white boulders placed ornamentally at the entrance to the Pescarmonas' driveway. Three more villas and he will be close to Natalia's, where he could ring, get a cup of coffee, recount . . .

'*No, not now,*' she counters, '*the children would wake up, they'd want to hear all about it too, and I don't think that's a good idea. Because just last night, not only Andrea but also Giudi struck me as being . . . I don't know, maybe the story of the Zemes disturbed them. But you yourself, how did you manage to stay there all that time, faced with that terrible sight?*'

'*I looked and I didn't look. And anyway, honestly, it didn't strike me as so very terrible. It was all very practical, very functional, everything a part of the procedure.*'

'*Boring then?*'

'*Well yes, a little bit, and while the doctor was giving a brief explanation of the details of the main injury, my mind started to wander, to reconstruct the tragedy outside the procedure, the stormy night with Delaude hobbling along the beach amid thunder and lightning, his eyes possessed, blinded by the rain, drunk maybe, until a much higher and more malevolent wave than the others smashed into him, knocked him down, dragged him away – unless, indeed, he himself went out to meet it somewhere along the beach, for some anguished reason of his own . . .*'

'*And during these fine wanderings,*' Perry Mason's secretary cuts in severely, '*Scalambra was making his way, inch by inch, fragment by fragment, towards a completely different kind of hypothesis.*'

'*Only a hypothesis, indeed a simple doubt, a note of perplexity, manifested in the most unemphatic fashion possible, I assure you ... I saw him take off his gloves, he sat down on the sand, lit a cigarette, but forgot his line about a breath of fresh air at last.'*

'And what did he say after the first drag?'

'He said, verbatim: "Aurelio, this blow on his head doesn't look right to me."'

'My God, but it's a terrible suspicion, frightful, impossible, I need my drops, give me my drops!'

'Not a suspicion, Signora, but a possibility, an idea that needs to be verified. Maybe that injury too, like the others, was due to his smashing against the wrecked ship or the rocks in the Old Ditch. And maybe not.'

'There's no doubt that this would change everything,' reflects the lawyer's secretary.

'For the moment it just changes the time of the autopsy, which will be brought forward to eight a.m. today at the Ospedale della Misericordia. A couple of hours should be enough to establish whether there is water in the lungs or not, that is to say whether Delaude entered the water alive or dead, and whether that nasty blow on the head could mean ...'

'My God, my God, I don't want to hear, I don't want to know, give me my drops!'

A simple doubt, voiced by Scalambra for the sake of correctness, and for the sake of procedural correctness already reported to Grosseto. And yet Monforti, as he trips over a root that has broken through the asphalt, regains his balance and, a few steps later, recognises the path up to his own house, cannot entirely silence his wandering interlocutors.

Nothing was said on the beach. Given the place, the time and the procedure, any inference would have been premature, rash, gratuitous. However, Signora Zeme has some cause to be upset over the link that seems to exist between her husband's disappearance and Delaude's death; and quite rightly Mason's secretary insists on the question of the dark-haired lady 'guest' of the Count's; and quite reasonably Natalia would like to know just what the victim was doing on the beach in the middle of the night; and probably his sister, Sandra, if Monforti were to wake her (which he won't) in order to tell her what has happened, would ask for details about the crash that Roggiolani witnessed; and his brother-in-law, Ettore, would say that he prefers Cortina, that the Gualdana is not what it used to be, and that he will have to remember to lock the doors and windows and to put in a stronger lock than the one which at this very moment opens and closes with a tiny click, leaving a cadaverous dawn-glow outside striped by the rigor mortis of 18,300 pine-trees.

IX

At Grosseto, Outside Porta Vecchia

I

AT GROSSETO, OUTSIDE Porta Vecchia, two Carabinieri are checking the cars coming into town along Via dei Barberi. One says to the other: 'It's almost midday. Shall we hand out three more fines and then go?'

'Well,' says the other, 'let's do six more.'

It definitely isn't funny. But it is not Max & Fortini's fault. Although there are very few officers on duty today, the two Carabinieri are not imaginary, and even less imaginary are the fines they are dishing out to drivers found without seatbelts.

'Great Christmas present!' says a driver to his passenger, as they both replace their wallets, which have been relieved of forty-five and fifteen thousand lire respectively. 'What about all the thefts, break-ins and murders they should be looking into?'

But there's nothing funny about this either, since the local Carabinieri – Christmas or no Christmas, and despite all the wisecracks made about them – are far from inclined to ignore these other matters.

Were anyone to go from Porta Vecchia to Via Santore di

Santarosa, where their Group and Company Headquarters are situated, and to pass through to the 'conference room' (next to the so-called operations room), they would find a terse, busy work-session under way, which started two hours ago, and in which those from the Headquarters taking part are:

Lieutenant-Colonel Papi, the Group Commander;

Captain Scheggi, Company Commander, with his direct subordinates Lieutenant Amidei and Lieutenant Scalera;

Marshal Ognibene, Station Commander, whose subordinate, Sergeant Francia, is not taking part in the meeting, but is liaising with the communications-officers in the operations room.

For the area within whose jurisdiction the Gualdana lies, the Station Commander Marshal Butti is also present.

The six officers are facing one another, sitting on either side of the long table. At the two ends of it sit two civilians, namely:

Dr Veglia, the Assistant Public Prosecutor who, early this morning, acting on information from Marshal Butti, authorised the removal of the presumed-drowned man from the beach and ordered his transfer to Grosseto, with a request for an autopsy at the local Ospedale della Misericordia;

Professor Dr Meocci, a pathologist from the aforesaid hospital, who undertook the autopsy in question and this same morning gave Dr Veglia the relevant conclusions: murder.

Professor Meocci's conclusions are based in the first place on the absence of water in the trachea and the lungs. This means that Delaude was already dead before the waves or whatever else dragged him out to sea: drowning, whether accidental or voluntary, can be ruled out.

As for the multiple lesions found on the face and cranium,

the autopsy made it possible to ascertain that they were all – except one – 'post-mortem', since they did not cause haemorrhagic lesions. The only 'ante-mortem' injury consists of a deep fracture in the left parietal bone, with a consequent protrusion of cerebral tissue. And there is no doubt that it was this that caused death.

It is very unlikely, furthermore, that this injury could have been caused, like the others, by the body colliding into breakwater-boulders, submerged wrecks or other such obstacles. The fracture (which partly involves the frontal bone as well) can be attributed to a violent blow inflicted by a makeshift but relatively sharp weapon, such as . . .

The example given by Professor Meocci, and which he has already discussed with Dr Veglia, is that of an iron bar about an eighth of an inch thick.

'But a bar of this sort,' observes Lieutenant Amidei, 'would have to be quite wide to have the necessary weight.'

'In that case, couldn't it be an agricultural implement such as a hoe or a spade?' asks Marshal Butti.

He does not say 'a gardener's tool' although, in fact, he immediately thought of Orfeo, whose presence in the wood the other night has yet to be explained. But he has no desire to draw the suspicions of the Group Command (and in particular those of the frowning Marshal Ognibene) on to the poor man's head. He will make it his own business to interrogate him at an opportune moment.

The hypothesis of the hoe or spade, in any case, obtains Professor Meocci's assent, and the approval of the Public Prosecutor and Colonel Papi himself. And Lieutenant Scali, who is keeping the minutes of the meeting, diligently takes note of it.

There follows a brief discussion of the time of death. But for the moment, all that can be said is that it did not occur more than twenty-four hours before the discovery of the corpse.

According to enquiries conducted by Marshal Butti yesterday ('with praiseworthy promptness', Colonel Papi is keen to emphasise) it was in fact at around midnight on the 23rd that Delaude, returning together with an alleged guest of his daughter's, crashed into Zeme's car; after which, according to the guest herself, who has not been properly identified and is at present untraceable, he went home with her but was then not seen again.

Furthermore, neither the body temperature (given its long submersion in cold water), nor the absence of rigidity (due, presumably, to the tossing and rolling of the body in the shallow water) have allowed Dr Scalambra to establish more precise limits. And as for the autopsy, the results of some analyses have not come through yet.

But at this point Sergeant Francia enters from the operations room with a fax from the laboratory for Professor Meocci. He reads it, underlines the concluding words and hands it to the Public Prosecutor, who examines it and hands it to the Colonel, who examines it and hands it to Marshal Butti, who thus attracts the concentrated attention of all present.

'If I understand this correctly,' says the Marshal after examining it, 'what needs to be ascertained, as precisely as possible, is the hour at which Delaude dined the other night.'

'Ideally it would be good to know what he ate as well,' says the doctor, 'but the most important thing is the time.'

Butti tries to remember, 'According to the alleged guest,' he says, 'the two of them dined in a trattoria or pizzeria, presumably in the village or near by. And so,' he says, making as if to stand up, 'if the Colonel will permit me, I will proceed at once to carry out the necessary enquiries by telephone.'

The Colonel permits him by all means, and the Marshal disappears with Sergeant Francia into the operations room.

*

With the assistance of Lieutenant Scalera, who runs over the minutes, Pub. Pros. Veglia makes use of the break to recapitulate the situation and the direction in which the initial enquiries are moving.

The Delaude family:

After the identification at the mortuary, the widow confirmed that she did not know why her husband, with whom she said she was not on 'close terms', was at the Gualdana. With a significant facial expression, she ruled out the idea that her own daughter was closely or even distantly acquainted with the alleged 'guest'. She then returned to Castellina, after instructing a local undertaker's firm to 'see to everything', and after granting the judicial authorities all such access to the villa as the case might demand.

Through the local Headquarters in Siena, in any case, the Carabinieri of Castellina have been instructed to gather any information that might be relevant to the enquiry, and send it forthwith to Grosseto.

Alleged guest:

The search for her has been entrusted to Marshal Butti, who will proceed to identify her and, should he judge it opportune, to detain her.

Antonio Zeme:

Apart from the crash, which in any case was settled with a civilised exchange of apologies and a decision to adjourn insurance-matters until the following day, there is no evidence that he had or had ever had any other relations with Delaude. That his disappearance should coincide with the murder does, however, justify serious suspicions in his direction. After killing Delaude in a fit of madness or for whatever other motive, he might have committed suicide (but how?) and then been dragged away by the stormy sea himself; or, seized by panic, he might have fled, making his way to Rome by whatever means possible.

The Carabinieri of the Prati area in Rome (where he has his home and office as a representative of 'Volvo' for Lazio) have thus been instructed to detain him immediately, should he reappear there.

Magda Zeme, maiden name, D'Alessio:

From the bar receipt and the platform ticket for S. Maria Novella station, found by Marshal Butti in her husband's coat, it would seem that her husband did indeed see her on to the *rapido* from Florence at 21.00 hours. But apart from the fact that her relatives in Bolzano are still awaiting her, it is still not known whether she even got to Milan, where the following morning she had an appointment with a well-known neurologist.

The Carabinieri in Milan are now trying to contact the neurologist in question, who is at present on holiday, and also to identify the hotel that Signora Zeme had booked over the phone.

Possible kidnapping for extortion purposes:

There seem to be no grounds whatsoever for the theory, aired by public opinion, of the kidnapping of the Zeme couple for extortion purposes. On the other hand it is impossible to establish any link between the two disappearances, just as it is between . . .

The recapitulation is interrupted by the return of Marshal Butti, who has succeeded in identifying the place where Delaude and his companion dined the other evening.

'It turns out,' he reports, 'to be the pizzeria "Las Vegas", the only one in the village that stays open till late. The couple arrived around eleven p.m. and in addition to a Coca-Cola and a quarter-litre of wine, as the till roll print-out informs us, they consumed two pizzas by the name of "Four Seasons", which is to say,' he explains, consulting his note, 'with ham, olives, artichokes and mushrooms.'

'Rather heavy,' nods Professor Meocci, as if he had foreseen it.

'I imagine so,' smiles the Marshal. 'And besides, although I have never verified it personally, the pizzas of the "Las Vegas" are said to be . . .'

'Particularly indigestible?'

'Pure poison, according to local reports.'

'Perfect,' nods the doctor again. 'Taking it together with the analysis of the gastric contents, and considering the only partial clearing of the stomach, this information enables us to state that death occurred at around two a.m. I'll deliver my written report as soon as possible,' he adds with a glance at his watch, 'but meanwhile . . .'

Everyone stands up to say goodbye and, as the Professor goes out, Sergeant Francia comes back in and announces that they have not yet managed to contact the neurologist on holiday, while the hotel booked by Signora Zeme in Milan has been identified. It is the 'Michelangelo', right next to the Central Station. But Signora Zeme never arrived there.

'If she was in a state of confusion,' says the Prosecutor, 'she could have forgotten she had booked in there, and have gone to another hotel.'

The Sergeant rules it out. From the enquiries, it appears that no Magda Zeme, maiden name D'Alessio, has turned up at any hotel in Milan, either near the Central Station or elsewhere.

'In a way,' observes Captain Scheggi, 'the hotels closest to stations are the most difficult to get to. No taxi will take you, and if you've got any luggage it's a problem getting there on foot.'

'Particularly in Milan, where the station and its immediate neighbourhood swarm with drug-addicts, thieves, muggers and worse,' comments Marshal Ognibene fiercely.

'My mother once . . .' says Marshal Butti. But he breaks off in embarrassment, as it strikes him as inappropriate to recount a personal case; he would not continue were it not for the fact that they are all staring at him in curiosity. From his concise account, it appears that his mother, having gone to Scandicci to visit a sick relative, left her suitcase at the station, sending someone to collect it later. Signora Zeme could have done the same, in which case it would be possible to ascertain whether, although she never arrived at the 'Michelangelo', she had deposited her bags at the station's left-luggage counter.

But they would need an exact description of this luggage, Captain Scheggi objects. Would Marshal Butti by any chance be able to give one?

Not there and then. But as it appears that the guard Vannuccini helped the Zemes to prepare for their departure, it would be an easy matter to verify by phone whether . . .

'Fine, go ahead and verify, my dear Butti,' approves Col. Papi.

And two minutes later the officer returns with the description provided by Vannuccini, which Sergeant Francia will now transmit to the Police Station at Milan Central. The luggage consisted of a single but voluminous grey hold-all with blue stripes, brown leather handles and a label, also in a brown leather frame, bearing the name and address.

It is past one o'clock.

They none of them – not the Prosecutor who got up this morning at three, nor Marshal Butti who went to bed at four, nor the five officers of Grosseto whose families are awaiting them to start their Christmas lunches – have any further desire to rack their brains over the unknown quantities of the equation, simple though it be:

$$\text{DELAUDE G.} + \frac{\text{ZEME A.}}{\text{ZEME M.}} = 0$$

As for the information to be given to the media, for the moment they decide to limit it just to the murder case. And this to prevent not only a mass invasion of the Gualdana on the part of the media, but also fanciful and alarmist speculation, which would be counterproductive to the aims of the enquiry.

Marshal Ognibene declares himself to be in full agreement, and opines that the enquiries must in point of fact be concentrated: firstly on the alleged guest and probable prostitute (drugs? relations with the underworld?) who arrived with the victim and whom they should, in his opinion, immediately proceed to detain, if not charge and arrest; and secondly on the widow Delaude, whom the Carabinieri in Castellina will have to investigate in order to ascertain whether she is in possession of an alibi for the night of the 24th.

When Marshal Butti points out that owing to the holidays the workforce at his station consists of himself and Corporal Macchia, Captain Scheggi decides to transfer Corporal Oliva, of the local Metropolitan Company, to the aforesaid station and to call Sergeant Farinelli back on emergency duty.

The Prosecutor announces that he will pay a 'trip to the pine-forest', and the meeting breaks up hurriedly with reciprocal expressions of Yuletide cheer.

2

Wandering through the countryside, Poverty met a man who was crying and complaining over the fact that he had lost all his goods.

'O man,' she reproached him, 'what are you complaining about? Have I deprived you of any real goods? Of temperance? Of equity? Of courage? Do you really lack what is needful? Look around yourself! Are there not bean-plants growing along the paths, and do not fresh-water founts abound?'

Ugo the Hermit repeats to himself this apologia of Bione of Boristhenes (IIIrd century BC) for the third time, but it affords him little relief. After his boiled roots last night, the carob soup thickened with flour that he has prepared as a Christmas lunch strikes him as even more depressing than ever, and just will not go down.

And yet today too, the Gherardinis or the Salvinis, or perhaps some of the Gualdana residents, would have been happy to invite him in. Or he could have gone to the Tavernelle, where his singular sermonising has always amused the regulars. Or, preaching and begging, he could have gone around the farms near by, coming back home with eggs and possibly some poultry.

But this is where the problem lies: it is his very desire to preach his cynical gospel that seems to have deserted him. And if you take that away – he reflects – what is the difference between a wandering philosopher and a mere parasite, a simple scrounger? The fact is that Everardo, by pulling out – no doubt deliberately – that blessed comb-seller, touched him on one of his weak spots. He does not feel himself to be of the stuff the blessed are made of. Loving his neighbour is not one of his strong points. And though Cratès was so highly appreciated for his wise advice, he basically prefers

Mison, the great misanthropist of the VIth century, who was once seen laughing in a deserted place:

'Who were you laughing at, there was nobody there?' they went and asked him.

'But that,' he answered, 'was just why I was laughing!'

However, not even this really corresponds to his mood today. Around his hut, on the bare hill and the fields that slope down towards the marsh, not a living soul is to be seen; but, faced with his naturist Christmas lunch, he has not the slightest desire to laugh.

3

Oh it's a really great Christmas for Orfeo Baldacci, a great day of family joy and peace, in the words of the priest. That tart – first she spends two hours washing her hair again and then she fills a big box with pies and puddings and slips off to brighten up that other fellow's day, friends and accomplices included. And he's left here, sitting by the door staring at the twenty-six terraced houses that have taken the place of an olive-grove, and the petrol-station, that's replaced Gori the woodcutter's timber-yard.

Twelve years ago, when Orfeo got married, this was all still country, there were nothing but little one-storey cottages like his, and fields, vegetable-gardens, paths. And that was fine by her, she never complained about a thing, she looked after her peas and lettuces, she cooked liver dishes and ribs of pork, she even sang. If she wanted anything, she would ask for it nicely. A bathroom? And he installed a nice tiled one for her, with some help from his friend Grechi, the plumber. Two more little rooms? And he put them up (without permission) with some help from his friend Marsilio, the builder. A scooter to go shopping? And here you are, one scooter ready and waiting, baby.

Much too generous, much too weak, for ever saying yes. And then that bloody inheritance, that bloody idea of the leghorn shop, of being independent, while along came the bulldozers, the cranes and the cement-mixers to hem him in on all sides, not to mention his dog Fede getting run over by a car and the fig-tree behind the chicken-run withering from old age or disease. One thing after another, day after day: but in the end the circle closes and the boar is left trapped in the middle with all the hounds slavering and the guns trained on it.

Orfeo lets out a threatening grunt, like a boar that senses danger, and spits on the ground at the very moment that Marshal Butti appears at the gate. So much the worse for him, he can make what he likes of it.

'Hello Orfeo. Happy Christmas.'

'Hello.'

It ought to be the Carabinieri's job to give him a hand, to investigate, try and see what and who are behind the situation he's got into. *Mammeglio*, this fellow's come back to pester him because he's on her side, of course, along with the priest, her fancy man and everybody else. He doesn't tell him to sit down but Butti sits down all the same on the bench beside him, takes off his cap, stretches his legs out.

'I'm exhausted, hardly slept at all last night.'

Orfeo says nothing.

'All alone?'

Orfeo looks down to the ground.

'You haven't even shaved.'

Orfeo shrugs. 'What's the point of shaving if I'm not going to the Gualdana?'

The Marshal yawns: 'But what were you really doing in the woods the other night? You wouldn't tell me. What were you up to?'

'Nothing, I told you. I worked in various houses and then

at the Prestifilippos', where I do everything when they're not there. And then since I'd brought some food along I stayed there. I had to keep myself going, didn't I? I had to build myself up. Because I'm not the kind of bloke who accepts everything, even though they think that by now . . .'

'They who?'

'Them,' says Orfeo. 'Those people.'

He doesn't say who they are but says they are all in it together to weaken him, to wear him out and then chuck him away like a cartload of dung. Only they want to be careful, when you provoke a boar, it turns nasty, it's got the means to defend itself and all right, a woman is a woman, but there are certain things she just can't do, she'll have to chuck this crap about independence and all the rest of it, a wife is a wife and he's the husband and the husband might put up with things for a while but in the end he knows how to pull himself together, regain his strength, and then they'll see what's what, then they'll see who'll come out on top.

'And what are you thinking of doing?'

Orfeo shakes his head angrily against all this arguing, arguments here, relationships there, all the stuff his wife is always hammering him with, but which they've hammered into her, swelling her head, and if they're talking about heads he'll show her who's got the harder head, and sooner or later she'll have to give him what she's got to give him.

The Marshal senses that this is a point of contention of a strictly intimate nature, for which he not only lacks jurisdictional competence but suitable terminology. Besides, he's here to use his own terminology.

'Listen, Orfeo, did you know Count Delaude at the Gualdana?'

Orfeo knows him and even looked after their garden five years ago for a year. But then he argued with the wife, a stubborn, tight-fisted woman, impossible to satisfy.

'You know he's dead?'

'No,' says Orfeo, without asking any questions.

'We found him dead on the beach, late last night.'

'Drowned?' Orfeo asks laconically.

'No. Murdered, struck on the head.'

Orfeo remains silent.

'He must have died the other night around two o'clock, when you were in the wood as well.'

Orfeo grunts, shrugs, looks down at the ground.

'He may have been killed on the beach, but equally they may have carried him there already dead. Did you see anything that night, by any chance? Cars driving around, strange movements, anything?'

Orfeo remains silent for a long while, slips his hand into his thick flannel shirt to scratch himself, then turns towards the Marshal, his little eyes gleaming above his grey beard.

'I saw someone.'

'Who?'

'The comb-seller.'

'What comb-seller?'

'The one the priest was talking about in his sermon. The one who only eats roots and carobs and goes around dressed in rags, scrounging eggs off people.'

'You mean the teacher? The one who lives up on that hill of the Gherardinis?'

'Yes, him. I saw him and I recognised him crossing the Grand-Duke's Bridge, with his lamp and his cloak. He was going towards Poggiomozzo.'

'What time was it? Do you remember?'

'Late. After midnight.'

'And where were you? What were you doing?'

'I was walking. First I watched the news, on the Prestifilippos' television, but all you ever see there is crap, you just hear crap, they're all eye-deep in shit, them too. So anyway I just got angry, and so I went out for a walk.'

'After the late-night news, you mean?'

'Yes, when they close down for the night.'

'So gone half-past twelve. And did he see you?'

'Nobody ever sees me, if I don't want them to.'

Now it is the Marshal who remains silent for a long while. Finally he puts his cap back on and gets to his feet.

'Listen, have you got a lawnmower that works properly?'

'Yes, can't complain about it,' says Orfeo malignantly. 'Everybody else complains, because it makes a terrible racket.'

'Show me it, would you, my brother up in San Savino is thinking of getting one.'

Talking about prices, petrol-consumption and maintenance they go into a corrugated-iron shed with a wickerwork roof, where the lawnmower and the vacuum-tube for leaves and pine needles (which is actually forbidden at the Gualdana on account of the noise) are kept, along with a complete assortment of scythes, sickles, pruning-hooks, rakes, brooms, shovels, spades, hoes, all lined up in order of use and size.

'Good, you look after them,' says the Marshal, passing his eyes over them one by one.

'I work with them,' says Orfeo. 'I work myself to death, and meanwhile she gets up to all her dirty tricks, and not only that, but decides that I'm not to . . . never, not even just once in a while! And everybody else saying she's right, well, I mean! But if they think they've . . .'

'Go and shave, Orfeo, do as I say.'

'And who's going to see me?'

'Me, for example.'

Orfeo shrugs and returns to his seat, his eyes to the ground, his hands calloused and black around the nails.

'I'll say goodbye, Orfeo, be seeing you.'

Orfeo remains silent, his chin in his hand, and as soon as the Marshal has left he spits into the distance.

4

What will be will be, thinks Eladia, deciding not to flank the Wheel with a new, superfluous controlling card, and what has been has been. But what has been? The games obscurely announced by the cards on the 23rd were already concluded in the early hours of the 24th, as the control card made clear yesterday. But what games?

Now that the wheel is motionless, with the twelve Major Arcana all set firmly, each in its own House, it will be possible to study the connections with individual events, people, animals, things.

The frightful *libeccio* storm, for example, and that dead man found on the beach, on the other side of the Old Ditch, appear to be clearly related to the malevolent influence of the Water – the Swords, that is – announced right from the beginning. Whereas the porcupine that caused a crash – apparently only a minor one – could correspond to the fall of the Magician from the House of *Life* into that of the *Enemies*, where animal nature has the upper hand. And as for the Fool who was initially in the House of the *Wife*, but whom the oscillation hurled into that of *Death*, he would seem undoubtedly to be identified with Delaude.

But be careful. The catastrophe inscribed in the Wheel is so complex and entangled that easy matches could well turn out to be the most deceptive. Better to reflect again on the general indications of the cards of Swords, whose deadly meanings range from 'duels' and 'break-ups' to 'morbid states' and 'perverse impulses', without forgetting, however, 'remorse' and 'deserved punishment'.

In the beneficent meaning of the Arcana, on the other hand, the Knight has already turned up tonight in the shape of Officer Butti: who, as Milagros heard from Vannuccini, was summoned to Grosseto this morning.

Therefore, as Eladia points out to Signora Borst, they can expect that today or tomorrow the King will arrive too, in the person of some magistrate or officer.

'But it remains to be seen whether they will manage to understand anything without the cards,' says Signora Borst.

'But meantime,' says Milagros, 'even with the cards it's impossible to make tail or head!'

5

The only thing that Marshal Butti has ever envied General Bonaparte for was his legendary ability to close his eyes in any situation and position and wake up five minutes later, refreshed and lively. As usual, on the route, 'Orfeo's gate–Gualdana barrier', not a single grain of weariness dissolves beneath his lowered eyelids, despite Corporal Oliva's considerately smooth driving.

Vannucci and Guerra mistake his haggard air for one of serious vexation and disguise their own evident curiosity behind the curiosity of the media.

'The *Nazione* and Telepadùle,' they announce, 'have already phoned to find out whether it was an accident or a suicide. And they want to send people by tomorrow morning at the latest. What do we say to them?'

A recent addendum to the community's rules states that no journalist, photographer or television reporter can be admitted to the Gualdana without the explicit authorisation of the resident or residents concerned. Sometimes the media have been given the go-ahead (for Maestro Kruysen's eightieth birthday, for example), sometimes they have been refused entrance by other more or less 'public' figures, both residents and visitors – they have even been awaited in vain (for example by the Hon. Bonanno, ever eager to express his opinion at crucial moments in national and international politics).

But a sensational occurrence is public property and in any case the Gualdana is not an impenetrable fortress; a thwarted reporter can always make his way in from the seaward side, wander around the villas asking questions and taking photographs, and then construct whatever fantasies he likes around them. Better to keep these people under control.

'Don't try and stall them if they come. And if they want to film the Count's villa, take them there, but without letting them inside of course.'

'And what about the beach, where the body was found?'

'Take them to the beach too. But as a special favour, five minutes and then off, you've got work to do, you have to come straight back here.'

'But suppose they want to interview us?'

'You?'

'Yes, us. If they ask us personally . . .'

But Vannucci has got his own line ready. 'Ah, I know nothing and I'm saying nothing.'

Guerri doesn't agree at all. 'We'd better co-operate, because they'll find out what happened anyway and then make you look a right fool.'

'But I'm not saying I don't admit what happened, I just say . . .'

'The less you say the better,' the Marshal advises. 'As little as possible, just the barest details.'

'Lips buttoned then,' Vannucci sums up.

'No, what do you mean, lips buttoned?' shouts the Marshal.

'Cautious admissions, then?'

'What admissions? You haven't got anything to admit, have you?'

'Well, for example: I admit that fellow Lotti found the dead man and that Roggiolani was on duty?'

'Leave Lotti and Roggiolani out of it. It's none of your business!'

'But suppose they know it already?'

The Marshal realises the infernal alternatives that can present themselves in relations with the media, and the idea that this pair should end up as more or less official spokesmen does not reassure him in the least. Moreover, Corporal Oliva does not seem up to this kind of confrontation either; he is young, blushes easily and his eyes seem somehow overcharged with seriousness.

'And what about the autopsy?' Guerri feels authorised to ask finally. 'Are there any details? Can we talk about it?'

Butti plumps for concision. 'It's a murder. Delaude was killed with a blow to the head at around two in the morning of the 24th.'

Guerri whistles, Vannucci exclaims *'Mammeglio!'* with the meaning 'it's incredible!'

'The police doctor's report will be published tomorrow, so there's no need to keep quiet about it. But I will ask you not to mention the story of the crash the other night, and the fact that Zeme has disappeared . . .'

'But his wife has disappeared too,' Guerri points out. 'Everybody knows by now.'

'Right, exactly, you just know what everybody knows, you haven't heard anything else, no links, no coincidences, no suspicions.'

'For the moment,' says Guerri.

'For the moment. And for the moment you don't know anything about the girl who arrived here with the victim either. You've never heard of her, you've never seen her, is that clear?'

'A big dark girl, taller than him, so Roggiolani says. A

nice piece of . . .' Vannucci bites his tongue, as if in the presence of journalists. 'Anyway, I didn't see her,' he concludes contritely.

'But I saw a dark girl like that,' says Guerri. 'I don't know if it was really her, because she seemed a bit shorter, about as tall as Roggiolani. It's true I was on my bike.'

'And when did you see her?' says the Marshal, very calmly.

'This morning, here in the wood. She was looking for dry cones for the fire, but they're all still soaking from the other night and she had to chuck away three out of every four. A beautiful girl, nice piece . . .'

'Where was she?'

'On the road. She had a plastic bag and she was . . .'

'I got that, but where, exactly? Near Delaude's villa?'

'Yes, somewhere around there. But five or six villas further on, where those two actors stay.'

'Max & Fortini,' specifies Vannucci. 'They're here too, they're preparing a new . . .' He breaks off and looks at the Marshal and Corporal Oliva disconsolately. 'Milagros told me,' he adds to justify himself. 'I don't know anything else and I'm not saying anything.'

The Marshal's laugh sounds like the first creak of a hundred-foot pine-tree about to topple. '*Maremma benedetta*, are you buttoning your lips with me?'

'No, it was because this morning Milagros . . .'

'Forget about Milagros! Or did she tell you something else . . . ?'

'No, or just that there's a girl staying with those two actors now, she met her at midnight mass and this girl . . .'

'But who the hell is this girl?'

'Nice sort, tall, dark, she says.'

'And what else did she say?'

'That first she was with the Count. She came here together with the Count from Florence and now she's moved in with Max & Fortini, and she says she's really happy. Her name's Katia, she says.'

The pine-tree does not topple; the Marshal sighs. '*Santa maremma,*' he says.

If this Katia were a ferocious murderess, as his ferocious colleague Ognibene thinks is quite possible, by this time, reflects the Marshal, she would already be miles away. Whereas yesterday, during the brief conversation at the door of the villa, she sounded as if she knew nothing about Delaude. Indeed, she seemed to have a grudge against the dead man, and talked like a woman who had been unceremoniously ditched by someone still alive.

Anyway, best to carry out a little check-up, entrusting the mortified Vannucci with it.

'Yes, I get it: if nobody answers, it's a sign they're out at lunch, but if someone does all I do is ask about Grechi, I get it.'

But it is the girl herself who answers, and she hasn't seen the plumber, she knows nothing about his being supposed to call, and if he does come she'll pass the message on.

'It was her, she's at home,' reports Vannucci, scarlet at having carried out his mission brilliantly.

'How do you know? Did you recognise her?' says Guerri sarcastically.

'No, it was her that didn't recognise me, you prat,' says Vannucci triumphantly. 'If she'd been one of the wives she'd have said hello, wished me a happy Christmas, wouldn't she?'

The Marshal knows enough to ask for the keys to the Delaude villa and to decide to start from there. Evidence might turn up that might be useful in interrogating the wanted woman. Ferocious evidence of a ferocious crime.

Before entering he makes Corporal Oliva put gloves on as

well, in case it should prove necessary to bring in the forensic experts. But it soon becomes clear that nothing has happened, there is no sign of a struggle in any of the rooms, nor are there traces of blood or cerebral tissue: Delaude was not killed in his own house. Maybe in one of the beach-huts? The Prosecutor will want that checked too, if nothing else turns up.

Several times during the search, the Marshal finds himself recalling matching images from the search in the Zemes' house. The bedrooms are smaller here perhaps, but the doors and handles are identical. The windows and french windows are protected by Venetian blinds instead of sliding shutters but, in both houses, the floors, bathrooms and showers have brightly coloured tiles. And there is that same impression of passing from one empty box to another, made apparently of damp cardboard, with those same twin beds and their flowered, chequered or striped coverlets, intended for high summer. One has been used and left in a rumpled state.

In the big double room, furnished much more soberly than the Zemes', the bed is also unmade. On the shelf near by there is a lamp, probably burnt out, a paper cup with an inch of water and a box of contraceptives.

There are three left out of eight, but that doesn't mean anything, thinks the Marshal.

There is a sudden distant rumble, as of horses galloping off, and Butti goes down to have a look at the basement, where a thermostat has turned the heating-system on.

'Shall we turn it off?' asks Oliva.

'Yes,' says the Marshal. But then he thinks of the chill of the mortuary and says: 'No, leave it, the wardens will see to it.'

They will also see to the dirty plates in the kitchen and the bottle of Calvados left on the living-room table, with its unscrewed top by its side. Just one glass, drunk after the 'Four

Seasons' pizza, to help digest it. Maybe while waiting for someone to come? Or to phone? His wife's Christmas greetings? The Marshal did not see her this morning in Grosseto, nor did she ask to see him or talk to him, to find out how her poor wretch of a husband had ended up lying there on the beach. A frighteningly cold woman, with a heart that countless contraceptives had turned to stone. Or were the contraceptives the consequence of that coldness?

'Relationships ... relationships ...' murmurs the Marshal, thinking of the Baldaccis.

'The wife and daughter are being checked up on, aren't they?' says Corporal Oliva. 'I don't believe there are any other close relations.'

Butti looks at him benevolently. 'No,' he says, 'I was talking of a different kind of relationship. Come on, let's go and see the car that crashed.'

The mechanic's report will be as long and complicated as the pathologist's, unless Signora Delaude, when she comes, decides to give the car away as scrap metal. A tremendous blow on the head for the Count, a tremendous blow on the bonnet of his old car. Morbid connections that might arise in Monforti's mind, thinks the Marshal, but which must not be allowed to influence one – although in actual fact Monforti, with his anxiety and his dark premonitions, wasn't that far from the truth ...

'Find anything?'

'Nothing special, the usual things,' says Corporal Oliva, in charge of the search.

He closes the boot again, opens the back door, bends down between the seats. A couple of advertising leaflets, a half-crumbled cheese-biscuit, and on the back shelf a beige waterproof hat and a 1978 Michelin guidebook.

'Come on,' says the Marshal. 'Maybe tomorrow we'll search the crash-victim's Volvo.'

The crash-instigator's car is left there like a forgotten tomb, strewn with pine needles, yellowing oleander and ilex leaves scampered over by tiny spiders.

6

Even from Canada, phoning to wish everybody a Merry Christmas, Signora Neri's ex-husband noticed that 'there was something the matter' with the children, they seemed 'a bit low'. But they said it was nothing, they'd just slept badly. Then they ran to the porter's lodge, where their father had said they might find a little present. And when they came back – on two luxurious, truly perfect mountain-bikes that had arrived the day before – that strange air had vanished. Even the news of the macabre discovery on the beach did not seem to affect them that much.

'Just think, Mamma, they found him over there, beyond the Old Ditch, just where the wreck of the *Viktor Hansen* used to be!' said Andrea, as if it were not Delaude's corpse that had surfaced beside the wreck but Captain Kydd's.

And after lunch (did they eat a little listlessly? wonders their mother), they get back on their mountain-bikes to go and carry out an on-the-spot inspection.

The sharp bends, sandy stretches, and steep ups and downs of the coast path provide excellent terrain for testing out their new bikes, with their twenty-one gears. They go back and forth across the Grand-Duke's Bridge and its rough approach-roads several times, by way of experiment.

But 'on the spot' there is in fact nothing interesting to see, apart from the lines of footprints that intertwine, thicken and blur around a central point which must be where the corpse had been drawn on to dry sand, before being carried off to Grosseto.

'*Madonnina!*' says Giudi none the less, imitating the guards, and taking advantage of the fact that her mother is not there to tell her off.

Then she goes with her brother right up to the water's edge, to examine the sea from close up. But amidst the jetsam cast up there by the *libecciata*, neither of them can make out anything that resembles the superstructure of the *Viktor Hansen*. And yet, according to Roggiolani, as reported by Vannucci, the *libecciata* had brought the wreck up from the sands below the shallow water.

'Roggiolani is a prat,' says Andrea. 'Gabriele said that the wreck has sunk for ever.'

The two of them remount their *montapicchi*, as they have decided to call them, and after crossing the Grand-Duke's Bridge, go into their highest gears, and hurtle along the asphalted roads at speeds not allowed by the rules of the residents' association, whirl past the Tavellas' villa, the Bonannos', the Kruysens' . . . after which they brake sharply and turn abruptly down a side path. Just ahead of them they have seen the Carabinieri's Uno, parked at the Cork-Tree Crossroads.

7

Katia has just finished writing on the board in the kitchen the various things that she will have to get in the village tomorrow (the shops are open on Boxing Day morning), when she hears a ring at the door. It'll be Grechi, the plumber, the one they rang from the lodge to ask about half an hour ago. And this Gualdana must be really exclusive, if you can get a plumber to come and work there on Christmas Day. Then she opens the door.

'Oh,' she says, surprised but perfectly calm, now under

the firm protection of Max & Fortini, who are working through there, in their 'funny-factory', as they call it.

The Marshal she met yesterday is there in front of her, and to her left, at the entrance to the drive, a second Carabiniere is standing next to their parked car, a young man who at once looks away. Yes, she's perfectly calm, but just the tiniest slip can dump you in the shit. Right from the first sentence – 'I have to speak to you' (and not: 'May I speak to you?' or 'I would like to speak to you') – Katia realises that the tune has changed.

What can she do? Call the masters of the house? Act as the mistress of the house herself, please come into the sitting-room? They stay standing in the hallway and this time he doesn't keep her waiting, he chucks the news right at her, like a handful of earth on to a coffin, stating that Gimo has been murdered, and telling her where and when. Katia forgets what she has seen a thousand times on television and does exactly what she has seen a thousand times on television.

'Oh my God,' she murmurs, turning white, closing her eyes, lifting one hand to her throat, with her legs trembling, truly. She leans against the door, truly. She is horrified, truly.

'But why?' she says hoarsely. 'What happened? Who was it?'

The Marshal takes her by the arm and it is he who leads her into the sitting-room. Then he lights the cigarette that Katia feels she absolutely must smoke, truly. Even her fingers and lips are trembling, truly.

She just manages to pull herself together a little and the Marshal brings out a notebook and asks for her name and address. Of course, this is what the Carabinieri always do in these cases: first of all they want your documents, to establish who you are, where you're from. And at a moment like that how are you supposed to remember where your handbag is with your identity card? The kitchen, the bedroom, the bathroom, God knows.

'It doesn't matter,' he says, 'we'll have a look at that afterwards. Are you from Florence?'

'No, from Prato, but I live in Florence with my aunt.'

She gives him the address of the 'DryCleaners 2000', the full name of her aunt who owns it.

'We live above the cleaner's, but I have my own room and pay for it.'

She explains, in broad outline, what she does for a living: a model for supermarket advertisements, a few fashion-shows, sometimes a hostess at trade fairs or conferences, a few TV adverts, a few appearances on Teleimpruneta, a little local broadcasting station. A modern, independent girl in a tough, ruthless world.

'No porn?' asks the Marshal as he might ask if she goes in for jogging.

Katia is hurt, denies it emphatically and sincerely. Not even Aunt Ines (who doesn't know about it, mind you) would consider the series of nudes that Giorgio did of her last year as pornographic; because in that case Marilyn Monroe herself, at the outset of her . . .

'It's just to get the picture clear,' explains the Marshal, 'to rule out certain possibilities. Better to find out from you directly.'

And again, in order to get the picture clear he makes her tell him everything about Gimo, punctiliously calling him 'Delaude', whereas she, now that he's dead (and in that awful way!), thinks of him once again as Gimo. A recent acquaintance, met him about a week ago. Never seen him before. Never seen his wife. No introduction, no mutual friends. A chance meeting at a party.

'No drugs?' the Marshal asks her as he might ask her if she says her prayers before going to sleep.

Tough, ruthless questions. Katia pulls up her left sleeve, then her right, and shows him the unblemished candour of her arms.

'I've never even been tempted to try them,' she says stubbornly, 'the heavy or the light stuff. They ruin your work.'

'True,' confirms the Marshal. 'And Delaude?'

'I don't know, I really don't think so. He didn't have much money to spare, poor Gimo . . .' She breaks off, shaking her head. 'I can't believe he's dead, it seems so . . . such a . . .'

But she is not allowed to wander. 'So at this party, Delaude . . .'

A party for the inauguration of a new branch of a furniture shop, with a councillor present, and the vice-chairman of the tradesmen's association. And Delaude, in his role as a Count. A lot of compliments, a lot of promises of important 'contacts', and the proposal of this 'trip' to the Gualdana to introduce her to some people.

'What sort of people?'

'People in the television world, producers, big advertising agents, sponsors, actors. It sounded like a good opportunity . . . Because if you don't get yourself known . . .'

'And who did he introduce you to? Who did you see?'

'Nobody,' snorts Katia. 'At a certain point I realised he was dead scared to be seen with me. Because of his wife.'

And she recounts his slow approach to the pine-forest, waiting for the dark, the sudden dash through the barriers close on the tail of Max & Fortini's car, and later, after the pizzeria, another sudden dash on the tail of the white Volvo, the porcupine, the screech of brakes, the crash.

'Did you get a good view?'

'Of the porcupine? No, not at all.'

But it is the driver of the Volvo he is interested in. What he said, what he did. Katia racks her brains. No, no quarrel, no angry words, she's sure of that. This Zeme was supposed to come along the next day to sort out insurance matters, that was all. But he didn't come.

'And after the accident did Delaude say anything about Zeme? Whether they knew each other at all, whether there were any old grudges? Or did he express an intention of going there himself, that very evening?'

'No, he didn't talk to me about it. I think he just knew him by sight, the way he knew most people here. By sight, no more. And that's why I sent him . . .'

Katia is overcome by remorse, truly. She had called him a worm, she had had a terrible row with someone who just a few hours later went off and got killed in that awful way. A nice memory for that final journey of his, truly. She feels ashamed but by way of expiation she confesses the terrible row to the Marshal, point by point.

'And so I went and locked myself in another room,' she concludes, mortified.

But he makes no comment. He just asks: 'What time?'

'I don't know, midnight, half past.'

'And you didn't see him again?'

'No.'

'Didn't even hear him? Did you hear whether he talked on the phone?'

'No, I went straight to sleep. I was shattered.'

'So you didn't hear him go out, or whether anyone came or rang?'

'No, nothing. Later I heard the thunder a bit, but I was dead tired, I slept right through.'

The Marshal closes his notebook slowly, as if trying to remember some more questions, and Katia's shoulders droop (truly) under a crushing thought: now she's had her interviewer, she's had her great inverview, a long, exhaustive one, ready to be passed on to the media.

'And now what happens to me?'

The Marshal puts away his notebook and pen, without replying.

'I mean, what do I do, what must I do?'

'You must stay here, on hand. Tomorrow the Public Prosecutor will drop by and he'll want to talk to you.'

Another interview, a shower of interviews.

'But here I'm not really . . .' stammers Katia. 'I don't know . . . I would rather . . .'

'It's best if you don't move from here,' says the Carabiniere, frowning. 'We must be sure of finding you, because otherwise . . .'

Otherwise what? shivers Katia. And returning to the hallway with the interviewer, a yell from the 'funny-factory' freezes her completely, truly.

'No, no, no, it's not funny, how many times must I tell you it's not funny!'

Those two saints pick her up literally off the street, they welcome her like Little Red Riding Hood, they give her food and a bed and she brings the wolf himself into their house, the Carabinieri! She just wants to sink through the floor, to die, truly.

'But . . .' she says, dry-throated, 'won't the papers and the television come round, for a crime like this?'

'The Gualdana Murder.' 'Max & Fortini questioned by the investigators.' 'Two famous actors take a strange girl into their house and the Public Prosecutor says to them: do you know that this top bitch is involved in a murder and now you're implicated as well?'

Now of all times, thinks Katia on the verge of tears, just when this breakthrough has come in her life, perhaps the final breakthrough . . .

A door slams, hasty footsteps approach. What a dark, severe, funereal uniform a Carabiniere wears, when seen against the background of a seaside home! What a great big pistol he has hanging by his side! What heavy, inexorable black leggings!

Max appears at the end of the corridor, sees them both, stops, says nothing. And behind him appears Fortini, who sees them, comes forward, offers his wrists and says resignedly: 'They've found us out at last. It's better this way, we can't stay on the run for ever.'

'No!' shouts Katia. 'No, no, it's not funny, it's not funny at all!'

8

Monforti's sister closes the second suitcase, jerkily zips up the Vuitton bag and, raising her head, says once again: 'It's no good, I feel guilty.'

'Will you drop this guilt nonsense?' Monforti growls.

'I really don't feel it's right, leaving you here on Christmas Day of all days.'

'Look, we've exchanged presents, haven't we? And we've had our family meal . . .'

'We could have stayed a bit longer, gone to Cortina for the New Year.'

'So I would feel guilty too. Ettore gets bored to death here at the Gualdana. He puts up with it for ten days in the summer, and that's already too much. All his friends, all the people he enjoys being with are up in Cortina. He only comes here so as not to feel guilty about you, you only come here so as not to feel guilty about me. What is all this, a new way of counting out, one two three, and you're guiltee?'

'There you are, see,' is Sandra's reply, 'you're all on edge, you're nervous, we'd have done better to stay.'

'I'm just tired, I didn't sleep much.'

Sandra waves her two hands like exasperated butterflies. 'Ah!' she restricts herself to sighing.

She cannot tell him that in his condition as an anxious-catastrophist, an aboulic-depressive, the last thing he should ever have done was spend the night on the beach with a corpse. But can Monforti reply that actually it is the corpse that has revived, re-animated, resurrected him? Sandra would not only find these words in poor taste but would take them as indications of a morbid and emotionally capricious condition.

'Anyway it was interesting. Damp but interesting.'

Sandra censures him with her eyes, but then laughs guiltily. 'How on earth did it happen? That's what I can't begin to imagine.'

They have talked about it for hours.

'Just think if Scalambra were right,' insinuates Monforti, bending down to pick up the cases. 'Think if it were a murder after all: "The Gualdana murder".'

Sandra has a definite air of regret when she answers: 'Well, what does it matter, I'll read about it in the papers.'

'What do you mean, the papers? You never read the papers,' says Ettore cheerfully, coming in and taking hold of the cases. 'Here, give them to me, I'll do it.'

He displays the virile smile of a man untroubled by guilty feelings. He has done his duty, he has spent Christmas with his brother-in-law, whom he is fond of but who does not amuse him, and were it of any use he would be prepared to stay in this unamusing pine-forest until the New Year. But apart from the fact that nothing is ever of any use with a depressive, his brother-in-law seems to be definitely on the mend, he appears stably vivacious, he has started driving again, he no longer dockets everything in a sandwich between bad and worse, and so there is no reason not to set out for Cortina, especially on a traffic-free day like Christmas.

This is what Monforti, with full understanding and sympathy, perceives as lying behind Ettore's vivacity, and he hands over the cases with a smile, picks up the bag and follows him to the car where the boot is already open. Bang!

Then they embrace, exchange Christmas greetings again.

'Don't stay too long by yourself, go to Natalia's, remember that you're having dinner with her tonight!' his sister exhorts him through the window.

And when the car sets off she shouts: 'Keep an eye on events, you'll have to tell me all about Delaude, I'll phone you!'

It is not a white Volvo, it is a dark red Alfa this time that drives off through the pine-trees, edges over to the right-hand side of the road and slows almost to a halt to let the Carabinieri's Uno past, and then sets off cumbersomely again and disappears around the bend.

As the Marshal gets out and walks towards him, Monforti gathers from the expression on his face and – to tell the truth – from the mere fact of his presence, that Dr Scalambra made no mistake, that it is and will be a murder case.

But meanwhile something has twitched at the corner of his mind.

Sandra and Ettore (once again a husband, a wife) setting off with their luggage ... At the bend, their car crossing with the Carabinieri's, which if it hadn't been driven by a Carabiniere, and if Ettore weren't the highly careful driver he is, could have caused a ... Not a nose-to-tail accident, of course. A head-on collision. But it was this very difference that had struck him, that had made something flash into his mind ... An idea? ... An image, rather, or at least the *shadow* of an image, but such a confused one that ...

What could it be?

*

The procedure certainly does not envisage – indeed, it probably precludes it – that an officer of the Carabinieri should pass on to an outsider all the information he possesses with regard to an investigation that is currently under way. But Monforti is not a real outsider, or is not an outsider any longer, as the night spent together on the beach must surely count for something. And what also counts is Butti's linguistic (so to speak) hypertension, because, apart from this morning sitting around the table at Group Headquarters, he has not been able to say a single casual or carefree word to anyone.

So, after a cup of instant coffee with a good deal of milk, he has allowed himself to slip into an informality, which, although dignified (in Monforti's opinion), is none the less exhaustive. All those phone-calls, those faxes, those check-ups . . . Dying in your own bed brings enough complications, as it is, but getting killed, and by an unknown hand to boot, sounds like something to be avoided at all costs.

'Not forgetting,' the Marshal goes on, gloomily, 'the problem of the media.'

'Yes, I was thinking of that,' says Monforti, and recites: "'Mysterious murder at the Gualdana. Nobleman barbarously butchered".'

They smile at each other cheerlessly, weighing up the senseless and inevitable transformations that will be forced upon that black body tossed about under the moon, that circle of silent dogs, the wet sand and the monotonous ebb and flow of the waves.

The investigators will try to move with the utmost discretion, this is obvious. They will not give the names of Lotti or Roggiolani or Monforti himself, nor of course of the two actors, Max & Fortini, who proved highly understanding, more than willing to provide hospitality for the victim's . . . companion for as long as necessary. But if the girl should be, so to speak, 'discovered' . . .

'"The Forest of Sin",' recites Monforti. '"The Count's Secret Life".'

'Tell me something about this Delaude . . .'

Monforti can tell him very little. Bad-tempered? Violent? Not at all. Notoriously tense relations with his wife, as the Marshal will already have deduced no doubt. An acrimonious rupture, years ago, with the Tavellas, over a jointly owned catamaran. A couple of little scandals, with public face-slapping, over German or English au-pairs. But what about enemies, rivals, jealous husbands under the sign of the contraceptives, with all the implied peccadilloes and suchlike seediness?

'Not here,' meditates Monforti, 'not at this time of year, at least.'

'No, I suppose not.'

Butti stays silent for a while, disoriented rather than worn out, before adding another shifting and ambiguous frond to his pine-forest of perplexities. 'And what about this Ugo de Meis, this teacher who . . .'

'The Hermit? But what's he got to do with the enquiries?'

'That remains to be seen. You never know. At any rate, did he know the victim?'

Monforti can say nothing on this score, except that Ugo the Hermit, a kind of vagabond philosopher, a harmless eccentric . . .

'Yes, we know that he has limited means of support and occasionally carries out works of propaganda and proselytism of an environmental, naturist kind . . .'

'But he's not at all fanatical and I just don't see what kind of relations he could have had with Delaude. He may have met him in some house or other that they both got invited to. They often invite him, around here. But how come . . .?'

Butti explains how come.

'But it's simple,' says Monforti, 'he came here to dinner that night. Orfeo must have seen him on his way home.'

'What time?'

'He left early. We offered to give him a lift but he insisted on walking back. He's like that, he has his principles. It must have been around ten.'

'Baldacci says half-past twelve, after the late-night news.'

A discrepancy of over two hours, which the Hermit must have spent . . . where? . . . doing what?

'After midnight on the Grand-Duke's Bridge? With his lantern?'

'That's what Baldacci says.'

'Strange.'

Something twitches at the corner of Monforti's mind again, a feather, a corpuscle, another ungraspable associative shadow. The Cynic and the Count? The Door-Opener and the Adulterer? The Naturist and the Consumer of Contraceptives? No link between these two figures, who maybe could only ever find a conjunction, a meaning, in Eladia's Tarot cards . . . Or could it be Orfeo's sharp, surly eyes during midnight mass, his stubbornly bent head, over there on the rocks of the Old Ditch, that combine arcanely with Father Everardo, with the Hermit, with Zeme and his wife? It is the wife that the Marshal is now discussing, with bewilderment, with frank, confidential bafflement.

'I can't make head or tail of it,' grumbles the officer. 'The only thing I can say at this point is that there must be a link between the murder and the two disappearances, even though officially we'll deny it, at least for the moment.'

But then he goes back on his tracks, denying himself in turn. 'In any case, it's still too early to talk of a real disappearance, the two Zemes could quite easily turn up again. Maybe we're here racking our brains and they're calmly sitting up there in Monteriggioni, who can tell? Things like that happen all the time.'

He gets up unwillingly, tormented by the thought of the report he will have to write now at the station.

'But can't you dictate it to that lad?' suggests Monforti who has accompanied him to the car, where Corporal Oliva is waiting.

Butti shrugs. 'He says he knows how to use the word-processor. We'll see.'

He pokes his head through the window. 'Call Grosseto for me.'

He pulls his head out again. 'First we'll see if he knows how to use the radio.'

And the radio, handled with supreme skill, informs them that Signora Zeme does not seem to have had the same idea as the Marshal's mother in Scandicci. At the left-luggage deposit at the Central Station no hold-all has been found that corresponds to Vannuccini's description, with or without a label.

9

The Kruysens are perhaps the only permanent residents in the Gualdana who do not make use of Ivella Vannuccini's information service. Not that she refuses to supply them with it, of course. On the contrary, during the hours she spends with them helping the old maid Emma to do the heavy work, she has always tried to interest Signora Kruysen in the local scandal and gossip. But the kind, silent smiles with which Frau Ute invariably responds have ended up by discouraging her. Furthermore, the maid, Emma, who never leaves the house, does not know a word of Italian; and as for the Old Maestro, always cooped up with his music and his old books, she cannot even imagine going in and recounting the day's news to him.

This explains why neither Ute nor Hans Ludwig, as they take their tea in a corner of their vast, impressive library-salon, knows anything about the recent events. He has spent the afternoon meditating on the *Small Treatise on the Organ* by J. S. Bach, which he possesses in a facsimile of the venerable autograph manuscript P 283 of the Berlin Staatsbibliothek. A couple of hours ago, she quite clearly saw the Carabinieri's car pass in front of the villa, and perhaps vaguely wondered what they were doing in the forest. But nothing really arouses her interest or curiosity, unless it concerns her husband in some way. Her attention was forlornly attracted, rather, by the fleeting appearance of Signora Neri's children: they would probably have stopped to greet her, they might even have stayed for tea, had their gleaming new bicycles not borne them away. And the Bonanno girls would still be guests here, if only the mice had had the good idea of staying in their house for Christmas as well . . .

Hans Ludwig has put his cup down and he reopens the *Orgelbüchlein*, adjusting his glasses. Ute guesses that he is contemplating the good-natured, craftsmanlike subtitle which 'offers the organist beginner the method to develop a chorale in all manner of ways', with the dedication below 'to almighty God to honour him, and to my neighbour that he might teach himself.'

She knows that the decision to remain secluded is his own, owing to kindness and a desire not to sadden or bore people with his old age, but this lonely Christmas afternoon must weigh on him none the less. He would be happy to see 'beginners' around him, even if not organists – like the two sharp-witted Neri children, or the affectionate though dim Bonanno girls, beginners themselves in their own way . . .

Only she can't ask Signora Neri yet again to send her children along to hear her husband playing the piano. But she could perhaps, one of these days, organise a musical entertainment to which anyone who wished could come along. In winter, even during the holidays, there are so few residents that Hans Ludwig would surely not refuse.

10

Standing in front of the open doors of the wardrobe in her bedroom, Natalia Neri has no idea what to put on, although of course her situation is very different from that of all other women who have no idea what to put on. It is not a real dinner, just a little something offered to Gabriele as a friend and neighbour all on his own on Christmas evening; and so one could even decide not to put anything on, just remain in trousers and three-year-old turtleneck. But he is still a guest, and thus deserves a show of respect of some sort. The red one with fringe definitely not. The black or the turquoise? They're over the top as well. The chalk-white one would do fine if it didn't have that low-cut neckline in which Gabriele – not to mention the children – might suspect an absurd intention to create a stir. On the other hand Gabriele will certainly turn up as he is, in a jumper, whether out of masculine thoughtlessness or, on the contrary, to be in keeping with the informality of the invitation. Which however *is* a Christmas invitation, with an exchange of presents, and therefore calls for something that is – well, not dazzling or glittering, of course not, but subduedly *habillé*, something soberly . . . elegantly . . . A nuance that is perfectly clear in Natalia's mind, but which unfortunately the wardrobe does not contain.

And at that moment Gabriele chooses to ring the doorbell.

A pity, thinks Natalia, realising that what she really regrets is the chance to wear something different from her usual clothes. But as she moves forward to receive her guest she tells herself something she tells herself all too often: better like this, one thing less to worry about.

The guest, with his three packages wrapped in shiny paper, has been let in by the children. He is wearing a silky cashmere jacket and even has a silk scarf tucked into his open shirt-collar. A pity, thinks Natalia once again.

'You've come early,' she tells him off with the air of apologising, 'I haven't even had time to get changed.'

'But a while ago Father Christmas called me on the radio from Grosseto,' says Gabriele with a wink to Giudi, 'and told me to hurry up.'

Giudi gives a hint of a forced smile, Andrea doesn't even try. What the devil is the matter with both of them? Gabriele's jokes, whether any good or not, always make them laugh.

'Here you are. For you . . .' says Gabriele, beginning with Giudi. 'And for you . . .' he continues, handing Andrea his package. 'This,' finishing with her, 'is for Mamma.'

This word, as pronounced by Gabriele, unexpectedly touches her.

'Come on, let's go and open them in there,' she says, already turning round.

'No,' says Giudi, 'the tree is here and I'm opening it here.'

The adults go through into the drawing-room, leaving the children in front of the tree, which is richly beribboned and decorated, but ecological, made of plastic.

'I don't understand these ups and downs,' murmurs Natalia. 'They're perfectly well, but one moment they're all frowns and half an hour later . .'

'They're getting bored, you should send them ski-ing with friends.'

'That's what I'll do. Now I want to open this.'

Monforti, who consulted with Sandra for ages, has an intense and disheartening vision: a drawer in Natalia's bedroom packed full of pendants similar or even identical to the one he has given her.

But success is total, satisfaction general. Giudi has already slipped the bracelet with the small silver compass ('so you won't get lost in the wood') on to her wrist, Andrea, from the door, is already scrutinising the horizon with the old navy telescope in shiny bronze ('so you can tell us when the fishing-boats have caught a swordfish'), and Natalia is slipping the little block of pyrites on the end of a black lace around her neck.

'It's not too heavy?'

'No, it's beautiful.'

'It ought to go with the colour of your eyes.'

Natalia rewards him with a brief non-maternal glance, Andrea catches her with the telescope and signals. 'Mamma hasn't got multicoloured eyes.'

'It was a compliment, prat,' Giudi says to her brother, *sottovoce.*

'It's pyrites from Massa Marittima,' explains Monforti. 'There have been mines there since the days of the Etruscans.'

'It's splendid. But this jersey kills it, I must go straight up and put on something that will set it off. Meanwhile you go and get the champagne.'

Cautiously twisting the cork, Monforti wonders whether and when it will be right to announce that Delaude was killed. Not that he was a friend of the family, not that Natalia and the children saw his caved-in skull. But a murder implies a murderer, and nobody knows yet who this murderer is. To think of him as free, and maybe somewhere close, very close, is not the most soothing way to round off a feast-day. They will have to check that all the shutters are properly closed, and as for the big veranda with its spectacular windows . . .

'Here we are.'

Natalia makes her entrance, feeling shy at her own exhibitionism. She has finally gone for the close-fitting dark blue one, which comes up to her throat, leaving her arms bare, and on which the glistening jewel stands out: numerous tiny prisms all reflecting and interreacting.

'You're perfect,' Gabriele admires her, with a happy absence of emphasis.

'A stone like that,' says Andrea, going over to weigh it, 'can also be used as a defensive weapon, if you get a mugger on the head with it.'

'Don't be boring now, be a good boy and set the table on the veranda, it's all there on the trolley.'

'And the champagne?'

'You can both have some later.'

Natalia picks up a plate where round slices of bread with foie gras are set out, puts it on the table by the sofa, raises her glass, puts it down again as she remembers ('how silly of me') that she hasn't given him his present.

Under the scarlet paper Monforti finds a box in elegant shiny-black cardboard, with the words:

BLIND JIGSAW
500

'A blind puzzle?' asks Monforti, perplexed.

'Yes. Open it.'

Inside there is a bag with 500 pieces.

'There's no picture,' notes Monforti, examining all sides of the box and its lid.

'Exactly, it's one of those really difficult ones, without a picture. Or rather, you'll only see it when you finish.'

'I'll never manage it, but I appreciate the idea: go blindly on hoping that in the end everything will come together, will have a sense. I take it as a therapeutic present, thanks.'

'No, take it as a challenge to your superior intelligence. That was the intention.'

'I see it as an allegory of my life.'

'Of all lives, to a degree, don't you think?' says Natalia, carefully cheerful. 'You always find out what the picture was afterwards.'

They look at each other with a sort of indulgent embarrassment, each of them evaluating the as-yet unfinished, fragmentary, and cackhanded assemblage of their own picture, and at the same time imagining how it must appear to the other: a beautiful woman like that who let herself get ditched by her husband; a pleasant man like that who let himself slide into depression.

'Let's drink.'

They drink to Christmas, but actually to the chance they may still have to put together the remaining pieces, to discover the complete picture. That husband was an idiot and anyway didn't deserve Natalia; depression picks on those it wants to and doesn't last for ever.

'And I'd like to drink to Marshal Butti as well,' suggests Monforti, 'and the puzzle he's been given.'

'What?'

Will the champagne bubbles be enough to lighten the news?

'It's a murder. Delaude was killed.'

'No! Who by? Why?'

'That is the puzzle. A blind one.'

With appropriate omissions, Monforti tells her the story.

'It seemed a bit strange yesterday with three people disappearing at the same time,' Natalia remarks at the end. 'And now they find one of them, but murdered. It can't possibly be all a coincidence.'

'That's what they think too, but they hope they're wrong in spite of everything. Tomorrow the Public Prosecutor will be coming here for further enquiries.'

'What's the matter, Andrea, have you finished?'

Andrea is standing rigid at the door, his arms hanging loosely by his sides.

'Shall I light the candles?'

'Yes, go ahead and light them.'

Andrea turns round, then turns a quarter way back. 'What's the Public Prosecutor?'

Gabriele (very good at this) expatiates, explaining his technical functions and prerogatives, in order to make the conclusion as bureaucratic as possible: 'You see, from certain clues they suspect that Delaude didn't die an accidental death but was killed, and in a case like that naturally . . .'

'So that's why . . .' Andrea begins in the tone of an exploding cork.

'That's why what?'

'No, nothing, I was just saying,' Andrea hesitates; 'the Carabinieri we saw in the woods today were looking for the murderer?'

'Yes, more or less. Not that he'd still be . . .'

'Let's hope they find him.'

Indifferent to investigations and clues, he goes back to the veranda and they hear him laughing excitedly with his sister.

'Luckily they're taking it well,' says Natalia.

'Actually, they're enjoying it, it's like the television for them. You'll see, tomorrow they'll have got over their edginess. Another drop?'

'Yes, thank you.'

But from the bottom of the glass the little bubbles of anxiety and apprehension insist on rising.

'And yet, I don't know . . . I wouldn't want . . .'

Is it correct, Natalia wonders, gazing at her placid suitor's crossed legs (he has forgotten to change his corduroy trousers, which are rather worn at the knees); is it prudent to ask an apprehensive person to reassure you?

'I mean: it crossed my mind that the children might know something, might have seen something.'

'About Delaude? I'd be surprised.'

'Or the Zemes, or anyway something connected with these disappearances. They seem edgy to me, but perhaps the real problem is they're frightened.'

Monforti emits the thoughtful grunt that he has unconsciously picked up from the Marshal over the last few days, but he is fully conscious of the advantages of the procedure, when he objects reasonably: 'Listen, if they saw anything, it can't be connected directly with the murder. Delaude was killed at night, and that night they were both with you, weren't they?'

'Yes, I saw them in their beds,' laughs Natalia at herself. 'When they were small they were afraid of thunder and so even now when there's a storm ... I'm an apprehensive mother, I have to admit.'

'But it means you can provide them with an alibi for the night,' points out Gabriele. 'And in the daytime what on earth could they have seen or heard that they daren't tell?'

'Or got up to? Or found?'

Monforti thinks of the murder weapon, of some conclusive clue against the unknown murderer, and the possibility that this unknown murderer might know that Andrea and Giudi ...

'Well, keep an eye on them,' he cuts himself short.

'I'd rather not ask them any direct questions,' continues Natalia, 'because they clam up at once, like cleaning-ladies when they break a cup, you know? Oh, it must have fallen, it broke by itself, they deny the evidence.'

Monforti, aware that cleaning-ladies can arouse even more interest than an unsolved crime, does not miss the chance to change the subject, complaining about his Giovanna.

'She rarely breaks anything and keeps the house perfect, she's a tornado when it comes to cleaning. But her cooking gets worse and worse.'

'But at least you've gone one, my Tiziana's leaving me on the 15th of January. She's getting married at last.'

'Who to?'

'Guerri's brother. He's a clerk in the Council Offices, but he's also a freelance electrician. She promised me she'd talk to Mori's daughter, but she can only come three hours in the morning.'

'But didn't Milagros have a friend in Rome who was working for a director but wasn't happy there, wanted to change . . . ?'

'Yes, but from what I heard . . .'

Thus these feminine figurines gradually take over from the criminals and investigators, from the suspects and suspectors, and the pine-forest of the enigmas returns to its familiar, affectionate self, the crib recomposes itself peacefully, the day finally recovers its traditional yuletide identity.

X

This December 26th

I

THIS DECEMBER 26th, St Stephen's Day (the first Christian martyr, stoned in Jerusalem) will linger long in the collective imagination of all the Gualdana residents with any interest in the ordinary maintenance of their homes. Despite the semi-festive nature of the day, who should turn up at the crack of dawn at the porter's lodge but the plumber Grechi, currently nicknamed the Arabian Phoenix, Temperani, an extremely rare example of a blacksmith, and Ciacci the electrician, alias the Perjurer?

Those who have seen them slip through their fingers for weeks or months cannot believe their eyes. 'So I can expect you about that wretched sink?' 'You'll be along for that aerial?'

The elusive artisans make promises. Not right away, but they'll be along, they'll find some way to drop by during the morning, that's what they're here for; and they stand around the illuminated ilex-tree, smoking and chatting with the Gualdana guards. But both to respect Marshal Butti's instructions, and to get their own back on these friends whose exasperating elusiveness often has repercussions on their own lives, the guards remain fairly laconic in their replies. Was Delaude alone? Yes, alone, why? But what about that girl who was with him in the pizzeria? Never met or seen her. Is it true that Roggiolani found the body? Roggiolani isn't on duty today. But hadn't the dead man already been seriously injured in a crash with another resident? As far as they know, he might have crashed into a tree. And the widow? She'll be along sooner or later. Wonder if the roof will need checking again for that owl's nest? Maybe, maybe.

Seeing the way the wind is blowing, nobody dares to ask Roggiolani anything when he gets off his moped and approaches the little group. And besides he himself gives a mere circular wave of the hand to those present and slips straight into the lodge like a long-awaited minister. Shortly afterwards, the barriers are raised for Marshal Butti and Corporal Oliva, who also disappear without saying a word. And five minutes later the barriers admit, not (as it was reasonable to hope) the Colonel with other officers, followed perhaps by the Prefect, the Quaestor, but an ordinary civilian in an ordinary car painted an ordinary green, quite unlike the greys and blues of officialdom.

He too, after a quick glance around, enters the lodge accompanied by Vannucci. The police-doctor, perhaps. Or a registrar who is to keep the minutes of the meeting. Or another witness. Or more probably a relative, or a lawyer of the dead man's relatives.

'So who is he?' Ciacci decides to ask at last. 'A relative?'

Vannuccini contemplates a pine cone, hanging high above him, before revealing through tight lips: 'No, he's the magistrate. The Public Prosecutor in charge of the enquiries.'

This sounds solemn even to his own ears.

'He's going to have a look round,' he tones it down, 'just to get an idea of the forest.'

But Dr Veglia knows the pine-forest well, he has friends

from Siena who invite him to their beach picnics in the summer, and he would rather like (and his wife would very much like) to have a villa in a place such as this, rich but unostentatious, restful, sheltered, with both nature and all mod cons on hand. That it is also full of mysteries does not surprise him in the least; these thousands upon thousands of intertwining branches naturally suggest the idea of an immense lid, beneath which all sorts of things might be seething away.

'A porcupine, eh?'

Roggiolani nods and proceeds with his scrupulous account, which, so as to be truly worthy of a magistrate, becomes embellished with superfluous details, his own private reactions, his perplexities or inner certainties. The Marshal every so often frowns at him, but in vain, and Veglia listens to him with only half an ear. A porcupine. Suppose it should all turn out to have happened on account of a porcupine . . .

They are aroused by a screech of brakes and the forceful slam of a car door. The chairman of the condominium committee, Ingegnere Laguzzi, enters, having hurried down from Bologna. He has a rather flustered but resolute air. An efficient man, used to command and to 'taking charge' of situations; like the other six counsellors (all well-known professional men), he freely devotes part of his precious time to managing the Gualdana. He does not say a single word in memory of Delaude, calls his murder 'the event' and on his way down from Bologna (at 120 miles per hour where possible) he must have already meditated on the other unpleasant 'event' that he had heard of from the guards: the disappearance of the Zemes.

'There's no point hiding our heads in the sand,' he declares. And he makes a gesture in the direction of the beach, as if indicating a spot suitable for such ingenuous self-concealment.

'I'll say just one thing,' he goes on, 'a short while ago I stopped in the village for a coffee, and what did I see opposite the "Il Molo" bar? A van from Telepadùle! The first warning-signs!'

'But they must be there for the demonstration,' says the Marshal. 'There's going to be some sort of ecological march this morning.'

'Maybe,' concedes Laguzzi, 'but then they'll come here, there's no getting away from it. And if the story of the Zemes comes out as well,' he says crossing the index and middle finger of his right hand with the corresponding fingers of his right hand, 'they'll soon put two and two together. And then – Telepadùle will be nothing! We'll have the RAI and the big networks on our backs, at the very least, plus all the newspapers and magazines in Italy. It'll become a national case, as you can imagine, I'm sure. So without wishing to hide anything, because here there's absolutely nothing to hide, indeed, placing ourselves entirely in the Law's hands . . .'

The Prosecutor, to whom this speech is directed, nods with befitting gratitude. Full co-operation, entirely at their disposal, other guards ready to be summoned on duty (the staff is reduced in the winter) for any searches, patrols, reconnaissance-duties, etc. But everything to be kept within the pine-forest, under the thick, green protective lid.

'In my opinion we must try to keep the lid on it,' the chairman says in fact, miming a tough struggle with a seething saucepan. 'Because, first point: in this way the enquiries will be able to proceed more calmly and efficiently, without unseemly interference, distortions, exaggerations. Am I correct?'

'Perfectly correct,' approves Dr Veglia, to whom the question is directed.

But it is the second point that the chairman of this

secluded oasis really has at heart. And how can one blame him? thinks Veglia. If he himself had a villa here he would do all he could to ward off scandal, to prevent any indecorous, morbid fuss about the Delaude 'event', the Zeme 'event', and thus avoid involving all the worthy, well-off, peaceful and even famous people, who would be living around him under their common lid . . .

'Within the limits imposed by circumstances and the law, of course . . .'

'Of course.'

'. . . and with the consent of the other counsellors, whom I will undertake to contact, there is just one piece of advice I would like to give to the residents and above all the staff of the Gualdana: ears open, lips sealed!'

He lifts his hands quickly to his ears, then squeezes his lips with six fingers. A born mime-artist.

The Prosecutor stands up, nods to the Marshal. 'Fine, thank you very much, Mr Chairman,' he says, shaking his hand. 'And now we must get to work.'

He places two fingers on the table and mimes two legs walking along.

2

Let us take – thinks Monforti before opening the box of the 'pictureless' puzzle – a blank sheet of paper and let us tear it into a thousand pieces. Well, a thousand, in a manner of speaking. If the paper is, let's say, the standard A4 size, we'll make two-hundred-and-fifty pieces. *What will we have?*

He has thought these last words out loud and Giovanna, Agostino the gardener's niece, who is cleaning the glass in the drawing-room door, looks at him nervously. Was he asking her or has he started talking to himself again, something he hasn't done for ages. Maybe his sister and brother-in-law leaving like that has made him anxious again.

'I don't know,' she says. 'Were you asking me?'

'What?'

'What we'll have.'

'Oh no, sorry, I was thinking if one took a piece of paper ... Nothing, it's just a bit of nonsense.'

But not entirely, because the two-hundred-and fifty or so pieces can, if one has patience enough and time, be put together to re-create the piece of paper exactly as it was. *And then what will we see? What picture will we be faced with?*

With her rag and her spray-can, Giovanna finds it more prudent to go and clean the windows in the hall.

The picture of Nothing! thinks Monforti with satisfaction, as if this nihilistic start prefigured the solution of all the 'pictureless' puzzles possible and imaginable.

But of course, once the box has been opened and the little bag of pieces has been shaken out, one has to bear in mind the different colours. The fact that there are so many fragments of variously shaded blue might suggest a marine landscape under an intensely azure sky, all the more so since there is an equal abundance of sand-coloured pieces, and green ones (tree-tops?) run them a close third. A seaside resort, therefore, like the Gualdana?

But it could equally well be a lake in the Alto Adige (one of those that Signora Zeme never reached?) or a close-up of a swimming-pool. It all depends on the perspective. One needs to identify some object of known dimensions, such as a ...

And there it is, in a piece with an amoeba-like outline, a tiny hand sliced off at the wrist which seems to be clutching a fragment of a stick. A little man on the beach?

Or even a big man, making due allowance for different proportions. The Hermit with his old cloak? Signor Zeme? Delaude's murderer, at any rate.

3

'The villa where those two actors are staying is over there, on the right-hand side,' indicates the Marshal. 'And the girl is with them, as their guest. It must be about two hundred metres.'

The Prosecutor gives a last glance at Delaude's mangled car ('on account of a porcupine . . .'), and asks: 'Guest . . . in what sense?'

'No, no,' says Butti. 'A real guest, this time. No funny . . . They're working day and night on a new show and they're not . . .'

'I see,' Veglia stops him. And he adds: 'I can't say I'm that keen on them, but for my daughter Max & Fortini are the . . .'

He waves one hand vaguely, and the Marshal thinks: 'Two abettors conceal a young murderess'. He lets out a half-laugh as he says: 'Mind you, in person, they're amusing.'

'Quite possibly, quite possibly,' the magistrate concedes. 'Anyway I think I'll go over later. First I want to have a quick look at that other house.'

He has walked around the deserted rooms of the Delaudes' without passing comment and now he is going to do the same at the Zemes'. Cold, unadorned homes, far from desirable, but it is the season itself that makes them look all equally suspicious, with or without corpses, with or without disappearances. In the summer, enlivened by more intense light, by the colourful bustle of the residents . . .

'And the neighbours? Have you spoken to them?'

'No,' says the Marshal, 'because here, for example, we have four empty houses, and in the front row by the sea it's the same. But I thought I'd get Oliva to check up none the less. At the lodge they'll get us an exact list of who's here and who isn't.'

'Of who was here and who wasn't,' Dr Veglia says more precisely.

With its tawny fringes fluttering in the wind an Irish setter comes bounding up, having outpaced the other three by a good few yards.

'Are these the dogs?'

'Yes, and now Lotti should be along too. Do you want to talk to him?'

'No, not now,' says the Prosecutor. 'Later perhaps. He must be a strange sort, this Lotti.'

He returns to the wheel of his Fiat Tipo and following the Marshal's instructions, drives slowly, carefully, to one of the round parking spots, that give on to the coast path and the beach.

'And this must be the route Delaude took on the night of the 23rd, supposing he came on foot?'

'Yes, it's the shortest way from his house to the sea. In the summer, the guards tell me, he leaves the car here to go down to the beach to his hut.'

'And if he had come to see Zeme he would have come the same way.'

'Yes, that's the way in, around the back, so to speak.'

He precedes him along a path that runs round the ground of another villa in the front row, which is empty. He stops in front of Zeme's front door, and takes out the key.

'But if you prefer to go by way of the garage . . .'

'As you like.'

The Prosecutor walks once around the Volvo and, after glancing at the interior, bends down to check the damage from the crash: nothing serious, it would seem. But the bumper has suffered and the boot no longer closes properly.

'It was enough to spark off a row,' he says, thinking of the various cases he has dealt with over the years in which drivers have injured or even murdered one another: for such matters as precedence, a parking-place ... 'Let's go upstairs.'

In the hall he searches the pockets of the coat hanging there.

'Is this where you found the platform ticket?'

'Yes, and the bar receipt. The shop receipt was in the car, in the bag with the present for Vannuccini's son.'

A great amount, an excessive amount of furniture in the living-room. A great many, too many medicines in the bedroom and the bathroom.

'And does the wife take all this muck?'

The Marshal repeats what Monforti said about the psychotropic drugs.

'Is he a doctor?'

'No, but he knows the illness well, he's been through it himself. He came to the beach with me for the identification, when the dead man was presumed to be Zeme. He's a cultivated and intelligent person, and offered his assistance freely.'

'Did he know the Zemes, this Monforti? Has he got some idea of his own about it?'

'He knew them, and I have to say he was the first to talk about a disappearance. He came to the station to let me know informally about this broken window quite some time before . . .'

'A pessimist, then.'

'Quite, but he was right.'

'Maybe we'll hear him again tomorrow, if things haven't been cleared up by then ... And this would seem to be where the Signora prepared that famous hold-all which wasn't found in Milan.'

'Exactly.'

'Putting two and two together,' the Prosecutor sums up, considering the confused state of the room, and by analogy, that of Signora Zeme, 'God only knows where the poor woman has ended up.'

On the coast path, almost opposite Villa Zeme, the Carabinieri's car is parked, with Corporal Oliva, Vannucci and Roggiolani awaiting orders. They all walk down through the bushes until they reach one of the farthest huts, almost at the water's edge, which has been badly mauled by the storm.

'Delaude's section is this one,' says Vannucci.

Roggiolani pushes the half-hinged door open: inside, between the battered cane walls, there is nothing but a plastic coat-hanger, dangling askew on a single nail.

'Did the sea carry everything away?' asks the Prosecutor.

'No, I don't think so, the Countess always takes her stuff away at the end of the season.'

'Right . . . And is the Zemes' hut near by?'

'Not that near, a bit farther up.'

They make their way there, treading carefully over the carpet of branches, twigs, bottles and boxes, aerosol-sprays, cans, skeletons of chairs. The Zemes' section is empty too.

'They don't keep anything here, they never come here, the Signora . . .'

'Yes, I see.'

The Prosecutor walks to the water's edge. After leaving the lodge he had asked to be taken to the place where the discovery had been made, on the other side of the Old Ditch. Now, just over a mile south of the point of arrival, what they have to do is ascertain the other essential point and establish Delaude's other nocturnal route, the one he followed in the sea, when already dead. Where was the corpse most likely to have set out from?

The magistrate's eye runs along the beach as far as the breakwater blocks of the Old Ditch and, in the other direction, as far as the distant promontory of the Capriola: an imperceptibly concave stretch, fringed all the way by a dark strip of algae that seems deliberately placed there to underline the accumulation of detritus. The possibilities seem infinite.

'Well . . .' hesitates Vannucci, shaking his head. 'I don't know . . .'

The Marshal realises that today it is a matter of timidity rather than reticence, but it irritates him none the less: 'Come on, come on, out with it!' he urges.

'I don't know, maybe I misunderstood things . . .'

He understood things perfectly: if Delaude had not been dead long when he was dragged out to the open sea by the storm, his corpse should have stayed at the bottom for a few days at least, before being forced to the surface by the gases and then drifting away.

'Yes, but there's open sea and open sea,' says Vannucci, turning to Roggiolani, as if seeking confirmation. The latter agrees and points to a spot on the beach to the left, more or less in front of Villa Borst, where nothing special, however, is to be seen.

But from their explanations it would seem there is a great difference. Because from there almost as far as the Capriola the sea gets deep almost at once: at just a short distance from the beach 'you can't touch the bottom', as the warning flags indicate in the summer. Whereas on this side children and inexpert swimmers can walk out for thirty yards and more, on account of a vast platform of sand that borders the beach all the way up to the wretched camp-site at Poggiomozzo. And it is along this platform that the *libecciata* and the currrents may have rolled the dead man up to the point where he was found.

Dr Veglia looks towards the Villa Borst.

'So we just need to start from there,' he says, addressing Corporal Oliva directly.

'All right, *dottore*.'

Dr Veglia walks a little farther out and turns to consider the generously spaced villas in the front row, whose roofs can just be glimpsed through the dips in the dunes, the bushes and the twisted pinasters. He asks whom they belong to and whether they are lived in at this time of year.

The one right opposite is known as the 'Dutch villa', they explain, because it belongs to some Dutch people who in fact never come, and who apparently want to sell it now. A little farther on, there's Signora Borst's, and in this direction the Zemes'. Then, continuing towards the Old Ditch, there's the architect Raimondi's, who was supposed to come but didn't. Then beyond that a whole lot more, all empty, then Signora Melis, who arrived this morning . . . Then . . .

'Which means,' says the Prosecutor, addressing Corporal Oliva and the guards directly, 'all you need do is start looking from here, more or less.'

The laborious search is for the murder weapon (bar, hoe, or whatever it might be), which may have been left at the scene of the crime. And by pointing out the differences between 'open sea and open sea', Vannucci has managed to spare them all a good deal of trouble. Otherwise, they would have had to begin practically from the Capriola.

But the real trouble, as Dr Veglia and Marshal Butti both think without saying so on the way back to the coast path, is the thought that all this may get them nowhere, that Delaude may have been killed somewhere else in the Gualdana, either in a house or in the open air, and then have been carried to the beach, where all traces were wiped away by the sea.

'And now,' says the Prosecutor, 'a comic interlude.'

A magistrate and a top model meet in a pine-forest, thinks the Marshal, swallowing a smile. He wouldn't mind witnessing this, but the magistrate decides otherwise.

'I'll have a chat with the girl, you go back to the village to your environmentalists. And when you have a moment, I'd suggest having a word with that wandering philosopher. If somebody saw him, he might have seen somebody or something with his lantern, on the night in question.'

The man in civilian clothes goes towards his Fiat Tipo parked in the lay-by. The man in uniform starts towards his Uno parked on the coast path. Not a single one of their movements has escaped the eyes of Special Agent Andrea Neri, who has had them under observation for some time now, with his powerful telescope.

To tell the truth, Agent Neri started the morning off as a world-champion cross-country cyclist on the Gualdana circuit, and it was only later, when he climbed on to the roof of the Raimondis' empty villa, that nostalgia for the daydreams of his infancy induced him to become an awesome cross between a pirate chief and a bosun of the *Viktor Hansen*, a smuggler's tramp-ship drifting in these treacherous waters.

Having pulled the telescope out to its full length, he began to scrutinise the isles of the Tuscan archipelago one by one: Elba, Montecristo, Giglio, Capraia, and, there on the horizon, a fretted line that an inexpert eye might interpret as clouds but which is in fact Corsica.

When the investigators arrived, the new Special Agent observed their clumsy manouevres with some disdain. How ridiculous to go looking for footprints on a beach that the storm had turned upside-down and strewn with jetsam. The murder weapon? It isn't that hard to deduce that the murderer will have hurled it out to sea and so what they really ought to do is search the sea bottom, entrusting the task to a skilled diver – which, it just so happens, they have on hand in the person of Special Agent A. N.

The Public Prosecutor (since that is who the man in civilian clothes must be) gets back into his car to continue his inept enquiries somewhere else. The Carabiniere is preparing to do the same thing himself, when an individual of medium height comes up behind him, wearing a green anorak and a checked cap, whom A. N.'s trained eyes easily identify as the Hon. Bonanno.

There is a part of the roof, reached by an external concrete staircase, that is used as a solarium or dance-floor for silly summer parties, and A. N. at once conceals himself behind the parapet that surrounds this area, without, however, taking his eye from the telescope.

It is difficult to tell where the *Onorevole* emerged from exactly, but the meeting does not seem to be a chance one. Prearranged? Not on the Marshal's part, since his expression, while respectful enough, is not particularly enthusiastic. So it is the other man who has come looking for him.

And it is in fact the other man who is doing the talking, and the sharp-eyed agent has never so strongly regretted not having learnt to lip-read. He talks emphatically and at length, with wide demonstrative gestures towards the overhanging pine fronds, and the officer listens with his head bowed, absorbed. It is clear that he is receiving information of particular importance.

He then speaks, briefly, formulating an indecipherable question which unstops a new gush of words and further gesticulations towards the treetops on the part of the heated *Onorevole*, who in his excitement even removes his cap. As a mark of respect, no doubt, the Carabiniere takes his own off, studies it, passes one hand over his hair and raises his eyes towards the top of the pine-trees. But his expression remains reserved, serious, when he speaks again. I will obey, he is clearly saying. I will do what is asked of me by a Member of Parliament elected by the Italian people. I will get to the bottom of this business, leaving no stone unturned. The other man listens to him with an expression that starts off as highly attentive, then gradually becomes more gratified, and is accompanied by lively nods of agreement. And when the Carabiniere looks at his watch, salutes him in military style and gets into his car, the *Onorevole* remains standing there, with his nose in the air and a meaningful smile of triumph on his face.

Andrea knows enough to close his telescope quickly, slide along behind the parapet to the concrete staircase, at the foot of which his faithful '*montapicchi*' awaits him, a present from a distant father, beyond Corsica.

4

After prolonged observation of jigsaw-pieces, the observer's eye (due to the phenomenon whereby images or pictures persist, even when the jigsaw in question is 'pictureless') can find itself projecting on to the surrounding world those snippeted shapes with their whimsical outlines: looping, gibbous, concave forms, cuneiform appendices, amoeboid flexures, all intended to dovetail with other segments, correspondingly fretted. Thus, for a while, it can seem as if the whole world is made to be cut up, dismounted and reassembled at pleasure.

Such was Monforti's psycho-physical state when, a short while ago, he raised his eyes and listened to Giovanna's warning pronouncement: there was no table salt or sugar in the kitchen, and they were almost out of coffee. The snippet of her face shone with a vindicatory air, dovetailing almost perfectly with the snippet of Signora Sandra, always so ready to object and criticise but then perfectly capable of leaving her brother without even the basic necessities of life.

Setting forth from the forest to remedy the situation, Monforti continued despite himself to snip the world into pieces: in the frame of the windscreen a fragment of Milagros (half a red boot) appeared, dovetailing with a fragment of Mongelli's bicycle (left pedal), waiting by the side of the road; then, in front of the lodge, a fragment of *Ingegnere* Laguzzi (one folded arm and wrist) and of Vannuccini (sloping shoulders on a trapezoid snippet).

When he reaches the village, the mild obsession persists, affecting objects of all dimensions: the grey castle on top of the hill, cut up into five thousand pieces, would take months of work to put back together; but the jar of coffee, split up into fifty shards, would be no joke either. Whereas a snippet of dark material with a shiny button can be easily clicked into place with the other ten thousand fragments that go together to make up the full picture of Marshal Butti.

'Giovanna sent me, we've run out of a few things,' Monforti confides at the entrance to the minimarket in Piazza Garibaldi. 'She looks after me wonderfully, looks after my every need – except my need to eat something decent.'

Butti shares his feelings with a deprecatory 'Eh . . .' which he then repeats in another context, when Monforti asks him what news there is. There is none, the Prosecutor's visit to the Gualdana has borne no fruit so far ('So you see, Marshal, nothing escaped our eyes, after all!' 'Eh, but nothing is still nothing'), unless one should choose to take the Hon. Bonanno and his theory seriously.

'About the crime?'

'About the crime.'

A theory with no basis in fact at all, and the Marshal's first thought was to brush it off as one of the many odd ideas that spring up around every case of murder that presents any sort of complexity (not to say 'mystery') at all. But he then reflected that for the purposes of warding off the media until the desired solution was attained, there was nothing better than to let a politician speak.

'The theory is crazy,' he says, 'but the good thing about it is that it makes no mention at all of the Zeme business. And so I suggested he should expound his hypothesis on television directly, go and get an interview with those people there.'

'Those people there' are the Telepadùle (i.e. Tele-bog) van, parked askew outside Righi's, the butcher's.

Monforti feels a moment of pity for the poor politician, who will undoubtedly cover himself with ridicule with his ridiculous theory, whatever it is. But he corrects himself: it will be a just punishment for the man – it must not be forgotten – who blighted the Gualdana with a hedge of sixty incongruous thujas (Mazzeschi himself, the nurseryman, was indignant as he laid them out). And he expresses amused perplexity on another point to the Marshal: 'But you're misleading the public, my dear Butti. This is pure misinformation.'

The Marshal lets out a snort of laughter, at once correcting it into a cough. 'And what's wrong with that? For them it's a scoop, Bonanno gets himself talked about for a while, we get left alone for twenty-four hours at least, and so we can spend a nice evening watching the interview on television. In fact, why don't you come and have dinner and we'll watch it together? My mother will feed you better than your Giovanna, I can guarantee that.'

Monforti accepts the informal invitation with informal cheerfulness, instantaneously reassembling the fragments of various bottles of Brunello di Montalcino he has in his house, which he can present to Signora Butti.

'Have they come just to hear Bonanno?' he asks, indicating the van.

'No, they're here for the Friends of the Ozone Layer, in Piazza del Municipio. Come and see for yourself.'

They enter the narrow alleyway that opens behind the newspaper-stand (which is closed) and make their way down to the piazza, where the demonstration is being held under the imperturbable eye of Sergeant Farinelli. The association of 'Friends of the Ozone Layer' does not yet have a real branch of its own in the village. It was founded in Livorno three years ago by a primary-school teacher and is spreading throughout Tuscany 'like wild-fire', as its supporters like to say.

Here in Piazza Grande, the 'friends' form a little group of about thirty people, some of them locals, and the rest from villages and hamlets near by, all with their blue flags and banners. 'We want to breathe', 'Save the planet', 'Ozone = Life'. They are gathered around a diesel lorry, which is parked under one of the four plane-trees and is being used as a podium, on the side by the town hall. Of course the town hall itself, where a delegation of ozonists would have liked to meet the mayor, is closed today, but Farinelli has none the less set himself in the doorway, with arms stiffly folded, as if defending the Bastille singlehanded. But the mood of the little crowd is not threatening, the terror that is being announced here is a fairly long-term one.

From up on the platform, an old man with a blue handkerchief around his head, apache-style, has just finished speaking and he receives scattered applause. A woman of about fifty now pulls herself on to the lorry, with a huge blue bubble stuck or painted on her forehead.

'Is ozone blue?' asks the Marshal.

'God knows.'

The woman (maybe the founder in person) has an incredible number of blood-curdling facts at her fingertips, and she begins to recount them into the microphone 'before it is too late'. Very soon such words as 'ethicality', 'full awareness', 'common heritage', 'humanity', begin to float up towards the ozone layer, and Monforti's attention drifts, he follows the swooping of two seagulls over the port, the manoeuvres of the cameraman of 'Telepadùle-News' around the group of demonstrators.

It is thus that he notes Fioravanti and Baldacci.

'Those two, that woman on the bench . . . ?'

The Marshal nods.

It is Signora Baldacci, the adulteress herself, sitting on one of the four stone benches arranged around the fountain between the plane-trees. She is sitting hunched up, with her hands clasped; it is hard to tell whether she is downcast or irritated, and her forehead is bare – without, that is, the blue circle (in recycled paper) that almost all the other women are flaunting. Fioravanti, a yard or so away, is leaning up against one of the trees; after rummaging in his pockets he at last finds his cigarettes and sticks one into his blond beard; but then, maybe out of respect towards his friend the ozone layer, puts it away furtively. He has nothing blue on him either.

'It has been calculated that by the year 2005, on account of the melting of the ice-caps, the level of the sea . . .' the orator is saying into the capricious microphone.

And the television camera does not miss a single word of these scientific prophecies.

Father Everardo and Ugo the Hermit, who now emerge from the direction of the port, each pushing his own two-wheeled vehicle by hand, have missed quite a few. The Hermit came down to the village to pick up the stale bread that Spini, the baker, always puts aside for him (since he only uses part of it for his hens), then dropped in at the monastery to say hello, receiving a gift of a jar of stewed blackberries, originally given to the priest by Marshal Butti's mother. The two men then had a friendly chat about the blessed comb-seller, each remaining firm in his own conviction. Hermitage not as proud isolation, according to the Capuchin, but as meditation, the fruits of which, in the form of humble preventive warnings, must then be redistributed among men wherever necessary. Which means everywhere, in the Hermit's opinion. But a hermit who goes wandering around with a warning-sign like a traffic-policeman is a hermit who loves his neighbours, so why should he have become a hermit in the first place?

They stop at the edge of the piazza, without knowing exactly what to say or do, each doubtful about the other's feelings on the question of the ozone layer; and so for a few minutes they both remain silent, looking and listening.

'Not many people,' the Hermit remarks at last.

'But that doesn't mean anything,' replies Father Everardo, thinking of the twelve Apostles.

'All the lands cultivated north of the 25th parallel will be . . .' foretells the woman on the podium.

'Save an entire planet!' says the Hermit. 'I don't think there's ever been such an absolute ambition in history.'

'But there's never been such absolute folly,' returns the priest.

'75 per cent of the equatorial flora . . .'

'But on the whole,' the Hermit says, declaring himself, 'I'd go along with the position of the Cyrenian Egesias. He wouldn't have supported the ozone layer, but rather the hole in the ozone layer: enlarging it, increasing it to the utmost, humbly helping it out day by day.'

'Millenaristic suicide,' says the priest compassionately. 'Somewhat primitive, apart from anything else.'

'Tens upon millions of Europeans will be forced . . .' continues the orator.

'But given that the planet is what it is,' the Hermit says, warming to his theme, 'and given that we didn't come here of our own will, we would at least have the satisfaction of doing away with it ourselves, without waiting for stellar catastrophes or other such interventions from on high. Like saying: "To hell with it!"'

Father Everardo turns and gazes at him with a smile that truly antagonises the Hermit. 'Ah,' says the admonisher, 'pride, ever the pride of Lucifer.'

'The truth is,' the follower of Egesias now exaggerates, 'I couldn't really give a damn about the human race, whether taken *en masse* or prat by prat.'

'Don't say that,' the Capuchin entreats him sorrowfully, 'you are a good man and a sensitive one, maybe even too sensitive, forcing yourself to . . .'

'And don't you,' the Hermit says, losing his temper, 'give me this priestly crap.'

But he blushes at his facile rebuttal and, seeing his opponent remount his scooter sadly, he suggests they should meet up at Signora Borst's at tea-time, where they will be able to continue the discussion more calmly. But Father Everardo will not be going to Signora Borst's, his 'Maremman' sermon at midnight mass was much appreciated by the Signori of the Rocca, and they are taking him to the Argentario for a sort of 're-run' in the villa of a friend of theirs, a 'well-known lady senator'.

A worthy man, thinks the Hermit, a man of good qualities, and yet so ingenuously flattered by what is merely a patronising summons. He is wondering how he himself, with his Cynic's severity, would react to the same summons when a voice by his side says: 'Might I have a word, *professore*?'

It is the summons, anything but patronising, of the Marshal of Carabinieri.

When Butti leaves him to go and question de Meis 'informally' about his nocturnal movements in the Gualdana,

Monforti makes his way back up to Piazza Garibaldi where he has left his car. But he is not the only one whose friendship for the ozone layer has cooled off. Influenced perhaps by the famines and sufferings impending over mankind, Signora Baldacci must have slipped furtively away from the demonstration to call on Spini.

Monforti sees her come out of the baker's and walk distractedly the few yards that separate the shop from the butcher's. Righi is standing at the door, thin and bespectacled, like a schoolmaster at an old-fashioned college. They exchange a few words, probably about the sun and the weather, then go into the shop together.

Something twitches at the corner of Monforti's mind. Should he go in too? Has he forgotten some request of Giovanna's? A steak? Ham?

But nothing takes shape in his mind, no fragment clicks into place, and Monforti goes off with his salt and his coffee thinking of the excellent dinner awaiting him tonight.

5

After washing the dishes, Katia is tidying up the kitchen and is already thinking what she will prepare tonight, when there is a knock at the kitchen window. It is Milagros, who has not rung at the door for fear the comedians might be resting.

'Resting? It's quite a surprise if they sleep at night, let alone during the day! In the daytime, as soon as they've finished eating, they rush straight off to the funny-factory to make up stories that just about kill you,' explains Katia proudly, elated at having heard of the 'funny-factory' from their own lips.

Anyway, Milagros explains, her mistresses didn't want to

disturb them by phoning, so they sent her to ask Max & Fortini whether they would all three like to drop in for tea, this afternoon.

'Me too?' asks Katia, shyly.

Poor Gimo really did bring her to paradise. With all that's happened, she's never been treated so kindly as in this pine-forest. After that visit from the really clever Marshal, not to mention Max & Fortini who spent a whole hour consoling her, even the magistrate who came from Grosseto, this morning, treated her like a daughter. And now to cap it all, two ladies who really are ladies such as Signora Borst and her friend invite her to tea!

'Of course!' says Milagros. 'We're all just one big happy family here!'

Only that if Gimo really was killed, thinks Katia, someone must have done it, mustn't they?

Unknown to Katia (who in any case is no longer interested in these seedy little provincial networks) a Telepadùle van has turned up at the barriers and is asking permission to enter. The Hon. Bonanno is said to have given his consent.

Consent to what, what are they there for? Barabesi and Guerri want to know.

The driver, who is also the operator, says impatiently that they're there for an exclusive interview about the murder: 'Telepadùle-News' was promised it by the *Onorevole* in person over the phone.

The lodge has not been informed, replies Guerri. And in any case, Barabesi points out, they surely don't think they can go wandering all over the Gualdana with their cameras? The rules of the residents' association expressly forbid . . .

They needn't worry about that, the interview is to be held in his house, says the director-cum-interviewer, Meniconi, in conciliatory fashion, and apart from that they'll make do with a couple of shots of the entrance here or the beach, in front of one of the villas in the front row.

No beach, no front row. Only Bonanno's villa and grounds, if it really is true that the *Onorevole* has promised this interview, which they really can't see the point of, since what can he possibly know about . . .

He has a theory, Meniconi tells them, which the news-editors found highly interesting and which cannot be revealed yet, but which all viewers of Telepadùle will hear from the *Onorevole*'s own lips after 'The case of the distracted typist', during the Tp-News at . . .

'What are you waiting for?' shouts the Member of Parliament, from a distance, as he approaches on foot. 'Why's it taken you so long? There won't be any light soon.'

The director explains that they were held up by the piece on the ozone layer, while the operator jumps down quickly and, without Barabesi or Guerri daring to offer any further protests, sets the camera up right in front of the entrance.

If the *Onorevole* would like to stand here, behind the lowered barriers, suggests Meniconi, in a thoughtful attitude, leaning on the barriers themselves? It would be an excellent opening shot, especially if he were to twirl a pine cone in his hands reflectively. Then as an amusing, witty effect he could climb into the van and sit at the wheel as if he were a reporter for 'Tp-News'. That would be an excellent . . . No?

No, Bonanno says firmly. It would hardly be dignified. That is to say, the barriers and the reflective attitude with the pine cone are fine, it would be a suitable act of symbolism after all. But sitting at the wheel of the van would be somewhat exhibitionistic, it would look as if . . .

'OK, forget I said it,' Meniconi withdraws at once jovially. 'So one pine cone if possible,' he asks the guards. 'Yes, this one's fine, thank you. But the barriers, let's keep one down and the other one halfway up. Like that, fine. And, *Onorevole*, if you could lean here. That's it. Perfect. Only showing the pine cone a little more clearly and with your elbows a little wider apart. Great.'

6

It is not out of petty curiosity that Wilhelmine Borst and her friend Eladia, after the encounter last night at mass, have invited Max & Fortini with their young 'au pair' along. The two comedians have always been welcome guests at the Borst house, and the girl seemed pleasant, of good character. She now reveals herself to be on the ball, at once helping Milagros as she bustles back and forth between the kitchen and the living-room, as if it were not a matter of tea with a few friends but a dinner party for thirty people.

'A slice of cake, Signor Ugo? . . . Some more tea, Signora Neri? . . . Signora Graham?'

She is perfectly aware of her anomalous situation; by now she must be known to everyone in the forest, and she has chosen the most intelligent way to avoid all embarrassment.

But the awkwardness remains. How can they refrain from openly asking the questions in everybody's mind?

Eladia would of course have the excuse of the Tarot cards. After all, just three days ago, when there was nothing to foreshadow the tragic death of one resident and the mysterious disappearance of two others, she warned that an enigmatic catastrophe was impending. But it is her religious, fatalistic faith in the cards that prevents her from referring to them or making tactless boasts.

Monforti thinks back to his puzzle, in which he has made no progress whatsoever, and tries by use of imagination to compose a picture for this other puzzle: a picture which might somehow contain this Katia girl and Orfeo, with or without a hoe, as well as the adulterous Friends of the Ozone Layer, Bonanno's freak rats, the Hermit, who, instead of returning to his hill the other night, is said to have . . .

But it is the Hermit himself who now turns to the subject in his own fashion. '*Rafel*,' he shouts, '*mai amech zabi almi!* . . . What, friends, do these obscure words mean?'

Katia and Milagros look at each other, disconcerted; nobody replies. Then Signora Graham, who spends all her time studying Italian, raises one finger: 'Nobody can say,' she informs them. 'Dante, in Canto XXXI of the *Inferno*, offers them as an example of an indecipherable glottological enigma. It is no accident that the giant who utters them is that same Nembrotto who raised the tower of Babel and thus created the confusion of languages.'

Everyone compliments Colin's mother on her gifts as an Italian scholar, but they all wait to see what the relevance of this other mystery is.

'Rafel and Mai Amech,' suggests Max, 'meet in hell and one says to the other: *Zabi almi*.'

'It's not funny!' Milagros laughs, having heard from Katia about Fortini's outbursts.

'No, but it corresponds to the obscurity of events,' says the Hermit. 'Signorina Eladia was quite right when she said that strange things would happen. And the first happened to me, that night, around one, when I thought I had arrived home but no: according to Orfeo I was still here, on the Grand-Duke's Bridge. The Marshal of the Carabinieri told me so. Can you get more obscure than that?'

Amidst the exclamations of surprise from all sides, Monforti recalls the poisonous glance that Orfeo had darted towards the Hermit and himself on his way out of church, while Everardo delivered his sermon on the Comb-Seller. Could it be that . . .

'And on the other hand,' continues de Meis, alias Ugo of Borgomanero, alias Cratès of Thebes known as the Door-Opener, 'where does Dante place, figuratively speaking, the towering Giants of Canto XXXI?'

'In Monteriggioni,' Signora Graham immediately replies. 'He says in fact that their gigantic figures crown the bank of the infernal pit just as

Monteriggion is crowned with towers.

And thus his guide promptly informs him:

Know that they are not towers, but giants.'

More compliments for the Italian scholar, who, since she is also a Spanish scholar in her spare time, observes that in her opinion Don Quixote's adventure with the windmills derives from this same Canto in Dante. With the difference that Sancho warns his imaginative master against making the reverse mistake: 'Take note, Sire,' he says in fact, 'that they are not giants, but windmills.'

Max attempts another joke on two windmills who meet up at Punta Ala, but a muttered warning from Fortini freezes him.

The Hermit comes to the point at last.

It was Father Everardo, he says, with his Dantean references to the Maremma, who set him thinking of the indecipherable enigma of 'zabi almi': the deranged Sapia, later redeemed by the Comb-Seller, was banished to Castiglione Alto, a couple of miles from Monteriggioni (the lord of which was Ghinibaldo Saracini), with its circle of towers. And this has led him to formulate his own theory on the Gualdana murder.

During the pause for effect that follows, Monforti's eyes

meet Signora Neri's. Oh dear me, they say to each other with anticipatory irony. But Monforti also thinks of the yet-to-be-divulged theory of that fool Bonanno (him and his thujas!), and this disposes him to indulgence. Without forgetting that Monteriggioni . . . When did they talk about this turreted town, which is *en route* for those travelling from the Gualdana to Florence or vice-versa? The Marshal had mentioned it the previous day, with jocular optimism, suggesting that the Zemes might both be there, having a good time. And before that . . . but when? He had also said . . . what?

'You're not trying to tell us, Signor Ugo,' Signora Graham has asked in the meantime, 'that Count Delaude was killed by a giant?'

'No, by an animal,' he says to the amazement of everybody and in particular of Monforti, who has remembered at that moment what it was that the Marshal had said.

But in a way it's the same thing, continues de Meis. Because according to Dante the giants – those of the Bible as well as Greek mythology – were actually animals: but prehistoric animals, fortunately now extinct, since their animal nature (which was why they did not speak, except for the incomprehensible Nembrotto) and their immense stature (about twenty metres) were matched only by their dangerous cunning. Which is why the poet praises nature for having ceased to create them:

Natura certo, quando lasciò l'arte
di siffatti animali, assai fe' bene!

But Signora Neri has had enough of this mockery.

'Listen, Ugo,' she says, 'I can't understand how you can joke about that poor man's death. Taking one mystery with another, I prefer to think that it was an accident after all.'

'But so do I,' the Hermit defends himself.

Let us remember, he says, that night when Signor Lopez was gored by a boar; suppose that Eladia and Signora Borst had not arrived before he died, what would the Carabinieri have thought when finding the body the next day?

'*Mammeglio*!' shouts Milagros, meaning 'but of course,' 'exactly'. 'They would have said: "this chappy here, he was killed by Orfeo with his pitchfork".'

'Or by somebody else with something else,' says the Hermit, 'but anyway someone would have got dragged into it. Whereas with the animal theory, there's no risk of doing anyone an injustice.'

Signora Neri and Monforti exchange a contrite glance. They had done poor Ugo an injustice, attributing to him some stupid joke, and associating him with the fanciful Bonanno. His 'theory', in fact, is simply an imaginative fable, urging prudence.

But Eladia does not take it as such.

She too, she says, has wondered about an animal. But what sort? There are many animals, usually harmless, that can become dangerous when the Magician is in the House of the *Enemies*.

The porcupine then! says Katia. Or the barn-owl. Can barn-owls be dangerous?

Not particularly, but if one isn't careful the really large sort of owl can be, says Signor Mongelli, who is an assiduous reader of the magazine *Natura*. And besides who knows how many 'synanthropic' animals might be concealed in the wood?

Lotti's dogs, suggests Fortini lugubriously, while Max expresses himself in favour of the Abominable Snowman.

No, explains Mongelli, by 'synanthropic animals' he means those ones which, while not actually domestic, are not completely wild either, being accustomed to share the same habitat as man. Such as the local tortoises, that trudge around quite calmly between the houses; or the squirrels and the more retiring 'big-moles', which came down exceptionally to nose around Bonanno's house; or the porcupine and the powerful badger, another nocturnal animal; not to mention the birds of all sorts and sizes that make their nests on house roofs, in steeples, towers . . .

'The Tower has ended up in the House of *Sickness*,' murmurs Eladia, 'which means that something has collapsed or someone has fallen. The only good thing in all this is that the Lover has passed into the House of the *Children*.'

Monforti feels himself blushing ridiculously; he doesn't know where to look, he would like to collapse and sink along with the Tower, while an embarrassed silence tells him that Eladia's gaffe (or her spinsterly, matchmaking encouragement?) has fallen on attentive ears.

The Hermit bails him out fraternally, remarking that with all these confused clues there is a risk of just getting totally bewildered.

'What is needed here is the *lectus lucubratorius*,' he says, and this arouses sufficient curiosity to distract all malignant attention from the Lover and the Queen of Wands, alias the beautiful Signora Neri, on whose lips Monforti, raising his eyes, sees that a smile – by no means a sorry one – is hovering.

The *lectus lucubratorius*, explains the Hermit, was a kind of hemp or rather *dormeuse*, but it did not help one to sleep but rather to *lucubrare* – stay awake, meditating. The scholar Varrone, the learned empress Julia Domna and even Seneca the philosopher, although a follower of stoicism, all kept one in their studies. Marcus Aurelius Antoninus, who as a true Stoic actually slept on the ground, had a horror of it. To think the desolate thoughts that he transcribed in his *Meditations*, he preferred to wander at night around his misty encampments on the Danube.

'Marcus Aurelius and a legionary sentinel meet on the Danube,' suggests Max, 'and one says to the other . . .'

'What is love? A simple emission of mucus,' says the Hermit.

It takes everyone a moment to realise that this is a disconsolate idea of Marcus Aurelius' and not a cynical joke of de Meis's, but Fortini definitely approves: this is the goods, this really *is* funny.

Mongelli agrees.

Signora Graham, Signora Neri and Milagros on the other hand express their revulsion, while Katia maintains a puzzled silence.

'Everything depends on the controlling card,' says Eladia impartially. 'When the controlling card is Swords, there could be something in the idea.'

'But what are swords? Mere shovels, after all,' observes Signora Graham, playing on the English meaning of the Italian word for swords, which is *spade*.

So this means everything happened under the sign of the hoe or shovel? Monforti wonders in amazement, moving over to the astromantic wheel and gazing at the Fool who smiles cynically at him from the House of the *Wife*. But whose wife?

But it is no good, he thinks, a lucubratory bed really is needed here; unless one chooses to lie on the ground or wander around the rarely misty villas of the Gualdana by night.

7

The procedure Signora Butti adopts is the following: home-made pasta separated into rolls the size of a little finger, then further reduced into little pieces the length of a finger-joint, which when plunged into boiling oil for a few seconds (how many? this is where intuition, the cook's eye or personal genius come into play) turn into those rustic delights known here as 'bighelloni'.

But the bighelloni, which Monforti helps himself to liberally, burning his fingers in the process, are there merely to while away the time until dinner, and their simple, not to say primitive, nature means that they cannot possibly be coupled with the vintage Brunello that Signor Monforti has so kindly brought with him. A less illustrious local wine is therefore served to the two men, as they sit in two armchairs facing the 26-inch television across a round table.

It is twenty-five past seven and Telepadùle's advertisements are following one another across the screen: a furniture shop, a gymnasium with indoor swimming-pool, a palmist, a shop selling wedding-dresses, another furniture shop . . . The Marshal has turned the sound down but he is holding the remote control, ready to flick it back up.

'I spent half the afternoon listening to theories,' says Monforti, once he has finished munching his last bighellone.

'Interesting?'

'Yes, but somewhat complicated . . .'

His hand reaches out by itself towards the plate, takes another bighellone between two fingers.

'*Mai amech zabi almi.*'

'Sorry?'

The bighellone disappears.

'It's an enigma without a solution. A Dantean enigma.'

'Ah, Dante . . .' says Butti, in a tone between deferential and nostalgic, pouring some wine into Monforti's glass.

Evocative sounds and aromas waft in from the kitchen where Signora Butti is hard at work. The table is laid in here, under the light hanging from the centre of the ceiling above the uncorked bottle of Brunello. As a mark of respect for his guest, the Marshal is still in uniform; on arrival, he merely took off his leggings in order to be able to put on his long trousers, which have gradually inched their way to an outstretched position across the 'oriental' carpet.

Carpets of similar origin flicker across the television-screen, followed by cars, leather garments and the window of a perfume shop in Ribolla.

'Ah, about time!' says Butti, pressing the button.

There is a sudden deafening roar around the room, but his finger at once reduces it to a tinny jingle, introducing 'Telepadùle-News'.

'And now our evening news, at seven-thirty,' announces a girl, whose appearance suggests a bun fresh from a visit to the hairdresser's.

Bevies of old men appear, displaying venerable smiles behind huge slices of panettone: it is the Christmas lunch offered by the local council, whose chairman longwindedly explains the charitable initiative. Modulating her voice to a register of sentimental festivity, the bun then passes on to present a group of handicapped children: the bishop wanders through their midst, caressing them, while his lay helpers distribute Christmas toys. Her voice becomes jovial when the Friends of the Ozone Layer appear on the screen. Although there is little of the yuletide spirit in their catastrophic forecasts (which in fact are omitted) the camera presents the demonstration as a kind of cheery gathering, all in the name of the sky, of universal solidarity and a better future for our children. A picture of Fioravanti's blond beard. A cruel close-up of Signora Baldacci. A weary face – thinks Monforti between one bighellone and another – a battered, defeated face. Maybe her lover has tired of her. Maybe the atmosphere at home is beginning to weigh on her, unless it is the Florentine leghorns that are going badly

. . . Or could it be a question of rape? Perhaps despite her refusals, Orfeo, small but brawny, threw her on to the bed and . . .

For the brutal murder in the Gualdana, the lively bun is substituted by a baritone announcer. Has anything new come up in the enquiries? Not officially. There is a shot of the Carabiniere station with Sergeant Farinelli appearing at the door and at once going back in. The sudden switch to two hands holding a pine cone is dramatic.

The Telepadùle-News team, reveals the announcer, have managed to enter the forest where the crime took place and have obtained an exclusive interview with one of the VIPs who resides there. The VIP makes his appearance, leaning on one of the barriers to the Gualdana: the hands with the pine cone are those of the *Onorevole* Giampaolo Bonanno, an influential member of the Commission for Agriculture and Forestry.

Another scene change, and there is a long-shot of the VIP in front of his villa, he walks slowly towards a thuja-hedge, stops, turns half-length and the interviewer hands him a spongy yellow microphone. Yes, he knew the victim, but only superficially. No, he has nothing to say about him, and in any case believes that the cause of Delaude's death is in no way connected with his private life.

But how has the *Onorevole* reached such an astonishing conclusion?

'I am not a policeman,' Bonanno states by way of premise, 'and I have every confidence in the work of the investigators, and of course fully recognise their right to follow up other hypotheses, to seek in other directions.'

'Good of him,' mutters the Marshal.

'I am not a doctor,' the politician states by way of premise again, 'and I have the utmost respect for the pathologist who carried out the autopsy, on the basis of which it was decided that what we are faced with is a case of murder.'

What then is your hypothesis? the interviewer prods him, fearing further premises.

'My modest hypothesis,' the *Onorevole* begins, with confident strokes, at last swimming in friendly waters, 'derives from my modest competence in the field of agriculture, and also from the fact that here, in this pine-forest, I have my *buen retiro*, where, like Cicero, I come to retire whenever I feel the need to abandon the *Urbe* in order to breathe a little fresh air and devote myself to my reading, to my . . .'

'The Hon. Bonanno,' the interviewer cuts in hastily, 'is a keen classical scholar, and it is in fact from a classical writer, Lamanna, a noted mathematician of the eighteenth century . . .'

'Alamanni, Luigi A-la-man-ni,' the scholar pronounces good-humouredly, 'and he wasn't a mathematician but a didactic poet of the sixteenth century, when it was the custom . . .'

'And so in a book by this poet . . . ?'

'Yes, in book III of the poem *Field-Farming*, which is a hymn to what Alamanni called 'The Invincible Hoer', and what today, more prosaically, but with equal respect and admiration, we call the owner-occupier farmer.'

'Quite right. But what did you find in this poem?'

Bonanno smiles as he rummages in a pocket of his country-casual anorak. His smile contracts when he passes to a second and then a third pocket. It broadens once again at the fourth. His hand is holding a sheet of paper.

'I found,' he says, 'these highly significant lines.'

And he proceeds to read them.

'Here the lofty Pine . . .'

But his dry throat impedes him, he is forced to swallow and to start, in more stentorian fashion, from the beginning:

'Here the lofty Pine darts to earth
Its hardest of fruits, to the risk
Of whoever lingers by

'Its hardest of fruits!' the interviewer shouts excitedly.

'Yes,' confirms Bonanno, 'which if flung, so to speak, from a lofty pine-tree, could quite reasonably . . .'

The camera tracks up the trunk of a lofty pine-tree, and zooms in on a pine-cone dangling murderously from the top.

'*Onorevole*, but this means you've found the murder-weapon!'

'Exactly. But at this point it is no longer a case of murder, but . . .'

'Marshal,' says Monforti, 'you have just committed a political assassination.'

Butti raises his shoulders and laughs. '*Mammeglio!*' he limits himself to saying, with the meaning, 'it takes more than a pine cone like this to bury a politician.'

And now the politician, without wishing to interfere in the enquiries under way, suggests that the case should be re-examined from this new angle. The interviewer approves, pine cones are notoriously dangerous, despite the proverb that says they have eyes, and it is quite possible that Delaude, struck on the head by a large, compact pine cone as he walked underneath . . .

'Now here comes the link with the *libecciata*,' says Butti, 'which began two hours later.'

'And let us not forget the *libeccio* of that night, which multiplied the speed of the missile, so to speak. And in this case, I wonder whether it might not be wise to seek an opinion from a ballistics expert . . .'

The *Onorevole* removes his cap, offering, as it were, his head to the enemy.

'Now,' he continues, 'if the wound was not immediately fatal, one can surmise that Delaude, stunned, half-conscious, without knowing what he was doing, dragged himself with his last reserves of strength to the beach, where subsequently . . . I repeat, I am not a doctor, but in my opinion, a re-examination of the wound from this point of view . . .'

'Dinner's ready!' orders the Marshal's mother, appearing at the door with a steaming soup tureen.

The two men sit down opposite each other, they are served, they grind pepper on to the pasta and chick-peas, keeping one eye and ear on the politician.

'Hey-eh . . .' Butti suddenly says, lowering his spoon in alarm, 'now he's going to get me with his rats.'

Bonanno, although remaining among his lofty pines, has allowed himself a cryptic digression (the message is clear enough for its intended recipients) on the huge 'big-moles' that make their nests there and which, inexplicably, left their arboreal habitat to come down into his house a few days ago. A rather mysterious, not to say suspicious invasion, which might have justified a small-scale investigation, not merely from a naturalist point of view.

'Hey-eh-eh . . .' murmurs the Marshal.

But there is no reason for it. The rats have not returned, the villa is once again habitable, the naturalist intends to forget all about the anomalous episode, whatever its cause, environmental, climatic or . . . even human.

'Quite a relief,' says Butti while Bonanno, after showing the hardest of fruits for the last time, disappears behind his thujas. 'I could already see myself interrogating the cats down at the station.'

'Let's return to serious matters,' suggests Monforti, 'this sublime soup that comes straight from the sixteenth century.'

Signora Butti parries, merely admitting that even the simplest dishes have to be made properly, thus suggesting that they are actually far more demanding than certain sophisticated, delicate concoctions that might look good but have no body. And when she sets on the table a rich dish of pork ribs and 'fegatelli' and sees her guest become radiant, she cannot conceal her pride. Signor Monforti will have to put up with this, she begs him hypocritically, these are simple things as well, a dish for peasants, poor people . . .

Butti cuts her short. 'She likes to be modest,' he says, 'but she's an exceptional cook. When it's the season, you must come and try her boar, her hare . . . and the way she prepares pheasant!'

Other animals, thinks Monforti, as something twitches at the corner of his mind.

The exceptional cook has placed a possessive hand on her son's shoulder.

'What I know,' she declares cheerfully, 'is that the only way to hold on to a man is by his stomach.'

Something twitches at Monforti's mind again, a snippet of an image, a fragment which in the chaotic heap seemed for one moment to dovetail with another fragment: Giovanna's broad back in front of the cooker? Natalia's hand spreading a canapé with foie-gras? the old men biting into their panettone a short while ago? the Hermit sipping his tea at Signora Borst's . . . ?

But the satisfactory click does not occur, or is at any rate overwhelmed by the wonderfully browned pork ribs that make it possible to hold on to a man, in this case Monforti, by the stomach.

XI

There Are Few Places in Italy

1

THERE ARE FEW places in Italy that have less in common with the pine-forest of the Gualdana than Milan's Central Railway Station. Erected in Assyrian-Teutonic style in an epoch when it was possible to conceive the development of civilisation in an Assyrian-Teutonic direction – along the ringing tracks, that is to say, of grandeur and order – it has today become what Telepadùle-News would define, with appropriate variations of tone, both a serious socio-humanitarian problem and an imposing temple of degradation, vice and crime.

Its immediate neighbourhood, its monumental entrances, its sidings, the mile-long meanderings of its underground passages, all swarm with hundreds of variously lost souls, barely kept at bay, and certainly not under control, by the guardians of the law. They know that they can take no resolutory action against this rabble, which remains in a state of furtive and continual parthenogenesis, and they restrict themselves to periodic 'cleansing' operations that leave things exactly the way they were.

At dawn the drug-addicts and thieves, the alcoholics and

small-time pushers, the beggars and immigrants from three continents, are prised from their stinking nooks and crannies, where the railway-police officers venture with caution, like Vannucci and Roggiolani on the Gualdana beach after a storm. Except that the jetsam scattered along this wild, tenebrous shore consists mostly of syringes and bottles, rags, newspapers, sheets of cardboard and plastic, miscellaneous scraps of food, as well as a plentiful supply of wallets, handbags, suitcases, rucksacks, documents, thrown away swiftly after bag snatches or muggings.

With no conviction but with resigned diligence, the officers collect everything that looks as if it has been removed illegally from the 'upper' world, from the 'Assyrian-Teutonic' people, and then with no undue haste but with resigned diligence they embark on the task of sifting it.

One of these cyclical scouring operations had been planned for last December 6th ('the station can't be left in that state over the holidays!'), had been postponed for a few weeks because of new emergencies, had then been fixed for the 20th ('is it really fair to pick on those wretches just before Christmas?'), and was finally launched in the early hours of this morning, December 27th, following the usual procedure: pointless identifications, platonic intimations, futile confiscations.

As was foreseeable, the material facing the two officers assigned to the sifting is more plentiful than usual, since the turmoil of pre-Christmas travellers offers particularly favourable conditions for slick pick-pocketing, dexterous pilferage and lightning snatches. The two colleagues – a man and a woman – set to work in an attempt to trace wherever possible the owners of these objects, and sooner or later, in typical Italian *fa niente* style, something will emerge from the heap.

2

To make any kind of serious headway with a puzzle of over 300 pieces, Monforti knows perfectly well that two tables are required, one to spread the pieces out and organise the first groupings by colour, the other for the actual assemblage. But seriousness as applied to a game or a sport has always struck him as a ridiculous waste, with the consequence (and this too he knows perfectly well) that he has found himself cut off from the company of many of his fellow creatures.

'Take up chess, one thing may lead to another, have a go at golf, I don't know, try sailing, play bowls, go fishing,' he has been told countless times by the 'specialists'. These are the famous 'interests' that one should take up when depressed, and the very word makes him shiver. Far better a Signora Zeme staring blankly at Perry Mason or wandering bewildered among bottles of medicine and suitcases, than a Signora Zeme with some 'interest' screwed on to her like a prosthesis. 'You know, she's much better now that she's in touch with those collectors of old postcards and plays bridge . . .' Atrocious.

The pictureless puzzle, spilled haphazardly over the living-room table next to a sofa, will just have to be assembled as it is, without any special preparations, without any system, and with the left hand. Here is a squared-off piece, cleanly sliced along one edge: a piece of the frame, evidently. And another one, with the same clean cut; and others, scattered here and there, to be collected and set in line, united by various shades of brown, from tawny to gilded to yellowish with a few dots of green. It surely isn't going to turn out to be a mocking picture of an omelette, one of those burnt vegetable ones that Giovanna is for ever serving up? And so the blue would be a tablecloth. But there's that little hand, how would the hand fit in?

'You know, I was thinking it might be an omelette, your picture,' he says to Natalia, when she phones later.

She pretends not to understand and to be offended.

'Me an omelette? Is that how you see me?'

'I see you as . . . good point, how do I see you? Nothing edible, anyway.'

'So I'm inedible, in your opinion. Well, that's just great.'

'No, I was looking for a rather less prosaic simile, I don't know, something from Dante, everybody knows Dante by heart here except me . . .'

'Listen, just say a rose and leave it at that.'

'A rose, fine. I'll look for it, but it'll have to be a rather faded yellow one, with dark, brownish edges . . .'

'Go on, say moth-eaten. Look, let's forget it, you're not on top form today, obviously that meal of Mamma Butti's hasn't settled properly.'

'Not at all, it was *haute cuisine* and what's more I learnt that the way to hold on to a man is by his stomach.'

'Only by the stomach?' Natalia replies boldly. 'That strikes me as rather limiting.'

Monforti, never quick at repartee, is unsure how to reply and Natalia switches at once to the subject of the Hon. Bonanno and his pine cone, which she saw on the Tp-News with the children.

'I was laughing, though I was embarrassed too. But they were literally rolling on the floor, as if it were a Max & Fortini show. What I mean is, this morning they're absolutely fine, it looks as if we can rule out what we were saying yesterday, they're just full of beans. So today we're going to visit the Tamburis, you know, she's Nicoletta's daughter, they've got that famous farm, above Scansano, and for a few days they're getting away from here, as you advised.'

'And you? Are you staying up there too?'

'No, heaven forbid, it's kids only, the three Tamburi children, my two, Berenice's two, and then she's going to take the whole lot along to her house in Volterra – the woman's a saint. No, no, I'm dumping them, I'll spend one night there and come back tomorrow evening, a single woman. Mamma Neri is shutting up kitchen for a while.'

'A pity,' Monforti says boldly, 'I was hoping to get taken by the stomach.'

'Is that all you ever think of?' Natalia replies boldly.

Monforti, tardy as ever with repartee, can merely say yes to what follows: yes, he too has been invited to the Kruysens' musical entertainment, yes, he'll be going along as well, no, he won't forget, from four p.m. to five-thirty, fine, sure, we'll meet there, get back to your omelette.

'There's also a lot of blue, in the picture,' Monforti says tentatively, by way of closure. 'Maybe it's ozone, ozone equals life, and you for me . . .'

'To be compared with a gas, that was my romantic dream when I was fifteen,' Natalia says with feeling.

Monforti says no more.

3

In the room (it cannot be called an office, but neither is it a warehouse) the task of examining the objects collected in the 'cleansing operation' at Milan Central Station is nearly over. Coffees have been drunk, cigarettes smoked, lists drawn up and compared with other lists. A futile job to be sure, but one that cannot be done unsystematically, with the left hand. Procedure pays off; not always, but often enough. With some assistance, of course, from memory.

On the table there is now a name that the woman inspector of the railway-police believes she has already seen in a fax sent yesterday or the day before from Grosseto, concerning an enquiry at the left-luggage deposit in the station.

'You know that check-up at the left-luggage they asked for from Grosseto?'

Her colleague instinctively shakes his head.

'Come on, the Carabinieri, it came from the Carabinieri in Grosseto. Didn't you deal with it?'

The man lets a few seconds slide past, not so much to reflect on the matter as to take his distance from it. 'When was this?'

'Yesterday or the day before.'

'I wasn't here yesterday. And the day before . . . well, it was Christmas.'

The woman passes him the object.

'This name doesn't ring a bell?'

'Not a tinkle . . .' says her colleague, plucking his lip. 'Try Marzio, ask him, if he's around.'

Marzio is not around. The inspector goes out under the huge glass vaults of the station, echoing with loud-speaker announcements in the mysterious Assyrian-Teutonic language. An old female tramp, probably one of those driven out a few hours ago, shuffles into a subway, muttering grimly; three Arabs are huddled in a corner like prawn-shells; a boy with a face like well-chewed chewing-gum tries to halt the less precipitate travellers with one outstretched hand.

Ten o'clock and all's well, thinks the inspector. She shrugs and sets off firmly with the object in her hand towards the cubbyhole where the ten Carabinieri appointed to Milan Central Station are based.

4

Forgetting about the ozone layer, Monforti has returned to the minuscule but unequivocal dark hand clasped tightly around a short section of a handle, telling himself that where there is a hand there is a face, there are feet. He looks for them unsuccessfully but none the less manages to pick out a few concordances: some sharp dots of dark green, that stand out against a beige background; some curious scales, halfway between hazel and grey; and those pieces striped with dark brown that made him think of bog grass but which also recall clipped stubble. The yellows and reds, all dull, neutralised by rippled hatchings, could also be the surface of Mars photographed by a space-probe; except that there's that 'invincible hoer's' hand.

Could it belong to a hermit labouring in an arid desert? But the Desert Fathers, who seemed to have been as depressed out there as in the centre of Milan, did not hoe, took no 'interest' in growing things – or at least that seemed to be the implication of the learned discourses at Signora Borst's house the other day. And anyway, in that case it would be a painting and not a photograph. Or even an enlarged detail from a painting. A sacred subject. St Anthony with his temptations, for example, and there in the background this little secondary scene. No brush-strokes can be seen, but the wretched quality of the reproduction could have flattened and smoothed everything out.

Monforti thinks of the Old and New Testament. Jesus tempted by the Devil (look for the Devil). Or the Exodus (look for an entire people on the march). Moses on Mount Sinai (look for Sinai and the Tablets of the Law). Moses at the rock gushing with water.

The plumber, Grechi, who has been wandering around the house for the last half an hour, appears at the door.

'Moses and the plumber Grechi meet in front of a rock in the desert,' thinks Monforti, 'and the plumber Grechi says':

'Two washers were worn right through and I changed them, but with the shower I'm afraid I'm going to have to change the whole unit.'

Sandra had called him with little hope some days ago, but it was the Gualdana murder that had really got him moving. Monforti heard him talking about it with Giovanna as he checked the taps in the kitchen, and it is clear, from the way he remains firmly by the door, that he would have no objection to going over it all again with him too.

Monforti resigns himself to: maudlin memories ('There was nothing stuck up about him, he'd stay there chatting away while I unblocked the sinks!'); contemptuous mistrust of the investigators and the authorities in general, including the Hon. Bonanno ('They're all the same, all in it together, living off our backs!'); a personal opinion on the crime ('It was someone from outside, a gipsy, a drug-addict, one of those criminals they let straight out again as soon as they've caught them!'); sarcastic remarks at Orfeo's expense.

'He says it was his wife!'

'Orfeo's wife?' Monforti says in surprise.

'No, the Countess. He says she's a determined woman, quite capable of a thing like that, if she felt like it. But I say: even if she had the muscles and the guts, she'd need the height too, and the Countess isn't what you'd call tall . . .'

'Is Orfeo in the wood?'

Grechi doesn't know, but he saw him last night at 'Il Molo', all cocky and jaunty, talking about this and that, laughing and joking and ready to take a joke.

'He must have made things up with his wife,' he says innocently, making it clear just what sort of joke Orfeo had been ready to take.

All three of them in a good mood again, thinks Monforti, slotting Orfeo in between the two Neri children, who had split their sides last night over Bonanno's show.

'So about this shower,' he says to Grechi, 'can you drop in tomorrow morning and replace it? Can I count on you?'

Grechi's prompt *'mammeglio'* is pronounced with an intonation that signifies 'you bet you can!'

Monforti wonders whether he should get an interview on Telepadùle-News to expound the following theory on the crime: Delaude was killed in a joint operation by the residents of the Gualdana to ensure that Grechi, Ciacci and all the other handymen, would finally show their inquisitive faces in their forest.

The spinach tortelli, boiled on far too high a flame, were mostly overcooked with split sides; the beef olives look rather limp.

'And for tonight I've made an omelette,' Giovanna announces invitingly.

'Ah, good,' says Monforti.

His sister Sandra is convinced that the woman is a sham, pretending not to know how to cook so as to be relieved of the task. But Monforti, who sees her at work every day, knows that Giovanna really does try. It is just the vocation that she lacks.

'Mmm . . .' murmurs the chewer, 'good these beef olives.'

Giovanna, who had remained there waiting to hear him pronounce, goes off happily.

A little later, when the Marshal phones, Monforti would like to express rather more heartfelt thanks than is usual for last night's dinner. But Butti does not allow him to, he has news from Milan via Grosseto: at the Central Station they have found the label that was attached to Signora Zeme's bag. Not the bag? No, just the leather label with the name and address, obviously torn off the handle and chucked away in an underground passage.

'The label just tells us that she got to Milan,' the Marshal remarks, 'that she got off the train with her bag, because otherwise the cleaners would have found it in the compartment, and probably that she was mugged or robbed inside the station. But it doesn't tell us where Signora Zeme has got to.'

All enquiries in the hospitals and in the hostels for down-and-outs and immigrants have led nowhere. The neurologist, tracked down in Taormina, confirms that he waited for her in vain on the morning of the 24th: Signora Zeme did not contact him, she simply did not turn up for the appointment, a fairly common occurrence with the sort of patients he deals with. From Bolzano, her sister, now extremely agitated, intends to mobilise the radio, the television and the newspapers with messages and photographs. And furthermore there is still no news of her husband, Zeme himself. In Rome, the Carabinieri of the Prati area have entered his flat, seeking any evidence of his having visited it and not ruling out the possibility of suicide. Not a trace. And not a trace in his office at the Volvo works, where no one has seen him or received any messages or instructions from him, either in writing or by phone.

'But in this Milan operation,' Monforti says, 'would they have found her if she had ended up among the tramps and drug-addicts?'

The Marshal thinks this over: 'In theory yes. I have never taken part in an action of this sort, but I imagine that they do things fairly thoroughly; they'll have mobilised more than a hundred men from both the Police and the Carabinieri. They search all the empty carriages, the subway passages, the abandoned warehouses ... True, it's a vast area, like a city ...' he admits, out of respect for Monforti's pessimism.

Monforti now recalls that first vision which had almost induced him to dissuade Magda Zeme from leaving: a frail solitary woman, swallowed up in the crowd and then driven brutally into some dark corner by subhuman louts, beaten, robbed, thrown down in a confused state into the infernal nether regions of the station, and left there, totally apathetic, an oblivious larva after the trauma.

But the pessimist is also Milanese and knows perfectly well that when each train gets to the Central Station, it is not the cleaners who rush on to it first. The last traveller has not yet dismounted before a mob of rapid raiders swarms through the carriages, grabbing anything that has been left in the compartments and jumping silently off with their booty. So, less pessimistically, the bag might have been forgotten by Signora Zeme, who got off, took a few steps along the platform, realised her hands were empty, went back with her heart in her mouth to her seat, but found nothing there; the bag had already gone, God knows where.

'And wouldn't she have gone to the police, then? Or she could have gone to the hotel, and phoned her husband from there, or her sister . . .'

But that is what someone who is well would do. With a depressive, one must take into account not only the extreme anxiety but also the extreme humiliation that such an incident would cause. It was she who had insisted on leaving all by herself, it was she who had wanted to demonstrate that she could get by perfectly well after years of dependence and passivity. It was a first step, a first rung on the ladder, a kind of test. And if she failed it . . .

'So you're saying . . . ?' says the Marshal.

'I'm saying that they might still find her at any moment, despite everything.'

'Alive . . . ?' suggests the Marshal, encouragingly.

'Yes.'

'But also dead,' the Marshal retreats, discouragingly.

'Oh yes, also dead, of course.'

Monforti returns to his sofa, depressed, and takes up his puzzle again with unexpected gratitude. A game, it is true, but one that serves to block out everything else while you are working on it. And so *this* is the real aim of all those hobbies – ski-ing, tennis, bridge: all practised seriously to keep the wolves at bay, for no other reason. A great discovery, at his age, a great intuition.

In order to keep this other old wolf at bay ('I have never understood anything at all in life'), Monforti now brings all his seriousness to bear on the game, and is soon rewarded. Another brown segment merges into the one clasped in the invincible hoer's hand. And then another, and a third, which also reveal the garment worn by the man, a kind of shapeless dark frock-coat, a fold of which hides his face. He is not a hoer, but a man clutching a long curved stick, pointed towards the brown stripes of bog-grass, stubble or whatever they are ... And there, just a little higher up, an eye opens up (*'mammeglio!'*), yes, a half-hidden eye, half-buried in the ... sand ... earth ... crust ... hedge ... straw?

But no, it's fur, bristling fur, it's the eye of some animal which briefly carries Monforti back to the Gospel ('the donkey on the flight to Egypt!'), but then a few more pieces help him to identify it: the big protruding lips, the long head, the sinuous neck, and then the arch of the hump, yes, a camel drawn by its bridle (not a stick) held by a camel-driver in a kaftan. The rest comes rapidly and automatically, the grey scales are palm trunks, the green points the lanceolate leaves, and all he has to do is upturn the sky to get the blue Nile in the foreground and there, on the other shore, more camels and camel-drivers against a varied, irregular background of desert. Nothing sacred. A simple photograph, an easy postcard which there is no longer any point in completing.

The solution of the game has not given Monforti much satisfaction, it has not called for any extraordinary commitment, and in the end the picture has turned out to be very ordinary. He was right, as usual: whichever way you look at them, these hobbies are always disappointing. The comparison with life ('so much effort, so much suffering, all to discover something entirely banal') is snarling away beneath the surface, and in order to avoid being mauled by it Monforti gets up and walks around the room, then goes out and walks twice around the house, listlessly kicking the pine cones that get in his way.

The fruit, he admits with a smile, really can be hard, if not quite the 'hardest'; you can feel it even through the cap of a robust shoe. A good man, poor Bonanno, but no less dangerous for all that – on the contrary. Better not to think about his initiatives in the field of agriculture and forestry, a man capable of planting 45 thujas in the Gualdana, someone as insensitive to botanic discordances as that, would not hesitate, in perfect good faith, to fill Rome with fir-trees, to strew the countryside of Lombardy or the banks of the Nile with cypresses. A bungler, a sower of incongruities . . .

But when he goes back into the house and sits on the sofa in boredom, with nothing to do until it is time for the 'musical entertainment', Monforti tries to imagine what would happen if Bonanno were a member of the parliamentary commission for puzzles. Impossible mixtures of palms and pines, of camel-drivers and petrol-pump attendants, of sands and skyscrapers, which would thus be far more difficult to distinguish, to separate, to break down. Maybe in some experimental shop in London there already exist games prepared in this way, or more simply perhaps there exist cravers of difficulty who buy two, three, or five pictureless puzzles, empty the bags on to the table and shuffle them, creating a random mixture, a Rembrandt with a view of Grosseto with the window of a supermarket with a Swiss glacier. After all, wouldn't this be a more faithful image of life, a game of infinite superimpositions and adulterations, of inextricable excrescences and anomalous fragments, like Bonanno's rats?

And in the end it is the Hon. Bonanno himself who gives Monforti his first idea as to the procedure he should adopt in order to make any sense of the enigmas of the Gualdana. Because suddenly the pine-cone theorist seems perfectly extricable. Not one of the pieces of his mystery can conceivably dovetail with any of the others, can combine in any way with Delaude, with Orfeo, with the Zemes, with the Hermit, with Katia. It is a mystery that can and must be expunged from the heterogenous heap of fragments. It is an intruder, a trespasser, that has come like the thujas to create confusion and incongruity and which must be eliminated as soon as possible. The breakdown process, that is what is needed in order to begin to see things clearly.

Political enemies plotting to introduce rats into his house? Poor old Butti being asked to carry out a discreet enquiry? Come off it! The plot (if it wasn't actually a kind of lesson, an ecological vendetta) can only have originated within the Gualdana, or must at any rate have had its motive within the Gualdana. And the culprit . . .

Monforti smiles. Various bits and pieces come together, the breakdown process is working. The culprit has given himself away several times; if one but looks properly, one can see that over the last few days he has left a glaring trail, a wake, which while apparently irregular and inconstant, is actually as uniform and straight as a pointing arrow. It will now be a matter of unmasking him, but Monforti is sure he can manage by himself, without any help – discreet or otherwise – from the Carabinieri.

5

Nobody applauds in the Kruysens' salon when the Maestro concludes Schumann's *Scenes from Childhood.* Applause is forbidden, but now Ute Kruysen, who took care to whisper this prohibition to the guests before the concert, regrets having done so. The instrument is old and decrepit, and besides the piano is not Hans Ludwig's real instrument: furthermore his hands are equally old and decrepit. The Maestro would feel the applause to be undeserved, out of place, unsuited to the occasion and the performance, and it might sadden him, reminding him of other audiences, other long-distant triumphs . . .

Ute had told herself all this, with what she now considers to have been excessive solicitude. Because after lifting his hands from the keyboard, Hans Ludwig turns round with a smile of winning familiarity, a smile that seems to admit – to require even – applause of equal familiarity, such as might be conferred by affectionate acquaintances here, in this salon, on this wintry day by the sea. The applause was, so to speak, included in the score, it was the final touch. But the young people obediently restrain the impulse, the adults respectfully refrain, and the moment passes, the chance is missed.

Ute serves the marzipan sweets, allowing Hans Ludwig two before Debussy. The Bonanno girls reluctantly nibble one each, out of politeness. With great dexterity, Andrea Neri throws one up in the air and catches it in his open mouth. A grandson of Signora Melis, bony, bespectacled, tries to do the same thing and the heartshaped sweet ends up on the carpet. And then Hans Ludwig himself has a go (set a bad example!), and succeeds at his first attempt. Andrea and his sister Giudi clap. The Maestro wears a smile of blessed impudence.

Signora Melis, who arrived in the Gualdana this morning with one of her grandchildren (ten-year-old Leonardo), is the only one who considers this gathering a social occasion. Her fingers are loaded with rings, her purple-streaked silver hair is set in a spreading baldachin of regal coils. A kind of generous snobbery leads her to attribute a supreme value to almost everything that enters the circle of her life, and in her presence one feels on the threshold of a definitive pantheon, admission to which actually requires very little.

Monforti – his depression not being connected with any artistic or intellectual activity, nor with a family drama or a tragically-concluded grand amour – does not even possess that very little, and yet Signora Melis continues to have hopes of him.

'He is still truly great,' she says, referring to the Maestro. 'He is an exquisite man.'

'Yes, he's nice,' says Monforti jarringly.

'You must see him often, you are always here.'

'Well, now and then. He keeps himself to himself.'

As an intimate friend of Kruysen's, he has failed the test.

'But has he prepared the first twelve Preludes of Debussy, or the other twelve? Or is he going to play us all twenty-four?'

'I don't know, I haven't seen the programme.'

The Bonanno girls have copied it out by hand and distributed it to the guests, but Monforti left it somewhere while he was talking to Natalia and Signora Borst.

'I can't find mine,' says Signora Melis, rummaging in her handbag. Then she turns to Eladia: 'My dear, might I have your programme for a moment?'

Eladia rises to hand it to her, but is anticipated by Mongelli, sitting closer to her.

'Thank you, my dear,' says Signora Melis, as if receiving a precious jewel lost at sea from a fisherman.

'Only the first twelve,' she informs Monforti. 'They're short pieces, two or three minutes each, but highly demanding. He will take a little rest between each one.'

A fingernail the colour of a Mafia massacre surmounted by a mighty ring points out the last two lines of the programme to her neighbour. 'Strange, he's changed the order, unless it's a mistake on the part of the two dear copyists.'

Ce qu'a vu le vent d'Ouest, Monforti reads, *La cathédrale engloutie*, and contemplating these two fascinating titles he finds himself not simply twitched, but submerged, carried back down to the sandy seabottom of the Gualdana enigma. Ah, if only he could interrogate it, could restrain it among the high fronds of the pine-trees – that wind that came not from the West but the South, that freak *libicocco*. The witness that saw everything, that knows everything, that blew indifferently over the scene of the crime, over the murderer fleeing with his bloody weapon, over the corpse and the waves that lapped at it, then engulfed and rolled it away.

'He doesn't have much strength left, and I expect he'll double the notes with the chords,' Signora Melis whispers doubtfully.

Entrance to her pantheon does not mean that one is any less exposed to her criticism. On the contrary, the guardian of the temple considers it her privilege to point out the failings of those on whom she has already bestowed eternal glory.

'Of course that liquid tone will be almost completely lost . . .'

She shakes her head imperceptibly, but Monforti is now swimming in the intense liquidity of that night, and the 'restraining' touch of the Maestro, the resonance pedal that prolongs the sounds, creating almost an organ 'legato', not only fail to disturb him but actually enchant him, transport him from Prelude to Prelude, ferry him across the pauses, cradle him like the gently rolling tug of the undertow. Down there in the abyss, he makes out the dim shape of the *Viktor Hansen* and his ears catch the arcane tolling of its bell. He allows himself to be assailed by the resounding squalls, fulminated by the 'B' of the antepenultimate bar, which crashes like a climactic burst of thunder . . .

'Tremendous, truly tremendous,' decides Signora Melis, joining her fingers with a jangle of rings. And as if yielding to a long-repressed impetus she rises and moves towards the statue of the Maestro, embracing him before anyone else dare approach.

In the road in front of the Kruysens' villa, the Hon. Bonanno invites everyone to dinner at the trattoria at the Tavernelle. He is in a merry mood: he enjoyed himself on television (in replay) and this concert has made him dream of the beautiful, pure things that still exist in this world: nature, music, family and friends.

'My dear, what a good idea,' says Signora Melis, taking him by the arm.

Even Mongelli accepts.

'And Monforti, if you're on your own too . . .' the politician says, fraternally.

Monforti doesn't feel like it, but he is indebted to this precious bungler who has put him on the right track, helping him to break the puzzle down. What does it cost him to lie? He refuses with an excuse but compensates for it, congratulating him on his interview on Tp-News.

'You're truly telegenic.'

'Oh heaven forbid!'

A happy man.

'Gabriele!' Andrea protests in a whisper as they set off on foot towards the Neris' house. 'You didn't mean that?'

Natalia is a few yards ahead, with Giudi.

'No, but I wanted to . . . make it up to him in some way, after what he went through with those rats, poor chap.'

Andrea walks on in silence.

'It was a real trauma, for him and the whole family. There are people who have a morbid, ancestral horror of rats, like snakes . . . I think it goes back to the time of the Black Death, the plague.'

'But in the fourteenth century, they didn't know it was the rats' fault,' Andrea argues. 'The germ was only discovered . . .'

'Whatever the reason, with some people a shock like that can even turn their brains. They go mad, they're never the same again.'

Andrea falls silent. Monforti has slowed his pace, the luminous oval of Natalia's torch is now about twenty yards ahead of them.

'And so,' Andrea asks cautiously, 'he could have pulled out that theory of the pine cone because he's gone mad?'

With considerable effort, Monforti maintains his gravity. 'It's too soon to say, but there's no doubt that whoever conceived the plan must have a criminal mind of the first order. Bonanno thought it might be a plot dreamt up by someone in Rome, but I don't think his political enemies would stoop to such perfidy. In my opinion it's all a local conspiracy, and what worries me is that the culprit, or the culprits, seem to have got clean away with it. And they could start up again from one day to the next with another house, with the Melis family, for example, don't you think?'

'What are you two doing back there?' Natalia calls to them. 'We have to get going, we're already late!'

'Yes, we're coming!'

But the two of them linger still, and lower their voices. At a certain point they even stop, one in front of the other in the dark, and only a few minutes later does their confabulation end with a peal of laughter from Andrea, who runs off, joins his mother and sister, and a moment later they are all gathered around the car, placing suitcases in the boot (bang!), running into the house for some last forgotten object, and listening to Monforti's warnings: it's late now, the road before and after Scansano is narrow, there are all those bends and counterbends, and there's that nasty climb up to Torracce which . . .

'No,' says Andrea, 'that's not there any more, they got rid of it last year, they cut away half the hill and now they do motor-cross on the old road and seeing as how Nicolò and Vittorio . . .'

'Nicolò and Vittorio are over sixteen,' Natalia reminds him severely, 'and I beg of you . . .'

'Anyway they won't even let him touch their motorbikes,' says Giudi.

'And what do you know about it?' says Andrea belligerently, seeking some devastating insult. 'Are you taking your teddy-bear for bye-byes?'

'And what about your invincible pirate's telescope?'

'And your "Swoon" perfume?'

'And your ring in the nose?'

'And your . . .'

'Come on now, that's enough, stop it, get in! *Ciao* Gabriele, see you tomorrow evening, I'll phone you when I get back.'

The headlights are switched on, the pine-trees detach themselves from the darkness, the engine comes to life. And in the gloom as the car drives off, Monforti starts to reflect.

6

The southern bank of the Old Ditch is not as misty as that of the Danube, and the northern one is not swarming with

Quadi and Marcomanni waiting to storm the Roman encampments. Nor are the sentinels of the 'Legio Fulminatrix' watching by night on the Grand-Duke's Bridge, as Marcus Aurelius Antoninus passes in his imperial cloak, absorbed in immortal contemplations.

Besides, although it is already dark, it is not exactly night. None the less Monforti prefers to come and meditate here, rather than go and ponder in his armchair at home. He feels the need to go back over various ideas, questions, vague fragments of pictures that were summoned up by Maestro Kruysen's piano.

What would the wind of the West have seen around dawn of December 24th – he asks himself again – if, instead of sweeping down on to the coast of Brittany (crowded from Douarnenez to Concarneau with mothers and wives peering at the horizon, their hands screening their eyes, straining to see fishing-boats that were never to return again), it had turned southwards and reached these shores, thrashing and whitening the sea from Castagneto Carducci to Porto Ercole?

But then, it strikes him again, he might as well wonder what the *libecciata* did see.

Except that this is precisely the point. The *libeccio* wind did not merely see. It also participated in the crime, even if only as an accessory, tugging and rolling the corpse to the spot where it was found. And it drove the sea on to the scene of the crime itself, using it to wipe out all traces. No point asking it for indications about cathedrals or any other submerged objects . . .

From the coast path on the far side of the bridge, he sees the traces of the other night's necrological bustle, black and sharp on the moon-glimmering pallor of the beach. No storm has cancelled these. And Monforti could probably, should he so desire, identify his own footprints in the sand.

But as he goes back the way he came, recrossing the Grand-Duke's Bridge and taking the path to the south, the image that once again presents itself to him is that of the cathedral of Ys: not merely submerged now, but engulfed, swallowed whole by the sands, buried like the wreck of the *Viktor Hansen* behind him, whose bell, on stormy nights, can still be heard tolling from the depths . . .

Interesting, undoubtedly. Haunting. But it cannot be said that the wind of the West has taken him far. And the most annoying thing, after having cleared the table, as it were, of an irrelevant enigma, of a 'parasitic puzzle' like that of the rats, is to find himself faced with an identical problem as regards Orfeo and Ugo the Hermit. Are they parasites as well, the one with his hoes, the other with his alleged presence at the spot after midnight? Do their colourful cut-outs slot in or not with the more faded ones of Gimo and the Zemes? And there is always the possibility that these last three belong to three different games, none of them having any connection with the others and each with – or rather without – its fine picture on the lid:

a) Gimo attacked on the beach by a man or an unknown animal, perhaps a prehistoric one like the giants of Monteriggioni, or struck down (why not, at this point?) by the hardest of fruits of a pine-tree, this too gigantic;

b) Signora Zeme, not only robbed of her bag, but also devoured by cannibal immigrants in the underground passages of Milan Central Station;

c) Signor Zeme, gradually infected by his wife's depression, taking advantage of the storm to throw himself like Sappho from a rock of the Capriola, but quite independently of Gimo's death.

No, he thinks, walking past the blazing lights of Villa Melis. It isn't possible. Let's forget about Orfeo and the Hermit, let's leave them aside for the moment. And let's even leave Gimo himself aside for the moment. But there has to be a link between Signora Zeme's disappearance in Milan (in Milan?) and her husband's disappearance here (yes, certainly here). The 'invincible hoer' of the puzzle, who turned out to be a humble camel-driver in fact, had already suggested an idea . . . a tiny fragment of a picture . . . which had nothing to do with Orfeo, or with the Hermit, or with Gimo, but which had taken him back to his own life as an (ex-?) depressive: wasn't it the Marshal who had said to him, talking about psychotropic drugs . . . ?

No, it was he who had said it to the Marshal, when discussing the destruction of inanimate objects and the fatal alternation, in manic-depressives, between fits of 'euphoric-logorrhoea' and states of total dejection:

'Marshal,' he had said to him, 'you have no idea . . .'

Only this road is getting him nowhere. Or rather: it breaks off half-way. Because it is impossible to say what would have happened next.

The 'rustic' omelette that Giovanna had left him for dinner has not sharpened his wit. He threw half of it in the rubbish-bin, had some coffee, and after half an hour of painful alternation on the television between euphoric-logorrhoic shows and wordy documentaries (which he himself reduced to silence with a squeeze of the thumb on the audio-button) he idly settled down to complete the camel-driver jigsaw.

But this presents no further uncertainties, apart from some fragments that are paler than the sand, and not so dark as the camels, with which he soon reconstructs a yellow dog, bringing up the rear of the procession.

It is in fact the silenced television that sets off his suspended associative mechanisms: 'You have no idea, dear Marshal, you cannot even imagine . . .'

But this gets him no further. It is he who ought to have

this idea. It is he who should imagine, given that the Marshal cannot, is unable to. But it's useless: beyond a certain point the fragments will not click together, and he cannot proceed with the picture he had started to compose, he is even tempted to unmake it, so as to . . .

> *Siena mi fe', disfecemi Maremma.*
> [Siena made me, Maremma unmade me.]

But Signora Zeme is (was) from Bolzano, and it could quite easily have been Milan or the Alto Adige that unmade her. But that was after she herself had unmade – destroyed – something that in the end was more than a simple inanimate object.

At any rate it is here that everything begins. But where does it finish? How?

This armchair, which has never been particularly comfortable, and which his aboulia has always prevented him from changing, is of no use as a lucubratorium. Much better to wander around after the Stoic fashion, now that it really is night, or even after the suspicious fashion (according to Orfeo) of the cynical Hermit.

No: he had made up his mind to leave the Hermit and Orfeo aside. Without letting himself be distracted by them, he will instead get to the point from which, it seems, Gimo rolled to the tomb of the *Viktor Hansen*.

But hadn't he decided to 'break down' Gimo as well, in order to concentrate solely on the Zemes?

He will see on the spot, he concludes. And so, after picking up his jacket and his tweed hat again, he goes to the garage to get the car out. There is no point walking all the way there, given that it is from there that he intends to wander around meditating.

After leaving the car in the asphalted lay-by, he makes his

way to the coast path. And from one of the dunes near the deserted, abandoned 'Dutch villa', he considers first the beach, then the Zemes' villa on the right and Signora Borst's a hundred yards to the left.

Not a glimmer of light is to be seen in any of the villas at this hour, and over towards the Old Ditch even Signora Melis' house has been in darkness for some time. However, the high and almost full moon illuminates the scene with almost daytime clarity, whereas that night – he reflects – it must have been impossible to see the palm of one's hand. In these conditions, it is doubtful whether his nocturnal wandering can really inspire him.

Automatically his footsteps carry him to the right, towards Villa Zeme. Automatically he slips into the narrow, tortuous passage through the bushes that Andrea took the other morning, towards the open french window, with its broken pane, banging behind the ill-closed shutter.

The shutter is still ill-closed, the window still open, the broken pane has not been replaced. Everything (on the instructions of the Public Prosecutor, probably) has been left as it was.

'You have no idea, Marshal . . .'

But that was before the Marshal came here to make his first inspection and saw with his own eyes the state the room had been left in. Here he had been able to get some kind of an idea by himself.

'You cannot imagine just how far . . .'

How far? Is he sure he can imagine it himself?

Not quite automatically – indeed, with some deliberation – he opens the shutter fully. He has no need to turn the light on in order to rediscover every detail of that well-remembered scene of desolation, which in the pale, spectral moonlight appears even more . . .

Frightening. This is the word, for anyone who knows

anything about these manic-depressive alternations: 'Oh how clever, how clever, thank you, thank you so much. Now I can go! Now I can go!'

'Yes, go and don't worry, Signora.'

'Vannucci has called, he's got the tickets.'

'Oh how clever. But the cases ... I'm not well, I'm not well, I'm not well.'

'But *how* are you not well, Magda? In what way?'

'Stop it, don't talk to me, I beg of you. I'm not going.'

One can have no idea.

In the living-room the windows are all closed. But the glimmer of light that filters through them enables him to reach the hall and the little staircase down to the basement and the garage, where the light can be turned on without attracting anyone's attention. Besides, it is unlikely that anyone (except for the Hermit? except for Orfeo?) will come wandering round here at one a.m. Just possibly Gimo might come here (return here?), if he weren't dead and (providing the Prosecutor has given the go-ahead) buried.

In the garage the Volvo has not changed: the boot is still dented and ill-closed like the shutter upstairs, and the front passenger-seat still holds the Pinocchio that took Signora Zeme's place on the return journey from Florence S. Maria Novella.

That's it, I'm not going.

However, she did go – she just didn't arrive, poor woman. Unless ...

But no, the road is still broken and the whole picture will not let itself be reconstructed: the moment he seems to glimpse it, it unmakes itself.

Siena mi fe' ...

Sapìa was from Siena too. And that blessed comb-seller,

who – now he comes to think of it – must have been the cause of Orfeo's rage at the end of the sermon: because Father Everardo was exalting his figure as a strict ascetic, an ecological consumer of berries and roots and even, perhaps, a saintly protector of the ozone layer, when Orfeo . . .

An imaginary whiff of ozone (maybe triggered by a spark from the switch) seems to waft around the garage when Monforti turns the light off and climbs back up the little staircase to the hall, on his way back to the disarranged room.

7

Sitting on the bed which is laden with empty or half-empty bags and cases, shoes and other randomly discarded clothes, Monforti knows now that Orfeo's puzzle is autonomous, like the rat one, although more complicated.

And in fact, one by one, each of the pieces clicks into place. The Hoes, the Swords, the Water (except for the fresh water) are not involved. Instead, what is involved is the wife 'who wouldn't let him have it', according to Butti's crude expression, but who by now must have let him have it, to judge from her behaviour during, and above all after, the ecological demonstration.

And the Hermit is involved too, but only in the role of the Door-Opener and of Bion of Boristhenes, whose macrobiotic theories he must have propagated in the presence of one or other of the two adulterers, or perhaps of both, at the 'Il Molo' bar or the Tavernelle.

Even Mamma Butti is involved, with her traditional conservative theory of holding on to men by the stomach. It was this that the adulteress should have reflected on (but then so should Father Everardo, instead of stirring up the flames), if she had wanted to continue her adultery in peace. Because as a cuckold, the ever-grumpy, taciturn Orfeo might even have closed an eye (like the philosophical emperor with his promiscuous wife, Faustina) on the principle that love is a mere emission of mucus. But as for that other matter, working hard all day as he did, never!

The moon is beginning its descent. On the bedside table, a little luminous alarm-clock shows two o'clock: more or less the time (so it seems) that Gimo died just a short distance from here (so again it seems). And now that gardeners, adulterers, hermits, preachers, ecologists are no longer around to confuse the issue, one might as well admit it. One cannot reasonably doubt that Gimo is in some way part of the same 'game' as the Zemes: duly recomposed, his picture must clearly fit somewhere into the same blind (as yet) lid.

But it's probably better not to start with him, as of course the Prosecutor and Carabinieri had no choice but to do.

Starting from scratch (or almost), the best tactic is to place in the centre of a hypothetical table the only piece of the puzzle that allows one to make an immediate clicking connection: the label found in the underground passage at Milan Central Station.

There. One of the bags left on the bed is a leather one, probably discarded because too heavy, but which had already been fitted with a label. Let us now imagine its handle grasped by the fragile fingers of

Magda D'Alessio Zeme
Via G. Ferrari 22
Roma

and let us trail our mind's eye up the slender arm, complete the minuscule picture of the poor woman, voluminous bag in hand, clambering on to the crowded train in Florence. And then, in Milan, another hand . . .

No. In Florence, her husband will probably have handed her the bag when she was already on board, or more probably he got on too to stow it on the rack. And then . . .

But this is not the right way either. The matter must be followed from a much closer angle, and indeed right from this very room: with Vannuccini turning up with the tickets, picking up the bag himself, putting it into the boot or on the back seat, from where Zeme takes it out again in Florence . . .

Yes, but just a moment. Or rather, several moments.

The luminous hands show that it has gone four when Monforti wakes up numb with cold. And in the almost pitch-dark room, with the moon now setting behind the Capriola, it takes him a while to work out where he is; he is bemused, finding himself in bed with his jacket on.

Then his hand, groping around, encounters miscellaneous objects and finally grasps the handles of the leather bag. His mind runs over the stages of the imaginary journey that he made several times, back and forth, before dozing off.

The road continued to break off, as he drowsed, but this time he had not allowed it to block him and he had managed to pick it up again, after an obstacle of which he had worked out the nature but not the position. The interruption was only on the outward journey, furthermore. On the way back, the bag was no longer there and the problem did not arise, although another one arose inevitably in its place.

He is now on his feet, and he considers the idea of really taking the bag with him, on the no-longer imaginary journey he intends to make in order to set himself on the same road, in the same situation as the lost couple. The bag, bearing the identical label and filled with the clothes strewn over the bed and others which he starts to grope around for on the floor, will symbolise that equally crammed, equally heavy one that Signora Zeme was supposed to take all the way to Bolzano.

In his (ex-?) manic-depressive perfectionism, he even remembers the Pinocchio that was intended for Vannuccini's son and which is now sitting in a foetal position on the passenger-seat of the Volvo. He will go and collect it from the garage and place it on the seat next to himself, as an appropriate symbol of Signora Zeme.

But this time he has to turn on the light in order to make his way through the maze of furniture in the living-room, even with the risk of attracting Roggiolani's attention, since he could well be making a nocturnal round on his bicycle. And returning from the garage with the Pinocchio in its transparent box, he also turns on the light in the hall: where he remembers that on a shelf, that afternoon when they were all looking for the phial of Enzed, there was a large electric torch. He will need it to reach his own car in the lay-by, particularly because the front door is locked and he will have to go out the way he came, making his way down through the bushes and walking all the way round along the coast path.

But the torch is no longer there on the shelf. Who could have taken it, if not Zeme himself, that night? And come to think of it: Gimo must have had a torch as well, although none was found on him.

At this point he recalls that he does in fact have one, in his jacket-pocket, and he turns it on. He switches off the other lights. In the bedroom he picks up the bag, and having stepped out on to the paved terrace he turns to push the shutter to. But he has to be careful not to close it completely, hampered as he is with his load: if the hook should click, he will not be able to get back in and replace everything. After all, the Prosecutor and even the Marshal himself would deplore his intrusion in no uncertain terms.

8

Roggiolani was not making any rounds in fact, when Monforti knocked on the glass to ask for the barrier to be raised. He had instead fallen asleep, and in his confusion, like a Danubian sentinel caught off-guard, he came out to justify himself.

What with *Ingegnere* Laguzzi and the Prosecutor and all the rest – he explained – he couldn't get any sleep even during the day.

He must have wondered what was up, seeing him drive out at that hour, but he did not make so bold as to ask.

The car now purrs through the darkness towards the village, with the folding puppet already unfolded and in a state of euphoria so that it never ceases to praise itself for having decided to leave, the neurologist for having agreed to receive it on December 24th, its sister and mother who are going to help it discover the infantile trauma that is to blame for everything, now it is sure of it, even though other people are partly to blame since they've never made life easy for it, this must be said, but now it's all water under the bridge, now it wants to start afresh and first of all it'll take lessons in English, history, computer-science, gymnastics and the piano which it used to love as a girl and then stopped because he never encouraged her, this must be said, but now she wants to take it up again because there's no reason why – even if she isn't Maestro Kruysen – she too can't get to play Schumann, Debussy, the Wind of the West but what are you doing? you've missed the crossroads! now to get on to the Maremma road we'll have to go all the way along that track through the bushes and that narrow road because it's impossible to make a U-turn here, it's forbidden, it's very dangerous, I forbid you, anyway it's too late now, my God we're going to be late, we'll never make it, I knew it, but it was you, you did it on purpose to stop me leaving, to keep me here, to destroy me, I know, it was you!

Magda, please.

That wasn't the crossroads, here it is now, but even if it had been – thinks the driver, turning – he might really have missed it, with that torrent of senseless sentences, which, after a strangled sob, has now become a silence loaded with grief and menace.

Magda, we're on the Maremma road, do you see?

S. S. 'Maremmana': km 2 . . . km 4 . . . km 7 . . .

Is she sleeping now? God, please let her sleep. But the wooden eye is open and adamantly fixed – not on the streaky surface of the illuminated asphalt, nor on the line dividing the traffic, nor on the white-ringed trunks of the pines and cypresses that flicker past alternately on either side – but on the black plastic dashboard where there is nothing to see except the mute radio.

Km 12, 13 . . .

Do you want me to turn the radio on? Shall I put some music on?

Km 14, 15, 16, 17 . . .

Yes.

Yes what, Magda?

Music. Debussy, or Chopin or even Grieg, Vivaldi, you see if I could find them, I'd like to devote more time to music but I don't even know if they've got a CD player at my sister's, I should have asked them, I could buy the discs in Bolzano or even now in Florence if we get there in time, at the station gift-shop they should have them, so when I get there I'll have them straightaway, although that isn't the problem, it's that they always have the television on, just imagine, without the slightest consideration for me or the fact I'd like to listen to my records, you know what they're like, if you don't know, I'll you tell you, no, don't contradict me please, and so in the end they'll make me feel really bad, I mean bad bad, do you know what really bad means? no, you don't know, don't say anything please, you're the last one who can ever understand me, you've never understood me, it's you who've reduced me to this state!

Magda, I beg you . . .

IT WAS YOU!

Km 42 . . .

Snap . . . snap . . . snap . . . snap . . .

The grim, gaping eye is fixed on a little silver box which the driver recognises, as her thin fingers open and shut it endlessly, making the enamelled lid click: snap . . . snap . . . snap . . . In the desperate silence that has now lasted for twenty-five kilometres, the rapid succession of clicks soon becomes obsessive, terrifying, announcing an even more deranged crisis.

Magda?

Snap . . . snap . . . snap . . .

The man at the wheel tries to keep his attention on the road, where the traffic is still very light but the hills have become more frequent, the bends more dangerous. We are approaching, he remembers, deathtrap bend at km 52, the victims of which are regularly deplored by the posters at the village news-stand. But he also feels that he is approaching the point where the road ought in some way to break off, or deviate, or . . .

With its headlights and its outer band of little red lights, a trailer-truck comes noisily down the hill, thunders and rattles past, and when the silence gradually re-establishes itself, the 'snap . . . snap . . .' has also stopped.

Instinctively the driver slows down but cannot bring himself to look to his side. His eyes continue automatically to register the warning-signs of bends and hills, a board bearing the sign km 49, the announcement of an emergency lay-by 200 metres ahead, a tourist notice with some towers . . .

I'M NOT GOING.

As if jolted by a hump in the road or a sudden turn of the wheel, the car skids violently to the left but then straightens up.

I KNOW IT WOULD SUIT YOU, BUT I'M NOT LEAVING. LET'S GO BACK.

The car, which has continued straight for a hundred metres or so, moves over to the right and pulls up in the emergency lay-by.

AND DON'T SAY ANYTHING PLEASE . . . DON'T SAY ANYTHING! DON'T SAY ANY-THING!!!

The driver doesn't say anything.

Having passed km 50, Monforti no longer looks at the signs. He watches the edge of the road and the trees that slide past on the right, looking for the point from which the 'Maremmana' used to wind its way up a hill that has now been half-flattened, like Andrea's hill near Scansano. The entrance to the old road, if he remembers rightly, is still fully visible when one passes in daylight.

There it is in fact, a little farther along on the right, in an opening through the trees; beyond it the asphalt becomes rough and broken but remains visible for quite a stretch, before disappearing into the high scrub. Was this the interruption or deviation he had imagined?

The headlights, a little way beyond the turning, illuminate a landslide of stones and tangled brambles and brushwood that make it impossible to go on. But from here the new road cannot be seen and consequently, with the headlights off, there is nothing to prevent the driver from getting out, opening the boot, and then taking the macabre simulacrum from its folded position on the front-seat and placing it in the boot. The problem of its final destination will arise later, but in the meantime he must resolve that of the bag.

Monforti closes the boot, returns to the wheel and switches on the headlights. The brambles and brushwood in front of him remind him of the jumble of jigsaw pieces that he had taken for sand and bog-grass, before identifying the camels. He thinks of the label again, which has allowed him to recompose one whole part of this other blind puzzle. But the 'key piece' of the remaining part is not in the shape of a label. Instead, it resembles the toy that little Colin had in his hand, last summer on the beach, when Signora Graham ran and dragged him away from his game with an alarmed cry and a sudden tug.

XII

Evaporating, the Night

I

EVAPORATING, THE NIGHT has left a dark deposit of hills along the horizon to the right, the gibbous outline of which is growing ever more distinct. The risk of dropping off to sleep has passed, thinks Monforti, stepping out of the car to stretch his legs.

An hour ago he stopped in this lay-by at the far end of a viaduct, and with the engine still running for warmth he closed his eyes and leant back in his seat, doing what one is supposed to do when one feels one's hands on the wheels threatened by that fatal loss of control. This rest was a duty more than a need: to guarantee the physical safety of the only person to have understood the case, who will now have to report, explain and make others understand in turn.

But he did not sleep; his brain continued to verify every join, to check every detail of the picture he had reconstructed in its entirety. And now he no longer has any doubts. The 'pieces' being what they are, there is no other way they can possibly be assembled. What he lacks, however, is concrete proof, and he does not see how he can obtain any.

The cold air and light do not help him. He stretches, stamps his feet hard on the ground, but no real proof comes to mind: he doesn't have any, there isn't any. Below him, the brooms clinging to the slope emerge from the darkness; densely clustered, they seem to impose their greyness on the whole vast valley.

Monforti paces with short rapid steps up and down the lay-by, but he is unable to shake off his torpor, which breeds insidious doubts and uncertainties. Material concrete proof is clearly needed and it is unlikely that he himself . . .

Dogs, he thinks when a car or lorry-engine starts up in a farm-house down below and a dog begins to bark, the noise gentled by distance. All he can do is talk to Butti about it, persuade him that dogs are needed.

He gets back into the car while from somewhere near by, half-way up the hill, one cockerel and then another add their contribution of noise. Yes, Butti will listen to him, if nothing else. And then maybe he will act, if for no other reason than because 'one never knows'. He will set the meticulous engine of procedure in motion.

2

The Marshal has not yet arrived but it just takes Sergeant Farinelli one glance to realise that this man with bristly cheeks, bloodshot eyes, and all the wrinkles and crinkles of a sleepless night, would not be presenting himself at the station at this hour, when the offices are still closed to the public, without some very good reason. I must look like a man who's made up his mind to make a clean breast of it, Monforti tells himself while the Sergeant takes him through to the Marshal's office, where the light is already on.

'He'll be here in a minute or two.'

Just so as to keep his eyes open, Monforti spends the minute or two looking through the *Police Handbook* which is there on a shelf between a dictionary of the Italian language, a copy of the new Penal Code and some other volumes of a legal appearance. He dips into it here and there, and then lingers (he needs to) on the definition of 'circumstantial evidence' or 'clue':

> Another means of proof is the *clue*: this is founded on induction and leads to the ascertainment of a fact of which one does not have or cannot have direct proof, but of which one infers the existence from a proven or otherwise known circumstance.
>
> Clues can refer to circumstances that precede the crime, that accompany it or follow it: they range from those concerning the capacity of the author of the felony to commit such an offence and the events that may have led to the crime, to those that accompanied the committing of the crime, and finally those clues that refer to the traces left by the crime, to the steps taken by the offender after the crime, and the criminal's demeanour itself.

How many of mine – Monforti wonders, feeling rather at bay – how many of the clues that slot together so perfectly in my head match this definition? All of them, *a posteriori*, if the picture turns out to be correct. But *a priori*, in the anonymous, procedural light of this office, they all appear completely unpresentable in a Carabinieri Station. 'What circumstantial evidence is your theory based on?' 'Well, you know, while walking along the banks of the Danube, I had a long chat with Pinocchio.'

When Butti enters, he has already decided to bid him good day, apologise and leave. And yet little Colin . . .

Butti too sees the exhausted criminal, ready to come clean. 'A difficult night?'

'I spent it thinking things over.'

'Ah,' says the Marshal.

He sits at the table and offers to send for some coffee from Celso's bar.

'Yes, thanks, I need it. And some mineral water.'

Then the cigarette, the proffered lighter. Everything necessary to facilitate the confession.

'The fact is that I can't explain anything, it's really too complicated,' Monforti says by way of aggressive premise. 'But I think I know what happened.'

The Marshal does not lose his composure but his eyes haze over slightly. Monforti anticipates him. 'I don't want an interview on Telepadùle-News,' he says. 'Not right away, at any rate. But I've come to you . . . I thought that if you could – without too much . . . too many complications, get those dogs sent over from Florence . . .'

'Which dogs?' says Butti, surprised.

'Those ones that were going to be used to find little Colin, the English boy, you remember last year on the beach? But then Vannucci . . .'

'Ah yes, of course. But now we've got them at Headquarters in Grosseto, we're fully equipped. Two. We were given them in September and so far . . .'

'Fine. To check my pine cone out, I mean my theory . . .'

'A pessimistic one?'

'Very pessimistic. But I'll point out to you that the bust of Garibaldi really was about to fall when I . . .'

'No, no, you're right,' says Butti seriously. 'You have an unblemished record in these matters.'

They both laugh, the Marshal gets up to turn off the light and notes that the day is still dim. He moves over to the window to look out at the square, the reinforced effigy of Garibaldi, and then announces: 'Here comes the coffee.'

He turns the light back on, sits down again, while Monforti ('I tried to sleep in the car') yields to a jaw-unhinging yawn.

'And the dogs are indispensable, you say.'

'The only way.'

Monforti gulps down his mineral water. Butti observes him, stirring the sugar in the cup.

'And you're asking me to bring the dogs in on the grounds of your pessimism. You won't or you can't tell me anything else.'

'I could, I could . . .' Monforti says feebly.

But he rouses himself. 'I'm afraid I wouldn't be at all convincing, do you see? In fact, I'm afraid I'd be the first to unpick myself, to pull myself to pieces, if I heard myself putting my . . . my clues, my evidence, into words.'

The Marshal looks at the volume that the other man has placed on the corner of the table. 'But that book,' he says, 'does not envisage acts of faith on the part of officers of the criminal investigation service.'

'Let's put it like this,' says Monforti. 'If things went the way I think they did, I'll explain everything afterwards. But if the whole thing turns out to be a non-starter, you'll never ask me anything again, you'll forget all about it and I promise to live the rest of my days with a photo of the Hon. Bonanno next to my bed.'

'And does that sound a fair offer to you?' asks the Marshal in as fair a tone as possible.

Monforti protests. 'You mustn't look upon it as an offer! According to this encyclopaedia you are authorised – I'll go further – urged, to receive it as a dutiful contribution, a possibility that has, let us say, presented itself spontaneously and which is worth checking out. Think of me as an anonymous letter.'

The Marshal gazes long and hard at the crumpled letter drinking coffee in front of him.

'But the main point,' he say, 'of this letter?'

'The main point,' says Monforti, 'is implicit.'

'I see.'

Butti drains his cup of coffee, looks at the time, pulls a black notebook out of a drawer and phones the Public Prosecutor, Dr Veglia, immediately. Nothing new has turned up in the enquiries, there is still no trace of the Zemes, and at this point, it may well be a good idea to carry out that search of the forest that Dr Veglia mentioned as a possibility yesterday morning; does Dr Veglia agree? Using police-dogs, of course, so as to save deploying too many men, which in the circumstances . . .

Monforti picks up the *Handbook*, reads through the definition of 'clue' line by line, and the sensation of dangling in the void grows upon him as the Marshal specifies his request, makes arrangements with the Prosecutor about the official procedure necesary to launch the operation, and finally receives informal consent.

'He'll call back,' says Butti, replacing the receiver, 'but he seemed fairly convinced. But then again it's true that we can't lose anything by trying, at this point.'

Silence falls.

The Marshal has compromised himself, he has taken his decision, thinks Monforti, he has taken my erratic and mimetic night upon his military shoulders, he has reduced it to the dimensions of a 'check-up', and is now waiting, calmly, impassively, incuriously.

The silence is prolonged, a placid, businesslike silence. It is as if they could hear the voices in Grosseto proposing, objecting, specifying, ordering. Until the incurious officer says in an incurious tone: 'At least tell me this: we couldn't have got there by ourselves, is that it? Are there things you know that we don't?'

'No, no, it's not like that at all,' Monforti assures him.

'There are things that only I could know and that I didn't know I knew, let's say.'

'And which you then gradually remembered, you put them together . . .'

'It's not like that either. Firstly, more than putting things together, I had to separate them, break them down, so to speak. It was Bonanno who gave me that idea.'

'With his pine cone?' says the Marshal, almost offended. 'I don't believe you.'

'No, with his rats. When I realised that the mystery of the rats could not really be connected with the rest, I had already taken a major step forward. Once I had solved that . . .'

Butti's impassivity diminishes noticeably. 'Solved it? What do you mean, solved it? Was there really a plot, are you telling me seriously that someone in Rome . . .'

'Not in Rome, not in Rome.'

And Monforti invites him to imagine by way of hypothesis that the Gualdana contains two very young people, two somewhat isolated and bored children, well versed in all the forest's ecological secrets, who, spurred by a rather flimsy motive ('to punish a barbaric planter of thuja-bushes'), got hold of some traps, prepared some appetising bait ('slivers of pear are irresistible, it appears') and placed the whole lot on the lowest branches of some pine-trees where the arboreal 'big-moles' are known to nest. Having captured some of these beasts and put them in a sack, they carried them at dawn to the Member of Parliament's villa, worked loose a rusty grating, released the animals, closed it up again, and waited to enjoy the joke.

'A strictly apolitical joke, then,' says Butti.

But which then assumed a political colouring, because the suspicious politician took alarm, and demanded an enquiry from the Carabinieri. A casual witness was present at the scene . . .

'On the Grand-Duke's Bridge . . .' says the Marshal.

Exactly. He casually informed the culprits (whose guilt he did not for one second suspect) of the turn things were taking, thus throwing them into consternation. From that moment on, every time they saw the Carabinieri's car pass by or saw the Marshal talking to Bonanno, the criminals trembled, a constant prey to changing emotions, from precarious relief to troubled uncertainty and the terror of cornered animals.

'"The criminal's demeanour after the crime,"' quotes Monforti, 'should have opened my eyes. Delaude's death didn't trouble them one jot. They imagined that they themselves were the real object of the enquiries. And then the other evening, when Bonanno chose to forgive his alleged enemies on television, they felt their worries were finally over, and now they're full of beans, according to a reliable witness.'

The Marshal raises his hand. 'But I couldn't know any of this. It was you who had all the clues under your nose – assuming that they're not imaginary clues.'

'I have a full oral confession,' says Monforti. 'What more do you want?'

'From both of them?'

'From the older one, and that is enough to consider the case closed, I'd say. And not only that, I've also broken down the mystery of Orfeo and the teacher, I've cleared it right out of the way, I feel. True, I have neither proof nor confessions, just more circumstantial evidence. But in this case you had everything under your nose, just like me, no more nor less. And furthermore you had direct access to the person who could have given you the idea.'

'The *Onorevole* again?' says Butti admiringly. 'He'll go far, that man.'

'No, Marshal, I'm talking about your mother,' says Monforti. 'And about her marvellous meat dishes: I'm talking about her pork ribs the other evening.'

At this moment the phone rings.

3

When everything has been duly authorised, ratified, organised and set in motion and there is still a good half-hour to while away, Celso's bar-cum-icecream-parlour seems the most natural destination. It is almost nine o'clock and Piazza Garibaldi is reasonably animated, considering that it is winter. The haberdasher's opposite the Carabiniere-station is closed, as is the near-by sports-shop. But there are three people waiting to pass through the elaborate double door of the bank on the corner, there are already customers at both the baker's and Righi the butcher's, and a girl is standing by the newspaper-stand leafing through a magazine she has just bought. ('Breakthrough in the Gualdana enquiry?' asks the *Tirreno* placard. 'The investigators weigh up the theory of an MP friend of the victim.')

The moment he steps into the bar, gleaming as a result of recent refurbishment and modernisation, Monforti totters, overcome by sudden pangs of hunger. Celso, the owner, notes his unshaven chin and rumpled appearance, darts a glance at the Marshal by his side, fleetingly imagines a sensational arrest and asks what he can offer them, while Monforti wanders towards the array of miscellaneously-filled sandwiches.

'As your mother wisely reminded us,' he says after his first mouthful, 'you hold on to a man by his stomach. And that's the whole point.'

True, the ozone layer helped. Signora Baldacci seemed

downcast, indifferent to a demonstration organised by a movement she belonged to, and then later, in the close-up shots on Tp-News, she actually looked unkempt, bruised, a woman drained of everything.

'I thought she might have been raped,' says Monforti.

A brutal outburst on Orfeo's part, an act of rebellion against the intolerable and humiliating situation he had allowed to engulf him, as he slaved away at his nineteen gardens and she just got more and more 'modern' and 'independent', confusing him, intimidating him with her totally arcane enthusiasms and fads, chipping away at his life bit by bit, with her crazy clothes, her Florentine leghorns, her strange exercises, her flute, her young lover flaunted before the whole village, her topless sunbathing, the ozone layer, vivisection no doubt, the Third World . . .

'It was as if,' says Monforti, taking a second salami-sandwich, 'she were gradually poisoning him with arsenic.'

'But why did he let her do it?' asks the Marshal.

'Because cultural arsenic,' says Monforti, 'is difficult for someone like Orfeo to identify.'

But dimly, in his own way, he grasped what was happening and ended up concentrating all his resentment on the Hermit, that dainty-fingered good-for-nothing layabout, that scrounger who saw no shame in going around begging worse than the Moroccans, and yet whom everyone seemed to respect as if he were the priest of some incomprehensible religion. Maybe he had heard him preaching here and there, in some garden or some public place, he had certainly heard his wife speaking of him with admiration, *il professore* here, *il professore* there. And he ended up convinced that the teacher was at the root of all his troubles. It was he, rather than Fioravanti, who had given his wife ideas, who had provided her with the arsenic. Then Father Everardo stuck his nose in too, singing the praises of the blessed comb-seller at midnight mass, another notable loafer, another fine example of a root-guzzling scrounger.

'At that point he was almost bursting, he got up from his pew and stormed out in a rage,' Monforti recalls. 'But as he passed in front he shot a glance at me that was positively scorching. Pure hatred. Only it wasn't for me, it was directed at the Hermit, who was by my side.'

'A glance . . .' says the Marshal. 'You can't prevent a glance.'

'But it was the glance of a madman; by now he was well on the way to persecution mania. Everyone against him, Father Everardo, all of us Gualdana residents who supported *il professore*, maybe you too, Marshal.'

'Another plot.'

Another plot, but one that Orfeo, in his state of impotent subjection, unable to defend or express himself, knew he could finally get free of by violence, by making his rifle speak for him.

'Luckily you offered him the means to vent his rage, Marshal,' says Monforti. 'You gave him the chance to avenge himself on the teacher in the only way, apart from his rifle, that was open to him.'

'You mean when he lied about the time?'

'Undoubtedly. He saw the Hermit cross the Grand-Duke's Bridge at ten o'clock, but when he realised he could put him in difficulty by false testimony he immediately took advantage of the fact, he said he saw him after midnight. And he would have carried it right through, he would have stuck by his version with the Public Prosecutor, he would have sworn it in court too, if necessary.'

'Stubborn brute,' says the Marshal.

He looks at the time and then at Monforti, who is stretching his hand out to the tray again.

'I could hardly stand up,' smiles Monforti. 'I felt I was about to faint.'

'We could have sat down for a moment,' says the Marshal, but looking around himself without enthusiasm.

Celso's brand-new tables are of shiny grey marble, as is the floor. All the chairs are in Viennese style, with gilded metal backs and seats of pseudo-wickerwork. The walls are all enlivened by historic Campari and Coca-Cola posters in thick steel frames. It is impossible to imagine Orfeo sitting in such a place now; the arsenic has penetrated here too.

But, thinks the Marshal, there remains the matter of the 'Il Molo' bar: a shabby old place, with no pretences, where sporting and political dissensions, local jokes and rows, are still the order of the day. Outside it, Baldacci and Fioravanti came to blows long before Delaude's corpse was washed up on the Gualdana beach. Cuckolded husband, acquiescent till that day, unexpectedly attacks his wife's lover. Inexplicable.

'But there's still "Il Molo",' he says, 'that night when he and the other chap had it out.'

'I know what your theory is,' smiles Monforti, 'the theory of the . . .'

Orfeo swallowing her infidelity just as he swallowed the tirades about the Amazon forest, river pollution, pesticides and asbestos. It was all part of that same hailstorm that had come flailing down on his life, but he clung to a few familiar solid things, and reckoned he could resist by closing his eyes and ears. He was a peasant, he hoed, dug, pruned, mowed the grass in nineteen gardens and his own vegetable-patch, and he would go on like that, hardened and resigned – not exactly to a compromise or to his horns, but rather to a bad season that sooner or later would pass. His was an age-old acceptance, it had nothing to do with multiple orgasm or with the hedonistic emancipation sung by the magazines that littered his house. But there is a limit to everything. He could take his wife's macrobiotic diet, he could put up with the kamasutra with Fioravanti, the cassettes pouring out English lessons or hysterical rock while the beetroots were cooking, the anti-drug concerts or the marches against hunting or fur coats; but a husband has his needs too, after all.

'That's what I say,' says the Marshal. 'When his wife came to me with Fioravanti she made a great long speech about her ideas, her principles and ideals, but the meaning was quite simple: that she refused to comply with her conjugal duties.'

'She wouldn't let him have it,' says Monforti, 'if I can quote your own words, Marshal.'

'Yes, it's the most likely cause,' says Butti, 'and an age-old one too, as you say.'

He looks at the time and makes as if to move towards the cash-desk, where Celso, who still wears an old home-made jumper, seems somewhat perplexed by the marble, crystalware and metalwork that surround him. Monforti restrains Butti.

'I've indulged in an absolute orgy.'

'But you're on duty, you're helping with my enquiries.'

'Don't speak too soon.'

The jeweller's shop has now opened in the square, and in front of Righi, the butcher's, Righi himself and a boy are unloading quarters of beef from a refrigerator-van.

'The fact is,' Monforti reveals, 'that yesterday morning I saw the Baldacci woman dump the ozone layer and enter Righi's. And then, in the evening, your mother practically closed the case.'

'My mother,' says Butti, 'knows nothing about any case, she knows what everyone else in the village knows about the Baldaccis, no more nor less.'

'A pity, because if you had talked to her about it, your mother would have spotted our mistake at once, our shortsightedness.'

'What short-sightedness?' protests the Marshal. 'If Signora Baldacci, apart from her strange principles, wouldn't let him have it any more . . .'

'What?'

'Well,' says the Marshal, 'it's obvious, there's a word for it.'

Monforti looks at him, shaking his head. 'There, that's the mistake!' he exclaims in an amused whisper. 'It was meat that she refused him, because of her vegetarian ideals! It was steaks and chops! It was the pork ribs that she wouldn't let him have!'

The Marshal lets five seconds go by and then says: 'We'd better go.'

The appointment with the dogs is at the Gualdana lodge, but in the Marshal's opinion Monforti is in no condition to get there on his own.

'I'd better drive.'

Oliva and Macchia get into the duty car.

'How do I bring the seat forward?' says the Marshal, who is shorter than Monforti.

'Under there, on the left.'

'Ah yes.'

Not until they reach the Shell service station does Butti start laughing.

'Pork ribs, eh?' he bursts out. '*Mammeglio!*'

For twenty yards he gives way to a plain-clothes, 'Il Molo'-style laugh. Then he restrains himself, toning his laughter down to a disciplined, uniformed chuckle, as if responding to a quip from a superior officer. But he remembers his report and bursts out again.

'And the report?' he says, almost sobbing. 'What do I write in the report?'

Instinctively he has slowed down.

'Don't write anything,' says Monforti. 'Forget all about it.'

'A steak,' stutters the Marshal, driving at 30km an hour, 'how can I forget that?'

He recovers himself, emerges from the farce and re-enters procedure. 'It all hangs together, I have to admit,' he says, accelerating. 'First she must have tried to convert him to soya, and then she'll have gone on and on to him about a vegetarian diet, and then, seeing that he wasn't having any of it, she took meat right off the menu, she actually forbade him to cook it in the house himself. The final humiliation.'

'But Orfeo,' says Monforti, 'must have taken it as the conspirators' final move to weaken him, to sap his blood and strength, to starve him to death. I reckon that when he came to the Gualdana that night he brought with him half a kilo of sausages and barbecued them in some villa. You can always check it out at Righi's.'

'Yes, that's how things went,' agrees the Marshal. 'It was his way of pulling himself together, of regaining strength, as you said. They wanted to bleed him dry and he countered with a three-inch steak. And when he felt ready for battle, he sent his wife back to Righi's with no questions asked.'

'"With no questions asked",' says Monforti, 'is perhaps a euphemism?'

'No doubt about it, I'd say. It stands for 'a smack in the gob', and that's what Signora Baldacci's face showed the other evening on the news. You're right, there was a kind of rape.'

'Via a third party of pork ribs,' meditates Monforti. 'Essentially it was a point of honour for both of them.'

'Honour,' says Butti, 'rules everything.'

But it is not clear to Monforti whether he pronounced this standing to attention, his hand to his Carabiniere cap, or jokingly, in the style of 'Il Molo'. Being unsure, he answers seriously. 'No,' he says, 'in my opinion, it's pain that rules everything.'

'You're a pessimist,' says the Marshal. 'Where are the indicators in this car?'

4

The barrier rises, the two cars pass through and stop a few yards farther up, but nobody gets out. Vannucci and Vannuccini, who have both emerged from the lodge eager to provide help, are not summoned to co-operate and they hang around the Christmas ilex-tree, trying not to appear either too inquisitive or too idle.

When Signor Mongelli turns up on his bicycle, they hand him his newspaper zealously. When Signora Melis drives out, they hasten to raise the barrier. But they linger, keeping an eye on the curious scene: Signor Monforti's car (which Roggiolani saw drive out at four a.m.!) with the Marshal at the wheel; and behind it, the blue Uno. Both of them parked, waiting, as if at a road-block, or a trap set for someone – ready perhaps to make an arrest.

Is it possible? Anything is possible at the Gualdana, at this point. The Chairman, *Ingegnere* Laguzzi, will certainly not be pleased to hear about this further visit, this further investigation or search, whatever its result. Maybe they had better call him. He should have a word with these representatives of the law, to find out what's happening.

What happens next is that the magistrate, Dr Veglia, turns up at the barrier in his ordinary little car, and falls in behind the other two cars. Then a blue Carabiniere van comes along, with two Carabinieri sitting in front and two German Shepherd dogs in the back, behind the grille. Police-dogs, by the Madonna, no doubt about it. The whole caravan sets off, and while Vannucci goes to call *Ingegnere*

Laguzzi, Vannuccini takes advantage of the moment to jump on one of the guards' duty bicycles and he rides off in pursuit of the others.

In the little lay-by where they all get out of their cars, Monforti, who has just shaken Dr Veglia's hand ('This'll be your pessimist friend, I imagine'; 'Yes, that's right'), is a witness to the following coded dialogue:

Butti – I didn't think you would come as well.

Veglia – And I didn't think I'd come either, when you rang.

Butti – We don't actually have any new data, it's just a check-up operation.

Veglia – Yes, of course, I understand, but by following it on the ground, one always learns something.

What they actually said to each other was:

Butti – I really didn't hope that you would come along and watch this probable non-event.

Veglia – You phoned me at home, very early in the morning, to make it clear to me that you had some new data that you held to be interesting although weak from a formal point of view. So, if I chose, I could stay in Grosseto and leave you with the entire responsibility for the non-event.

Butti – The truth is that we're acting on an unspecified hypothesis or intuition or deduction of the pessimist here present.

Veglia – I understand that too, but if you're taking it seriously it must be a hypothesis that could possibly lead to results and in that case it is best that the Public Prosecutor be present.

Neither of them has mentioned the Zemes.

The dogs have come out as well, under the charge of Marshal Ognibene and Corporal Rosi – who is the real expert. But Ognibene has followed the appropriate course too, just as he has followed the courses in parachuting, diving and computer-technology and is currently, seeing the way things are going in Italy, taking a course in Arabic (which he finds very difficult).

The Prosecutor and Butti walk up to them.

'Good boy,' says Ognibene to his dog, which appears to be a very good boy indeed. 'Good boy, Diki.'

'So we're ready,' says the Prosecutor. 'Let's go and get these clothes of the husband's.'

'Ready,' says Ognibene, tugging the animal.

'And the wife's,' says Monforti, who has hung back. 'And the wife's, while you're there.'

'No problem,' says Ognibene, as if doubt had been cast on Diki's abilities.

The Prosecutor and Butti do not look at one another, nor at Monforti, as if they had not heard him, and they separate, the Marshal setting off with Monforti towards the beach, Veglia, followed by the dogs, towards the french window of the Zemes' villa, where he rolls the shutter open and enters.

'Careful with their paws,' Ognibene warns Rosi, 'there's broken glass.'

The Prosecutor has the immediate impression that something has changed since yesterday, when he came with Butti: the chaos is different, the scattered clothes look as if they have been moved, shuffled around, and they seem fewer in number too. It is not order, but a different kind of disorder. The overturned drawers are not in the same position, the bed-cover has several wrinkles, and between the bed and table a strange hat has got wedged, which was definitely not there yesterday.

The Prosecutor picks it up and turns it round in his hands. 'This wasn't here,' he says.

'Shall I give it to Diki?' Ognibene offers.

'No.'

It is a sporting hat which has neither a lining nor any initials inside and is made of several cuts of tweed, each different from the other. Patchwork. The Prosecutor's wife sewed herself a blanket of this kind, years ago, which she found 'amusing'.

'You take it, Marshal. This has got nothing to do with it, put it in your pocket.'

'But whose is it?'

'Someone who came here after me,' says Veglia, casting his eyes around again. 'And who took something away with him . . . There were some skirts, thrown down on the ground here . . . there was a pile of shirts . . .'

'A thief?'

'We'll see later.'

'Items have been removed, at any rate?'

'We'll see.'

The dogs have already started to sniff among the scattered garments, but Ognibene assists them, picking things up, smelling them, laying aside freshly-laundered shirts and socks, pullovers that smell of naphthalene, ironed pyjamas. He goes into the bathroom and returns with Zeme's pyjama jacket.

'A shoe will do as well,' says Rosi. 'Or a slipper.'

'I think underwear's better.'

In the end they choose a pink polo-neck, a shoe, a little white bra with a touch of padding, and then move into the hall, where they pick out Zeme's scarf, the gloves next to the phone, and make the dogs sniff his coat.

'Go get,' says Ognibene, stepping through the french window before anyone else.

Outside, Diki puts his nose to the ground and starts to move with a certain phlegm along the terrace carpeted with pine needles and cones; he reaches the barbecue-niche set into the side wall of the villa, comes back, crossing with Rosi's dog.

'The *libecciata*'s swept everything away,' says Ognibene, shaking his head in dissatisfaction.

The dog raises his nose, stands there immobile, then sets off firmly towards the forest, dragging Ognibene into the thick of the scrub.

'Hey!' shouts Ognibene, trying to restrain him. 'Hey! Hey!'

They disappear noisily into the undergrowth. The dog starts barking and is answered by other canine voices; a moment later there is a full chorus of yelping and shouting. It is Lotti's setters, who have come exploring; however, they quickly abandon the field of combat or play, obeying their master's distant and secret summons.

Ognibene reappears, pushing aside the broom and rosemary bushes, and places the polo-neck under Diki's nose once again; but meanwhile his colleague has started along the track that leads to the coast path, following his dog with outstretched arm, as it moves forward with only occasional hesitations, occasional changes of direction, and then reaches the line of huts, passes beyond them, passes beyond the line of shelters that were uprooted, disembowelled and mutilated by the *libeccio*, and finally goes down to the beach, moving towards the group of men waiting by the silent mother-of-pearl of the sea.

It is the stretch that Roggiolani and Corporal Oliva swept vainly the day before yesterday with wide wooden rakes, looking for a possible murder-weapon. Starting from a line drawn at about the level of Villa Borst, they made their way for about two hundred metres towards the Old Ditch, here and there amassing the miscellaneous detritus into heaps bristling with reeds and branches, like the nests of gigantic birds.

Between these scattered heaps the sand appears clean and combed, although it still contains innumerable blobs of diesel-oil.

'We had already got this far,' says Dr Veglia. 'This is more or less the point where Delaude must have ended up in the sea.'

He has turned to Butti, but he said it for Monforti, who is hanging around distractedly, absently, looking at the dogs, the distant promontory of the Capriola, the two men holding the clothes, the shoe, the pink polo-neck.

The Prosecutor's chin and eyes tacitly ask where they should start from.

Butti's head and eyes tacitly indicate all around.

Diki goes straight up to sniff Vannuccini, who strokes his head, smoothing his ears.

'What do you think you're doing?' Ognibene says brusquely. 'He's working, he doesn't want to play.'

The dogs sniff, walk around one of the heaps, move back up towards the forest, return to the water's edge, one of them stops in front of Monforti but abandons him immediately, Diki ventures farther south with Marshal Ognibene who is both urging him on and pulling him back by the short lead. But the circumvolutions of their footprints on the sand are getting gradually less uncoordinated, the wayward cobweb woven by deviations and changes of mind seems gradually to be condensing itself into a kind of system, a kind of olfactory geometry, as if the two animals were intent on a process of successive eliminations so as to draw ever more clearly a series of concentric ellipses.

Nobody speaks, nobody moves, nobody smokes, there is only the low panting of the dogs and the occasional sharp cry of a seagull.

Rosi and Ognibene let go of the leads and the animals now remain within the boundaries of a well-defined territory, they come and go restlessly within a narrow grid of smells, they suddenly start scratching at the sand, and it is then that the two men go and fetch them back, dragging them away by the leads with straining sharp-angled elbows and firmly dug-in heels, talking to them, calming them in a tone of bluff bonhomie.

The area scoured by the dogs is on the upper part of the beach, where the dunes begin, more or less opposite the empty 'Dutch villa' and in a recess between the dunes themselves. The Public Prosecutor exchanges a few businesslike words with Butti, arranges for some snapped-off canes to be set around the area, with a generous margin, to form a square of operations. Oliva and Macchia are ready with their short military spades, but Ognibene, who has left Diki to his colleague, comes to the fore again; he suggests using shovels and rakes, sends Vannuccini off to get some from the lodge, starts digging himself with Oliva's spade, attacking the square from one corner and working along one side. But almost at once it is Macchia's spade on the opposite side that bangs against something hard, which the Corporal lifts on the blade to show to Butti and the Prosecutor.

'It's Delaude's torch,' says Monforti.

What the others see is a red torch, of the dynamo sort, which could have lain there, one foot under the sand, since last summer, for all they know.

But nobody raises any objection or asks Monforti anything, and the Prosecutor gestures to Macchia to put it back where he found it and go on digging.

'Should I photograph it?' asks Oliva.

'Let's wait,' says Butti.

They do not have to wait long, because when Vannucci and Vannuccini come down with shovels and rakes, Ognibene has already struck and uncovered a second object: a spade, which, like the torch, appears to be in good shape, with no corrosion in the wooden handle or rust in the thick blade. The Prosecutor pores over it for some time before straightening up and saying to Butti: 'Let's take some photos, for the position.'

But meanwhile he gazes at Monforti, who remains silent, his hands in his pockets, once again a picture of exhaustion, of dejection.

When Oliva returns with his tripod they all stand aside to let him photograph the two objects from a short distance and from various angles; the objects are then removed and placed on a plastic sheet.

'Gently, for God's sake, gently,' Ognibene urges when the two guards set to work with their large shovels.

There are now four of them digging along the sides, with slow suspicious movements, stopping to examine whatever emerges from the slippery uniformity of the sand – a rag of kelp, a bottle-top, a piece of glass, a thin root that has wormed its way here from the two nearest dunes. Little by little a square parapet has begun to take shape, as if in preparation for some childish game, a medieval castle or car racing track, whose walls are for ever being shored up and for ever caving in, even though the men are now up to their knees and their spades and shovels are tossing up darker and thicker sand.

Nobody talks, nobody stops, only Vannuccini breaks the rhythm of the shovelling to take off his jacket and wipe away the sweat. Gradually the four walls mount up, the corners are bevelled, the square rounds out into a circle and Ognibene signals to the two Carabinieri to climb out; the hole is narrowing to a funnel and the four men cannot all go on digging without getting in one another's way.

'Come on, up you come,' says Ognibene, stretching his hand down to Corporal Macchia, who is in up to his shoulders and finds it hard to climb out. Oliva clambers out by himself, sending a mass of sand slithering back into the hole.

Only the dogs break the silence. From the shelter where Rosi has taken them, they burst into shrill yelping, they yank their leads taut, with their noses lifted skywards, their muscular bodies straining towards the hole.

Which a moment later becomes a grave, when Vannucci and Vannuccini stop digging simultaneously, and bend down to something their shovels have both met.

Vannuccini raises his eyes towards the row of observers standing immobile along the crumbling brink.

'There's some cloth,' he reports punctiliously, but implying that it is not up to him, that he has no wish to be the one to discover what lies beneath the cloth.

Butti helps him out and goes down to take his place, kneels, and starts scraping away the sand with both hands; then his fingers gather more delicately around the 'cloth' which lengthens, rounds out, takes on the contours of a shoulder of an outstretched arm, and then stops. Butti's fingers, almost tender now, summarily free a contracted hand, a head, a profile, a closed eyelid, a clenched mouth, and at that point the Marshal stands up and although he can count on other witnesses – the guards or even himself – it is Monforti that he addresses.

'Is it him?'

'Yes, it's him,' says Monforti, barely leaning over the ditch, 'it's Zeme.'

The diggers are now set to work lowering the brow of the ditch, making it as compact as possible for Oliva's tripod, so that more photos can be taken. Butti has already climbed out and gone to phone through to Grosseto, to summon the police doctor and the forensic specialists with their instruments. *Ingegnere* Laguzzi has turned up, striding down from the coast path with guard Barabesi. They do not come too close, but all the same Ognibene makes it his duty to keep them at a suitable distance, and there is a touch of reproachful roughness in his manner, as if the sensational events that are disturbing the peace of this residential pine-forest were due to some default or negligence on the part of the management.

When Oliva has finished, the Public Prosecutor moves towards Monforti, and stands next to him for a while, but in the end says nothing to him. Together they observe the shape as it emerges from the bottom: lying there on its side, with its left arm stretched out, its fist closed, most of its bulk still trapped in the sand, and the protruding part wattled and discoloured by residues of sand, it resembles not so much a corpse as an archaeological discovery, unearthed after millennia, in danger of crumbling into dust at the slightest touch.

Veglia orders that the body be dug out.

Macchia and Oliva pull their gloves on and descend slantwise so as to reduce landslips and cave-ins to the minimum. They kneel at the two ends of the corpse and without touching it dig a little trench all around, so that it gradually emerges on a short plinth that more or less follows its shape, the knees joined and crooked, the left foot, the left arm, and then the right shoulder and the other arm, the elbow bent, the hand . . .

But the hand, when they raise it from its damp bed, does not correspond. It is open and dangles at the end of a thin wrist, the fingers are very thin and long, with lacquered nails.

'There's a woman underneath!' Macchia shouts.

They dig again just enough to bring to light the outline of the second corpse, which is lying neatly face upwards beneath Zeme's. The Prosecutor stops them, makes them climb out and goes down himself with Butti, who has returned in the meantime.

'I wouldn't touch anything,' he says, 'until our men get here.'

'They'll be here in twenty minutes,' says Butti.

Once again Veglia has the impression he is contemplating two figures encrusted in a dim and distant past, far beyond any small gesture of pity; however, he accepts Laguzzi's suggestion of covering the bodies with a tarpaulin.

'Husband and wife,' he says to Butti. 'As on the Etruscan sarcophagi.'

'Eeeh,' sighs Butti philosophically.

'And where's your friend? The pessimist?'

They look around for him.

'I saw him going off,' says Ognibene. 'As soon as we found the woman, he went off.'

'He knew Signora Zeme well,' says Butti. 'Maybe he preferred not to see her in this state.'

'Or he's gone off to sleep,' says the Prosecutor. 'He looked shattered.'

'Yes, possibly.'

They walk along slowly, smoking, and moving away from the ditch which is already beginning to attract the first onlookers. Milagros's fur hat bobs up among the bushes that line the coast path and a little while later the girl herself is on the beach. Lotti arrives, having left his dogs at home, and he starts to talk in a low voice to Vannucci. Mongelli turns up too, makes a wide circuit around the sepulchre and joins Milagros, who on the contrary has already leaned over and had a good look, and he gets her to tell him about it. Lotti goes up to the shelter where the German Shepherd dogs are being held and chats with Rosi. *Ingegnere* Laguzzi goes restlessly from one guard to another, from one Carabiniere to another, until Signora Melis pays her visit, asking him to escort her to the scene of the discovery and accepting the prolonged homage of his explicatory and anxious gesticulations.

And finally guard Guerri, called back on special duty, comes down at the head of a long procession of officers and civilians, and Ognibene makes them all retire from the immediate vicinity of the hole and as they retire they all cluster into little groups, huddling close to one another, and they remain thus in silence on their gently warm beach under the winter sun, a few steps from the rhythmical benevolence of the sea.

Then the friable sarcophagus is bureaucratically profaned and Antonio Zeme (Signor) and Magda Zeme (Signora) enter procedure and are expedited to Grosseto for the autopsy.

5

Woken abruptly by the telephone, which he had forgotten to unplug, and recognising his sister's voice, Monforti calculates the immense length of time he would be kept talking there if . . .

He thus restricts himself to saying that he is fine, that everything is going splendidly, and that with Natalia too, well, he can't say that things are going badly, though you know how it is, better not cherish illusions that might later . . . What? Ah, no, there's no news down here, although the Marshal has confided to him that he expects developments.

'And how are things up there? Is there any snow? Is Ettore enjoying himself? Wonderful. Excuse me, somebody's rung the doorbell, it must be Grechi about those new units. Yes, I called him back – you see, I do remember. So all the best, *ciao*, keep in touch.'

His recaptured skill at casual lying must be another sign of his psychic health. He'll say so to Sandra, he thinks, when she reproaches him for not keeping her up to date on things.

He opens the door.

'Signor Monforti?'

Of course he hadn't been expecting Grechi. But neither was he expecting (or was he?) this well-mannered Carabiniere officer, who introduces himself as Lieutenant Scalera, assures him that he has come above all to thank him, on behalf of the Group Headquarters, for his valuable help in their enquiries, and wonders whether (at his own convenience, of course, he hastens to add, noticing the pyjamas under the dressing-gown) he would have any objection to coming to Grosseto with him 'and with our esteemed colleague Butti', in order to . . .

At the wheel of the car parked across the driveway – an official car, with the licence-plate E.I., but without the blue light or the word CARABINIERI along its side – sits Marshal Butti, who gives him a wave of greeting.

'Please, come in, Lieutenant. I had a rather . . . eventful night, let's say . . . and I haven't been able to get any sleep till now. But if you'd like to sit down and wait a moment, in a minute or two I'll . . .'

'Thank you so much, and so sorry to have woken you. We thought . . . the Public Prosecutor thought . . . that some further assistance on your part might well prove conclusive in wrapping up the investigation.'

Conclusive? thinks the assistant when the car is already at Grosseto. It might clear up several details, no doubt about that, but why conclusive? What remains to be concluded?

Lieutenant Scalera, on the short journey, cautiously circumscribes the conversation to matters of general interest, if not strictly to the rain and sunshine. Butti too remains on similar ground, apart from one specific reference to Signor Monforti's powers of observation: although the bust of Garibaldi was right opposite the station, he was the only one to notice . . .

And when they get to Via Santorre di Santarosa and the assistant is solicitously and ceremoniously escorted into the conference-room, things get no clearer. The Colonel and three of his officers (plus the omnipresent Marshal Ognibene), who are already in conference with Prosecutor Dr Veglia, installed at the head of the table, jerk to their feet in military fashion and introduce themselves, express their greetings, gratitude and compliments to Dr Monforti, who is to be credited with the great step forward that has been made . . .

But how do they know he has the title of Dr? He himself has long forgotten all about his degree in economics and business studies, and he has no recollection of having ever used 'Dr' on calling-cards or elsewhere. To discover this detail, he concludes, the Carabinieri of Grosseto must have assembled a good deal of documentary evidence about him.

'Dr, please . . .' Scalera invites him, using the title that he must previously have forgotten to use (or had he, more prudently than the others, reflected on his celebrated 'powers of observation'?), 'take a seat here.'

When they all sit down again, Monforti finds himself installed between the two Marshals and opposite the Public Prosecutor, who is sitting at the far end of the table between the Colonel and Captain Scheggi, while Scalera, opposite Lieutenant Amidei, keeps the minutes of the meeting.

'Fine,' Dr Veglia begins. 'I think that first of all we had best explain to Dr Monforti just what point we have reached.'

The officers all nod.

'The preliminary inspection of the bodies,' proceeds the Prosecutor, 'did not enable us to ascertain the cause of death with regard to Signor Zeme. As for Signora Zeme, Professor Meocci has reached some provisional conclusions which only the autopsy will be able to confirm. And the results of both autopsies will not be available for . . .'

'A couple of hours, if we're lucky,' says Captain Scheggi, who is responsible for liaising with the Ospedale della Misericordia.

'Whereas the urgency of the matter . . .' intervenes the Colonel, without, however, specifying the nature of the urgency.

'Yes, there's the usual question of the press conference,' says Veglia confidentially to Monforti.

He himself, he explains, would have been happy to postpone the conference with the media until the following day and think no more about it. But it wasn't possible. Three corpses found in three days in a place like the Gualdana could not be kept under wraps so easily. And it is in nobody's interest that the reporters should be left to their own devices, putting forward whatever theories they like without the criminal investigation service being able to confirm or refute them.

Colonel Papi, Captain Scheggi and Lieutenant Amidei concur. Lieutenant Scalera diligently enters their approval in the minutes. Marshal Butti says nothing. Marshal Ognibene seems to wish to say something but thinks better of it, frowning harder than ever.

'I don't understand,' says Monforti.

But at that very instant he luminously *does* understand: *they* haven't understood yet. That is why they thought that 'some further assistance' on his part (in the form of an informal although concise interrogation) might be conclusive.

Meanwhile his blunt 'I don't understand' has created an embarrassed hiatus, which Marshal Ognibene fills by muttering, as if to himself, but making himself heard quite clearly: 'The hat . . . The witness's nocturnal visit to the residence of the . . .'

Dr Veglia raises one hand severely. 'Dr Monforti is here

for this very purpose,' he says. 'What we wish is that he himself should clarify . . . illuminate us . . . on the particular circumstantial procedure that enabled him to conclude, with enviable acumen, that Signor Zeme had been killed and buried just a short distance from his residence, and indeed from the place where Delaude himself was presumably killed.'

Everybody approves this new homage paid to Dr Monforti's speculative powers.

He, however, in his meditative silence, appears more preoccupied than flattered. He does not seem to appreciate the opportunity that is being offered him to provide urgent clarification and illumination.

'But the spade?' he asks finally.

'Quite right,' says the Colonel, turning to Captain Scheggi, who having also liaised with the laboratory should have already made his report on the spade.

The Captain makes his report. The spade found on the spot, eight inches or so beneath the surface of the sand, and which was probably used to dig the ditch for the Zemes, is also the one that then killed Delaude. The traces of blood and cerebral tissue discovered on the tool leave no doubts as to that.

'Therefore,' says the Prosecutor to the ingenious but reticent assistant, 'you can see the alternatives that face us. The Zemes were killed, we don't know how, we don't know where, we don't know why; and while the murderer was concealing the bodies in the sand, Delaude turned up unexpectedly, and was therefore killed in turn.'

'But not concealed,' observes Monforti.

'Exactly. But the *libecciata*, which dragged the corpse away, may have erupted before the murderer or the murderers had time to conceal it.'

Monforti shakes his head. It is clear that this line of reasoning does not convince him.

'Or,' continues the magistrate somewhat curtly, 'we can formulate the contrary hypothesis: Delaude killed the Zemes and buried them on the beach, and then someone else killed him. But in both cases we are left with someone guilty of homicide to discover, and we have no other testimony, nor any of those clues that obviously enabled you, Dr Monforti, to . . .'

'Yes, of course, I understand,' Monforti interrupts him, arousing optimistic expectations. 'But,' he continues, dashing them, 'with regard to clues, I don't think I can be of any assistance. On the contrary, I'm afraid I rather confused things by leaving that hat there, which revealed my nocturnal and probably illicit visit to the Zemes' house.'

At this frank admission, the atmosphere relaxes and the expectations are renewed. But Marshal Ognibene's brows, despite the conciliatory smile that Monforti turns on him, do not unpucker. 'There is also a question of removed articles of clothing,' he says, before a deprecatory gesture of the Colonel's can stop him, 'and a nocturnal departure from the Gualdana, witnessed by the Licensed Guard Roggiolani.'

'Listen, Ognibene,' says Marshal Butti, 'we mustn't . . .'

But it is the Colonel himself who cuts him short. The articles of clothing have already been discussed, he says, and it is evident that they could not have constituted a clue. They merely served for the dogs. And as for his arrivals or departures from the Gualdana, whether nocturnal or diurnal, Dr Monforti is under no obligation to account for them to anyone. However, if, as Dr Veglia was saying, he had indeed assembled data that could throw . . .

'Yes, quite,' says the Prosecutor. 'In that case . . .'

'Excuse my breaking in here,' says Monforti, 'but the clothes were not for the dogs. I used them to fill a bag belonging to Signora Zeme, which roughly resembled the one she had with her when she set out, and which I took with me on my nocturnal departure. I also removed the Pinocchio purchased at the station in Florence. Both of them are now in the boot of my car, since I haven't had time to replace them. But can one say,' he asks, 'that they have any value as clues? In a certain sense they did, since they were of assistance in ascertaining the facts of the case. But now I really don't see . . .'

'Excuse me,' Dr Veglia excuses himself in turn, 'but you speak as if the facts were now known. Whereas they are exactly what we are endeavouring to ascertain! We do not even know how Signora Zeme, who is supposed to have arrived in Milan, ended up where she did.'

Monforti remains in thought for so long that even Butti begins to give signs of uneasiness.

'I would say that the facts,' he says finally, 'can simply be left to speak for themselves. Indeed, I must say quite frankly that when I came here I thought they had already spoken for themselves. I had absolutely no idea that another murderer was being sought. Who, after all,' he adds after a pause, 'could well be myself.'

'Come, come, Signor Monforti!' shouts the Prosecutor, forgetting the 'Dr' and raising his arms. 'Please don't imagine that we . . .'

'And why not?' says the ex-Doctor. 'I was a friend of poor Signora Zeme, who was afflicted by depression just as I was, having suffered from it for years, and I might have wished to avenge her. Around midnight on the 23rd, in fact, having gone out on one of my nocturnal rambles, I might have witnessed, unseen, the car-crash, and the scene that then followed might have aroused a vague suspicion in my mind. After which . . .'

The surprising reference to the crash puts an end to the gestures and exclamations of protest with which everyone present, with the exception of Ognibene, was endeavouring to stress the complete lack of any suspicion attached to Monforti.

'After which,' he resumes, 'having returned home and stretched out on my *lectus lucubratorius*, that vague suspicion . . .'

But at this point, after the ex-depressive has opened a parenthesis to explain what the *lectus* in question was, another suspicion begins to take root: that from depression he has passed directly into paranoia. And thus who knows but he might actually . . . ?

His vague suspicion, continues the paranoiac, might have continued to grow and take definite shape, forcing him to get up again and go and inspect the Zemes' house. Peering through the half-closed shutter and seeing no one, he might then have gone down to the beach with his torch, where he might have heard a muffled sound of digging. Catching Zeme in the act of burying his strangled wife, he might have hurled himself upon him, causing him to fall into the ditch he had just dug, and then taken advantage of his surprise to push the sand heaped up on the sides down upon him. But then Delaude might have turned up – not with any intention of avenging Signora Zeme, but with vague ideas of suicide; thus caught out, Monforti might have killed him but, surprised by the *libecciata*, not have had time to conceal the body.

The first person who apparently wishes to speak after this hypothetical (?) reconstruction of the facts is Colonel Papi, who, however, changes his mind and looks at Prosecutor Veglia, who in turn looks at Captain Scheggi, who gets up and disappears into the operations room.

'This morning,' says the Prosecutor, turning to Monforti, 'you were with us when the bodies were found in the ditch. But I don't think you were present at their exhumation and inspection by the police-doctor?'

'No. I went off as soon as I had confirmation of the fact that along with Zeme's corpse, there was that of his wife as well.'

'You had confirmation, you say,' observes the Colonel, resolving to participate in what now looks like becoming a formal interrogation. 'But you haven't told us yet how you had reached the conclusion that his wife . . .'

'That was what I was explaining with regard to the crash. I added the hypothesis of my participation in the crime in order to see things from your point of view, since both of your reconstructions require a second murderer.'

'But anyway, did you really witness this crash or not?' the Prosecutor asks impatiently.

'No, but I heard about it the next day from guard Roggiolani. That is, from the very same witness who described it to you.'

The implication, the Prosecutor realises with some alarm, is that Monforti may have seen a clue, and begun to suspect something, where he himself saw and suspected nothing.

'Ah, I see,' he says, moderating his tone. 'And from the crash, in any case, you deduced . . .'

'I began to deduce,' Monforti specifies. 'I finally reached my conclusions on the grounds of the clue of the luggage label found in Milan. A double-edged clue, so to speak, which was not taken into due account.'

A glance from Marshal Butti reminds Dr Veglia of the bust of Garibaldi, which the Carabinieri never noticed although they had it under their very noses. He should have proceeded more cautiously, he thinks, in talking about clues to which the other man apparently had exclusive access and which he failed to bring to the attention of the law.

'The label,' continues Monforti, 'proves in fact that the bag got to Milan. But it in no way proves . . .'

He is interrupted by Captain Scheggi who returns from

talking on the phone to Professor Meocci. The autopsy, he announces, has confirmed the outcome of the first examination that was carried out on Signora Zeme.

'You mean that she was strangled?' asks the Colonel.

'Yes, as Signor Monforti had . . . deduced. And as for Signor Zeme, it seems likely that he died of suffocation, and precisely in the way Signor Monforti described.'

Marshal Ognibene turns menacingly to the presumed murderer: 'So then . . .'

'Ognibene, keep calm,' Lieutenant Amidei, his direct superior, chides him, with an apologetic smile, as to a guest molested by the house dog. He has noticed Dr Veglia's cautious retreat and tells himself that prudence is required with this Monforti: otherwise, he could end up holding the press-conference all by himself.

The Colonel has been thinking the very same thing but he feels the need to get to the point, in some way or other.

'And suppose we begin with the label,' he proposes, 'Dr Monforti?'

6

Monforti thanks Col. Papi for his friendly and concrete proposal. But he prefers to begin not with the label, which might be a little premature, but with the crash. And he proceeds with his statement in an orderly fashion, although occasionally indulging in reflections that might be considered marginal, if not actually futile and irrelevant – at least, at a session at the Group Headquarters. Lt Scalera, however, dutifully enters everything in the minutes under the title:

Statement of Dr Monforti

CRASH

The accident in itself, meticulously recounted by Roggiolani, was in no way suspicious: the porcupine could not have chosen deliberately to cross the road at that moment (apart of course from the possible influence of the stars); nor could Delaude for some obscure reason (again with the above reservation) have premeditated crashing into Zeme. But it is the behaviour of the latter after the accident that appears strange, or at least contradictory. Having got out of his car, he immediately concerns himself with insurance matters, to the point of pulling out a piece of paper and leaning on his wet, damaged boot in order to make a record of the facts in the presence of the guard Roggiolani. After which, he drops the matter and rushes off urgently, having established that he will call on Delaude the following day to settle it.

It is easy to understand exactly what suspicion the husband's behaviour aroused in my mind after the wife's failure to turn up in Bolzano.

NB, Lt Scalera – Monforti does not clarify what this suspicion was, but says that it was confirmed by the entrance ticket to the station of S. M. Novella, as well as the receipt from the bar of the same station and the Pinocchio, this too with respective receipt and indication of origin, purchased at the gift-shop of said station.

TICKET AND RECEIPTS

Here too, as in the case of the label found later at Milan Central Station, we have a double-edged clue. There is no doubt, in fact, that the ticket and receipts prove the arrival in Florence. But don't they prove it, as it were, a little too thoroughly?

Because it is true that at S. Maria Novella, as in every station with controlled ingress, a ticket is required to pass through to the platforms. But this obligation is purely theoretical. Nobody helping a relative with luggage to a train would think of obtaining the ticket in question. Particularly with the added factors of the pre-Christmas crowds, and the dual encumbrance of a heavy bag and a manic-depressive wife.

The same thing applies to the bar receipt, which Zeme was indeed legally bound to preserve while 'within a reasonable distance' of the public hostelry or shop in which he had 'partaken of the refreshment'. But in a bar – and particularly in a station bar, where one pays *before* taking the refreshment – we all know how things work in actual fact: the customer pays at the cash-desk and hands the receipt to the barman, who checks it, tears it halfway across, and puts it back on the counter together with the coffee, the whisky or whatever; but who would ever dream of picking it up again and putting it in his pocket? I wonder whether you yourselves in this room, although no doubt all highly law-abiding, would ever have . . .

> *NB* – Hilarity. Apart from Marshal Ognibene who does not pronounce on the matter, all those present admit they would never have thought of retrieving the receipt. Both the Sig. Colonel and Dr Veglia find the witness's observations 'most interesting' and invite him to proceed.

As for the Pinocchio, it seems that Signor Zeme had indeed been entrusted with the task of purchasing a toy for the Vannuccinis' son. But it is strange, given that it was a present, that he had not removed the receipt with the price from the bag. A temporary omission? Or the deliberate intention to provide Vannuccini, and later you yourselves, when you began to look into his wife's disappearance, with evidence that he had indeed accompanied her on to the *rapido* to Milan? The evidence would be even more persuasive, since it would not be provided directly by Zeme himself.

THE LABEL

Furthermore, he could not have anticipated the discovery of such a favourable clue as that of the label, which was held to confirm his wife's arrival in Milan. He merely hoped that the staff responsible would find the bag, together with its label, on the rack. Thus you would think that Signora Zeme, arriving in a state of confusion, had got off and left it there and then ended up herself God knows where. But he was perfectly aware that you could have thought something else as well.

However, the discovery of the label by itself made you conclude that if the poor woman had been robbed of the bag, she must have actually arrived there. But in my pessimism I do not believe that a bag, suitcase or haversack left on the train at Milan Central, has any chance of being found by the staff and thus ending up at the Lost Property Office. And that is why, without allowing myself to be misled by that illusory clue, I ended up by imagining the following 'departure scene' at the station of S. Maria Novella.

DEPARTURE SCENE

The *rapido* from Rome for Bologna and Milan is announced and finally arrives at Track 5. Those Christmas travellers who have reached their destination find their descent from the train impeded by the outward-bound travellers, swarming on board in a mad rush to occupy every seat, whether booked or not. Signor Zeme is one of the first to get on and I consider it quite likely that, for the benefit of possible witnesses, he turns round and says *'Magda, I'll go ahead and stow the bag'* or something similar. Then a possible altercation with the illicit occupier of the reserved seat, and the installation of the bag on the rack. Probable installation on the seat of newspapers and magazines purchased for the journey. Hasty return through the crammed carriage, because the train is about to leave. Descent and farewell gestures towards some window or other, possibly accompanied by loud comments on the disorganised nature of the service.

Departure of the train with the bag.

Stroll to the bar for a whisky, both necessary in itself and productive of favourable circumstantial evidence on account of the receipt. Purchase of the additionally circumstantial Pinocchio. Return to the superintended car-park, back into the car and then the grim journey home, while the tension slackens but the other nightmare begins: 'Now what's to be done?'

WHAT'S TO BE DONE?

NB – Dr Monforti wishes to make it clear that in his reconstruction of events he has not been able to follow a strictly chronological order. The scene of the false departure from Florence, he states, is what he reconstructed first. But he then had to travel several times – theoretically, that is – along the route Gualdana–Florence–Gualdana: seeking the spot where, on the way out at least, there must have been an interruption or a deviation. Said spot he reckons to have identified approximately last night, after his illicit visit to the Zemes' house, when he really did travel a part of the aforementioned route.

Dr Monforti furthermore wishes to make it clear that

he had mentioned, in a conversation with Marshal Butti, the impossibility for a non-depressive (or non-close-relative-of-depressive) to imagine just how destructive depressives can be, not only with regard to inanimate objects such as ornaments or french-window-panes, but also – and even more so – the psychic integrity of their own families.

Therefore, he explains, it is perfectly understandable that non-depressive investigators should not have grasped the dynamics of the crime. He, on the other hand, had the advantage of recalling, among other things, how Signora Zeme had left in the midst of a fit of euphoric logorrhoea and, with the aid of a similar bag and a symbolic representation of the lady herself by his side, he had been able to reconstruct the outward journey up to the 50th km, more or less, of the Maremmana Superstrada. After this preliminary clarification, he continues:

Near this point, just a short way before the so-called 'death-trap bend', there is an emergency lay-by. It was in this lay-by that Signor Zeme, having totally lost control of himself, must have stopped and strangled his wife. Another mile or two, I think, and the aforementioned bend would have claimed two further victims. And thus the corpses would have been found in their crashed car at the foot of the hill, and not six feet below ground in front of the 'Dutch villa'.

At this point, however, for the wretched uxoricide the problem of his own safety poses itself: in the first place he must get rid of the corpse. But a moment later he thinks, no: in the first place it must be believed that his wife disappeared *after* getting to Milan. And it is at this point that his mind, long before my own, conceived the scene of the presumed departure. All that remains is to effect it without wasting any more time, after transferring the corpse from the seat to the boot.

But he cannot carry out the transfer there in the lay-by, with the risk of being seen. He therefore sets off again, seeking a more suitable spot, and he finds it probably near the 50 km post, where the old route of the 'Maremmana' can still be followed to a site that is hidden from the present road. He carries out the transfer.

NB – Here attached: the rough sketch, traced by M. himself, of the site indicated. Dr V. observes that an on-the-spot inspection might enable them to find traces of the Volvo's tyres. M. doubts it, given the torrential rain that night, but thinks that an inspection might lead to the discovery of other traces.

Signor Zeme sets out again for Florence, where he leaves the car, with the corpse in the boot, at the superintended car-park of S. Maria Novella. He proceeds with the *mise-en-scène* already described. He returns to the car-park and gets back into his car.

WHAT'S TO BE DONE? (Part Two)
And now we're back, as it were, on the journey back. We're on the Florence–Siena motorway, having already passed San Casciano, Poggibonsi, Colle Val d'Elsa . . . and still with Signora Zeme's corpse in the boot. What's to be done?

I do not rule out the possibility that Signor Zeme might have left the motorway at Monteriggioni, which is directly associated with Sapìa and indirectly with Pia who was undone by the Maremma . . .

NB – This is a Dantesque allusion which the Sig. Colonel proceeds to clarify, explaining how a killer had seized the aforementioned Pia by her feet and hurled her into a deep ravine.

. . . and he might have conceived of getting rid of the corpse in the same fashion. But the risk of discovery was too great, even though there was no lack of ravines of a suitable depth in that area. And it is also quite possible that a little earlier, at the junction for Volterra, he might have been struck by a similar idea on seeing the steep and crumbling *Balze* or crags that have been gnawing away at this city for centuries. I know they suggested it to me, on my theoretical journeys up and down the same road, but not only in relation to Signora Zeme. I will return to this point, in any case, with regard to the *Cathédrale engloutie* and *Ce qu'a vu le vent d'Ouest*.

> *NB* – According to our Lt Amidei, these are compositions for piano by the French composer Debussy: 'The submerged cathedral' and 'What the West Wind saw'.

We are now on the Maremmana motorway and once again approaching the 50 km post; the idea that presents itself is that of a burial in the secluded site I have already described. But Signor Zeme, whose crime, as is evident from this very detail, had been entirely unpremeditated, does not have a suitable tool.

The only thing possible, he persuades himself while the numbers on the kilometre-posts diminish and the Gualdana approaches, is to bury his wife in the Gualdana itself. He has all the garden tools he can possibly need in the garage, and it will be easier to dig a shallow ditch on the beach than elsewhere.

CRASH (Part Two)
But here we are back at the scene of the crash, with the difference that now there is nothing contradictory about Zeme's behaviour at all. It is now perfectly understandable

that on seeing the boot crumpled and ajar, he should have hastened to lean on it under the pretext of 'making a record of the facts', but actually in order to prevent if from springing open. And it is equally understandable that he should then get away as quickly as possible.

I will pass over his arrival in the garage and then the removal of the slender corpse, the choice of the robust spade, the journey upstairs with both burdens, the long wait until at least one o'clock before descending to the beach along the path through the bushes. Instead I will momentarily draw your attention to his departure from the bedroom via the french-window.

This had not been left open in fact, nor had the sliding shutter been left ajar. But once he had stepped out with his load – the spade in one hand, the big torch in the other and the corpse over his shoulder – even a large man like Zeme must have found it difficult to close them again without at the same time releasing the catch on the shutter: which would have prevented him from returning the same way, as he intended to do. I myself was in this situation last night, although my load was less cumbersome.

NB – Marshal Butti doubts whether Dr Monforti who had been so brusquely summoned from his home, had had time to take a cup of coffee. Everyone apologises and Marshal Ognibene, who is responsible for liaising with the bar, immediately orders aforesaid coffee and indeed, on the orders of the Public Prosecutor Dr Veglia, coffee for everyone. The meeting then proceeds in a more animated fashion, which does, however, make the minute-taking a little more problematic, given the plurivocal nature of the discussion.

ON THE BEACH

NB – The Pub. Pros. proposes that at this point each person present should give his opinion on the hypotheses put forward so far by Dr Monf. in his personal reconst. of the events. – The Sig. Col. proposes that Marsh. Ognib. should give his opinion first. – Ognib. says he is unable to express any opinion until Dr Monf. has clearly explained the question of the double burial. None the less he must acknowledge the soundness of his hypotheses with regard to the failure to close the french w. and the shutter-catch. – Marsh. Butti confesses that until a mo. ago he would have shared his colleague's reservations. But he adds that having sudd.ly recalled certain events that have actually taken place in certain seaside resorts, he shares not only the premises but also the foreseeable conclusions of the reconstr. under discussion. – Lt Amidei, though not cognizant of the events Butti refers to, says he is sure that the conclusions will be on a par with the premises. – The undersigned Lt Scalera sudd.ly realises what the events are that took place in aforesaid resorts, but refrains from enunciating them so as not to ruin the effect of Monf.'s irrefut. final solut. – Capt. Scheggi, though clearly chafing at not having reconstructed events himself first, puts brave face on it and declares himself 'in anticipatory agreement with the cited composit.s of Debussy'. – Sig. Col. and the Pub. Pros. prudently avoid compromising themselves, adducing their inadequate grounding in matters musical. Both none the less declare themselves in agreement with above-mentioned hypotheses up to moment in which Zeme, arriving on beach, begins his digging op. – Dr Veglia then invites Dr Monf. to proceed. – The latter asks to examine the photographs taken on the spot, and examining them proceeds:

There was no reason for Zeme to walk any distance from his house with his macabre burden. Despite the hour and the darkness, someone might see him passing; and besides, if the remains should ever be found, his guilt would transpire immediately. It is understandable therefore that he should have chosen this spot on the beach.

NB – Monf. shows the first photos.

Conveniently situated in a recess between the dunes and directly in front of the near-by but deserted 'Dutch villa', the spot offered the optimum conditions for burying the corpse without risk of discovery (or so at least it seemed).

There was only one non-optimum – indeed *far from* optimum – condition, which the burier had not taken into account and which seems to have escaped you as well, although you have had it under your eyes all this time.

NB – Monf. shows the subsequent photos.

As for me, I had suspected it and this morning's excavation merely confirmed it. Because, to put it simply, we return to the initial dilemma:

Q. – If it was Zeme who buried his wife, who buried Zeme?
R. – Delaude maybe.
Q. – But in that case, who killed Delaude?

And it is here that the enigmatic towers of Monteriggioni came to my aid once again, reviving a whole series of momentary impressions, fragmentary ideas, more or less vague memories, which all finally came together to form one single picture.

NB – Monf. pauses lengthily, undoubtedly to recollect

the above-mentioned impress., but arousing appreh. among those present, since the time of the press-conf. has already arrived.

The dogs, to begin with. Not Sig. Lotti's but the ones that had to be sent for from Florence last year, since Marsh. Ognibene's brave animals were not yet in Grosseto, and which got as far as Monteriggioni before being driven back again, the Grahams' child having been found in the meantime. But these dogs, undoubtedly useful as a general indication, distracted me from the specific and conclusive clue that I should have perceived in **little Colin** himself. And thus I had to made a wide circle to get back there, setting out from the **Tower of the Tarot cards**, which collapses, involving two people in its fall, and which symbolises the **Tower of Babel** and thus leads on the one hand to the giant **Nembrotto** (Zeme himself?) with his brutish grunting, and on the other to the **Cathédrale Engloutie**, whose bell tolls on stormy nights. But then the cathedral itself, engulfed as it is, led me back to the buried wreck of the **Viktor Hansen** and hence to the fatal **Two of Swords** (or of **shovels**?), a symbol itself of catastrophes that are no less natural than human, and also to the plunging **Balze** that are inexorably engulfing Volterra, the ancient Felathri, the Volaterrae of the Romans, a city whose status as the most powerful of the twelve Etruscan 'lucumonie' was of no avail, since it was founded on **sandy layers** precariously placed on top of marly clays.

NB – The suspicion that Monf. is having us on begins to take root and even to bud and sprout, but nobody dares to urge him to hurry up. After all, we were the ones who asked him for an exhaustive explanation. Besides, Marshal Ognibene seems enchanted by the praise for his dogs, while Butti seems to be having a whale of a time at our expense (so let's send him down to pacify the chafing men of the press!)

And so here we are . . . that is, here we almost are . . . at the aforementioned conclusive clue, which I arrived at thanks to the **camels**, which in my 'pictureless' puzzle I had confused with the surrounding **sand**. Having recognised them for what they were, their teeth reminded me slightly of the somewhat equine teeth of the none the less attractive Signora Graham, who last summer . . . And here is the sand as well . . . Here is **little Colin**, barely two years old, using his toy spade to dig a hole in the sand deep enough to climb in up to his neck . . . And here comes his mother: she had wandered off for a moment but now comes running back with a shout and yanks him out, admonishing him with upraised finger and destroying the hole by kicking its sides so they cave in.

I didn't understand, at the time, just what risk the child was running, digging away without anyone taking any notice. Only later did I hear of tragedies that had occurred in other seaside resorts for the same reason. But not until tonight, when I had become convinced that Zeme had killed his wife and was reflecting on the mysterious disappearance of **both** husband and wife, did I realise what the solution was.

And then, when . . .

NB – Monf. raises one hand to silence the exclam.s of those pres. (some of whom seem on the point of rising both to express hearty congrat.s and to rush off as fast as poss. to the conf.) and proceeds:

When I was watching the digging this morning, in that recess between the dunes, I saw how the mass of sand heaped on the sides was for ever sliding back down into the ditch, and I also realised how the disaster, for Zeme, was almost inevitable.

However, things needn't necessarily have gone the way they did: in which case the mysterious disappearances, which might have remained unsolved, would have been those of **Signora Zeme and Delaude**. But let us begin by observing the last photograph.

Signora Zeme does not appear to have been thrown down but laid out decorously at the bottom as if her husband, after digging the deep ditch, had climbed down again to arrange her compassionately. I do not doubt that this is exactly how the unhappy man behaved, and I beg you to mention this in the conference. It is a detail that says far more than any comment can.

And now let us complete the reconstruction of events.

Delaude, having made his way down to the beach, not with any serious suicidal intentions, I think, but under the influence of vague existential reflections, has his attention drawn by noises in the recess and he approaches, lighting the way with his Crickett torch. Zeme, at the bottom of the ditch, jerks round and turns his own torch on the unlucky man as he leans over to look; Zeme then leaps out, grasping his spade and strikes the fatal blow. But at the same time his feet slip, and he falls back bringing all the sand heaped on the sides slithering down upon himself.

NB – The undersigned puts in a word to recall the tragic case of the beach of Tarquinia: where it was not a child, but a boy of sixteen who died from suffocation, buried in the hole he had dug himself; and this despite the presence of a friend, who could not dig fast enough to save him. – Marshal Butti recalls similar incidents on Adriatic beaches, when he was serving as a young corporal at the station of Cervignano (Udine). – Dr Veglia, for his part, expresses the hope that the Zeme case, with the publicity the media will give it, will at least serve to avert any other accidents of this nature. – Monf. agrees but asks for just one more moment of attention:

There remains to be considered, he says, **the West wind**. Which, in its local form of the *libeccio*, had not yet risen and so could not have seen anything. But when it rose, it did more than simply see. Let us picture the scene as it must have appeared after the collapse: Delaude's corpse lying by the partially filled ditch and all the signs of the landslip still evident. On the morning of the 24th, when the residents and the guards came down to the beach to ascertain the damage, the discovery of the one corpse would inevitably have led to the discovery of the other two as well. Instead, the *libecciata*, sweeping up in the night, dragging the body away, and levelling the sand perfectly, concealed all clues and wiped away all traces. She was the 'third man' that you sought in vain.

NB – The fact that the media have been waiting for half an hour now does not prevent the Pub. Pros. and the Sig. Col., on behalf of the Headquarters in general, from expressing their heartiest congrats. to Dr Monf., who is furthermore urged to take part in the conf.

But Monf. refuses firmly, stating that his first consid. is his privacy, and begs that no ref. should be made to his part in the reconstr.; all the more so, he says, since he would never have got anywhere at all without the trust and friendship bestowed upon him by Marshal Butti, as well as by his mother.

Aforesaid Marshal is unable to exempt himself, as his wish would be, from the task of assisting with the formal, detailed report that the undersigned will now have to compile for the Attorney, transmitting a copy, for cognizance, to the Legion Headquarters in Florence. So who will drive Dr Monf. back to the Gualdana? Who but Marshal Ognibene, by now almost convinced of his innocence and clearly desirous of hearing further praise for his dogs.

Closed, re-read and undersigned at the above date, time and place.

(*signed*) Lt Alberico Scalera.

7

Late one evening towards the end of December a dark car may turn up at the lodge of the Gualdana, be admitted by one of the guards (Barabesi perhaps) and make its way into the depths of the wood. And after a few hundred yards a voice, perhaps that of Signor Monforti, may say to the driver:

'Turn down there, on the left.'

Marshal Ognibene will carry out the manoeuvre promptly and the headlights, which were illuminating a dense screen of trunks will swivel and illuminate another identical screen of trunks.

'But how do you find your way around here?' the officer will remark perhaps. 'There should be lamp-posts, for safety reasons as well.'

Thus implying that so tenebrous a pine-forest cannot but favour all sorts of felonious misdeeds, if not actually instigate them.

'There, to the right now.'

Far off, a little light will gleam and vanish, gleam and vanish, between one tree and the next, apparently wishing to escape correct identification. Until one is actually in front of it, it is impossible to say which door it is hanging at.

'You can put me down here, this is fine.'

The officer will stop, get out and stand there as if uncertain whether to shake hands or give a military salute. Then, with the reluctance of one executing an order he is not entirely convinced of, will slip his hand into his pocket, pulling out a tweed hat.

'Ah, thank you, my hat. Good thing you found it.'

'Dr Veglia told me to give it back to you. Next time try not to leave it lying around.'

'But your dogs would find it again straightaway, Marshal!'

Ognibene will let a smile escape him but will scrutinise Signor Monforti and his dark arboreal background, with the air of one assessing the likelihood of possible relapses.

'That's true,' he will say complacently. And he will listen attentively to a few essential directions on how to leave the place, and set off mistrustfully through the treacherous labyrinth.

At the open door the beautiful Signora Neri will undoubtedly be awaiting him, one hand resting high on the door-frame.

'I dropped by to see if there was a light on and . . .'

'I heard the car and thought . . .'

'The Carabinieri brought me back.'

'So I heard. Out on bail or free?'

'Free, and with raised hats all round,' Signor Monforti will say. 'They had even impounded mine as evidence.'

It is then probable, and indeed natural, that from the hat he should start to recount his own story, of course not without first gratefully accepting a vodka or gin-and-tonic and settling on a divan next to the beautiful lady of the house, whose neck is adorned with the beautiful pyrites pendant that is so chromatically suited to her eyes. And fingering it, dangling it, swinging it, lifting it to her chin, squeezing it in her fist, the listener will betray a full sequence of emotions: surprise, rapt attention, dismay, intense horror, doleful commiseration and boundless admiration.

'But you did everything yourself! You see I was right to believe in your superior intelligence!'

Signor Monforti, whose timing always fails him when faced with a certain kind of smiling élan, restricts himself to a bashful murmur and deems it the right moment to address a mother who still knows nothing of the criminal plot conceived and carried out by her children against the Hon. Bonanno.

'I can't believe it! It was them?! And I never guessed that all their . . . But does Bonanno know?'

'Nobody knows, except Butti and myself, and now you too.'

'What do you think, should I pretend to know nothing?'

'Certainly. In a month's time they'll tell you all about it themselves, because, let's face it, they enjoyed it. And Andrea seemed quite proud of the operation.'

'A sack full of those "big-moles", my God how awful! What monsters I've got!'

Signor Monforti, disconcerted by a beautiful right hand that has begun to squeeze his forearm, merely pats it reassuringly with his left hand; and goes on to narrate by what paths, through what simple pictures and enlightening mottoes from village-life – the Piazza Grande, Righi in his shop-doorway, the ozone layer, the Tp-News, Mamma Butti's ancient proverb – he managed to decipher the obscure enigma of Orfeo as well.

'A purely verbal equivocation. What the wife wouldn't let him have, you see, was pork ribs, steaks! It wasn't . . .'

After a flummoxed pause in which he tries desperately to

extricate himself, beautiful Signora Neri bursts into uncontrollable laughter, with renewed bouts that go on for a good minute. Then suddenly she calms down.

'What about you,' she asks, 'do you believe in that old proverb?'

'That the way to hold on to a man is by his stomach? . . . Well, it depends on the kind of man. And also on the attractiveness of the woman, to put it in a nutshell. Because . . .'

But now it is he who feels embarrassed, and the fact that he is in the house alone with her does not help him at all, indeed it just increases his awkwardness.

They both look at the flames in the fireplace, in one of those silences that often precede solemn decisions.

'Well,' says beautiful Signora Neri, 'at this point I too feel I ought to let you h . . . well, you know what I want to say.'

Epilogue

APART FROM THE lazy creaking of the old trunks and the occasional black twitch of a bird, nothing now disturbs the nocturnal quiet of the Gualdana. Behind the closely-woven bushes glimmer rare but affable squares of light, and here and there chimneys waft into the air the aromatic tang of blazing cones and pinewood.

Signora Borst's imperfect hearing cannot catch the slightest sound from the sea and the flames of her hearth are placidly reducing the last flakes of this inevitable day to ashes. What has been has been, what had to happen has happened, as always.

Opposite her, her friend is dozing in the somewhat threadbare present of the armchair, but on the table by her side there is the pack of the future that contains dizzyingly everything. A little while ago she yielded to the insistence of **Milagros**, who after these shattering events has asked (but does she know if she comes to the point that it is not wise to ask, that it is unpropitious to know?) what fortunes the Arcana hold in store for her young self. Eladia contented her with the simple method known as 'the Judge's' and the four cards drawn for the girl are still lying there, in their open fan of possibilities.

There are no menacing Swords, fortunately, while the Empress, supported by a Seven of Cups guarantees a highly satisfactory settlement as far as physical well-being and authority are concerned. But what about love? The Knight of Coins is a far from sure candidate, while the Chariot may allude to a journey Milagros is to make to distant lands, back to the Philippines perhaps, but could also intimate the van driven by Ciacci, the skilful, hard-working, but expensive, electrician.

A rather drab projection for the lively Oceanian, who has after all caught the eye of the wealthy **Mongelli**, now weary of solitude. As she drowses, Eladia sees his cards laid out: the Lover (he himself, when he timidly imagined – and why not? – a compensatory and symmetrical set-up with beautiful Natalia Neri) crossed by the disenchanting presence of the Queen of Swords but perhaps succoured by the High Priestess (the widowed daughter of **Signora Melis**? It seems unlikely – hardly his type).

In the torpor of the room other destinies are proposed and portrayed by other Arcana. **Signor Lotti** is threatened by the severe Queen of Swords. Will he lose the lawsuit he has been pressing for years against an ex-partner, somewhat casual in his business dealings, not to say a thief, scoundrel and utter bastard? To judge by the adjacent Magician, normally positive, he will actually win it, although a King of Wands perhaps menaces two of his precious setters.

Max & Fortini have now got over the crisis that was blocking them, as is indicated by the Arcana XVIII, the Sun, with which Eladia infallibly associates them. The star that pours its golden drops on the twins below is a clear sign: the pair of comedians will prepare a highly successful show, sure to be acclaimed by everyone (bar a few peevish wretches) as excellent. But in this same show, who will play the role of the Sun, if not **Katia**? Sitting on a low divan, she will act as an incomparable au pair to Max & Fortini, killing herself laughing at their every joke. In vain will other comedians and their powerful sponsors bid for her charms, offering her astronomical sums: since (as she herself will say happily) money doesn't come into it: the simple fact is that *no one* will ever succeed in making her laugh the way those two do.

But the Arcana XVI that forecasts the existential-political itinerary of the **Hon. Bonanno** is imprecise and ambivalent. The flame that falls upon the Tower, destroying its crenellated battlements obviously indicates a government crisis. But whom do the two toppling figures correspond to? To the inept premier and the shifty Under-secretary Ciaffi? One can always hope so, but there is nothing to indicate whether the Hon. Bonanno will be swept away too in the downfall or whether in the next cabinet he will occupy a position worthier of his skills – at the ministry of 'pictureless' puzzles, for examples.

Two different Arcana seem to compete ambiguously for the future of **Orfeo**. Strength, symbolised by a woman engaged in opening the jaws of a lion (Orfeo himself, tamed, resigned to gulping down spoonfuls of soya?) and the Devil, presiding over two little demons of opposite sex yoked to his pedestal (Orfeo again, but with the two adulterers at his carnivorous mercy?).

Signora Borst sighs, rearranges the logs with the tongs, indulges herself with a Swiss chocolate. Eladia sighs, opens her eyes, smiles, refuses the box with a gesture, returns to her divinatory languor, which is now dangling the sinister sickle-bearing skeleton of Arcana XIII over **Maestro Kruysen**'s head . . . But no, there's been a mistake in the villa, the impending Death concerns **Signor Tavella** (heart-attack) and the Arcana of the Maestro is actually number XVII, the

Star, with its cosmic harmonies and the gushing torrents of limpid musical inspiration (it is the chaste virgin with two vases) for many happy years to come – or at least moments.

The High Priestess (Arcana V) transmits an unclear signal and whispers a name that Eladia is unable to catch. Is it perhaps that of **Ugo the Hermit** who will become the venerated leader of an increasingly numerous sect, who will distil his cynical meditations into the 286 pages of a bestseller and will be interviewed not only by the Tp-News? Or is it rather **Father Everardo**, destined on his motorscooter to pursue a sensational career in the ecclesiastical hierarchy? Eladia opens her inner eyelids wider . . . No, the Arcana that draws itself from the unfathomable depths of the universe and settles on the priest is number XX, Judgement. Not that the worldly successes of the Argentario have swollen the Capuchin's head and deluded him into taking himself for the Angel blowing his irrevocable trump from on high. On the contrary, informed of the tragedy, Father Everardo now blames himself for having failed to prevent it and is already intending, with next Sunday's sermon, to implore the Angel to have pity on himself, and indiscriminate pity on the three naked figures around the black ditch, two men and a woman, undoubtedly the incautious adulterer Gimo, the tormented Signora Zeme and the desperate murderer of them both.

'Will **Signora Neri** and **Monforti** get married, do you think?' says Signora Borst.

Eladia half-closes her eyes, then opens them wide. 'Not at once, if they've any sense,' she replies, rather unmystically. 'Here they can take all the time they want to see how things go, and then maybe . . . Anyway it's unlikely that he'll be able to shake off his anxiety and his pessimism completely.'

'Oh well, if that's the problem, he can always go into the village and check the bust of Garibaldi.'

'And then he can vent his feelings on the Marshal, he's now quite at home at the station.'

The two women laugh knowingly and serenely, help themselves to chocolates, throw the silver papers into the hearth where they are blackened at once by the fire, and sit careless of the details of the future, forgetting all about the Tarot cards which must, none the less, in some supreme combination of Arcana, contain, perhaps not the name, but the gesture of an ageing prostitute whose fingers, next autumn, as she rises from her bed of weeds and dead leaves on the side of a disused road, will encounter a small hard object and pick up an earth-encrusted silver box, with the initials M Z on the enamelled lid.

Appendix
The Principal People and Animals in the Story

Pine-Forest of the Gualdana

PERMANENT RESIDENTS AND REGULAR VISITORS

Sig. Gabriele Monforti, a depressive on the mend who occasionally puts up his sister **Sandra** and his brother-in-law **Ettore**.

Sig.ra Natalia Neri, abandoned by her husband and living in the pine-forest with her two children **Andrea**, thirteen years old, and **Giudi**, twelve years old.

Sig. Mongelli, whose wife left him to marry Sig.ra Neri's ex-husband.

Sig. Lotti, a Florentine ex-jeweller who gets his dogs to obey him with an ultrasonic whistle.

Sig.ra Borst, from Zurich, who lives with her old friend, **Eladia**, from Lugano, an expert in Tarot cards.

Milagros, Sig.ra Borst's Filipino servant, with Tuscan tendencies.

Hans Ludwig Kruysen, a famous retired musician, with his wife **Ute**, and their old servant **Emma**.

Giovanna, Sig. Monforti's domestic help.

Father Everardo, a Capuchin from a near-by monastery.

Ugo de Meis known as Ugo the Hermit, a hermit on a near-by hill.

SEASONAL RESIDENTS

Sigg. Antonio and Magda Zeme, who have come from Rome for the Christmas holidays.

Count Girolamo Delaude, who has come from Florence with **Katia**, an aspiring top model.

Hon. Giampaolo Bonanno, a Roman Member of Parliament who harbours suspicion of his party colleague, the Hon. Ciaffi, Under-secretary at the Ministry of Agriculture and Forestry.

Max & Fortini, well-known television comedians.

Sig.ra Melis, a lover of music and bougainvillaeas.

Sigg. Graham, parents of little **Colin**.

GUARDS

Vannuccini with his wife **Ivella** and son **Luca**;

Vannucci; Barabesi; Guerri; Roggiolani.

HANDYMEN

Orfeo Baldacci, whose wife **Amelia** maintains a cultural relationship with young **Dino Fioravanti**;

Grechi (plumber); **Ciacci** (electrician); other gardeners.

ANIMALS

Sig. Lotti's **four Irish Setters**;

Marshal Ognibene's **two Police dogs**;

The large **Rats** that introduced themselves, or were surreptitiously introduced, into the Bonannos' villa.

A **Barn-Owl** roosting in the Delaudes' roof.

A **Porcupine** that unexpectedly crosses the road.

A wounded **Boar**, which, many years ago, attacked and killed Sig. Lopez.

Owls, Tortoises, Squirrels and other 'synanthropic animals'.

In the Near-by Village

Marshal Aurelio Butti, commander of the local Carabiniere Station, and his mother **Sig.ra Butti.**

Father Albino, parish-priest of Santa Maria delle Preci.

Dr Scalambra, national health doctor.

Favilli (hardware); **Spini** (bakery); **Righi** (butcher); **Lilli** (electrical repairs); **Sguanci** (barber); **Magnolfi** (bricklayer); **Nannini** (petrol-pumps);

'Il Molo' (bar); **'Il Patio'** (discothèque); **'Las Vegas'** (pizzeria); **'L'Omino Blu'** ('The Little Blue Man') (knick-knacks).

In Grosseto

Procura of the Republic: Assistant Public Prosecutor (magistrate) **Dr Veglia.**

Group Headquarters of the Carabinieri: Commander **Lt.-Colonel Papi; Capt. Scheggi; Lt Amidei; Lt Scalera; Marshal Ognibene.**

Ospedale della Misericordia: **Prof. Meocci**, pathologist.

Team of Telepadùle-News: **Meniconi**, director and interviewer; a **driver** who is also an operator.